The Forb

MW00929244

STORM PHASE BOOK THREE

DAVID ALASTAIR HAYDEN

THE FORBIDDEN LIBRARY

Storm Phase Book Three

by David Alastair Hayden

Published by Typing Cat Press

Version 3.0 | May 2014

Cover illustration by Leos Ng "Okita"

Graphic Design by Pepper Thorn

Prologue

A lone girl knelt on the ice, a white-steel longsword clutched in her hand. Blood dripped from the blade's tip. Gore stained her tattered, mismatched clothes, and dark bruises splotched her pale, baojendari skin — evidence of the battle that had left her stranded alone in this frozen waste.

Her panting breaths turned to anguished grunts as her slight frame stretched and expanded. Over the span of mere moments, she grew several inches, and cords of muscle knotted along her limbs. The lines of a pentagram formed like a bruise on her forehead, matching the ghoulish purple in her once-bright blue eyes. Her fingernails lengthened into wicked claws. Fangs extended down from her gums.

In Awasa's mind, hatred and love battled, and the object of both was the same: Chonda Turesobei. She was no longer the Awasa who had foolishly set off from Ekaran weeks ago, driven by the desperate hopes of a silly girl afraid of losing the boy she thought she loved. She wasn't even the same Awasa from a few minutes ago. As her body had changed, so too had her mind.

A crimson sun sank into the horizon, casting shadows across the endless expanse of ice that was the Ancient Cold and Deep. With snow crusting in her unkempt, black hair, Awasa stood and snarled at her enemies.

She was surrounded by massive yomon: nightmarish savages, beings of chaos and destruction. Ragged pelts covered their vermillion skin, and heavy tusks protruded out from under their white, broom-bristle mustaches. Their onyx weapons, razor-sharp, glittered in the dying light. Less than an hour ago, they had numbered one hundred and eight. Now they were but ninety-one.

Their solid black eyes locked onto her as they trudged forward, seething with anger. The Winter Gate — the way to Okoro, the way to freedom and vengeance — was closed to them once again.

Awasa did not fear them.

Howling, a yomon charged her. Awasa ducked under its spear-strike and plunged the white-steel sword into its gut. The yomon screamed and died. She pulled the blade free.

Ninety.

From opposite sides, two more ran at her. With blazing reflexes she had never before possessed, she slipped out from between them and spun on her heel, swinging the sword in a wicked arc. Such skill was new to her, as well. The blade sliced deep into both yomon, who then collided with one another. They dropped their clubs and stumbled, grasping at their wounds, their magical flesh smoking and peeling away.

Awasa slashed deep into the shoulder of one of the wounded yomon. It crumpled and turned to dust.

Eighty-nine.

The other collapsed to his knees, and Awasa stabbed him in the throat.

Eighty-eight.

The rest of the yomon closed on her.

"Enough!" she screamed. "Enough!"

She pulled out a medallion she had tucked into a belt. She held it up. The air shimmered, and suddenly eight copies of Awasa appeared, identical to her in every way, except that long claws extended from their fingers and their faces were blank — no eyes or noses or mouths.

The yomon paused.

Awasa glanced at her copies and grinned devilishly. Proudly, she hung the medallion of Barakaros the Warlock from her neck. Despite this magic, the yomon could have overwhelmed her easily, but they hesitated. They were unused to fear, but they had suffered greater losses this day than they had experienced in centuries. None wanted to face the white-steel sword, and they had seen this girl transform from a soft child to a killing machine in moments. What more surprises did she hold in store?

Spinning slowly around, Awasa pointed the white-steel sword at them. "You will not attack me. You will follow me. I am your mistress now. You will obey me!"

A yomon stepped forward and growled, "Why? We outnumber you. You can't kill us all."

"If you wish to try, then go ahead." The yomon did nothing. "I didn't think so. You need me. I can get you what you want. I can get you out of here."

"The gate's closed again," the yomon replied. "There's no way out."

"Trust me on this, Chonda Turesobei will find a way out."

"The Storm Dragon? We don't want to face him again."

"You can, and you will. I was too weak when he brought us here — too weak to slay him when he fled with the others. But I'm strong now, and my power's still growing. Besides, he can't keep that form forever. He will become human again."

"Who are you?"

Ignoring the question, she held up her hand. It was coated in drying blood. Though cold ravaged most of her bare skin, the places coated in blood were as warm as if bathed in the summer sun. She glanced down. The body of a child lay on the ice before her, a child she had killed. Awasa dipped her hand into the Winter Child's wound. She took the blood and smeared it onto her bare forearm. The cold vanished from that spot. She knelt, and painted her face with the blood. Fangs extended, she bit into the child's neck and drank until she could stomach no more. The yomon watched silently, unmoving; puzzled, perhaps. Warmth spread throughout Awasa's body. As the Winter Child had been immune to the cold, so now was she.

Awasa smeared her hair back from her face and licked her fangs. "I am Ninefold Awasa. You are my yomon. Kneel before me."

One yomon fell to his knees, then another, and another. In a wave, the eighty-eight yomon knelt and bowed their heads.

Awasa laughed and shouted into the sky. "I'm coming for you, my love — my betrothed! Wherever you are, I will find you! And after I kill the others, we will return to Okoro!"

Chapter One

A large crystal embedded in the wall gave off timid, pinkish light, but as dawn approached, the crystal brightened and added a hint of warmth to the cramped, underground room. Gravelly voices rumbled through the hallway outside. A curtain of white fur drawn across the doorway muffled the voices, but it couldn't hold back the smoky scent of roasting meat wafting from the kitchens.

Amidst thick fur blankets piled on the far side of the room writhed a lanky, pale-skinned, fifteen-year-old baojendari boy. Sweat pouring from his brow, he gnashed his teeth and muttered incoherently. Neither scents nor sounds nor light stirred him. Only nightmares penetrated his exhaustion.

The *Mark of the Storm Dragon*, a lightning bolt spiking through a storm cloud in a circle of black, sparkled on Turesobei's cheek. The sigil had appeared after he had shattered the heart of the ancient Storm Dragon, Naruwakiru, and absorbed most of the released energy.

After struggling for weeks not to become like Naruwakiru himself, he had embraced the Storm Dragon to save his companions from the assassins known as the Deadly Twelve, who had tried to plunge Okoro into eternal winter and release the demonic yomon. Success had come at a price. He and his companions, save for the vampire Aikonshi and the monster hunter Hakamoro, were now trapped in the Ancient Cold and Deep.

Forever.

With the yomon bearing down on them, Turesobei had whisked his friends away and dropped them off near a village he hoped was safe. Unable to shift back into his human form, he had flown leagues away, until his winged fetch Lu Bei helped him return to himself. Then he crashed into the ice and was rescued by three white-furred, bear-like people known as the goronku.

Turesobei groaned, "Naruwakiru ..."

Even now, in his dreams, he fought the urge to become the dragon, because he was certain that if he ever became the storm dragon again, he would lose himself forever.

Nearby, two ancient books lay on top of his folded clothes and battered armor. One was a musty volume adorned with the Chonda Goshawk. The other was a diary with a polished leather cover, bound with silver wire and embossed with strange runes.

The amber kavaru, a wizard's channeling stone that hung from Turesobei's neck, began to glow in response to his struggles against the dragon. The diary woke. Pages flipped rapidly, and then the book spun into a dazzling cloud that coalesced into the form of a supernatural fetch. The fluttering pages turned to fluttering batwings. As big as a house cat and twice the trouble, Lu Bei was on the loose.

The fetch, whose amber skin matched Turesobei's kavaru, pounced onto Turesobei's chest and shook him.

"Master," he said in a tinny voice. "Master, wake up!" Lu Bei chewed on his lip with his tiny fangs. His large, black eyes swelled with worry. "Master, you must fight it. You can't become the dragon again."

Until six months ago, Lu Bei had hibernated in a pocket of the Shadowland, where he had gone after the death of Chonda Lu, the founder of Turesobei's clan. Turesobei carried the kavaru that housed Chonda Lu's dormant soul, but apparently their connection went much deeper because it had called Lu Bei back. The little fetch was always going on about Turesobei's special destiny.

Turesobei stirred and groaned as he opened his eyes. "Lu Bei?"

The fetch sat back with a sigh of relief. "I'm here, master."

"Where are we?"

"Underground, master."

"How ... why?"

"Ah, you don't remember then. Thought you might not. You were fading out when we arrived. The goronku, the ones who rescued you ..."

"I remember them."

"They brought you here, to their village below the ice. They tended your wounds and gave you a sip of drugged soup. You said it tasted like evil, and then fell asleep."

That explained the foul, metallic taste in his mouth. "I ... I remember some of that now. But not this room."

Turesobei reached toward his shirt and winced in pain. His left arm was broken and now fixed to a splint. His entire body ached, but the pain alone couldn't keep him awake. His spirit was depleted. Eyes sagging from fatigue and the last of the sleeping draught, he nearly fell back asleep.

But then he remembered Iniru and Enashoma.

His eyes shot open, and he sat up. "What time is it?!"

Lu Bei eyed the brightening stone on the wall. "I'm guessing nearly dawn. The goronku are awake already."

The scent of cooking meats finally struck Turesobei. His stomach growled. A bowl of water sat nearby, but they hadn't brought him any food.

He reached for his shirt again.

"I wouldn't," Lu Bei said. "It's filthy and torn. Besides, it's useless here anyway. Not nearly warm enough to help you."

It was cold in this room, far colder than it ever got inside the High Wizard's Tower back home, even on the worst days of winter.

"As you were falling asleep, the goronku medicine woman said they'd find you appropriate clothing. Why don't you lay back down, master? Let me go find Narbenu. He's the one that led the scouting party that rescued us. He's our sponsor here."

"No, I've got to get to Iniru and Shoma. I've got to —"

"Let me get him, master. Then we can worry about all that. One step at a time. If they survived the coldest hours of the night, they should be fine. Motekeru and the hounds are with them. I'm sure they're safe."

Lu Bei flew off. Turesobei lay back down. He wanted to believe Lu Bei was right, but he remembered the look in Narbenu's eyes when he'd told him about dropping his companions off near a village. It wasn't just the fear of Turesobei's companions facing the horrors that hunted this land at night and exposure to the extreme cold. There was a more specific fear that had danced through the bear-man's eyes.

The curtain pulled back. Narbenu and Lu Bei entered.

Narbenu looked a lot like a k'chasan, except that k'chasans sort of resembled cats — something one never dared point out in their presence. The goronku resembled bears in the same way, only with white, yellow-tinged fur. And they were a little more bearlike than k'chasans were catlike. The goronku had wide hands and feet, stunted snouts, round ears, beady black eyes, and thick frames.

Narbenu, who had a prominent belly and a grizzled beard, wasn't wearing his leather breastplate or carrying his hafted axe like before. He was wearing gray leather pants and a gray shirt trimmed in blue. Both the shirt and the pants were thick, so Turesobei guessed that fur lined their insides. Great, it was so cold here that people with fur wore fur.

Narbenu nodded. "Are you feeling better, lad?"

Turesobei shrugged. "I've been worse. I could use a lot more sleep, but ..."

"Your friends, yes. I was on my way to wake you when I ran into the little creature."

Lu Bei bowed.

"We need to get moving if we're going after your friends. Tell me everything you remember about the village."

Turesobei tried, but he had been lost in the dragon form at the time. He remembered little, but fortunately, Lu Bei knew more.

"It was a quaint village," the fetch said. "Stone buildings with tiled roofs. Looked ancient. Like it had been there for centuries, but it was all still in one piece."

"You were on the high plain northeast of here?"

"I believe so," Lu Bei said.

Narbenu frowned and glanced away. "It is ancient. And it may look nice, but ..." Narbenu shook his head. "We'll get a rescue party together. Hopefully ... hopefully your companions ... I'll have someone bring you food and medicine. And clothes. You'll want to be on your feet and after them right away."

"You're not going to tell me to wait here and rest while you do it?" Turesobei asked with surprise.

"Why on earth would I do that?"

"Because that's what adults do."

"Maybe where you come from, but not here. Here you fight for your own so long as you're able. I'd never insult your honor by making you stay behind. Nor will I insult you by giving you false hope. You'll be lucky if they're alive still."

"What's there? It looked like a decent village to me."

"Decent? Hardly. It's a place of the damned."

"What exactly —"

"Think no more of it for now," said Narbenu. "Worrying will do you no good. Rest while we get everything ready."

"You're going to help me find them?"

"We'll do our best."

Chapter Two

The light from the crystal on the wall was almost white now, with only a trace of pink, but it wasn't much brighter than a big candle. Lu Bei claimed the darkness made him sleepy, and turned back into a book. Turesobei drank the water they'd left him, then dozed until an old goronku woman, wearing a spectacular cloak woven of black feathers, shuffled into the room. She locked her milky eyes on Turesobei and took a deep sniff of the room. Her ears twitched. She smiled, and eased over to him.

"Hello, Chonda Turesobei. I doubt you remember me treating you last night." He shook his head. "My name is Eira. I'm a shaman, and I'm here to examine you again." She circled her hands above him. "Your spirit has improved, but it's still weak. Hardly stronger than that of a dying man. Except here." She pointed to the storm sigil. "There's tremendous spirit locked into this one part of you, as strong as a hundred souls combined. How can you contain so much?"

"Willpower," he answered, "and that's fading. I don't dare tap into the mark, or I'll become the Storm Dragon, and if I did that again I'd never turn back into myself."

"Too bad. I'd have loved to see the dragon, not that I can see much farther than my nose." She chuckled. "You're strong to resist so much. And you have yet another source of power ..." She gestured at his kavaru. "You have a second soul."

"That's my kavaru. It's a channeling stone, a gem my people can use to do magic. Well, not all of my people. You must be in a certain bloodline. The soul in the gem is that of my clan's founder, Chonda Lu."

She cocked her head. "It's not your soul in the gem?"

"No. Chonda Lu was a Kaiaru. The Kaiaru were an ancient race. Very powerful and not exactly human. Their souls resided in their kavaru gems, which allowed them to be resurrected into new human bodies using rituals that are now forgotten. But eventually, most of the Kaiaru were destroyed or gave up on being reborn. Only one Kaiaru remains on Okoro, the island continent where I am from."

"You are certain your soul is separate? Because the soul I sense in this kavaru ... it's no different from your own. They are the same — as if one were your left eye and the other your right."

"Well, I am a direct descendant of Chonda Lu, and according to my fetch, Lu Bei, I'm special somehow ... I'm Chonda Lu's heir in a unique way I don't understand. Sometimes

I think that maybe I'm ..."

He woke to the old woman's hand on his forehead. She frowned down at him, concerned. "You need more rest."

"That's what happens when I think too hard about Chonda Lu and how I'm different than other wizards."

"I have decided," Eira said. "You and Chonda Lu ... you have twin souls."

"Twin souls ... sure, maybe ... but I'm not going to think about it."

She laughed. "Probably wise. If something powerful keeps you from thinking about it, there's a good reason." She took his wrist, felt his pulse, and frowned. "Your spirit will return in time, though what damage you've done internally, I don't know. It's not healthy to give so much of your spirit away."

"Didn't have much choice. Say, how is it that I can speak your language? When I concentrate, I realize I'm speaking it, but I've never heard it before."

"We have discussed that, the priestesses and I. I'm afraid the answer is that we simply don't know. We thought you might."

"Maybe something about passing through the gate," he suggested with a shrug that made him wince as pain shot through his arm.

"My assistant put the splint on your arm last night. I suspect the pain medicine I gave you is wearing off. Is the pain getting worse?"

He nodded, and she pulled out a vial of dark liquid.

"I'm going after my friends," he said. "I can't take more. I'll sleep all day."

"I know. This will dull the pain without making you sleepy."

He drank the liquid and gagged, but he managed to keep it down. Whatever it was, it tasted coppery and sweet ... like blood and herbs ... he wouldn't ask.

"It will take maybe six or seven weeks for your arm to heal," she said. "Don't pull the splint off before then."

"Once my spirit recovers, I can cast a healing spell." Turesobei tapped his kavaru. "One of the benefits of being a wizard."

"How miraculous. Your people must be incredibly long lived."

"Magic can slow the progression of a poison or disease, but it can't stop them. It only speeds natural recovery. And you still have to sew up a wound, put a bone back in place, all those sorts of things. And you can only apply healing magic to an injury once."

"Still, better than what I can do." She groaned as she stood. "Too bad it can't fix old joints."

"It could help them a bit, for a while."

"Well then, you can pay me for my services once you're in better health." She gave him another vial of dark liquid. "Take sips as needed."

"Thank you."

"My pleasure. When you reach my age, you don't expect to learn wondrously new things. I feel blessed to have encountered you."

Turesobei woke with a snap as a striking, young goronku girl bustled in with a heaping bundle of clothing in her arms. She had soft, white fur, sparkling green eyes, full lips, and a golden mane tied into a braid that hung over her shoulder. She was very ... curvy ... and suddenly he was all too aware that he was naked under the fur covers.

She smiled broadly, and somehow that brightened the room. "I have clothes for you."

He gathered the furs tight around him and sat up. "Thanks."

"I'm Kurine."

"Turesobei."

She winked. "I know. Everyone's talking about you."

He looked at the clothes. "I — I can't believe you had anything that would fit me."

"We didn't. You're as thin as a child but as tall as an adult. And our clothes aren't warm enough for you anyway, what with you not having any fur. All that bare skin." She cocked her eyebrows saucily. He clutched the furs tighter. "Had to stay up all night with my mother, sewing. She's the head seamstress. We took your measurements from the clothes you were wearing."

"I'm sorry you had to stay up working."

"Oh no. Don't be sorry." She winked again. "I really do love a challenge." She knelt beside him, and started to sort out the bundle of clothes.

"That's a whole lot of clothing. You didn't make spares for me, did you?"

"Never been out in our kind of cold before, huh? Poor fellow. Poor, poor fellow. Afraid you're going to need all of these out there. And I suspect you'll still be miserable. There is one spare shirt here, and Mother is rigging up a basic spare coat for you. In case yours gets torn. You know how beasts are ..."

The more he learned about the Ancient Cold and Deep, the less he liked it. He was starting to think he might be safer in the Shadowland.

"Don't worry. We know what we're doing. We make clothes like this twice each year and trade them to the bare-skins."

"Bare-skins? So there are other people that look like me here?"

"Yes, but I've never seen one of them." She gave him a long, hard stare. "And I think they're coloring is different, and I've heard they're hairy. Not as bare as you. We trade with them for iron, and wood when it's available."

Kurine was pretty, and the way she looked at him made him incredibly uncomfortable. Probably because he was a novelty here. He wanted to clutch the furs tighter, but they were as tight as he could get them.

Poof! Lu Bei woke up, zipped around the room once, and landed in front of Kurine. He yawned, then bowed. "I am the grand, illustrious Lu Bei — diary, fetch, and fearsome guardian for Master Chonda Turesobei."

Kurine laughed and clapped her hands. "The little demon! I was hoping I'd get to see you."

Lu Bei frowned and shook his head. "Not a demon, madam. Not a demon. I'm a fetch."

"We don't have demon servants," she said wistfully. "Oh, how I wish."

Lu Bei pouted. "Not a demon."

"We only have one book, too. For records, and it's not a demon either."

"Not a demon."

"Does everyone in your world have demons, Turesobei?"

Sparks blasted from Lu Bei's eyes. "Not a demon!"

Kurine gasped and shuffled back.

Lu Bei threw a hand over his mouth, then he drooped his shoulders and wings. "Sorry ... so sorry, madam. I got a little carried away. Just wanted to say, most demonstrably, that I'm a fetch, not a demon."

Laughing, she reached out and pinched Lu Bei's cheek. His eyes went wide as saucers. "And so cute!"

Turesobei laughed. "Lu Bei's one of a kind. I'm the only person anywhere who has a book that turns into a fetch. Well, hardly anyone else has a fetch, for that matter."

"Too bad. Well, back to business, eh?" She picked up a shirt of leathery, blue-grey animal skin with the gray fur still on it. It matched the shirt Narbenu wore, but Kurine turned it inside-out. "Sonoke skin shirt. Wear it with the fur toward your skin."

"Toward my skin?"

"Keeps the heat in better that way. And it's softer. She ran her hands along it. "The sonoke skin would chafe against your pretty, smooth skin."

He reached a hand out and touched the fur. It was very soft. As she turned the shirt over, her hand brushed his, as if by accident. But he was certain it wasn't an accident.

"You ... you weren't here when ... you didn't undress me, did you?"

Kurine sighed wistfully. "No, I wasn't here." She glanced toward the doorway. "Oh, by the way, you aren't going to tell anyone I was in here alone with you, right?"

"Er ... I don't ... guess so. Why?"

"It's not allowed, you know. Boy and a girl alone in a room together. Big no-no. I was supposed to go get Narbenu, but he was busy and, you know ..."

He was afraid he did know. "I would never tell on you. I swear."

She patted him on the cheek. "I knew you'd understand." She picked up another, larger shirt. "This is the jacket. Same material. Wear it on top of your shirt but with the fur pointing out." She showed him the laces at the neckline and the sleeves of both garments. "You've got to keep them tight. Don't let the heat out. Now, these are underpants. I'd wager you want the fur inward on these since —"

"Yeah, yeah, got it."

Smiling, she lifted a pair of pants. "Trousers. Notice the fur inside and out. Already sewn together, works better that way for pants. Laces at the top and bottom." She raised a giant coat with a smooth outer surface. "A parka with seal skin on the outside."

"We have seals!" said Lu Bei, drowsily. "I've seen them."

"We don't use their skins for anything, though," Turesobei added.

"You should," Kurine said. "The seal skin is water resistant, especially when treated properly. I can't stress this enough: do not get wet when you're outside. Never. Now, the inside of the coat is sonoke skin and fur. The padding inside is hair."

"Like people hair?" he asked, a little queasy.

"Yep. Some of it's mine."

"Oh ... um ... okay."

"You can think of me when you wear it. Really, this is a coat fit for a king. It would sell for a lot of iron. Most of the ones we make don't have padding like this."

"I really don't deserve something so fancy."

"It's not every day that we have a guest who comes from the world beyond the gate and can turn into a dragon and cast spells."

"I guess not."

"I think you could wear your leather breastplate beneath the parka."

Next, she showed him the waterproof mittens which fit over his gloves. How he would be able to handle anything while wearing them, he had no idea. Then she showed him the stockings and socks. The boots were made of one layer of sonoke skin and fur and another layer of skin that had been boiled and hardened. The treads on the bottom were surprisingly basic. He was about to ask why when she showed him the shoes that went on top of those.

"The overboots are waterproof with seal skin, and these tiny bits of bone on the bottom of the sole will give you traction when walking on the ice. You won't need them inside, of course."

"Wow. You must have worked really, really hard last night. That's a lot of clothes for one person."

"Like I said, we make similar ones for trading. We've done it before and had the materials ready and some parts already cut and in progress."

"How come the bare-skins don't make their own clothes?"

"They do, but theirs aren't as good as ours. We use secret treatments on the sonoke fur. We're the best at it. Now, you need to try it all on. I might need to make some adjustments."

Turesobei waited for her to leave, but she didn't budge. He glanced at Lu Bei, but he was falling asleep.

Kurine eyed the doorway, cocked an ear, and said, "Well, go on."

"Okay, I'll try them on now."

"Good. It's very important that you do." When he didn't move she added, "Well ..."

"Aren't you going to leave?"

"Aw, is that necessary?"

"It would be where I'm from."

"Well, it is here, too, of course. But no one's around."

"Woo woo!" cried Lu Bei, suddenly fully awake. "Show it off, master!"

Chapter Three

Turesobei elbowed Lu Bei. "I don't have fur. I would be naked. It wouldn't be right."

"Aww, but we don't have humans here in the Southeast," Kurine whined. "And even if we did, I'm sure they wouldn't be as cute as you. I was just hoping to see —"

"No. Sorry. You're going to have to leave or turn around."

"Oh fine," she huffed. "Spoil my fun." She spun around, but then glanced back and winked. "I won't hold it against you, though."

Sheesh.

With an eye on Kurine, he climbed to his feet, wobbled half a step, then caught his balance. He reached toward the underpants, grimaced, started to bend his knees ...

"I'll fetch it for you, master!"

"Thanks. I could use the help."

"I would be happy to help," Kurine said.

"Oh no," Turesobei said. "You stay right like you are."

With Lu Bei's help, he managed to get on his pants and stockings easily enough. The shirt was another matter. The splint was made from a thin piece of bone, and it ran from the back of his hand to his elbow. The shirt was tight, and he was having trouble pulling it on. He got both arms in, but couldn't pull it over his head. Lu Bei perched on Turesobei's shoulders, reached over his head, and pulled at the collar, but that led to it getting stuck under Turesobei's chin, and then slapping him in the nose.

Turesobei sighed. "Okay Kurine, you can help me now."

She skipped over. As she pulled the shirt over his head, she lightly stroked one hand down his back along the spine. Turesobei shuddered from a mixture of pleasure, tickles, and fear. Otherwise, she went easy on him and neither said nor did anything else flirtatious. In fact, she soon got down to business by inspecting how everything fit and tut-tutting over her work. The sleeves were a tad too long, and so were the pants, but she said she'd erred on the side of too long, since it was easier to make it smaller than bigger.

"How old are you, Turesobei?"

"Fifteen." He rapidly calculated the days and weeks that had passed since he had left Ekaran to rescue Iniru. "Actually, I'll be sixteen in several weeks."

"That's fantastic! You're almost a man! If you're still here in Aikora then, we must throw you a feast."

"So goronku are adults when they turn sixteen?"

"Naturally. Wait, are you … say, what are you exactly?"

"I'm baojendari."

"Ah. Are baojendari not adults at sixteen?"

"Eighteen," he muttered.

"If we did that, I'd still be three months away from adulthood. It's silly to wait until then. What's the point?"

"That's exactly what Iniru said when she found out. Her people become adults at sixteen, too."

"What's an Iniru?"

"She's my …" Was Iniru his girlfriend? Was that the right term? They'd never really discussed their relationship. They hadn't actually spent that much time together. She obviously wasn't his betrothed …

"She's your …" Kurine prompted, frowning ever so slightly.

"She's … a very good friend."

"Oh," Kurine said brightly.

"Do you have a betrothed, Kurine?"

"What's a betrothed?"

"Someone you're supposed to marry."

"Goronku women select their husbands," she replied, as if doing it any other way were ludicrous. "Do you have a betrothed?"

"Yeah. It was arranged when I was still too young to even speak."

"That's terrible! Why would someone do that?"

"I'm a prince in my clan. It was a political thing."

Her eyes went wide. "You're a wizard, a dragon, and a prince?! How wonderful."

"It's really not."

"Is your betrothed this Iniru person?"

"No, my betrothed is Awasa and … I think she died … when we came through the gate. I can't imagine how she could've survived. And she wasn't herself anymore — she'd been attacked and possessed by a demon sorcerer. It's a long story."

Kurine touched his shoulder. "I'm so sorry. You must be devastated."

"I haven't really had time to be. It just happened yesterday, and I'm trying not to think about it. Trying just to focus on rescuing my sister Enashoma, Iniru, and my other companions. I can be upset later and … Awasa and I didn't get along. I cared for her, but we never loved one another. I don't think."

"Well, if you want to save your friends, I'd best get back to work. Walk around, and let's see how well you can move with all of it on."

With the parka, the clothes weighed almost as much as his full suit of armor, and it was far more bulky. He walked around, awkwardly. "If I wear my breastplate, I'm not going to be able to move. Are you sure I'll need all this?"

"I'm afraid so." She took some measurements. "All right. Clothes off. I need to make

16

some quick adjustments before you leave here."

She helped him undress all the way to his pants, at which point he said, "Turn around."

Kurine didn't complain. Swiftly, once he was naked, he crawled back into the covers. She picked up the clothes and hurried out. He napped until a plump goronku man bounded in with a tray of food.

"Don't know if it's what you're used to, lad, but it's what passes for food around here. Cooked it up special for you. A real fancy meal. Enjoy!" He kissed his fingers and left.

"Thank you!" he called out as the man disappeared.

One bowl had three different kinds of smoked meat. The second bowl had smoked fish on top of a thin layer of purplish leafy vegetables. And the third held steaming broth with bits of ... something. He didn't care. He was starving. He drank down the broth, which wasn't soothing. His lips and the back of his throat burned by the time he finished. The fish tasted great, as did one of the meats. The other two were chewy and tangy, and heavily spiced as well. He drank all the water available, and his mouth still burned.

Narbenu entered carrying a bowl of water with some herbs mixed in. "How's it going, lad?"

Turesobei took the bowl and stared into it with dread. Sweat dripped down his forehead and from his lips.

"You look like you need a drink."

"It's not spicy, is it? I can't take any more spice."

Narbenu laughed. "No, it's just cold water and a few soothing herbs. Cook likes his spice, more than most of us, and it occurred to me you might not eat spice in your world."

"We have loads of spices in my world. We use them a lot. But they're not this hot."

"Lots of spices? Huh. We only have the one. You'll have to tell Cook about them."

Turesobei drank the water. It helped, but the burn didn't go away completely.

Kurine stepped into the room with the bundle of clothes. "Alterations are done." She spotted Narbenu and made an oh-no face.

"You've already been in here?" Narbenu asked suspiciously. "You were supposed to come get me. You weren't in here alone, were you? You know that's forbidden, Kurine."

Turesobei quickly replied, "She came in and —"

"I was here!" Lu Bei said, popping into fetch form. "I made sure nothing improper happened. Very sure."

"It's true," Kurine said.

Narbenu frowned. "Well ... no offense to the little demon —" Lu Bei slapped himself in the forehead. "— but he takes orders from young Turesobei. I don't think it's quite all right. Next time, make sure another adult goronku is with you, okay?"

She sighed. "Of course, Narbenu." Kurine set out the clothes. "Everything should fit perfectly now."

"I'm going to need some help getting dressed," Turesobei said. Seeing that Narbenu was about to ask Kurine if she had helped, he added, "Lu Bei helped me before, but it was clumsy. And poor Kurine had to stand over in the corner with her back turned listening to us fumble about for half an hour."

"I'll help you," Narbenu said.

"I've got to get something anyway," Kurine said.

Narbenu and Lu Bei helped him get all the clothes on. This time he added his breast-plate, and immediately thought he might collapse under all the weight. Finishing that, he put on his sword belt and instinctively reached toward where the scabbard would hang. But it wasn't there. Sumada was gone. He cursed.

"What's the matter, lad?"

"My father's white-steel sword ... I lost it while I was fighting the yomon." Awasa had it. Out on the plain where ... he couldn't let himself think about it. Survive and save the ones you can — mourn later — that's what he had to do. Something he'd sadly already done before, something that was becoming far too common.

"White-steel? I don't know what that is."

Turesobei thought about the weapons he'd seen Narbenu and the other goronku carrying the evening before: all iron. "You don't have steel, do you?"

"We do, but it is rare, and a single steel sword would cost a fortune. Most weapons here are iron, or blessed onyx which is harder than iron but also rare."

"White-steel is ... well, it looks like regular steel except it's almost as white as paper. It can cut through magic and demons. It's made from white ore that has fallen from Avida."

"That sounds most useful! We don't have any way to kill demon-beasts. All we can do is wound them temporarily and flee."

"White-steel is rare in my world. My father's sword was nearly pure — incredibly rare and valuable."

He touched the spot on his belt where his spell pouch would hang. No spell strips with castings prepared in advance — all his castings would be slow or quick-cast, which was a draining technique except for the simplest of spells. He moved his hand a little farther along the belt and tapped a spot where he kept an emergency spell strip. Whew. Still there. He was going to need that one, though using it might kill him.

"I'll get you a weapon," Narbenu said, "though it won't be as fine as what you're used to."

Kurine returned with a knitted sweater, scarf, and hat — all of them tiny. "For the little demon."

"Argh! I'm a book fetch!"

"You really do look like a little demon."

"But I'm not. Watch this. Master, would you like a bowl?"

"Why not?" Turesobei replied.

Lu Bei bounded over to a bowl, grabbed it, and took it to Turesobei. "See what I did just there? I fetched it. Now watch this." Lu Bei turned into a book, and then back into his fetch form. "Book then fetch. I'm a book fetch. See?"

"So you're a book fetch demon?"

Lu Bei bounced up and down huffing and grumbling, and Turesobei thought he might explode. Kurine laughed and poked him in the belly. "Don't get your wings tangled. I'm only messing with you. Here, take your clothes."

Turesobei laughed appreciatively. Not many people could best Lu Bei.

"I don't need clothes," Lu Bei pronounced. "I don't get cold."

"Everyone gets cold here," Kurine replied, "sooner or later. Don't you want to be cozy?"

Lu Bei held a staring contest with her ... and finally relented. He bowed and said, "Thank you, miss. I shall wear them outside when I'm in this form. Master can hold onto them for me."

"You've got to try them on first," she said.

Lu Bei did. Turesobei was certain if Shoma were here she would cackle with delight at how cute Lu Bei was. Turesobei bit his lip and commented as sedately as possible. "They seem to fit you well."

Lu Bei handed them to Turesobei, and turned back into a book. Kurine winked at Turesobei, and he smiled back.

"Take a few minutes more to rest," Narbenu said. "I know you're eager, but I've got a few more things to take care of before we can set off."

Turesobei was amazed at how nothing fazed the goronku. Him crash landing after transforming back from being a dragon, him being a wizard and looking different and hailing from another world, Lu Bei's nature. It also worried him. If things like that didn't alarm them, then that could only mean they faced plenty of horrors and a few wonders regularly.

"I'm never going to make it."

Lu Bei patted him on the shoulder. "You'll make it, master. We'll get there and save them."

"Putting on clothes exhausted me. Walking to ... however far away it is ..."

"Narbenu said something about mounts, master."

"Any mount here I'd have to learn how to ride." He tapped the spell strip tucked away in his belt. He had no choice. "Lu Bei, return to book form. Do not record again until I tell you to do so."

"Master, what are you —"

"Just do it, okay? Don't make this difficult."

"Master, don't do anything —"

"That's an order ... I'm sorry."

Lu Bei stomped his feet, and then disappeared. Turesobei pulled out the only spell strip left to him — a spell of last resort, but made for just this sort of situation. A spell that he'd kept hidden from Lu Bei. A spell that allowed him to do a special trick, a very dangerous and costly one. A moment of regret flickered across his face. He chanted and released the spell. The magic activated. Pain shot through this body, but once that ended, he felt energized, as if he'd had several days of rest. He tucked the still-active spell strip back into his belt.

"You can come out now, Lu Bei."

Lu Bei reappeared and sniffed around the room. "I smell magic. Powerful magic, and it's still active."

"I'm not going to talk about it."

"What did you do, master?" His black eyes narrowed. "You look refreshed."

"It was a small spell I'd like to keep secret. It will wear off. I have my reasons for keeping it from you. Let it go."

"As you wish, master."

Narbenu drew back the curtain. He was carrying a cloth-wrapped bundle in his arms. "Ready to go, lad?"

Chapter Four

"As ready as I'm going to be," Turesobei replied.

"Our party will be large enough that you can nap along the way without fear of danger ... once you get the hang of riding."

"I'm a skilled rider."

"I doubt your mounts are the same as our sonoke." Narbenu unwrapped the bundle, revealing a knife and a hand axe not all that much larger than the axe Turesobei had carried in his now lost pack. The blades of both were iron. "I thought you might like the axe. We don't have many swords here, and our hafted axes look a bit heavy for you. We have maces if you'd prefer."

"This will do." He sheathed the knife, and took a few awkward swings with the axe. "I'll just have to get used to it. Most of my training was with a sword, though I'm decent enough with a spear. Don't guess you have any of those?"

"There's a spear sheathed on your mount's saddle."

"A spear or a lance?"

"Is there a difference?"

"On my world there is."

"It's not as long as you are tall."

"A spear, then. Perfect."

Waddling in his giant suit of furs, Turesobei followed Narbenu into a wide hallway. More of the crystal lights were embedded in the ceiling. Turesobei pointed to one. "What are those?"

"Star stones."

"We don't have anything like them in my world."

"We trade the Westerners for them. They dig them out of the mountains and polish them."

They passed many doorways. Some had the curtains drawn back, revealing small apartments the size of the room Turesobei had stayed in, while others had large living rooms that led to multiple bedrooms. The hallway branched off in several places.

"How many people live here?" Turesobei asked.

"Twelve hundred. We're a large community. We have a big oasis."

"Oasis?"

"You'll see. This is a hard land to survive in. Those who have access to game and plants can ... well, I wouldn't call it thrive, exactly."

They entered a large common area about sixty paces across. Rugs and cushions were arranged into seating sections on one side. Tables were set up for eating on the other side. The doorway to the right led into the clanging, smoky kitchens. Warmth flowed out from the kitchens and from a vent in the center of the chamber. Geothermal heat, he guessed. There must be volcanic activity deep below. Some people in Okoro used heating like that. Southern Batsakun was famous for its hot springs. Now that he thought about it, there had been a small vent in his room. But if that was all the warmth it put out, no wonder these people needed fur.

The entrance across from him led to another long hallway. Perhaps that was where the goronku worked, since two merchant stalls were set up to each side of that door: one sold odds and ends and weapons, while the other sold clothing and jewelry. Kurine was at the clothing stall. She spotted him and waved. He waved back. She blew him a kiss. He hesitated, then waved again.

Narbenu raised an eyebrow at him.

"I don't know why she's taken such an interest in me."

"You're different, unusual. She craves a challenge, that one. I'd be careful if I were you. Our customs may not be to your advantage."

"Why is that?"

"Because you don't know them. I suspect we're very different from your people."

An ornately carved door stood to Turesobei's left. Guards with hafted axes flanked the door. He remembered now coming through this door last night, though he didn't remember the common room. Probably because they had drugged him right after he'd arrived. Narbenu pushed open the door, revealing a staircase about forty steps long that led to a wide landing and a stone door at the top. Another guard stood at the top of the steps. He nodded to Narbenu, and then helped him push the door open. The entrance to the town was built into the side of a low hill. Two more guards stood to each side of the door outside.

The blast of cold air punched Turesobei in the face. He'd been so exhausted and battered yesterday that he'd barely registered the cold. Shivering, he drew the crimson scarf Kurine had made him up over his face. He had to get home.

On top of the hill was a cleverly disguised watchtower: a pale, stone building with ice piled around it so that it would match the surrounding terrain. Turesobei had noticed it upon arriving last night, though he'd missed a lot of other things. It was strange how in delirium, one could pick out something hidden and miss the obvious.

The goronku had four other buildings outside. Turesobei was certain one was a stable. What purposes the other three served, he had no idea, though a sound almost like that of dogs barking came from one building, along with an unpleasant odor.

To the right was a steaming lake the size of the crescent-shaped lake that lay between the High Wizard's Tower and the Palace in Ekaran. There was no ice within fifty paces of the lake, and the ground sloped down toward the lakeshore. Judging from the difference in height between where he stood on the ice and the top of the lake, he guessed the ice was nearly as deep as he was tall. Out of the thawed soil around the lake grew a thick stand of spindly trees and thorny shrubs alongside dense patches of herbs and vines with purple leaves. Those he recognized, having eaten some this morning. A dozen goronku were out tending the plants.

A rock wall, taller than a goronku, surrounded the area, protecting their buildings and the lake. In the direct center stood a tall column with hideous faces carved into it: faces of demonic birds, bears, and creatures he couldn't identify. Probably to ward off demons. If he were a demon, it would've driven him off.

Narbenu stomped ahead, and Turesobei followed, the treads of his new overboots crunching into the ice. They rounded the large building — Turesobei stopped — his jaw dropped.

A war party of nineteen armed goronku awaited them — on their ice drake mounts. The beasts, the sonoke, were slender with smoky fur that turned white on the ends, except on their opalescent, scaled bellies. Their armless, legless bodies were thick at the front and tapered to a thin tail. All told, they were the length of five men. Whiskers like those of a catfish trailed from their snouts. Ram horns curled from their foreheads. One of the beasts turned toward him and locked its slitted, reptilian eyes on him. It blinked three times, snorted, and looked away.

"Everyone ready?" Narbenu asked.

The goronku nodded silently. They were staring at Turesobei, not menacingly, but with keen interest and a bit of suspicion.

"I'm Chonda Turesobei," he announced. "Thank you for helping me. I will be indebted to you."

Many heads bobbed in acknowledgement, but no one said anything. He was starting to think that other than Shaman Eira and Kurine, the goronku were a mostly silent people. Narbenu said little that wasn't necessary.

Narbenu led him forward to meet the goronku at the head of all the others. "I'm the leader of our scouts, so normally I would command such an expedition. However, this is a special situation requiring many warriors, and it could involve some delicate negotiations with some of our enemies. Therefore, our party is led by Sudorga, our war chief."

War Chief Sudorga wore a coat of banded mail many times nicked, just like his face, which bore a number of battle scars. His fur was steel gray, and a white beard hung halfway down his chest. He half-bowed and said in a surprisingly airy voice, "We will do our best to find your friends and save them if we can, Chonda Turesobei. We owe that to you."

"You really don't owe me anything. I appreciate the help you're giving me, but I am imposing on your people."

"You are stranded in need, and we took you in. What kind of people would we be if we didn't do our best to help you? We would shame our ancestors and insult the gods otherwise."

Four mounts without riders were positioned behind Sudorga's mount. Narbenu led Turesobei to the front of one. "This is your mount, KZ 1304. Hold your hand out so that he can sniff it."

"That's a strange name."

"It designates which sonoke sired him, his birth order, and which year."

"You don't name your mounts?"

"Some do. Most do not. This one is young and has finished his training. He is yours. Our gift to you no matter what happens this day. If you wish to name him, you may."

Turesobei held his hand out. "Iyei," he told the sonoke without a moment's thought. "Iyei is what I shall name you, if you will have me."

The mount Turesobei had ridden into Wakaro in search of the Storm Dragon's Heart and that had ultimately plunged into the river from high up on a rope bridge had been named Iyei.

The sonoke sniffed Turesobei's hand, snorted, shut his eyes, and bowed his head. Turesobei patted him between the horns. The fur was thick and soft, not at all unlike the fur Turesobei was wearing. In fact, it seemed identical. Surely not ... that would be like wearing denekon scales back home.

"Well done," said Narbenu. "Now, climb in the saddle and I will teach you the rest. You said you had riding beasts at home?"

"They are very different, but I'm guessing from the saddle most things will be the same."

Turesobei climbed into the saddle, which was comfortable, though a little big for him, even in all his thick clothing. He took up the reins and learned all the spoken orders, rein flicks, and sidekicks that Iyei would respond to. While the commands were strange, it wasn't all that different from riding a denekon. Riding was riding, he supposed.

After he recited all the commands a third time without error, Narbenu said, "You're a fast learner."

"To cast spells you have to be able to memorize a lot of phrases and commands. I've been working at that sort of thing all my life."

"You have supplies in the pack behind your saddle, enough food to survive at least a week out in the wilderness. Your spear is hooked into the side of the saddle. There's a place you can hang your axe, as well."

A mount edged up next to his. The goronku who rode it was young, probably not much older than Turesobei. He would've thought the young goronku was handsome, with his refined facial features and bright blue eyes, but he had no idea what standards the goronku held. The goronku boy wore a copper collar around his neck that was locked into place. None of the other goronku wore anything like it, including two others who looked roughly the same age as this one.

"I'm Kemsu," the young man said in a deep voice. "If you need anything along the way, I'd be happy to help you."

"Excuse me if I'm impolite, but I don't know anything about your customs. What does the collar represent?"

"I'm a slave," Kemsu replied, almost proudly.

"Kemsu belongs to me," Narbenu said. "That is a story for another time. Are you ready to ride?"

Turesobei nodded. He decided to withhold judging Narbenu for owning a slave. He didn't know their customs, and he hadn't seen any other slaves. Of course, slavery wasn't all that much worse than how most baojendari treated zaboko, with indenture and segregation, practices that were thankfully less extreme amongst the Chonda. And Kemsu didn't seem disagreeable about it.

War Chief Sudorga barked an order, and the group set out. The sonoke slithered along the ice like snakes, moving and sliding with ease. The sensation of riding was strange as he urged his mount to go. Turesobei could feel constant tugs side-to-side, even though the beast kept an even, straight-ahead course. With denekon, the motion was an up-and-down bounce. This was going to take some getting used to.

To help Turesobei get a feel for what the sonoke were capable of, they went slow and then sped up to the beasts' full speed, which was even faster than a denekon sprint, though the sonoke couldn't maintain that pace for even half as long.

As they slowed back down into the natural pace for traveling over distances, Turesobei asked Narbenu, "How far is it to the village?"

"A day and a half. We'll have to stop during the night. But with a party this large, we'll be spared most of the dangers."

"Most?"

"This is a harsh world," Kemsu answered. "And there are many things that even a group of heavily armed goronku can't scare off."

"Like the yomon?"

"The yomon are the worst things here," Narbenu said. "But even the yomon don't wander out alone."

Chapter Five

Once Aikora, the goronku village, fell out of sight, Turesobei was officially lost. Endless fields of ice stretched in every direction. No trees. No villages, farms, or rock formations. No mountains in the distance.

"How do you navigate?" he asked Narbenu.

"By sighting the stars when we can," Narbenu replied. "The stars come out in late afternoon and stay till mid-morning, if your eyes are sharp enough to discern them."

Turesobei craned his head back. Only a deep, purplish blue sky hung above. "Too close to noon now?"

Narbenu nodded.

"Our stars do not come out until darkness falls."

"Your sun is bright? It is said that our sun was once bright."

"And yellow." Zhura, the Dark Moon, was a faint, waning smudge in the sky; Turesobei could barely see it. "Even our moons are brighter. I can barely see Zhura today."

"When sight fails us, we rely on our sense of smell."

"That wouldn't get me anywhere."

Narbenu tapped his large, bearlike nose. "That's why we have these. Out here, you need them. Of course, not all of the Ancient Cold and Deep is as barren as the plain we live on."

"You promised to tell me what we're facing. Why are you so afraid that my friends are in danger?"

"The village you described ..." Narbenu sighed. "If you're right, and your friends made it there ... the inhabitants, the reitsu, they aren't friendly. They're wraiths ... vampires."

Turesobei thought about Aikonshi, whom he'd left behind, whom Chonda Lu had created to be a monster hunter. "I'm familiar with vampires. We have them in our world."

"I doubt yours are like ours," said Kemsu, riding alongside them. "The reitsu steal the warmth from your body."

"They drain away body heat?" Turesobei said, puzzled. "Ours drink blood, though a few drain life force instead."

"To survive in these elder days, some people evolved thick fur." Narbenu patted his belly. "And blubber. Others developed more cold resistant skin and learned how to survive wearing thick clothes. But the reitsu were a magical people. A lot like you. Tall and pale-skinned. According to legend, when the cold swept suddenly across the world, the reitsu tried to protect their bodies using magic.

"But it didn't go the way they hoped. The magic warped them. They became immortal and resistant to the cold, but they couldn't bear children any longer, and to maintain their warmth, they had to steal it from others. The reitsu turned on one another, and many were wiped out. Those that remained fed on other races. The warmth of one goronku will keep a reitsu toasty for decades. But most wanted more than what they needed; their hunger was insatiable. Those that remain now are the ones who learned to control the hunger. The rest fed and fought until they were slain by those they hunted, except a few who trade their services as assassins. The reitsu of today, when they begin to lack warmth, go into hibernation until someone comes near."

"They can't feed on animals?" Turesobei asked.

"It's a poor solution. When they feed on animals, they begin to take on the animals' traits and lose their humanity, such that it is. Turns them into mindless creatures. Most of the reitsu are jaded and prefer to hibernate, actively dreaming of days long gone when there was yet warmth, days they still remember."

"Have your people fought them? You seem to know them well."

"We goronku know far too much about the reitsu. We warred with the wraiths for centuries. We outnumbered them, but they are incredible warriors. Fighting nearly ruined both our races. We have a truce now, a truce that has lasted well over a century. They don't feed on us; we don't make war on them. It's easy because there's so few of both our races now, and we have plenty of other enemies."

Turesobei furrowed his brow. "But you will help me retrieve my friends from them, right? If that's necessary."

Narbenu glanced at War Chief Sudorga. "We shall see, my young friend. You present an unusual circumstance. Our world is in a careful balance, which you have already thrown off by stirring up the yomon."

"I'm sorry."

"Well, no one likes the yomon. They terrorize all of us now and then. Your killing a few of them was a good thing. Look, your companions ... I don't want you to get your hopes up. You should know that if they wandered into the wraith village, they're already dead."

"A few of my friends are amazing warriors, one of them is supernatural — more magic and machine than man."

"He would have to be incredible to fight off the reitsu," Narbenu said. "The reitsu are lightning fast and deadly with their claws. And it takes only one good grasp for them to drain warmth from you. Your best hope is if they kept your companions for sport. That's not likely, and I can't tell you we'll be able to get them away even if they have."

At noon, they stopped for a quick lunch. The goronku dismounted and walked around, circling their arms as they did so. Figuring it was to maintain circulation out in the cold, Turesobei did the same. He had noticed his body temperature dropping as they went. Lu Bei refused to come out. Either he needed rest, or the cold affected him more than he wanted to admit. As the goronku began to eat, Turesobei opened his pack and fumbled through the rations and gear, not certain what the purpose of most of it was. He thought of how clueless Awasa had been with the trail rations at first, and now sympathized with her.

Kemsu helped him. "Your food rations." He lifted the largest pack. "Sonoke cheese. Do you have cheese in your world?"

"From goats and sheep."

"Don't know what a goat is, but sheep cheese is good. Mild compared to this."

"You have sheep?"

"The Westerners do. They're the ones that look a bit like you, but are kind of fat and hairy. They always gift us a small amount of cheese when we trade with them."

Kemsu took a block out of the pack and unwrapped it. "Butter. Eat it straight or melt it onto any game you kill, if you have access to a star stone. Out here, you need to eat a lot of fat to keep warm. Cheese is your basic ration. Butter for extra energy; it's dense and worth a fortune if you're starving."

"A star stone? Like the ones on the walls in the village?"

"The same, though we carry smaller ones with us." Kemsu lifted a dimly glowing crystal from Turesobei's pack. "Always good to have with you at night and for a little extra warmth. Better than burning blubber, which poorer people are forced to do. When you tap on the star stone, the surface heats up. Tap a lot, quickly, to get it hot enough to melt butter. Tap just a few times to make it warm and give a bit of light. It will slowly cool. The more you make it hot, the faster it will burn out. The one you've been given is new. It can provide light like it does now for many years."

"The one in my room was brighter in the day than at night."

"Yeah, that's a bit of a disadvantage. Works best when you need it least. It'll grow brighter at night if you tap it. Otherwise, it seems to somehow reflect sunlight, even through ice and earth. No one understands why. At maximum heat, a star stone will last several weeks, so only do that for emergencies. Six taps just to take the chill out of a room. Using it that way, it'll last maybe a year. Night use drains it more."

Kemsu wrapped the star stone back up, and lifted out another food pack. "Dried sonoke strips. Stringy, bitter. Made from old sonoke or wild ones. Better if you melt some butter on it. And then this last pack is seal fat. Tastes pretty good, gives lots of energy. Eat the sonoke first, though. Course, you'll want to hunt as much as possible while traveling, to keep your supplies up. Someone as scrawny as you, you'll be eating all the time to stay warm out here."

Turesobei took out a strip of dried sonoke and chewed on it. Tasted like old goat, or what he imagined old goat would taste like, and it took him a long time to chew it up. He got it down, and drank from the small canteen they'd given him.

"Sure you don't want more?" Kemsu asked with a crooked smile.

"I had a large breakfast. I'll eat more tonight. Or if I get cold."

"You get cold enough," Narbenu said, joining them, "and anything will taste good. You'll see."

War Chief Sudorga barked out a command, and everyone returned to their mounts and rode. Turesobei stayed beside Narbenu and asked him questions. He needed to learn everything he could about this place, and fast, if he was going to have any chance of finding a way back home. And it was easier to talk than to worry about Iniru and Shoma.

"How far out does the continent extend?" he asked. "You mentioned the Westerners and the Fire Mountain — how far away are those places?"

"Both are many weeks of travel away from here," Narbenu answered. "The continent extends out to the edge of the world, to the Boundary."

"The edge of the world?"

"If you travel too far, you step out of the Ancient Cold and Deep and into ... nothing. Looks like the world keeps going on in the distance. Ice and hills or whatever, like normal. Except you cross over, and then you disappear."

"You can't see the person who crossed the barrier on the other side?"

Narbenu shook his head. "Nothing looks any different, the person just vanishes."

"But how can you step into nothing?"

Narbenu shrugged. "You take a step past the Boundary, and then you're gone from this world. Those who go past the Boundary never return."

"So there might be something on the other side?"

"Perhaps. We have no way of actually knowing. But every tale we have says that going past the Boundary means you cease to exist. It's worse than death." Narbenu gave him an inquisitive look. "So you don't have a Boundary in your world?"

"The continent extends out to the ocean, and if you sail across the ocean, you will find other lands."

Narbenu nodded. "Just as the legends tell us. And is it true that your world's seas are melted ice?"

"Yep, just water."

"Amazing," Narbenu said. "I can't even begin to imagine such a thing."

Lu Bei popped out of the pack and fluttered ahead. While flying backward, he patted the sonoke on the nose. The beast grunted, and then Lu Bei landed on the back of its head. The sonoke didn't mind; animals always liked Lu Bei. The other warriors in the party stared at Lu Bei with wide eyes. They muttered amongst themselves. Lu Bei waved at them. A few waved back. A few, including Kemsu, rode a little farther away.

"Hello, fetch," Narbenu said.

"Hello, big furry man. Thought I'd stretch my wings."

"Do you want your hat and scarf?" Turesobei asked.

Lu Bei tilted his head back. "I do not need them. Now, what's this about a Boundary? If it looks like the world keeps going beyond it, how would you know that you've reached it?"

"You wouldn't necessarily," Narbenu said. "You have to be careful. There are giant stone pillars in a lot of places to warn you you're getting close. And some people who live near the Boundary have built walls in front of it. If you think you're getting close, best to move away."

"How close are we to the Boundary?" Turesobei asked.

"Sixty leagues to the south and nearly the same to the east. Three hundred fifty to the north and two hundred forty to the west."

"Where is the gate?" Lu Bei asked. "North and east of here?"

"Indeed. The gate is only a few hundred paces from the Eastern Boundary. The Northern Boundary lies beyond the coast of what we call the Glass Sea. An expanse of smooth ice that extends over a hundred leagues beyond the land."

Lu Bei stroked his chin. "Master, this world sounds like it's about the same size as —"

"Zangaiden?" Zangaiden was a nation in Central Okoro.

"Indeed, and in our world, the gate was on the Zangaiden side of the Orichomo Mountains. Plus, the distance from the gate to the coast here sounds about the same. I wonder if, under all this ice, the rest of the geography would match as well."

"So you think this world is somehow an ice-covered copy of our Zangaiden?"

"Maybe." Lu Bei scratched his head. "Although if it's true, I don't see how the knowledge does us any good."

Narbenu looked at them blankly. None of that would have made any sense to him.

Turesobei shrugged. "What about the yomon?"

"The yomon live at the Fire Mountain due north of the Winter Gate. Sometimes the yomon indiscriminately raid other lands and people. We goronku have suffered them many times over the years. Thankfully, the yomon mostly sleep, like the wraiths do. Don't know why they aren't content at the Fire Mountain, where they live in luxury. What could be so much better in your world that makes them so desperate to go there?"

"Beyond the plentiful food and forests?" Turesobei said. "That's simple. Revenge."

"We heard about the yomon moving nearer to the gate a few weeks ago. Figured they sensed something was going to happen. No offense to your world, but everyone here hoped they'd move on if the gate ever opened."

"I can understand why," Turesobei said. "What's in the middle of your land?"

"The Barrens," Narbenu said. "It is coldest there, very few hot springs, not much life, not many people. A few caravan routes cross that area, but that's about it."

"No cities or towns?" Turesobei asked.

"You mean big villages? There are a few big villages in the West. That's rare, though. Mostly it's like our region everywhere, with tiny villages based around hot springs. A bit different here, in that the goronku villages are interspersed with reitsu villages which aren't built at hot springs."

"No giant temples or anything like that?"

Narbenu shook his head. "No temples. There is the Forbidden Library, though. It's on an island that lies on the Glass Sea."

Lu Bei batted his wings, his eyes wide. "That sounds promising."

"If there was information anywhere about returning to my world," said Turesobei, "it would probably be there, right?"

"I'd guess so," Narbenu replied. "But it'd be nearly impossible for you to reach it. The trek would be incredibly dangerous, not to mention the important part about its accessibility."

"You mean the *forbidden* part?" Lu Bei said.

"Legend says that no one is permitted to enter the library," said Narbenu.

"Then why have one?" said Lu Bei.

Narbenu shrugged. "I've no idea. From what I've heard, demons guard it."

The wind kicked up. The color of the sun deepened from rose to crimson to blood as it began to set. The temperature dropped rapidly. Turesobei shivered.

Lu Bei folded his wings around his body. "If you don't need me, master ..." The fetch climbed into the pack and returned to book form.

A beast howled in the distance. Something responded. It sounded like a girl screaming.

Chapter Six

Turesobei turned toward the sound instinctively. "Do you think —"

Narbenu shook his head. "A demon."

"Are you certain?"

Narbenu sighed. "Nothing out here is certain. There are so many dangers. But it's definitely not one of your friends. They couldn't have made it this far on foot in a night. Not a chance."

"What are the biggest dangers to worry about?" Turesobei asked. "I may be stuck here. I'm going to need to know."

"Well, there's the bomokagi," said Kemsu. "They're larger than four goronku combined. Razor tusks to rend you, if they don't just trample you. Big and hairy and hard to kill."

"The kusokagi," said Narbenu. "Also known as scourers. Winged demons that swoop down on you. Usually at night, but sometimes in the day, especially if it snows. No one even knows where they live or come from."

"And then there are wild sonoke," said Kemsu. "Don't underestimate them just because these sonoke we're riding seem so peaceful."

"All manner of demons and beasts unnamed prowl our lands," Narbenu added. "Hardly any two are alike. The worst things come out at night."

The sun was halfway down the horizon. War Chief Sudorga called everyone to a halt to set up camp for the night.

"When will we get to the reitsu village?" Turesobei asked.

"Just before dark tomorrow," Narbenu said.

"That won't be soon enough to do anything." He rode forward to speak to War Chief Sudorga. "Can we travel a few more hours? Avida is rising. That will give us some light."

"Not enough," Sudorga replied. "Maybe in your world, but Avida is not bright enough to travel safely by. Travel is more dangerous at night anyway."

"I can see in the dark if I wish and can lead us," Turesobei said. "And I can summon a light to guide us. Just two more hours, please."

War Chief Sudorga stroked his beard and studied Turesobei. "Show me."

Turesobei chanted the *spell of the dancing fire globe*, hiding the pain that casting even such a simple spell caused him. Three globes of fire the size of his head appeared. Everyone gasped in amazement. But then fire globes fizzled out.

"That's — that's strange."

Someone said something to him, but Turesobei ignored them. He opened his kenja-sight and studied the terrain. Bright blue and white energies flared across the landscape, mixed with thin green and yellow currents. The only traces of fire energy came from him, the goronku, and the star-stones.

"Of course," he said, "there's not much fire energy for me to draw on here. Hold on, I'll have to use another spell."

A harder one, unfortunately. He cast the *spell of the moon mirrors*, which relied on air energy and was easiest when Avida was in the sky like it was now. Six white disks, like glass mirrors, appeared. Light radiated from one side of each of them. By concentrating, he angled them to shine ahead of the column.

"It's a simple enough spell. I can keep this going for two hours."

"There will be dangers," Sudorga said.

"I have no desire to put your people into too much danger," Turesobei replied. "If you wish to stop, that's your choice. I'm just trying to get to my friends in time."

Sudorga narrowed his eyes. "You swear that the spell is simple?"

"There are easier spells, like the fire globes, but it is a basic one."

"It's hurting you to do even that spell, isn't it?"

Turesobei sighed and admitted the truth. "It does, but I can manage."

"If you are so brave and strong that you would dare the night and go to such effort in your condition and in a world you're not suited for, then how can we proud warriors of this land not continue on? We ride!" As everyone set into motion, Sudorga added, "I have honored your strength, but be smart. If you start to falter, let me know, and we will stop. Don't wait until your spell fails. We need light and half an hour to make camp."

After another hour of riding, Turesobei grew tired. Summoning the moon mirrors wasn't much harder than the fire globes, but maintaining them was. If not for the overabundance of air kenja here, he wouldn't have dared the spell in his condition. Narbenu chose a location to set up camp. Turesobei sent the mirrors up above them and illuminated the site. Beasts howled in the distance. He hoped the lights wouldn't attract them.

The goronku drew their long knives and began to cut into the ice and packed snow. Turesobei drew his knife as well, but Narbenu shook his head.

"You rest and watch me do it. If you don't know what you're doing, you'll just waste your strength and make a mess."

The goronku cut ice and compacted snow into blocks, making a trench as they went. They stacked the blocks in a circle, and then laid the blocks on top of one another until they built a domed structure with a short entrance tunnel jutting off to one side. As they stacked blocks, they shaved them so they'd fit together perfectly. Three goronku worked on the outside of the structure while two work inside, building the dome overhead. He was certain it would collapse on them, but the structure held.

"A house of ice?" Turesobei said. "I don't understand."

"It's a snow house," said Kemsu. "Keeps the wind off you, and it keeps in warmth, from your body or your star stone."

"Five goronku to each," said Kemsu. "It's a tight fit."

"What about the mounts?"

"They'll sleep in the trench," Kemsu replied. "It gets them out of the wind. They really don't even need that. They can huddle together and survive just fine on their own out here. But the trench keeps them cozy, and more importantly, it makes it harder for predators to spot them."

They cut angled slopes into each end of the trench, and led the sonoke within. The sonoke, trained for this, fell quiet and snuggled up together. Following War Chief Sudorga, Kemsu, Narbenu, and a goronku whose name he'd forgotten, Turesobei crawled through the entrance tunnel into one of the snow houses. The central chamber was only as tall as a goronku could reach, since they had to set the blocks by hand. There wasn't a lot of space for all of them. It was cold, but not as cold as he would have expected. In the center of the snow house, Kemsu placed a star stone on its wrappings and tapped it three times. The light was dim and only a little warmth came out.

"Don't want to melt the ice," Kemsu said.

Turesobei dismissed the moon mirrors, unfurled the blanket from his pack, and placed it on the ice.

"Best to eat something first," Narbenu said. "You'll ..."

Falling into a deep sleep, Turesobei never heard the rest.

Chapter Seven

Turesobei woke in a surprisingly warm space, relatively speaking. It was like sleeping in a plush tent in a regular Okoro winter. The snow house had captured all their body heat. He still felt the chill in his bones, and he was ravenous. He stuffed himself on dried meat strips and cheese.

The goronku left the snow houses intact. It wasn't worth the effort to dismantle them, and some other traveler might benefit from them later.

By mid-afternoon, they neared the reitsu village.

War Chief Sudorga stopped the group. "We need to approach carefully. They may think we're attacking and overreact. Once they get riled ..."

"I could send my fetch to scout ahead."

"He can do that?" Sudorga asked.

Lu Bei popped out, landed on the head of Sudorga's mount, spun on his heel, and took a deep bow. "I am, sir, so very much most talented."

"I believe it," Sudorga said in a high-pitched chuckle.

"He has a limited range," Turesobei said. "He can only about two hundred paces away from me."

"I can't reach the village from here," said Lu Bei, "But I can fly up and get a good look ahead."

Turesobei cast the *spell of blending* on Lu Bei, and his skin turned a milky gray color to match the sky.

"So sorry you had to see that," Lu Bei told the goronku. "It is quite embarrassing. Please think no less of me. In my younger days I could do that on my own."

Lu Bei shot up into the sky.

Narbenu laughed. "Why on earth would I think less of him? He can fly!"

"He's self-conscious about not being able to blend himself anymore. Though, honestly, I'm not certain I believe him when he says that he used to be able to."

A few minutes later, Lu Bei dove down and landed, shivering. "Even colder up there. We've got to ride. Now and fast!"

"As he says," Sudorga commanded, and the group set off.

Lu Bei dug through the pack and pulled out the scarf and hat. The goronku snickered when he put them on. Lu Bei narrowed his eyes, bit his lip, then shrugged it off. "I really could blend back in the day. Don't know why no one believes me."

"You've got good ears," Narbenu said.

"He can magically record anything that I say or do, even from that distance," Turesobei said. "That's his purpose when he's not fetching. Now, Lu Bei, what'd you see?"

"I saw a half-dozen charred corpses in the village." Turesobei's heart stopped until Lu Bei added, "Not our companions. The whole village is massing around a tiny house. They've fashioned a sort of battering ram. I think they're about to break down the door."

Lu Bei tightened the scarf and shot back into the sky.

They raced the sonoke at full speed. After climbing a slight incline, the reitsu village came into view. Sudorga called them to a normal pace so they wouldn't alarm the reitsu.

Lu Bei returned. "The door is cracking but holding so far. Something — or someone — is bracing it."

"Think your friends are inside?" Sudorga asked.

"We're close enough now that I can find out. Are you certain we can't go any faster?"

"I'll send someone ahead to announce us. One goronku coming fast shouldn't rile them up too much."

Narbenu flicked his reins. "I'll do it."

Still riding, Turesobei cast the *spell of sensing presences*. He was too far away to detect anything except all the goronku around him, so he attuned the spell to seek out energies related to his kavaru. That harmony would resonate much farther. He picked up three signatures.

"Motekeru, Rig, and Ohma are inside. I can sense them because of their bond with my channeling stone. I'm too far away to sense whether Enashoma, Iniru, and Zaiporo are with them. I'm sure Motekeru is bracing the door. He's incredibly strong. They must've fought the reitsu and took shelter in the house during the night."

"Can they use magic like you?" Sudorga asked. "Is that what charred the corpses?"

"The reitsu drain warmth by touching their victims, right?"

"More than just touch," Sudorga replied. "They have to lock a hand on you and focus, but yes, that's basically how it works, and they can do it fast."

"Then I have a theory about how the corpses were charred. I think that —"

Lu Bei swooped down. "A contingent of reitsu met Narbenu ... peacefully. Looks like he's talked them into halting their efforts; they're not battering the door anymore."

"You'd best you climb into my pack now, Lu Bei. Be ready. I might need you to surprise them."

Lu Bei unwound the scarf and packed it up with the hat. "You got it, master."

Not that far ahead, Narbenu and a small group of reitsu were talking.

"So what do we do now?" Turesobei asked Sudorga.

"We approach cautiously, and then ask if we can have your friends," Sudorga replied.

"And if that doesn't work?"

Sudorga sighed. "I cannot risk war between our peoples. No matter how much I want to help you."

"I understand. Do you think they will let them go?"

"Hard to say whether they would under even the best circumstances. If your friends have killed some of them ... I'll do what I can."

"I know you will. Listen, let's not mention the Storm Dragon to them. I may need that as a bargaining chip."

Turesobei cast a simple glamor spell to cover the storm sigil on his cheek. The goronku stopped and dismounted before approaching the six reitsu standing near Narbenu. The reitsu were tall and skeletal thin with blue-black hair and skin so pale it was nearly transparent. From a dozen paces away, Turesobei could see veins on their faces and necks. He couldn't figure out the gender of any of them; they all looked roughly the same. The reitsu wore simple tunics, stockings, and boots — hardly enough to keep out the cold in an Okoro winter. Turesobei couldn't imagine what sort of magic they had bound themselves to for that clothing to be warm enough.

War Chief Sudorga half-bowed to a reitsu who wore a copper torc and matching rings on all his, or perhaps her, fingers. "Greetings, Lady Umora. Thank you for meeting us in peace."

The reitsu nodded respectfully. "Welcome, War Chief Sudorga. An interesting day this is."

Umora spotted Turesobei. Her pink eyes narrowed.

He bowed. "Greetings, Lady Umora."

She didn't return the greeting. "Your companions have caused much trouble since they arrived last night."

"Are they all alive?" Turesobei asked quickly.

She pointed back toward the village. "Two girls, a boy, a machine man, and two strange animals are hiding inside that house."

Turesobei sighed with relief — all of them were safe. Now he just needed to get them out of here.

"The boy and his friends have come from the land beyond the gate," Sudorga said.

"So they told me when they arrived here yesterday, when the dragon dropped them nearby. They sought shelter in our village. We do not provide shelter. Our lands are ours and ours alone. They are trespassers, and trespassers are food."

"I understand this," Turesobei said, "but my friends didn't know. We know nothing about your world. And my companions had little choice. The dragon dropped them here, and they are lucky it didn't consume them. I beg you to let them go."

"They have killed seven of my people," she seethed. "Seven! We have not lost so many at once in ages."

"Please. They were just defending themselves. You would do the same. They were stranded here by accident. They didn't know."

"What do you have to barter for their lives? What wergild can you possibly offer us? It would have to be immense for something so vile as what the machine did."

"Machine?" Sudorga asked.

"Motekeru, one of my companions," Turesobei said. "What is wergild?"

"Blood price," Narbenu said. "If you take someone's life, you must pay their family for their loss or suffer the same fate. Seven wergilds would be a fortune."

"I have nothing that you would value," Turesobei said. "Except perhaps knowledge from the world beyond. Stories you've never heard. Things you may not know."

"We would care for such things," Lady Umora replied, "but not so much that we would bargain even one life for them."

"Then I have nothing else. I can only beg your mercy."

"Please consider the boy's wishes," War Chief Sudorga replied. "He is an honored guest of ours, and it would please us greatly if you did."

"I am sorry, Sudorga. I cannot grant you your wish. I assume, given the peace between us, that you do not wish to make this an issue ..."

War Chief Sudorga sighed heavily. "No, Lady Umora. We do not, but we are disappointed."

Turesobei quietly uttered the *spell of compelling obedience.*

Umora shrugged and turned to one of the reitsu beside her. "Break down that door and take them."

"Wait," Turesobei commanded. "You will let my friends go, or you will suffer the consequences."

Unaffected, Lady Umora hissed, "Whatever sorcerous trick you are attempting to play on me, it will not work. We are a magical people."

Turesobei turned to War Chief Sudorga. "Back off, all of you. I won't involve you in this any further. Thank you for bringing me here. I must now fight the reitsu."

"Turesobei, think twice before you do anything rash," Narbenu said.

"Go," Turesobei told them, then he dropped the glamor, revealing the storm sigil on his cheek.

The goronku returned to their mounts, but didn't leave. Lady Umora watched Turesobei cautiously.

"I am the Storm Dragon," Turesobei said. "You will let my friends go, or I will destroy all of you and raze this village until not even a trace of you exists. I killed over a dozen yomon. You will pose no greater threat to me than they did. The goronku have no part of this."

He hesitated to unleash any of the energy, afraid that tapping even the slightest bit of the power would plunge him into the dragon dream too long or transform him into the dragon again. And he was certain that if he became the dragon, he would lose his humanity.

Lady Umora sneered, even as her fellows took a step back. "Become the dragon, then."

"What?"

"Become the dragon, and I will let them go."

Chapter Eight

"You — you don't think I'm the dragon?" Turesobei asked, thinking that Lady Umora was challenging him to prove it.

"Oh, I have no reason to doubt you. I recognize power when I see it."

"Then you should know that I can destroy you."

"I believe you can. However, I do not think you can turn into this storm dragon again. Something is stopping you. Perhaps you do not have control over the monster within. Why else would you drop your friends beside a strange village, unequipped to survive this cold, and then fly off?" She licked her fangs and cocked an eyebrow. "So my offer stands. Turn into the dragon, and I will free your companions."

Turesobei clenched his eyes and thought. He wouldn't hesitate to become the Storm Dragon if that's what it would take to save his friends, but only as a last resort. There had to be some other way.

"Just as I thought," said Lady Umora.

Turesobei chose honesty. "I can do it, and if you give me no alternative, I will do it. If I become the Storm Dragon again, it is likely I will be the Storm Dragon forever. I will destroy you and your people. I have enough control not to kill my friends. I would lose only myself. I am willing to die to save them."

"Are you certain? Many say they love someone so much that they would die for them, but it is another thing to actually do it."

"How do you think I came to be the Storm Dragon before? I did it to save my sister and my companions from the yomon and a cult of assassins."

Lady Umora bit at her lip. "One of them is your sister?"

"Yes, and her friend and my ... um ... girlfriend."

"And what are the others to you?"

"Well, they're all my family in a way. The hounds and the machine were made by my ancestor —" he lifted the kavaru "— the wizard who passed this stone down to me. It's called a —"

"I know what a kavaru is. They exist still in our legends. If one of the girls is your sister and the other your mate, we may be able to work something out. But you will not like it."

"I'm listening." He didn't bother to explain that Iniru wasn't his mate. It was probably better if they believed that she was.

"In our society, disputes that involve a relative may be settled by a fight to the death."

"Fine," Turesobei said. "Name your champion. I will fight him to the death, and if I win, you will let us all go."

"That is not how we do things." She eyed his arm. He didn't know how she could tell, but she clearly knew it was broken. "If you win, you and your companions may go, except for the machine man. If you lose, only one of the others may go free."

"All of us go free," Turesobei countered, "if I win."

"The machine man must pay for killing seven of my people."

"If I win, I will not command him to surrender. You can try to take him if you dare, but he will fight to the death. Unless you have stronger weapons than what I see here, you will have to sacrifice most of your people to kill him."

Through clenched teeth she said, "Fine. We agree to this. He may go free, as well … if you win. However, we do have a weapon that will kill him."

"Whatever it is, you'd rather not use it."

She tilted her head and smiled. "And you'd rather not become the Storm Dragon."

"I want the goronku to bear witness that the fight is fair."

"That is acceptable," she replied.

Turesobei marched over and presented the plan to War Chief Sudorga.

"Are you certain you want to do it this way?" Sudorga asked.

"I feel confident in my success."

"Lad," said Narbenu, "the reitsu are fast and deadly. Whatever your machine man did, I don't think you can duplicate that. No single one of us could take on a reitsu and survive, much less face their champion."

"Their champion," Turesobei whispered, "he will feed to kill me, won't he? He won't just stab me and leave me for dead because I'm no good to eat if I'm dead, right?"

Narbenu nodded. "They would never turn down feeding. You would keep him warm for many years."

"Then I think I have a decent chance at winning."

War Chief Sudorga went to Lady Umora. "If you don't treat the boy fairly, it will mean war between our peoples."

"I accept that," she replied, confidently. She turned to Turesobei. "Are you ready to face our champion and die, boy?"

Chapter Nine

"I'm ready," Turesobei said, "but I won't fight until my friends are brought out so that I can see that they're well."

Lady Umora dispatched several of her people, but they returned without Turesobei's companions.

"The machine man won't come out," a reitsu reported.

"I will have to go to them," Turesobei said.

On Lady Umora's orders, a group of reitsu escorted Turesobei, Narbenu, and Kemsu through the village. The goronku went along to ensure the reitsu didn't betray their word. The houses they passed were in terrible condition — cracked walls, loose roof tiles, crumbling window frames. Apparently, the condition of their village was not a reitsu priority. They passed seven charred corpses. The reitsu had made no effort to move them. Turesobei stepped carefully around them and approached a tiny house on the edge of the village. The decaying wood door was splintered in many places. Another few minutes and the reitsu would've broken through by shattering the door into pieces.

"Shoma?" Turesobei called out. "Iniru? Zaiporo? I've come to rescue you!"

"Sobei!" Shoma called out weakly.

"Shoma! Are you all right? Is everyone else with you?"

"We're all here. And alive. I think we —"

"It might be a trap," Iniru muttered.

"It's not a trap," Turesobei said. "How could they know how to duplicate my voice?"

Muffled discussions followed. They were taking too long. Turesobei invoked energy from his kavaru. "Motekeru, I command you to open the door."

The door crumbled as Motekeru opened it. Metal joints creaking, a battered Motekeru stepped forward. His bamboo cable tail thrashed back and forth with agitation, the spiked ball on the end scraping across the flagstones. The reitsu and goronku backed away.

The mechanical ... man ... had a body of petrified oak. Bronze plates reinforced his forearms, shins, thighs, and chest. His horrible head made entirely of bronze had a mouth so jagged and misshapen Turesobei wondered if it had been cut by a three-year-old. Within the mouth were two rows of razor-sharp, ivory teeth — few matched in length and some were missing. Amber energy blazed from eyes that curled upward on the ends.

Battling the yomon and the Deadly Twelve had left Motekeru in rough shape. The bronze plates were dented, the oak body scorched and nicked and scarred, the nose on his head crushed flat. His movements were slowing. The fire in his eyes sputtered at times.

Motekeru retracted his claws and knelt. "Apologies for not believing it was you, master."

"You don't have to kneel or apologize. I would have done the same." Turesobei patted him on the shoulder in what he hoped would be taken as a friendly manner. Though Motekeru obeyed him, Turesobei still feared him. Motekeru hadn't wanted to return to the world from wherever it was he'd been while sleeping the last few centuries.

The two amber wolfhounds, Rig and Ohma, charged Turesobei. Chonda Lu had apparently preserved his favorite pets so they could live on forever. Turesobei scratched behind the hounds' ears as they rubbed against his legs. They backed away, and Enashoma plowed into him. He wrapped his good arm around her and held her tight. "It's going to be okay."

Gently, Turesobei pushed Enashoma away. Her long hair was a tangled mess, matted with grime and blood, and she'd lost weight. Shoma's wide hips were slim now, her cheeks hollow. A cut on her chin festered. Her lips were cracked and bleeding. She shivered uncontrollably. Turesobei removed his parka, awkwardly with his broken arm, then he helped her into it.

"I'll get you out of this, Little Blossom. I promise."

Eyes tearing with relief, Zaiporo clapped Turesobei on the shoulder. Bruises covered Zaiporo's face and neck. A cut on his forehead had sealed, but blood stained his ash-gray zaboko skin and his clothes. The handsome, fifteen-year-old, former house-guard was broad-shouldered and stout, especially compared to taller, thinner baojendari like Turesobei and Enashoma.

Turesobei spun around, looking for Iniru. She stood at the doorway, peeking around the corner, probably sizing up the enemy and analyzing escape routes. How she could keep going, he had no idea. She had been near death when he had healed her in the Lair, and all he had done was accelerate her recovery. She needed weeks of rest. Now she had dozens of new bruises, scrapes, and cuts. A bloodstain darkened the back of her charcoal uniform. The wound on her back that his spell had sealed had reopened. Another bloodstain spread from her left hamstring. One of her eyelids drooped.

She turned and sized him up with a small spark in her eyes. Her lips twitched. "You look ridiculous in all those clothes."

"Thanks. You look terrible."

Limping toward him, she smiled. "Jerk."

He embraced her ... they kissed. Her lips were cold and dry, her breath ragged.

"It's time," one of the reitsu outside hissed.

Iniru's lips were tinged blue, and like Shoma, she was shivering.

"You're going to freeze."

"My fur's not enough in cold like this." She patted his chest. "Looks like you'll be fine, though. You adjusted fast. Already made a home here, have you?"

"I got lucky and made some friends." He nodded toward the goronku. "First time I've caught a break in a while."

"How are you getting us out of here? These ... whatever they are ... they aren't friendly."

"I'm going to have to fight their champion to the death."

Iniru tapped his splinted arm, and he winced. "You're going to fight one of them with a broken arm?"

"How did you know it was broken? Never mind. Yes, with a broken arm. If I win, we all go free. If I lose ... I die. But one of you can still go free ... my choice."

Iniru took his face in her hands. He stared into her deep amber eyes with their slitted pupils. "You must choose Shoma."

"I know that, Niru."

"I know you know that," Iniru replied. "But I don't want you to feel bad because you didn't pick me."

"I love you," he blurted out. His cheeks reddened.

She patted his cheeks. "I know that."

"I know you know that," he stammered in a poor attempt to be clever.

As they shuffled out, Enashoma tugged on Turesobei's sleeve. "I'm a bad choice. Iniru can survive in this place. I can't. I'm not cut out for it."

"The goronku, the people who brought me here, who gave me the clothes, they're good people. They would take care of you."

Nodding toward Narbenu and Kemsu who walked ahead of them, Zaiporo whispered, "If they're good people, why aren't they fighting to free us?"

"War would break out between the reitsu and the goronku — all through the region — and the last time these two peoples fought they nearly destroyed one another."

"I could fight these reitsu, master," said Motekeru. "You and the others could make a run for it."

"I made a deal, Motekeru. I will fight their champion."

"They cannot defeat me, master."

"They are bringing out a weapon they believe will harm you. Trust me, it will be best this way. Besides, I won't lose."

"Have you seen how fast they are?" Iniru said with worry. "You sure you know what you're doing?"

"I'm certain," he replied.

Motekeru rumbled, glaring at Lady Umora. "I do not think the reitsu will honor their bargain with you."

Joining them, War Chief Sudorga said, "The goronku will see to it that the bargain is kept."

Reitsu and goronku, eyeing one another nervously, gathered in the village commons, forming a circle. Along with the reitsu guarding them, Turesobei and his companions followed Sudorga and Umora into the middle of the circle.

"How did you break your arm?" Enashoma asked.

"When I crashed," he murmured. "Took all I could do to stop being the dragon. When

I did, I was in mid-flight."

"Why haven't you healed it?"

"I don't have the strength yet. My spirit's too depleted. All I've got is storm energy, and I don't dare tap into it."

"And you think you can win?" Iniru said.

"Only other thing to do is to let the reitsu and Motekeru fight it out and hope he beats them all while we run away. And I don't think we'd make it far. We're not in good shape and this land is inhospitable. And while I don't like the reitsu, I don't want to kill them all."

Shoma shrugged and Zaiporo said, "You didn't have them attack you when you sought shelter. You didn't have them pin you and try to ... I don't know what it was they tried on me. But it was like —"

"All the warmth inside you began to drain away?" Turesobei asked.

"How'd you know?" Iniru asked.

"Because that's what they do," he replied. "That's how they feed."

Enashoma shivered. "That's ... that's sick. I hate this place."

The reitsu in the circle remained eerily silent as Lady Umora explained the bargain. "Choose the one who goes free when you lose, Chonda Turesobei."

He placed his good arm around Enashoma. "My sister, Enashoma, goes free no matter the outcome."

"So be it," Lady Umora proclaimed. She pointed to Enashoma. "This one goes free no matter what. We will do no harm to her, now or ever."

The goronku brought blankets out for Turesobei's companions. Iniru and Zaiporo eagerly wrapped themselves up. Enashoma had Turesobei's coat, but she still took a blanket and wrapped it around her legs.

"They won't need those for long," Lady Umora told War Chief Sudorga.

"They should be comfortable while they can," he said. "You wouldn't want them to lose too much warmth, would you?"

She licked her lips. "You make a good point. Chonda Turesobei, say goodbye to your friends."

He kissed Enashoma and told her all would be well. She nodded, trying to be brave and confident. He faced Motekeru.

"You will surrender if I am defeated. That's an order."

Motekeru had only the one facial expression Chonda Lu had given him. But Turesobei knew, perhaps through their bond, that Motekeru understood him perfectly well. If Turesobei fell, Motekeru should fight and do his best to save the others.

Iniru kissed him. "Good luck." She said nothing else. What more could be said?

Chapter Ten

War Chief Sudorga and Lady Umora faced each other in the center of the circle and bowed.

Lady Umora folded her hands together and kissed them. "I swear by the ghosts of my ancestors that I will honor this deal."

War Chief Sudorga gazed into the sky and held his arms out. "I swear by the Crimson Sun that we will see to it that you honor this bargain."

Lady Umora looked to Turesobei. "Who do you swear to, boy? Who will be dishonored if you should not fight fairly?"

"I swear to no gods. I swear by my own honor."

War Chief Sudorga frowned. "You must honor some god in your land?"

"My people respect and honor many lesser deities and the greater deities of the earth, the sun, and the moons. But we do not swear by them."

"That's not good enough," Umora said. "You must swear by more than your own honor."

He gritted his teeth and flared his eyes. His friends were freezing, and their lives hung in the balance. This was ridiculous. "Fine. I swear by myself, the Storm Dragon, who was a god for centuries in my land."

Lady Umora furrowed her brow. "I do not think —"

"I don't care what you think! If I wanted to, I'd become a god right now and smite you all into nothing but ashes. Let's get on with it."

War Chief Sudorga shrugged, though fear flickered in his eyes. Lady Umora stared at Turesobei several moments, then sneered and said, "So be it. We fight hand-to-hand, but you may select a weapon if you wish. It won't matter."

Narbenu brought him a spear. Turesobei did a few practice jabs to test the weight and balance. He wouldn't have much chance with it. He'd only done basic training in using a spear, and the spears the Chonda used were a foot shorter than this one.

"Remember, lad, the touch of a wraith will only take a smidgen of warmth from you," Narbenu said. "They must lock a hand on you and focus to really draw it out. Their claws are sharp and have a mild toxin that causes pain. It doesn't do anything more than that, so don't be alarmed." He patted him on both shoulders. "If you should fall, my people will see that your sister is taken care of for all her days, and we will never forget you."

He was pretty sure Narbenu actually meant "when you fall," since no one thought he stood a chance.

A tall reitsu with corded muscles stepped into the circle. He moved gracefully but languidly, as if wandering through a dream. He took one look at Turesobei and said, frowning, "Sister, you have woken me to face this ... alien boy? Surely you could've dealt with him on your own?"

She pointed toward the charred corpses and nodded toward Motekeru. "The boy claims to be a god, brother. He is fighting to free his friends. But we did not wake you up for this. We woke you to fight the machine man. This is better. If you beat the boy, the machine surrenders to us."

The reitsu took a pale-bladed knife from a sheath on his hip and handed it to Umora. White-steel; so they did have the ability to injure Motekeru, after all. Not that taking on Motekeru with a knife would've been pleasant.

The reitsu champion bowed before Turesobei, who returned the bow then asked, "Do we have any rules?"

"No one may interfere to aid either combatant," said Lady Umora, "and you fight to the death. There are no other rules."

Enashoma rushed forward and gave Turesobei a hug. He kissed her, and shoved her toward Iniru, who had followed her. "It'll be okay. I promise."

"Watch yourself," Iniru whispered. "They're wicked fast. Faster than me."

Turesobei smiled. "It'll be okay." He closed his eyes, took a few deep breaths, then said to the wraith, "I'm ready when you are."

Almost instantly, razor-sharp claws struck Turesobei's chest and tore through clothing and armor to scratch him. Despite only hitting the surface, pain sparked deep into his flesh. Turesobei stumbled backward and jabbed clumsily with the spear. The wraith darted away, and then moved back in so fast Turesobei barely saw him. Another swipe struck him across the face, cutting into his cheek. This time, a chill went deep into his bones along with the pain. He felt a trickle of fire kenja leave him.

Turesobei jabbed again with the spear, trying to make a good show of it. He missed again, badly. All the reitsu in the circle laughed and taunted him. The reitsu champion circled him, grinning.

"You shouldn't play with your food," Turesobei told him.

Snarling, the reitsu darted toward him — and then past him without attacking. Before Turesobei could spin around, claws scratched hard across the back of his neck and jabbed into his side, near his kidneys. The pain was so intense he cried out.

He stumbled, turned, and swept the spear out in an arc. The reitsu caught it by the shaft, and snapped it in half. With his fist, the wraith hammered Turesobei's broken arm. Again he cried out, bending over in agony. Claws jabbed into and out of both thighs — and then both his arms. Pain wracked him, while cold burrowed deep into his soul.

An elbow struck his chin and downed him.

Turesobei's eyes rolled. He took deep, rapid breaths and tried to focus on staying awake. He couldn't fall unconscious — he had to be awake when the reitsu tried to drain him. The wraith knelt on Turesobei's chest, pinning him down. Laughing, he latched both hands around Turesobei's neck. Warmth fled from Turesobei; his internal kenja depleted rapidly. The wraith threw his head back, rolled his eyes, took in a deep breath, and licked his lips. Chill bumps spread across Turesobei's skin. He felt as if he were lying naked on the ice. Aches like those from a fever set into his bones. His mind became muddled. He hadn't expected the process to happen so fast.

But if the reitsu wanted warmth, Turesobei had more than enough kenja to give him. Focusing, Turesobei altered the channel the wraith instinctively used to draw energy and rerouted it to the *Mark of the Storm Dragon*. He wouldn't have to risk opening it; he could just let the wraith draw from it instead.

The channel shifted. Raw power flowed into the wraith. The reitsu screamed as he burst into flames. Turesobei kicked free and rolled away. A burst of fire shot outward, and the wraith disintegrated into a pile of ashes.

Unfortunately, the wraith's draw on the sigil resulted in a leak of storm kenja into Turesobei. Even though he hadn't opened the channel, Turesobei fell into the dream of the Storm Dragon.

Chapter Eleven

Turesobei fought against the dragon. "I did not call on you," he said. "I did not call on this power. I do not accept it."

He woke to himself suddenly, covered in ashes. Motekeru stood guard over him. The amber hounds, Rig and Ohma, flanked him. Based on their positioning, he had, apparently, strayed only mentally into the dragon dream, without physically shifting.

War Chief Sudorga was arguing with Lady Umora, who was snarling — eyes blazing — and screaming. The wraiths and the goronku had separated and were facing off, each side prepared to fight. Iniru had drawn Enashoma and Zaiporo away from the conflict.

Fighting through the tremendous pain from his injuries, Turesobei grabbed onto Motekeru and pulled himself up. Lady Umora spotted him, and then stormed over, pointing. Motekeru put himself between them.

"You cheated!" she shouted.

"I received no outside help, and we fought to the death," Turesobei gasped. He clutched a hand to the wound in his side to stop the blood that was flowing out. "Those were the rules. It was fair fight, and a deal is a deal."

"You burned him away like the machine did to those it murdered! You knew that would happen. You knew you would beat him!"

"I thought it might happen, yes. But I was far from certain. He could've killed me and won easily at any point. I was no match for him physically. If he had killed me instead of feeding, the storm energies would never have touched him. Some restraint from him, and you could've feasted on all of us. But that was his choice."

War Chief Sudorga pleaded with Lady Umora. "He followed the rules. You made a deal."

"You risk war between our peoples," she seethed.

"We had an agreement," Sudorga replied. "And we didn't interfere."

"He's your ally, Sudorga, and he deceived us!"

"Enough!" Turesobei shouted, eyes narrowing. "I have had enough! This ends now. I'm exhausted, cold, wounded, bleeding, half-dead, and trapped in an alien land, perhaps forever. War Chief Sudorga, would you please withdraw from the commons. Take my companions with you."

"Sobei," Iniru said, "I don't think —"

"I said go."

"I'm staying with you," she said.

"You're a liability right now. Go, Iniru. Protect Shoma and Zai — please."

Her nostrils flared with irritation, but she nodded and backed away. War Chief Sudorga started to say something, but Turesobei shook his head. The goronku withdrew. The gathered reitsu closed on Turesobei, Motekeru, and the wolfhounds.

"You cannot defeat us," Lady Umora said.

Turesobei patted Motekeru on the back. "Are you ready?"

"We will kill them all, master," he replied in his deep mechanical tones. "We should've done it this way from the start. These ... reitsu ... they're no better than beasts. No honor at all."

"You are the ones without honor," Umora said.

"We followed your rules," Turesobei said, looking not at her but the other reitsu. "Your actions now bring dishonor upon you."

Lady Umora brandished the white-steel knife. "I do not fear the machine, and I do not fear you."

"They have a white-steel blade," Turesobei said to Motekeru. "They think they can kill you with it."

"That little knife? Barely worth mentioning."

"It would take quite a lot of stabs, I should think."

"Many stabs," Motekeru replied. "It would be better for slicing cheese than harming me."

Lady Umora hesitated. The other reitsu stopped moving forward. It was time for Turesobei to throw in one more element to make them doubt.

"Lu Bei!"

From the pack on the mount, the fetch popped out and zoomed overhead, circling downward until he hovered beside Turesobei. Attempting a growl that was more of a high-pitched whine, the fetch cast sparks between his palms as menacingly as he could. The reitsu wouldn't know how little power those sparks carried.

"Master, I am ready to wipe the ice with the blood of these creatures." Lu Bei bowed toward Lady Umora. "You will die first, Lady Umora. Those without honor always die first."

Lady Umora backed away, snarling, as did the other reitsu. A grizzled wraith with stringy hair stepped in front of her.

"The elders have voted, Lady Umora. You are hereby removed from power. You have brought dishonor to us, and you're risking many lives. A deal is a deal." He turned to Turesobei. "Leave here, boy. Never return to our lands. If you do, your life is forfeit, no matter the cost to us."

Turesobei bowed. "Thank you for honoring the bargain."

"Are you sure it wouldn't be better to kill them, master?" Motekeru asked.

"A deal is a deal."

"As you wish, master."

The reitsu parted and allowed them to pass. Turesobei, Motekeru, and the hounds joined the goronku who were gathered around their mounts.

Lu Bei zoomed around Motekeru. "You haven't forgotten how to play the game."

"I would have killed them," Motekeru replied.

"That's what makes you such a good player," Lu Bei responded.

"I have never understood you, fetch. And I still don't like you."

Lu Bei shrugged, and when Motekeru wasn't looking, the fetch stuck his tongue out at him.

"One day, fetch, I'm going to rip that tongue out," said Motekeru, though how he knew Lu Bei had made a face at him, Turesobei had no idea.

Lu Bei's eyes went wide. He flew into Turesobei's pack, and transformed back into a book. Turesobei wasn't certain, but he thought Motekeru's body might have shuddered as he suppressed something like a laugh.

"That was gutsy what you did," Narbenu said, nodding to Turesobei.

Iniru kissed Turesobei on the cheek. "He's good at gutsy." She looked him over. "You're a mess. You're wounded again. Why are you always wounded?"

"Because ..." He sighed. "Because I'm always in over my head. And frankly, whatever my special destiny is that Lu Bei's always going on about ... well, it sucks. Also, I'm very brave."

"Stupid, more like," Iniru said.

"I am never sure whose side you're on."

She grinned. "Mine." She looked at the sonoke for the first time. "Oh wow. You ride these?"

"Sonoke," Kemsu said stepping forward. He bowed and smiled warmly at her. "They're called sonoke. We have three extras. Some of you will have to double up. The machine man looks heavy. Probably should take one by himself. I'm Kemsu, by the way."

"Iniru," she replied absently, staring at the sonoke.

"Shoma, you and Iniru ride together," Turesobei said. "Zai, you can double up with me. Motekeru, take the hounds with you. No more questions until we're moving. I want to get out of here before they change their minds."

"What about your wounds?" Shoma asked. "You're bleeding. You need to bind them."

"My injuries will have to wait, at least until we're out of sight."

A half-hour later, they stopped, and Narbenu wrapped a strip of cloth around Turesobei's midsection, to keep the wound in his side from bleeding any further. The others injuries would have to wait.

"You didn't earn any friends today," War Chief Sudorga said.

"You think they'll hold it against your people?" Turesobei asked.

"I don't think so. If they do, we can handle ourselves. But know this: if you leave our lands, they may come after you. How did you do that, anyway?"

"What, kill the reitsu champion?" Turesobei asked. "I altered the channel his warmth-feeding used, so it would tap my storm sigil instead of my soul."

"You took a big risk," Zaiporo said.

"I knew it could work. They tried to drain Motekeru of his warmth, but he is powered by magical fire, so it incinerated them. That's how the corpses ended up charred, right?"

"Indeed," Motekeru replied. "I barely touched them. It was their strikes against me that did them in."

"It was too much warmth for them to contain," Turesobei said. "I just had to make sure the champion didn't kill me or knock me out, so I could redirect the energy at the right time."

"You're lucky he didn't kill you," Zaiporo said.

"How did all of you survive them last night?" Turesobei said.

"When we wandered into the village," Zaiporo said, "only a few of them met us at first. They attacked us, but the hounds intercepted them, and then Motekeru reached them. They fought him and the hounds, and ignored the rest of us. Don't think they thought we were much of a threat. I guess they were right. Anyway, Iniru found the little house. It was empty, and the door was unlocked. Motekeru killed the seven nearest wraiths and joined us inside. Don't know why it took them all day to mount a decent attack."

"I think it must take them a while to wake up from their hibernation," Turesobei said. "Their best fighter didn't even wake until after we got to you."

"Their champion slumbered because he was already full," Narbenu said. "The reitsu are slow to rouse, especially if they don't anticipate a threat. Usually, no more than a quarter of the village will be out of hibernation at once."

It was late in the day, so they only rode for a few more hours. Only the active spell strip tucked into his belt kept Turesobei going. His injuries were far worse than he let the others know. As they rode, he let the mount follow along and dozed, with his scarf pulled over his face. He was left shivering without the parka, but his companions had it far worse, with only blankets to wrap around themselves. He was afraid they'd get frostbite before they made it back to Aikora.

Turesobei offered to summon the moon mirrors again, but War Chief Sudorga took one look at him and declined. The goronku cut blocks of ice to make snow houses, while Turesobei and his companions watched, except Motekeru. The goronku told him to rest, but Motekeru replied, "I am tireless. I will help."

Wearing his scarf and hat, Lu Bei flew around observing the goronku's snow house work and asking them endless questions about it, which they didn't seem to mind. Turesobei was glad, because they might need to know how to do it on their own soon, and he was too tired to pay enough attention.

"My companions and I, we'll all sleep in a snow house together," Turesobei said while snuggled between Iniru and Enashoma.

"No," Narbenu replied. "That is not proper. The girls must have their own snow house."

Turesobei sighed, but didn't argue it. Technically, it wouldn't have been allowable where he was from, either — not that he cared.

"Will we be safe?" Shoma asked, shivering despite Turesobei's coat and the blanket she had wrapped around her.

"The hounds and I will stay with them," Motekeru said.

Stable hands took the sonoke from them as soon as they reached Aikora. Bedraggled, exhausted, and bitterly cold, Turesobei and his companions limped down the stairs into the village, following War Chief Sudorga. When they reached the common area at the bottom of the stairs, the goronku people massed around them to hear the news. Turesobei guessed the spotters in the watchtower had announced their impending arrival.

"Everyone has returned safe and well!" War Chief Sudorga proclaimed. "And our friend the dragon wizard Turesobei defeated a reitsu champion in single combat!" The crowd oohed in amazement. "And he won the freedom of his companions, who now join us!"

Raucous cheers followed, but they ceased as Motekeru clanged down the steps into the common room.

"Worry not, my people, over this metal man!" Sudorga put an arm around Motekeru. "He may be frightening to behold, but he is honorable and mighty. He defeated seven reitsu in combat." Gasps spread around the room, then the people applauded again. "Now, our new guests need food, clothing, and treatment for their injuries. Make way!"

A goronku girl shoved forward, barreled into Turesobei, picked him up, swung him around, and put him back down.

"Kurine," he gasped in a mixture of surprise and pain. "Careful — I'm badly hurt."

"You poor, brave dear," she said, taking his face in her hands. "My champion. I was so worried you'd never return. I hardly slept a wink the last two nights. But you're back safe, and I couldn't be happier."

Turesobei smiled, not having a clue how to respond.

Kurine's eyes creased, and she chewed on her lip, as if in deep in thought. He tried to pull away, but she wouldn't let him. Kurine released a deep breath, blinked, and then said, quietly but formally, "Chonda Turesobei, will you accept my kiss?"

The common room fell into complete silence. Eyes pleading, cheeks blushing, Kurine leaned toward him. He should tell her no. Iniru was standing only a few paces away. Surely it wasn't proper for him to kiss her, given how strict the goronku were about boys and girls being alone in a room together. But none of them were responding as if it were a problem. If anything, they were waiting expectantly for his reply. Would it be rude if he kissed her? Would it be rude if he refused? Everyone was watching. Her friends and family, most of her people. Would she feel rejected if declined? Would they mock her? He imagined how hurt he would feel if he were rejected publicly. He could explain to Kurine afterward that it was only a friendly kiss, that it didn't mean anything more. And Iniru would understand. Maybe. Once she let him explain. And she'd forgive him ... eventually.

"Yeah, okay."

Kurine hopped, squealed, and planted a big wet kiss on his lips. While there was certainly nothing wrong with the kiss ... her lips were soft, warm, and inviting ... he returned it as simply as he could. When she broke away, tears streamed from her eyes. She hugged him tight.

"Thank you," she muttered, "you've made me so happy."

People in the crowd oohed. A few men whooped out congratulations, while women rubbed tears from their eyes. Turesobei squirmed free and took a step away, while Kurine smiled innocently and waved to a lady in the crowd. Was that her mother?

This ... this was not the reaction he'd expected. Not even close. His friends stood — silent, unmoving, completely stunned — except Iniru. Shaking her head, she clenched her fists tight while her eyes blazed with fury.

She whispered to him, calmly, too calmly, "You just can't help yourself, can you?"

Turesobei started to respond, but his mouth seized up. A tremor quaked through his muscles. Vertigo hit him. Aches far greater than any physical pain struck deep into his soul. He collapsed into convulsions, his body twitching, his limbs jerking and flailing.

Chapter Twelve

Turesobei tried to stop flailing, but his body wouldn't respond. His face twitched, his insides twisted, his soul burned. He chomped his teeth down hard, over and over. He knew why he was having a seizure; not that knowing why did him any good. His internal kenja was depleted, his soul starved. His body reacted the way anybody would react in such a situation: by going haywire.

There was one way he could stop it. He could tap the *Mark of the Storm Dragon* and replenish his internal stores. But if he did, his internal kenja would be completely replaced with storm energy. He would become the Storm Dragon forever, possibly without any memory of his original self. He'd just have to hope he survived.

Thinking about the sigil resulted in a sudden tug at its energy. His survival instinct was reaching out for the only power source it could find. Turesobei gave all of his will-power over to blocking access to the sigil's power.

Kemsu ripped his knife from its sheath and tossed the blade aside. "Someone pin him!"

Motekeru locked his giant, mechanical hands around Turesobei's upper arms and held him in place. Narbenu pinned Turesobei's kicking feet. Kemsu dove onto him, and shoved the knife sheath into his mouth. Turesobei clamped down on the leather.

Kemsu rocked back onto his haunches. "That ought to keep him from biting off his tongue."

Iniru knelt beside him and nodded to Kemsu. "Good thinking."

"I've done it before. My mother had seizures ... until she died a few years ago."

"I'm sorry about your mother," Iniru said to Kemsu while stroking Turesobei's cheek.

Crying, Kurine took Turesobei's left hand, trying to hold onto it while it flexed and thrashed. "Eira is on her way. Please be well. Please be well."

Enashoma took the other hand. She was crying, too. "He's done too much for us. His wounds are killing him."

Turesobei couldn't respond to them. All he could do was concentrate on blocking out the storm energies.

With a screech of pain, Lu Bei popped back into fetch form. "No energy from ... Master," he panted. "Hard to transform. Had to use my own. Both of us depleted now." He hopped onto Turesobei's chest and tried to look him in the eyes. "Where is it, master?"

Turesobei couldn't focus on him, couldn't even gesture with his eyes. Lu Bei started checking under his collar.

"What is it?" Enashoma asked. "What are you looking for?"

"A spell strip, Lady Shoma. A burned-out spell strip. He'll have it hidden on him somewhere. I knew he was up to something before we left here. But he wouldn't let me see what he'd done. I had a bad feeling about it."

"You should've done something," Enashoma said. "You should've made him talk. Why didn't you at least spy on him?"

"He is my master. If he says I can't know, I can't know. Besides, he had to rescue you. I know he did what he did because he had no choice."

Iniru patted Turesobei's chest and sides while Kurine checked his legs. The others continued holding him down.

Iniru glared at Kurine, and then snapped, "Don't you think you should be ... elsewhere? I don't think it's right, you touching him like that."

"I don't think you should be touching him at all," Kurine replied indignantly. "He kissed me."

"He's kissed me loads of times."

"I don't see how that's possible," Kurine said, feeling the inside of his thigh. He wished he was well enough to run away and hide.

"Enough!" Enashoma shouted. "He's my brother, and I don't think either of you need to be feeling him up while he's having a fit! Back off and let me and Lu Bei search."

Stunned by Enashoma's uncharacteristic outburst, Iniru and Kurine both backed off. With Kemsu's help, Enashoma removed Turesobei's breastplate and jacket.

Lu Bei pulled off Turesobei's shoes and pinched his own nose. "Nothing here." Lu Bei then ripped Turesobei's belt free, and the spell strip fell out. "Aha! Got it."

"Now what?" Iniru asked.

"We destroy it."

Narbenu pulled out his knife, and picked up the bamboo strip.

Lu Bei snatched it away from him, peered closely at it, and then groaned. "Curses. Just remembered. Gotta destroy it with magic. Tricky stuff."

"Why hadn't he gotten rid of it already?" Iniru asked. "He'd already saved us."

"I'm betting he was going to cancel it out as soon as he got back here to rest. With a few more minutes, he could've done it. Hmm, I bet his wounds are worse than he's letting on. This is dangerous magic."

"You're magical, right?" Enashoma said. "Use your claws."

"I don't think that would work."

Motekeru let go of Turesobei's shoulders, took the spell strip, popped it into his mouth, and swallowed. He belched a tiny flame and shrugged. "Burned up in the fires of my gut. That should do it. Tasted bad. Going to upset my stomach."

"I didn't know you ate!" Zaiporo said.

"I don't like to, but it's useful sometimes. I really need to, have for some time now, but I don't want to."

"What do you eat?" Zaiporo asked.

"The hearts of Master's enemies."

Several of them chuckled, until Lu Bei said, "Not a joke."

Everyone went silent and looked away from Motekeru.

Turesobei's convulsions stopped. But the pain, from his skin down into his bones, was extreme, and the pounding in his head hurt worse than when the reitsu had hammered his broken arm. He leaned over and spat up blood.

"Sobei?" Shoma exclaimed with worry.

"I'll ... be ... okay ... lungs bleeding a bit ... I'll ... survive."

Shaman Eira arrived in her cloak of black feathers. She knelt and tut-tutted loudly as she moved her hands over him. "Don't know what he did, but his spirit is more depleted than when he arrived. Nearly gone. Almost nothing left."

"Chonda Turesobei!" Enashoma nearly shouted. "How could you?! I know what kenja depletion does. I'm ... I'm *very* cross with you."

"Inexcusable," Iniru hissed.

"What's the problem?" Kemsu asked.

"Any time a wizard depletes his inner kenja," Enashoma explained, "he weakens his organs and drains months, maybe years from his life. If it doesn't kill him. To drain himself this much ..." She clenched her eyes shut. "I hope he hasn't killed himself."

Narbenu brought a bowl of water. Kurine took it and held it to Turesobei's lips. Her face was nearly frozen in shock.

He took several sips of water and lay back. "I had to. Not enough ... not enough energy to ... stay awake and ... to save you all. Couldn't have ... done it ... otherwise."

"But I don't understand," Iniru said. "How could you cast a spell to keep yourself awake and active without the spell quitting because you lacked the strength to do anything?"

"Lu Bei ... explain it."

"Fine," Lu Bei snapped. "Normally, if a wizard overexerts himself with a spell, he passes out. You've seen Master Turesobei do that before. With too much drain on internal kenja, the body shuts down to protect itself. A single spell can rip away enough to cause a shutdown, and that can permanently damage organs and strip years from the wizard's lifespan. I'm sure Master is short quite a few already. If a wizard is already exhausted physically, it gets much harder to cast, and Master's kenja was already depleted before we set out to rescue you. He could barely stay awake.

"The spell he used on the strip, the *spell of relentless need*, allows the user to burn internal kenja to keep himself going physically. But there's a catch. External kenja won't help. The *spell of relentless need* can only use internal kenja. Master Turesobei created a loop on the spell strip so that the spell would remain active, even though his body's natural response should've prevented the spell from working. That's how most wizards use that spell. It's for extreme emergencies. When using it, a wizard also shouldn't be casting any other spells at all. But Master did, and that made it doubly dangerous. I don't know how he managed to, but he did."

Lu Bei slapped the top of Turesobei's head.

"Ouch!"

"That's for hiding what you were doing from me, Master. It was too dangerous." Lu Bei slapped him again. "And that's for hiding the spell strip from me. How long have you had that tucked into your belt?"

"Since ... came back from Wakaro ... sneaked the spell past you. Was worth it. Saved the ones I love."

Chapter Thirteen

Waves of sharp pain woke Turesobei. He curled into a fetal position and groaned. He peeled his eyes open to a room that was almost entirely dark. A few taps like a fingernail on a window sounded. Pinkish light brightened the room to the level of a few candles. A hand touched his shoulder.

His face creased with worry, Zaiporo leaned over him. "You okay? Should I get someone?"

"Pain ... I'm in ... pain."

Zaiporo sighed with relief, and sank to his haunches. "Thank the gods. That's the best thing I've heard in a while."

Turesobei groaned. "This is ... good ... how?"

"Well, you weren't feeling *anything* before. No response. No reflexes."

"Comatose?"

"Nearly dead. For seven days now."

Seven?! It seemed nothing more than a blink of an eye to him. Last he remembered was Lu Bei and Shoma scolding him.

"You almost died ... twice. Eira revived you the second time by beating on your chest and throwing ashes in your face. She's been doing all sorts of weird things to keep you going. I doubt most of it works, but apparently some of it does. None of us could do anything, so we just let her do whatever she thought was best. I should go get her now."

"Water ... first."

Turesobei took a few sips, then curled back up. Zaiporo hurried out of the room. It seemed to Turesobei that Zaiporo was gone for hours. Pain swept through him in waves from head to toe, always pausing at his navel, where the spirit meridians all met, forming his kenja-heart. There, the pain grew so deep it felt like he was being stabbed, slowly and steadily, with the blade being twisted — like a hole was being torn open in him.

Sharp, terrible scents assaulted him suddenly. Pungent herbs, decay, and other foul things. He glanced around. Incense smoldered in burners. Long, gray feathers speckled with blood lay all around him. A thick pigment that smelled of excrement was smeared all over him. Torment's flames! How had he not noticed that before?

Zaiporo returned with Eira. Iniru and Shoma followed them. Like Zaiporo, they were now dressed in cold weather outfits like Turesobei's, though Kurine had added decorative stitching to Enashoma's. He wanted to tease Iniru about how she was puffed out in clothes now, too, but couldn't manage the strength.

The medicine woman placed her wrist on his head, and then on his neck. She licked his sweat off her wrist, grumbled, and started to pull the covers back.

"Ladies," Eira said, "if you would please turn away."

Iniru rolled her eyes, and spun around with Shoma. The medicine woman placed one palm high on his chest and the other on his navel. She chanted a moment, swayed, and then shook her head.

"I have no idea how you survived, but your spirit is renewing, growing stronger every moment."

"My kavaru," he muttered in between groans. "The life force in it ... keeping me alive ... can feel it."

She held her hand over it and nodded. "Yes, it has been feeding you. Not much, but enough. The fetch is bound to it, yes? That's why he sleeps."

"He will ... survive so long as ... the kavaru ... survives."

Shaman Eira covered Turesobei up, and Shoma stepped over and took his hand. "Are you feeling any better?"

"Body feels like it's on fire inside and ... everything hurts like ... you know that feeling ... when your arm falls asleep ... and you get sharp needle pricks as it wakes up? Like that, but worse, all over and inside."

"I cannot give you medicine for the pain like I did before," Eira said. "It would kill you in this stage. You're just going to have to endure it."

"Didn't feel anything ... until I woke up."

"Ah," Eira said, "my apologies then, for it is Torment you will endure now."

"How long ... to recover?"

"Hard to say ... weeks, maybe."

He nodded and squeezed Shoma's hand. "You okay?"

"How do I look?" she asked.

"Terrible, but not ... as bad as I probably do."

"You look like a corpse, but I am proud of you, big brother. You said you'd get me through it. You did. Don't know how, but you did."

"Got you trapped in ... eternal winter, though."

"I'm alive. We're all still alive thanks to you."

He doubled up in pain, and when it abated, he said, "Not all. Awasa."

Iniru knelt beside him and stroked his brow. "You did everything you could. She was the only one we lost. We fought the Deadly Twelve and won. Even Chonda Lu died fighting them. We fought the yomon, who the Shogakami imprisoned here because they were so dangerous. And we won."

"Isashiara ... Tochibi," he said.

"Okay, okay — we lost them too," Iniru admitted. "But you did everything possible. The odds were way against us. But you saved us. You even overcame the Storm Dragon.

You may not believe it, but I'm really sorry about what happened to Awasa."

"You were right ... I should've forced ... her back."

"That's on all of us," Zaiporo said. "Awasa wasn't strong enough. We all knew it. And the Warlock ... if he'd taken his time, I know he would've broken me."

"Could've broken any of us ... given time," Turesobei replied. "He took the quickest ... route. She didn't ... deserve it. Won't ... forgive myself."

Iniru kissed his forehead. "Don't think about it. You just rest for now."

Chapter Fourteen

Enemy horns blared a note of retreat. The clatter of weapons ceased; the screams of the dying faded. Head spinning, a knot swelling on his head, Turesobei picked himself up from the mud. Fallen friends and slain enemies lay all around. A banner snapped overhead. He looked at the emerald goshawk on a field of gray and sighed with relief. The blood-soaked standard-bearer nodded back grimly. The Chonda Clan wasn't finished — not yet.

He surveyed the battlefield. His clan of ten thousand now stood but a thousand strong. Forty thousand enemy mercenaries lay dead, their charge broken by Chonda warriors who had sacrificed their lives to save their homeland. Turesobei pulled his blade from the chest of the mercenary warlord. The greater threat was on its way. He'd stopped only the weaker advance force.

A column of the most fearsome knights to ever ride emerged from the pass through the Mountains of the Stars. Behind them marched a hundred thousand spears. The figure that led the knights, Vôl Ultharma, Emperor of Pawan Kor and Lord of the Sun, glowed so bright it was impossible to discern any features beyond his red-gold armor, copper helm, and white cloak. A wave of heat preceded him.

The surviving Chonda bravely formed into their battle lines. Vôl Ultharma's war cry thundered across the plain, and his cavalry launched into a charge.

Turesobei drew out a spell strip made of bronze with glyphs etched onto it. "Steady! We are Chonda. We bow before no one save the Jade Emperor. This invasion ends here!"

A voice that boomed and sang and whispered all at once entered Turesobei's mind. "Chonda Lu, greatest of the Kaiaru wizards. We meet at last."

"I know what you are, Ultharma."

"Then you know that no one can defeat me. Tengba Ren will be mine. The sacrifice of your people today ... it's meaningless."

"I know that you can never be slain." Ultharma's infantry marched out of the pass and onto the Yundragos Plain. "But I also know that you cannot rule a nation as large as mine without an army, Vôl."

Vôl Ultharma held his spear above his head and summoned a beam of fire. The beam struck Turesobei in the chest, and he was blown backward, somersaulting through the air. The bronze spell strip fell from his hand.

A scream tearing from his throat, Turesobei snapped up from his bed of furs.

Lu Bei sped over to him. "Master?"

Turesobei grabbed the fetch by the shoulders. "Ultharma — on the plains — have to stop him!" He fell back, clutching his stomach, and groaned as pain bore through him like a drill. "The bronze spell strip ... have to get it."

Lu Bei's eyes flared with surprise. "Ultharma? How — how do you know that name?"

"On the battlefield ... we have to stop him ..."

"Ultharma's invasion was stopped, master. That battle was long ago. Before my time. You were badly injured, but you saved the day with a most spectacular spell." Lu Bei dipped his shoulders and cringed. "I mean, Master Chonda Lu, not you."

Zaiporo knelt beside him. "Turesobei, are you okay?" He put a hand on Turesobei's brow. "You're feverish. Let me get you some water, then I'll go get Eira."

"Turesobei ... I am ... Turesobei."

"Yes, master," Lu Bei said. "You've had ... you've had a nightmare. Rest now. Everything is fine."

Turesobei lay back down, eyes closing from drowsiness — in spite of all the pain.

"I dreamed I was Chonda Lu."

"I know, master. I know."

For days, Turesobei endured continuous pain and feverish nightmares. He dreamt of lost loves, of children dying in his arms, of passing through plague-stricken cities and trying to bring relief to the sick. He dreamt of the weight of too many centuries upon his soul. Many times, he dreamed of fighting a demonic woman who reminded him of Aikonshi, or Awasa when he last saw her with the purple in her eyes and the madness on her face.

Every time he woke up, someone was with him. Zaiporo slept in the room, so he was almost always there, resting and recovering. Enashoma or Iniru visited sometimes in the day, though he saw them less than he would have expected. Kurine came every day, with Narbenu or Eira as a chaperone, and she would stay by his side most of the night. Kurine insisted on feeding him, and he was so exhausted he let her. She dabbed ice across his forehead and sang him lullabies. Her voice was as pure and sweet as any he'd ever heard, but the songs made no sense to him. She often sang herself to sleep, but would wake if he even budged.

Turesobei tried to talk to all of his visitors, but he rarely got out more than a sentence or two before pain or drowsiness overwhelmed him.

As his internal kenja returned, the pain worsened. He had sacrificed years of his life to save his friends. A decade at least, maybe more. Assuming he'd ever live to reach an old age — which was laughable. The way his life was going, he'd be lucky if he reached eighteen. So long as he recovered to his former strength, he'd be grateful for however many years remained to him. He had survived and saved most of his companions, despite the odds piled against him.

The defiant blaze in Awasa's eyes burned into him. It was the last time he'd seen her. The last time he would ever see her. "I hate you," she screamed at him. "I hate you." And she should — it was all his fault.

Turesobei woke. The room was almost entirely dark. No one was there. No one at all. That was strange.

"Zaiporo?" he whispered. "Kurine?"

No one answered. Had something happened? He was drenched in sweat. His fever had broken. The pain wasn't half as bad as it had been the last time he was awake. He thought about calling Lu Bei, but decided not to. If no one was here watching him, then they weren't worried about him anymore. He was well enough to help himself for a change. He sat up and drank the bowl of water they'd left him.

He felt closed in, trapped, like he was in a tomb. He desperately wanted to be outside, to be in the open ... just a window would do. The vision of Awasa was still swimming through his mind. He'd dreamt of her over and over — until he thought it might drive him insane.

Turesobei clutched his kavaru and bowed, touching his head against the cold stone floor. He wasn't devout. Most Chonda weren't. They performed the basic rituals honoring their ancestors, the Great Deities, and the Shogakami, and they observed all the major festivals. But Turesobei prayed now, earnestly and fervently, naming every deity he knew. He prayed for forgiveness. He prayed that he would find some way to return his companions home safely. Whether the gods could hear him, whether they would help him, whether they ever helped anyone ... he didn't care. Prayer was all he could offer.

"Goddess Kaiwen, Earth Mother, here I lie in your womb. In some strange, cold place and time. Help me take my companions home. Help us. In any way that you can. I am your humble —"

With a sound like giant wings whipping out, a shadow filled the room, plunging it into complete darkness. Along with that shadow came a cold that was beyond the cold of ice and wind, a cold of emptiness and despair. Two catlike eyes amidst the shadow opened, baleful eyes that burned and flickered like scarlet flames.

"You returned," a deep but feminine voice rumbled. "I knew you would. I have dreamt of you for thousands of years. Of how I would devour you and how delicious and slow and painful my revenge on you would be." The flaming eyes bore down on him. "The day of my revenge draws close. I know. I know, because you must come to me. You will have no other choice."

Chapter Fifteen

Turesobei cried out and scrambled back. He tore free from the covers. His heart pounded; pain raced through his limbs and thundered in his head. The fiery eyes and the relentless shadow had vanished. A dim, pink light illuminated the room.

Kurine grabbed his hand. "Are you okay? Are you in pain?"

"Where ... where did you come from?"

"I've been here with you all night," she replied, frowning.

"But I was alone just now."

Narbenu knelt beside him. "We were here the whole time, lad."

Rubbing his eyes, Zaiporo tapped on the star stone a few times to brighten the room. "All three of us were."

Turesobei shook his head. "But you were all gone, and I wasn't in the covers. I was kneeling, praying. The room fell into darkness ... then it ... she ... came for me." He began to tremble uncontrollably.

Lu Bei popped free from the pack, raced over, and hugged him. "Master, master, it's okay. Nothing can harm you here."

"I saw ... I saw ..."

"What was it, master?"

"Wings. Shadow. Flaming eyes."

"Probably another memory from the kavaru, master. Like the dream with Vôl Ultharma." Lu Bei shivered. "When the kavaru gave you enough energy to survive, I think echoes of Chonda Lu's past leaked through. Master fought many demons over the millennia."

Turesobei shook his head. "But this ... this was real ... somehow. I know it was."

"But we were here," Kurine said. "I was awake. Nothing happened. One minute you were sleeping peacefully, the next you cried out."

"That's true, lad," Narbenu added.

"In that case, she was in my mind. Maybe she infiltrated my dreams. She — she said I would come to her soon, that I had to because it was the only way. She said she would have her revenge, she would torture me, devour me."

"If you are right, master, then this being is confusing you with Master Chonda Lu. But I don't know of any old enemy of his that would be here in the Ancient Cold and Deep, especially not one made of shadow and with flaming eyes."

Kurine smoothed the hair back from his face. "I'm sure it was nothing, my love. A vivid nightmare. You have gone through a lot. But you are safe now. Nothing will harm you here in Aikora."

He smiled at her and nodded. If the encounter had occurred in his mind, then there was no way he could convince them it had really happened. And maybe they were right. Maybe.

"Can I get you anything?" Kurine asked.

"I am hungry," Turesobei said. He wanted fruit, but the goronku didn't have anything like fruit. "Something light. And I need to speak to Lu Bei for a minute. Alone."

"Of course. I'll be back in a few minutes."

Everyone left, and Lu Bei frowned at him in concern.

"Lu Bei, what do you know about Vôl Ultharma? The very name makes you cringe."

Lu Bei's wings flared out and tucked back in. A tremor ran through him, and he sat down suddenly, as if all the energy were drained out of him. He took a few deep breaths and regained his composure.

"If I knew anything of consequence ... anything at all ... I wouldn't dare speak it. Vôl Ultharma is lost to history for good reason. Only a Kaiaru or someone of their descent could even keep his name in mind for more than a few minutes. Kurine, Narbenu, Zaiporo, even if they heard the name, they wouldn't remember it tomorrow. Without your kavaru, the memory of the name would fade from you, as well."

"So you do know something?"

"I know that he once ruled the entire subcontinent of Pawan Kor, across the sea. He killed many Kaiaru, and he tried to conquer Tengba Ren —"

"But Chonda Lu stopped him. I was ... there ... in the dream. Chonda Lu said he knew what Ultharma truly was, but the dream didn't give me that information."

"Master kept that to himself. He never told me. He spoke only of the aftermath, of his long recovery from the blast Ultharma hit him with. Ultharma is lost to history, and Master said he would never return." Lu Bei sighed. "It was just a memory. Don't trouble yourself about it."

"You're bothered that I'm dreaming things from Chonda Lu's past, aren't you?"

Lu Bei scratched his chin thoughtfully. "Not really, master. I was, at first. But these memories are just echoes from the kavaru — a side effect from it transferring energy to you. It's nothing to worry about."

"If those dreams are the price of me being alive, I'm okay with it."

"Your pain must have gotten much better, master. You're talking, and you seem stronger. That's good."

"Well, I feel like I've only got one foot in Torment now, instead of two."

With a start, Turesobei woke from a dream of flaming eyes within shadow. Zaiporo was doing pushups on the other side of the room. He stopped and tapped the star stone to full brightness.

"Can I get you anything?"

"Food. Water." Wincing, Turesobei rotated his shoulders. "I feel like I've slept forever."

Zaiporo handed him a bowl of water. "Two weeks."

"Two weeks? Has it really been that long? I don't remember much of anything."

"You only woke to use the bathroom and eat. Half the time I think you were still asleep when you did. Like you were sleepwalking. The medicine woman said that was a good thing, that you needed deep sleep. Shoma and Kurine would try to talk to you, but you barely responded. Last time you were awake and coherent was when you woke up after that dreams about the shadow with the flaming eyes."

Turesobei nodded. "I kind of remember the girls coming by. And Narbenu."

"Kurine is here every night. All night. Poor Narbenu has to accompany her here and stay for as long as she does, though Shaman Eira took that duty a few times."

"I don't remember Iniru visiting, though ..."

Zaiporo looked away. "She ... she's been resting a lot. Ever since it looked like you'd survive. She was in pretty rough shape, you know?"

"She's mad at me, isn't she?"

"That too."

"Well, she's almost always mad at me."

"I doubt she's usually *this* mad at you. You'll be lucky if she doesn't beat the crap out of you."

"Bet it's about that kiss."

"Yeah." Zaiporo spilled some of the cold broth he was pouring into a bowl. "Definitely about the kiss."

Turesobei drank down the broth and wiped his lips. "I'm hungry enough that that tasted good."

"Then you must be starving."

Turesobei went to the bathroom, and then walked three circuits around the room with Zaiporo holding onto him.

"I'm never going to be able to thank you enough," Turesobei said.

"We've fought the worst together. We'd both die for Shoma. We're friends. You don't ever need to thank me for anything."

Turesobei sat down, panting.

"I'll tell the others you're awake and get you some more food."

"Tell them I'm awake, but that I don't want any visitors for a few days."

"You want me to leave?"

"No," Turesobei replied. "I'm going to need you here. I just don't want to be bothered. And Kurine needs to rest. I'm going to start meditating and walking circuits. Build my strength up and set my mind straight. I need peace for that." Turesobei looked at the diary. "That goes for you too, fetch. Rest until I call you."

After a week of walking circuits and meditating longer each day, Turesobei dressed and walked to the commons on his own. Enashoma, Zaiporo, and Iniru were eating lunch at one of the tables. They all looked much healthier than before, but they were clearly downcast. Not that he could blame them.

Enashoma jumped up and hugged him. "Sobei! You're all better."

"I wouldn't say that. Not yet. But I'm getting there."

"You should've told me you wanted to get out," Zaiporo said. "I could've helped you here."

"I needed to do it myself." He broke away from Enashoma and approached Iniru. She had her back to him, and other than an ear-flick when he approached, she hadn't acknowledged him in any way. "Hi, Niru."

"Un-huh," she replied.

He leaned down to kiss her on the cheek, but she recoiled. "I don't think so."

"You're mad at me?"

"And why wouldn't I be?"

"You're not going to let me give you an I'm-so-incredibly-sorry-for-being-stupid kiss?"

"You've given out enough kisses, don't you think?" she snapped.

He shrugged.

"You can't kiss me, period. Kissing is a big deal here."

"Niru, I didn't mean anything by it. Kurine had been kind to me. I thought it was just going to be an I'm-glad-you're-alive kiss. I didn't know she was going to be that passionate. And I didn't want to refuse her in front of everyone. I couldn't embarrass her like that."

"He still doesn't know, does he?" Iniru said to the others.

Zaiporo shook his head. "I didn't think he was ready to hear it. Thought it best to wait until he was up and around."

"What don't I know?" Turesobei asked, nervously.

Enashoma took his hand and guided him to the table. "You'll want to sit down for this."

"That bad?"

Enashoma patted his hand. "When Kurine asked you if you'd accept her kiss, you really should've said no."

"That was a major question," Zaiporo said, "and you gave the wrong answer."

A sinking feeling struck Turesobei in the pit of his stomach. "Oh no. What have I done?"

Chapter Sixteen

Iniru struck him across the back. It was a lot harder than a friendly pat.

"Ow!"

"Congratulations," she snarled. "You're engaged. Again."

"What?!" he shouted.

Goronku at other tables in the room spun around and glared at him.

"Sorry," he mouthed, ducking his head.

"Kurine is your new betrothed," Iniru said, acidly. "You lost one and gained another in less than a week."

"Which, to be honest," Zaiporo said, "is an impressive feat."

"It's true, Sobei," Enashoma said. "I couldn't believe it when I found out. Thought it had to be a joke. When you accepted her kiss, that was saying yes to her marriage proposal."

Turesobei groaned and plopped his forehead down on the table. "No. No. Nooooo. This can't — Niru, I love you. You know that. I didn't mean to — I didn't intend — I don't want to ..."

Iniru patted him on the cheek. "I know you didn't mean to. And while you've been recovering, I've come to realize something about you."

"What's that?" he asked with trepidation.

"That you really are an idiot. Truly and deeply."

"But only when it comes to girls," Enashoma added. "He's pretty smart otherwise."

"And brave," Iniru said. "I had planned to give you a nice big kiss to reward you for saving us, after you took on the reitsu champion and all that."

"Maybe later," he suggested.

"Oh, I don't think so, lover boy. You're engaged. It wouldn't be right. Got to keep the peace around here."

"They take being engaged seriously," Enashoma said.

Zaiporo picked the last bit of flesh from a roasted fish and said, "As much as our people back home. Maybe more. But you can't blame Kurine. Apparently, you're considered quite the catch around here."

"Why me?" Turesobei whined.

"You're decent to look at," Iniru said. "Don't get too full of yourself. I only said decent.

You're unique and exotic. They don't have baojendari or wizards. You can do things no one else here can. And you're brave. And some girls might find that whole dragon thing sexy."

"Do you?" he asked, hopefully.

"The Storm Dragon's Heart almost got me killed, what do you think?"

"The power saved you, too, against the yomon ..."

Iniru shrugged. "Guess it's a wash, then."

"What am I going to do?" he asked, keeping his voice low so only they could hear him. "Kurine is a sweet girl, a bit demanding and overeager, but also very sweet."

"And pretty," Zaiporo added.

Enashoma scowled at him. "Don't you go getting in trouble, too."

"She's not as pretty as you, of course," Zaiporo replied quickly.

"You're going to have to go along with it," Iniru said. "We've got nowhere else to go, and they're helping us. Just go along with it, and try to put her off. I doubt you can, but you do surprise me from time to time."

"Maybe you and me, if we're discreet, we can —"

"Not a chance," she replied. "There will be no alone time for us. Not here. These people are prudes, and we can't afford to offend them."

"Sobei, you're not an adult yet," Enashoma said. "Tell Kurine. That will buy you a few years at least."

"Sixteen is the age of an adult here," he said, "like with Iniru's people."

"So just tell her you're fifteen and won't turn sixteen for months," Zaiporo said.

Turesobei put his head down on the table and groaned again. "She knows how old I am already. I explained about not being an adult when she brought the clothes she made for me. I told her I turned sixteen in several weeks ... just three days now. And she said that she would see that I had a birthday celebration to honor my adulthood amongst her people."

"Yeah, that's the thing that I'd forgotten to ask," Iniru said. "I've been too nice about this, on account of you being nearly dead and all, but not anymore. How did she get so close to you that fast? You were only here for less than a day."

"She brought me the clothes, and she kept flirting with me while I tried them on, and I didn't know how to deal with her, and —"

Iniru scowled. "While you tried them on?"

Zaiporo shook his head. Enashoma sank back with a sigh.

"Well, I had to try them on, right? I made her turn around."

"But they won't let single men and women be alone in a room together."

"I didn't know that at first. She snuck in and didn't tell me the rules here. She was friendly, but I didn't really flirt back. We just talked. I was hurt, exhausted. I wasn't thinking clearly."

Iniru crossed her arms and huffed. "Well, if just talking got you this far, I'm sure we'll be planning a wedding soon."

"Niru, please ..."

"You're an idiot. I don't want to talk to you right now. You led her on."

"No, I didn't. At least, I didn't mean to. If I did, I don't know how."

"Well you did it somehow," Iniru snapped.

He started to apologize again, but what was the point? The only thing he could do to make it up to Iniru was find some way to get out of the engagement.

Iniru narrowed her eyes at him, then perked up and smiled at someone over his shoulder. Turesobei followed her gaze, and frowned. Kemsu was walking toward them, grinning.

"You're up and around," Kemsu said, glancing at Turesobei and then looking back to Iniru.

"Only just," he replied.

"Kurine will be delighted," Kemsu said, with a tone of ... irritation? ... resentment? "Iniru, are you ready for that sparring practice?"

"Not yet," she said. "I'm still recovering. I was sick and injured for a long time before I came here. I still really need the rest."

"No problem. We'll get to it eventually." He flashed a smile at her again. "Wish I could stay and chat, but Narbenu is going hunting today."

Kemsu strutted away, and Turesobei decided that he didn't actually like Kemsu much. He also didn't like the way Iniru had ... well, she hadn't actually flirted with him. But she hadn't discouraged him, either.

"Iniru," he said.

"Yes?"

Turesobei realized he was straying into dangerous territory with her, especially given his new betrothal. "Nothing."

She raised an eyebrow at him, but let it go, thankfully.

A goronku man he didn't know brought him a plate of food. As he ate, everyone fell into a depressed silence.

"Well, we're a happy lot," he said. "Should I be the one to bring it up?"

"You mean," said Enashoma, "the fact that we're never going to get out of here?"

"We decided not to discuss it while you were recovering," Zaiporo said.

"What have you been talking about, then?" Turesobei asked. "I figured you would be talking about that all the time."

"We haven't really spent a lot of time together," Enashoma said. "We eat together every day, and that's about it, except when we're visiting you. You're not the only one who needed a lot of rest, you know. That's most of what we've done. Sleep, eat, try to recover. We're all exhausted. We've been through a lot."

"Even Motekeru is resting," said Zaiporo. "Or meditating. Hibernating? I don't know, really. He and the hounds have a room, and they're resting there away from everyone. He prefers that, but I think the hounds should roam around and enjoy themselves more."

"I'll get them out later," Turesobei replied.

"Mostly we didn't talk about escaping the Ancient Cold and Deep," said Iniru, "because what hope do we have? And if you hadn't recovered, we'd all be stuck for certain. So we waited."

"You do have some idea about how we can get back, don't you?" Enashoma asked.

He shook his head. "I'm ... I'm really sorry. I've got nothing."

"We're trapped here permanently?" Enashoma asked with tears welling in her eyes. "It's so cold and so ... so far from home."

"I thought you'd have some ideas, at least," Iniru said.

"The Winter Child was the only way I know of."

"There has to be another way, though," Zaiporo said.

"The Shogakami used this land as a prison," Turesobei replied. "Which stinks for the people who live here, by the way. If there was a way to get out of here, the yomon would've used it."

"Could it be something you could do that the yomon couldn't?" Zaiporo suggested. "Something wizardly?"

Turesobei shrugged. "There is a chance to find a way that we could take but the yomon couldn't. Narbenu mentioned a place called the Forbidden Library. There might be knowledge there that I could use. But I wouldn't get my hopes up, since it's forbidden and the goronku don't know much about it. The odds seem poor at best."

"We can't give up hope," Zaiporo said.

"I agree," Turesobei replied. "But for now, we need rest. And we won't be able to reach the Forbidden Library if we don't learn how to survive in this environment first."

"Turesobei! You're up!" Kurine called out, having emerged from the door on the far side of the common area.

Iniru stood. "I'm taking a nap now."

"I'll join you," Enashoma said.

"I'm going to check on Motekeru and the hounds," Zaiporo chimed in.

Chapter Seventeen

While Turesobei's companions escaped, Kurine wrapped him into a giant ... bear ... hug and lifted him. "You're better!" she squealed. "At last!"

She set him down. Her expression was radiant. He was so screwed.

He squirmed free. "I still need a lot more rest."

"But you're up walking ..."

"I am."

"We haven't talked in ages."

"I know, and we really need to talk about —"

"About your birthday? I've already made all the plans. I know it's in three days ..."

"It is."

"But I'm thinking you're definitely not well enough for partying yet."

"Definitely," he replied. He took her hand and led her to sit down beside him. "But it's not about my birthday, Kurine. It's about us — you and me."

Her lips puckered into a frown. "That sounds serious."

"Well, it is. I just found out we're ... supposedly ... engaged."

"Not *supposedly*. We *are* engaged."

"But I didn't agree to it, Kurine."

She pinched him on the cheek. "Oh, yes you did, silly. You accepted my kiss."

"But I didn't know that's what it meant." He wanted to say he'd just done it to be nice, but he couldn't bring himself to do that. "I kissed you because ..."

"Because you like me. Obviously."

"Well ... in my world, that's all accepting a kiss would mean."

"I know."

"You do?!"

She sighed. "I didn't know you didn't know then, but I do know now. The little demon told me. I'm so sorry. I wasn't trying to take advantage of you. I promise I didn't know. I was so excited when you returned. You were a hero, and I really like you. And it's not like there are any decent men my age around here. I honestly didn't think you'd accept, especially not so soon. I was being rash, but you *did* accept — you were as much into me as I was into you." She smiled. "It was one of the best days of my life."

"It was?" Turesobei blurted out.

"My life's not as exciting as yours. I make clothes. I do chores. I've only once traveled more than a day away from the village." She stroked his cheek. "I knew you had just lost your betrothed, but I didn't really understand, and I didn't know everything you'd been through. You, poor, poor boy. If I'd known, I promise I would have waited longer before asking you."

"Well, maybe since we had different ideas about what the kiss meant, we can back up and —"

She recoiled as if he'd struck her. "You don't want me?"

"No, no. It's not that. It's just ..." What in Torment was he supposed to say? That he didn't want to marry her, no matter how pretty and perky she was? That he thought she would make a terrific friend? She wouldn't want to hear that. As he hesitated, tears welled up in her eyes. He had to give her some hope. "I want to get to know you. To get married ... we'd need to spend time together first."

"We have chemistry. That's all you need."

"It — it is?"

She cheered up. "Un-huh. We're really going to get to know each other well once we're married. We'll have the rest of our lives to grow close."

"Don't you think it's best that we get to know each other before we decide to get married? What if after a few days together we don't like each other?"

"I can't imagine that. I know you're attracted to me. I know you like me enough to marry me."

"You — you do?" It was news to him. "How?"

"I just know. Just like I know you'll get over your infatuation with the assassin girl."

"You know about me and Iniru?"

"The little demon told me all about your history together."

"Then ... you must know how much Iniru means to me."

"It was a boyhood crush. You'll outgrow it."

"I risked my life, my sister, my clan ... everything for Iniru."

"For love. You risked everything for love, not her. There's a difference."

"There is?" He shook his head. "Never mind. The point I'm trying to make is, if we're to get married —"

"But Turesobei," she said with frustration, "we *are* getting married."

"I didn't know what I was agreeing to."

"To accept the kiss is to enter a sacred and binding contract. It is a promise between the two of us and the gods. You honor it, or you risk damnation and shame. Only death can break it."

"Maybe we can appeal to ... your clergy, the gods, the Council of Aikora ... to make an exception, since I'm a foreigner and didn't know the ways of your people or what I was agreeing to."

Kurine stared at him in silent horror, then broke down sobbing. He put his arms around her and tried to hide her tears from the other goronku in the commons.

"Kurine, I'm not trying to ... I really do like you, but ..."

"No, you don't have to make up a lie. Just tell the truth. You don't want me. I offered, and now that you know what your acceptance means, you're backing out. Because you don't want me. It's okay. I'll free you from your promise."

"You will? But how? You just said we couldn't break the agreement."

"There's a convent at a Crimson Sun enclave fifty leagues away. I can become a priestess. Devoting myself to the gods will spare me my shame. I'll live out my years there. It won't free you from your part of the promise ... but that doesn't matter to you. You can continue on with your ... *girlfriend* and ..." She threw her head into her hands and broke down completely.

A convent? He couldn't do that to her. "Kurine, maybe ..." He was so completely screwed. "*Maybe* we could get married."

She looked up at him, her eyes red. "You're just saying that because I'm upset."

"Honestly, I think you're beautiful. And you're lively and smart and ... a challenge." He thought of Awasa and Iniru. "I like challenges ... apparently. That's a lot to work with."

"You need more?" she sobbed.

"I need to know you first. I mean, I hated Iniru for weeks when I met her."

"You did?"

"Oh yeah. She got on my nerves."

"I bet she still does."

"Well ... yeah," he said, then added quickly, "but in a good way."

"So you will marry me after we get to know one another ... or you'll decide you don't like me, so I'll have to go to the convent and ..."

"That's not going to happen. You are *not* going to the convent."

"Then why should we wait? There are no other options."

"Two reasons," he replied, thinking quickly. "First, I might not still be here. If I find a way to return to my world, I might as well be dead, as far as it would concern you. Then you'd be free to choose another."

"I ... I guess so." She wiped away her tears. "Does that mean you've figured out a way back?"

"Not hardly, but I'm not giving up hope. The other reason is that in my world, in my culture, it is wrong to marry before the age of eighteen. I'm too young. But two years, that's plenty of time for us to get to know one another, and a lot could happen in two years. This is a dangerous world, and I'm going to be searching for a way back. And if there is one, I'm going to take it. I must wait to marry, or else I will dishonor my ancestors and the traditions of my people."

It was ironic that he fell upon this excuse. He spent so much of his time angry at the way his society treated him like he was a child, despite all the responsibilities they heaped on him, despite all the sacrifices he'd made and the dangers he'd faced.

"But if you stay here," she said, "you will be one of us. Then you should follow our customs."

"Despite what I grew up with?"

Kurine furrowed her brow. "How about a compromise between our two cultures? If you stay here and become one of us, you will marry me on your seventeenth birthday. We are allowed to postpone our engagement for a year, if we so desire."

One year. A lot could happen in a year. He could die of cold exposure, be slain by a reitsu, return home, become the Storm Dragon, even possibly fall in love with Kurine. The chances of him living a year seemed slim anyway.

"Okay," he answered in defeat. "It's a deal. One year."

It was *not* going to be fun explaining this to Iniru. Even if ... an incredibly large if ... Iniru understood his reasoning, she wasn't going to accept it. Would she break up with him? Were they something that could be broken up? Why did girls complicate his life? Were prophecies and dragons and enemy clans and ancient demonic enemies not enough?

Smiling again now, she kissed him. "You won't regret it. And once you get to know me, you'll fall in love with me. You won't be able to wait until you're seventeen."

He laughed. "You could rival Shoma for being upbeat."

"Shoma ... why do you shorten each other's names?"

"In our world, to use a short, informal version of someone's name means you are close to them. It represents a deep bond of friendship or love. You don't do that here?"

She shook her head. "Your friends call you Sobei, right? Can I call you that, too?"

"Of course. Can I call you ... I can't think what I would shorten your name to."

"Just stick to Kurine."

"I'm going to go rest now. This discussion has tired me out, I'm afraid."

She helped him up. "Thank you ... Sobei. I know it's not ..."

He nodded. "It's all fine," he lied.

Turesobei returned to the room.

"How did it go?" Zaiporo asked.

"Not well."

Lu Bei popped out. "You saw Kurine, master?"

Turesobei nodded. "Thank you for telling her what you did."

"Did it help, master?"

"It helped, but ... I'm stuck with my engagement. I couldn't break her heart. She'd have to become a priestess if I abandoned her. I can't do that to her. The only other way out is for me to get back home or die."

Lu Bei rubbed his hands together as he suppressed a laugh. "I can't wait till you explain it to Iniru, master."

"You sounded way too happy when you said that."

"Oh, master, I am sorry," Lu Bei drawled in an overly sweet voice. "I am so very *very* apologetic."

Sighing, Turesobei rolled his eyes. "If we can't get back home and have to stay here, she's agreed to let our marriage wait until I'm seventeen. A compromise between our cultural norms."

"Well, that gives you some time to find a way out, master. Clever as you are, I'm certain you will be able to disentangle yourself from her. Or add a couple more betrothals."

Turesobei grabbed a washcloth and threw it at Lu Bei, but the fetch dodged it, stuck out his tongue, and turned back into a book.

"You've gotten yourself in over your head for sure," Zaiporo said.

"That's my motto, don't you think?"

"We all seem to live by that."

"Wish you had stayed back in Ekaran?" Turesobei asked.

Zaiporo stared off into space for a few moments, then shook his head. "You know, this is going to sound crazy, but I'm still glad I came. Though I wish Shoma had stayed behind where she'd be safe."

"You're glad you came? Seriously?"

"For years, I thought I'd spend my life guarding Awasa. Then, I thought I'd run away and start a new life, a simple life as a merchant or farmer. But I've fought monsters, rode the back of a dragon, and traveled to a new world. How many people can say they did that? I helped you fight off a threat to all Okoro. I saved the world! My life, even if it ends frozen here, has been extraordinary and surprisingly meaningful."

"I could do with a bit ordinary," Turesobei sighed.

"You do realize that you will never have an ordinary life, right? I might get to settle down one day if I survive. Not you. You have power and responsibility and some sort of huge, inescapable destiny."

"That also, apparently, includes difficult women."

Chapter Eighteen

Over the next seven days, Turesobei slept less and less, and spent as much time as he could meditating and stretching. He refused visitors, even on his birthday, and Zaiporo brought him all his food. The only way he could avoid Kurine's affections, Shoma's questions, and a confrontation with Iniru was to keep everyone out. Zaiporo would head out first thing after waking up to give Turesobei space. He also delivered messages to the others, which Turesobei thanked him for profusely, because Kurine was insistent on making sure he was well and not mad at her. Iniru didn't send any messages back, which meant either she was still mad, or had found out the engagement was still on and was even madder.

On the eighth day, he cast the *spell of the moon mirrors* three times without pain and was satisfied he would make a full recovery. Knowing he couldn't avoid confrontations any longer, he went out to eat with the others and found them all in the common room, dressed in full cold weather gear. Kurine was showing them how to tighten all of the garments. She bounced over and kissed him on the cheek. Iniru huffed and scowled. Kemsu scowled, as well. Apparently, he didn't approve of Turesobei's engagement to Kurine, either.

"What's going on?" Turesobei asked.

"We're going outside for sparring practice," Zaiporo said.

"I'm going out to watch and test my clothes," Enashoma said.

"Iniru has promised to show us some of her moves," Kemsu said. "She claims to be a deadly assassin." He tapped her on the arm. "I doubt it, though. She looks too sweet for that."

She unveiled a smile of sharp teeth. "Oh, you'll see. I'm way more than you can handle."

"I'm joining you," Turesobei said suddenly. "I just need to go get my parka and overboots."

Iniru sized him up. "You're not in any shape to fight."

"I'm not going to practice, but ..." He bit his lip. He had to think of something fast. All he really wanted to do was not let her spend time with Kemsu without him there. "I'm feeling cooped up. I haven't seen the sky in ages."

"Well ... I can understand that," she said suspiciously.

Glaring at Iniru, Kurine said, "Unfortunately, I can't come along with you. I have work to do."

"I'll see you later ... at dinner, maybe," Turesobei said.

"You're on!" she replied. "Meet me at the commons, and we'll go to my home from there."

He gulped. "Your home?"

"Since you're well now, I think it's time you met my parents. My dad just returned from his latest expedition. I can't wait for you to meet him! I mean, you'll have to soon, anyway; he's on the Council. And Mom's been pestering me every day, asking when she's going to get to meet you."

She bounded off, and Turesobei threw his head in his hands. So much for the plan he'd been bouncing around in his head of getting the Council to negate his marriage to Kurine. Unless after meeting him, her father hated him ... but if her father ended up hating him, that would probably make other things go poorly, since this was the only place they had to live for now.

"Big night for you," Iniru remarked.

"Very big," Kemsu said coarsely. "Kurine's dad is the biggest goronku in Aikora. He's a monster of a man."

"Zai, my friend," Turesobei said, "you're right. No ordinary life for me."

Zaiporo patted him apologetically on the back.

Turesobei dressed in his cold weather gear and went outside. The sky was grey and the landscape an endless white. He'd forgotten how harsh it was ... and somehow, he'd even forgotten how cold it was. It was unimaginably cold, like his mind just couldn't retain the knowledge as soon as he was out of it. Following the sounds of them talking, Turesobei found the others on the opposite side of the stable. A circle of small stones marked off a well-trodden area that he assumed was intended for just this sort of thing. He stood beside Enashoma.

Kemsu was in the midst of a spear form which involved a lot of powerful thrusts with a few swipes and blocks mixed in. He finished and looked very impressed with himself. It was a good form. Better than anything Turesobei could've done. But it was certainly not the best he'd seen. As Iniru took one of the goronku spears and stepped into the circle, he knew Kemsu was about to feel far less competent. In fact, Turesobei was willing to bet that Kemsu would never again think highly of his combat skills.

Iniru blocked, stabbed, spun, kicked high, kicked low, somersaulted, swiped, threw the spear up and caught it, and bent backward so far Turesobei could hardly bear to watch. It was a fighting dance of pure beauty, and it was done so fast that it was hard to track all the little extra twists and special moves she did along the way. He knew there were many, because she had broken down a few sword forms for him along the way back from Wakaro. She had tried to show him all the details, but most had been lost on him, since they were far beyond his ability. He did notice that she moved a little slower than normal. Not that she wasn't still above and beyond amazing.

She finished. "Wow. All this gear really slows me down. That was terrible."

"No," said Kemsu, staring at her. "That was the most amazing thing I've ever seen."

"Then you haven't seen much," Iniru replied, clearly unimpressed that he was so impressed. Iniru was a young k'chasan qengai, and Turesobei often wondered what her teachers and elders must be capable of after many more years of study.

"You were beautiful," Zaiporo said, also enraptured. It was the first time he'd seen a healthy Iniru in action like this. Enashoma glared at him. He noticed and added, "The *form* was beautiful."

"Your turn, Zai," Iniru said.

Zaiporo frowned. "I've little experience with the spear, I can't do anything to compare with that."

"It's not a contest. Do the form you know best, and we'll work on the techniques. Trust me, you're going to feel like a clown in all this gear anyway. You'll need to get used to it. You don't want to look like Sobei against the reitsu champion."

"Hey!" Turesobei said. "That guy was super-fast."

"You don't think you could've dodged a few of those attacks of his? Maybe get off one block?"

"He was their champion, you know. Best fighter they had. And I was trying to let him win without getting killed."

Iniru shrugged. "Well, I think some blocks would've helped that."

Enashoma leaned in and whispered, "She's just giving you a hard time because of Kurine."

"It's not fair," Turesobei whispered back.

"Nothing ever is," she said, with a sigh as Zaiporo entered the circle nervously, eyeing Iniru with reverence.

Zaiporo performed the same spear form Turesobei knew, though more competently than he could've done. Iniru stepped in when he was done and praised him.

"It wasn't that good," he argued.

"Don't compare yourself to me, Zai. I'm a qengai. I did my first complete spear form when I was five years old. I trained ten hours every day of my life until I was sent out to help Turesobei. Fighting is all I've ever done. Now, let me give you some pointers."

She took the spear and began to demonstrate new techniques to Zaiporo and Kemsu, who crowded in on her.

"Well, Iniru is certainly popular now," Enashoma said.

"Jealous?"

"What about you, mister?"

They both looked at each other and laughed.

"Maybe we should be paying attention, too," Enashoma said. "I only know the staff and some other basics. Sure am glad Dad made them give me more lessons than the other girls. What about you?"

"I'm not much in the mood for learning the finer points of spear combat," he replied.

"Sulking?"

"I've earned the right, I think."

"If you say so."

When they took a break, Kemsu said he didn't want to rest too long, because Narbenu would want him back soon.

"How is it you're a slave?" Zaiporo asked. "No one else here is. And why aren't you angry about it? I'd be furious all the time. I ran away because I wanted to be completely free, and I had a lot more freedom than you."

"I'm paying a blood debt," Kemsu said proudly. "My father killed Narbenu's brother. My father didn't face the repercussions. Instead, he ran. So I'm enslaved to the murdered man's closest kin. That's Narbenu. I'm doing what my father wouldn't do. I'm doing what our laws demand. I'm doing what's right."

"Will you be enslaved forever?" Zaiporo asked.

"Until Narbenu releases me, but before he will do that, I must serve him at least five years *and* prove myself worthy. I must do something noble and brave. I have served four years already, but I haven't had any good opportunities to prove myself. And though he may not seem it, Narbenu is a tough man. He will want to see something amazing out of me. He's still angry about the murder. The worst thing is that as long as I'm a slave, I can't ..." He looked away from Iniru. "I can't marry or have a family. But the gods will favor me for doing what's right. I know they will. And once I prove myself, I can do anything I want."

They returned to the forms and practiced a half-hour more, trying to learn from Iniru as she got used to fighting in the heavy garments and worked to get back to full fighting strength. But then Narbenu arrived and said to Turesobei, "The full Council has gathered, and they wish to see you as soon as possible."

Chapter Nineteen

Faded tapestries adorned the walls of the Council Chamber. Turesobei nervously paced along the walls, scanning them. The stitching depicted battles, festivals, and religious processions. None bore any writing.

"Narbenu, do your people read and write?"

"The priestesses do, so they can maintain our record book. Why?"

"I hadn't seen any books since I arrived."

"Paper is rare and precious. We maintain oral histories and sing stories."

"So do we, though not as much as we did in the past. We read and write more now."

Seven cushions lined the far wall. Another cushion sat in the middle of the room. "Is this where I'll sit when they arrive?"

Narbenu nodded. "You should stand until they sit. You should also bow when they enter."

"Am I in trouble?"

"I don't think so."

"Why haven't I met with the Council before?"

"You have met two members already: Eira and Sudorga. But the Council wasn't complete until Trade Chief Tsuroko returned last night ... Kurine's dad."

Was Kurine's dad angry about her betrothal to a foreigner from another race? That might explain the sudden summons. Hope that they'd annul the engagement flickered through him. That would save him. Though it would probably leave Kurine shamed, which he didn't want, and he and his companions kicked out into the cold with little to survive on and no knowledge of the land.

"Narbenu, why are you here? You're not in trouble because of me, are you?"

"Not likely. I am here because I was your sponsor in admitting you to the village. Not every stranger gets the sort of hospitality you have been given."

Seven taps on a tinny drum announced the Council, and the members entered the room from a doorway to the side: War Chief Sudorga, Shaman Eira, four goronku he didn't know, and an enormous goronku he feared he'd soon know all too well.

Turesobei bowed. The councilors took their seats. Kurine's father, Tsuroko, thudded down onto his cushion, bones creaking. He was easily a head taller than War Chief Sudorga and bigger around by far. Scars marked his face, hands, and arms.

"Please be seated, friend Chonda Turesobei," War Chief Sudorga said.

Turesobei sat. Narbenu knelt to the side and just behind him.

"You already know Shaman Eira," War Chief Sudorga said. He gestured to the others, each in turn. "This is Sun Priestess Oroki, Earth Priestess Faika, Herd Chief Boronaru, and Trade Chief Tsuroko."

Turesobei's eyes skipped across them and landed on Tsuroko, who showed no reaction to him — none whatsoever. Turesobei squirmed.

"Respected elders, I hope that I have in no way offended you."

War Chief Sudorga glanced down the line to Tsuroko whose face remained as still as a statue's. "You haven't offended us," Sudorga said. "This is simply the first chance we've had for the full Council to meet since you arrived, and so we thought it was time to discuss your situation."

"My situation?" Turesobei asked.

"You were in dire need of our assistance, and we gave you hospitality," said Earth Priestess Faika, "as the gods command us to do."

"But you have recovered from your injuries now," added Sun Priestess Oroki, "and though you are trapped in this world with no place to call home, the time for mere hospitality alone has come to an end."

An image of him and his companions fighting to survive out on the ice, with Enashoma and Iniru freezing to death, flashed through his mind. Turesobei restrained a wrench of panic in his gut and spoke with as even a voice as he could manage.

"If it's time for us to move on, I understand. You have given us so much, and we have taken more than we had any right to ask for: shelter, food, help in rescuing my companions, expensive clothing ..."

"You misunderstand us," said Eira. "We are not kicking you out into the wild. We know you cannot handle that on your own."

Turesobei sighed with relief.

"There is, however, a limit to the generosity we can freely provide," said Herd Chief Boronaru. "We are not a wealthy people, though we are perhaps the most prosperous of the goronku clans in this region."

"You are free to leave if you so desire," said War Chief Sudorga. "But to remain you must —"

"Pull our own weight?" Turesobei said.

"Indeed," said War Chief Sudorga.

"With my power returning, I may be able to repay you somewhat with a bit of magic, but it won't match what you've given us. We have little else to offer your people. We will have to move on."

Trade Chief Tsuroko walked across the room, and hunched over Turesobei. Staring down at Turesobei with cold eyes, he dropped his hands, like mallets, onto Turesobei's shoulders. The impact squashed him deep into the cushion. Turesobei swallowed hard, and stammered out an incoherent apology, though what he was apologizing for, he wasn't certain. Actually, he *was* certain. He had stolen the man's daughter without his permission. Only ... she had stolen him, hadn't she? Turesobei was confused.

"Stay," Tsuroko bellowed. "Stay and become one of us. Learn our ways, take on trades so that you might contribute to the community." Tsuroko lifted Turesobei up by the shoulders. With a deep chuckle, he added, "Stay, and I'll be happy to call you my son."

After Tsuroko set him down, Turesobei bowed to him. "I would be most honored to stay and to ... marry Kurine ... sir, I would. But we *must* seek a way back our world. My people need me desperately. War is coming to our clan, and without me, there is no hope for victory. But if I can't find a way home, I'd be happy to stay here and become one of you." Not that he would have much of a choice. "But for the sake of my people, I must try to return home."

Anger flashed across Tsuroko's face, but then he smiled warmly. "Well said, my boy. Well said. We must all do what is right in serving our people."

As Tsuroko returned to his seat, War Chief Sudorga asked, "Do you know of some way you might return?"

Turesobei shook his head. "My plan is to seek out the Forbidden Library. If knowledge of a way to return to my world exists, surely it must be there."

"The Forbidden Library lies on an island on the Glass Sea in the North," said Sun Priestess Oroki. "It is a long way to travel, and we know little about it."

"They say winged demons guard the library and its knowledge jealously, sharing it with no one," said Earth Priestess Faika. "Never do they venture out, which is good, for they are supposed to be mightier than even the yomon."

"I must try, though," said Turesobei. "And I've faced yomon and demons before."

"But the ice," said Tsuroko. "That is a challenge you are not accustomed to. Unless you go the long way around, the trek to the shores of the Glass Sea is treacherous, taking you across the Central Wastes. And the sea itself ... the clans of this region do not send caravans in that direction, though some peoples in other lands do send ships and caravans to and across the sea. I myself have never journeyed to the Glass Sea, and I have been many places."

Tsuroko led their trade expeditions ... across *this world* ... no wonder he was battle scarred and huge.

"To get there, you would need sonoke to ride," said Tsuroko, thoughtfully scratching through his crudely chopped beard. "You'd never make it there on foot. Supplies, of course. A guide and guards. Knowledge of how to survive on your own, if it came to it."

"I could do it without guards," said Turesobei. "I have Motekeru and the hounds, my spells, and Iniru's qengai skills. I would need a guide and supplies, though ... but I have no way to pay for those things. So we'd have to travel on our own."

"You would never make it without a guide," Tsuroko said. "Trust me. This land is less hospitable than you think."

"It seems harsh to me now."

"You've only seen our little region," said War Chief Sudorga. "This area is quite tame."

"And as I said before," Herd Chief Boronaru commented, "we are not wealthy. We trade clothing for iron and herbs, but otherwise we subsist on what we hunt and grow. You would need food and equipment, four mounts at least. A guide. All that would cost you a small fortune. Which you do not possess."

"But you could stay here and work to earn these things," said Earth Priestess Faika. "If all of you worked hard for two or three years, we could give you what you would need."

"And you could travel part of the way along a trade expedition," said Tsuroko.

"Two years?!" Turesobei said, alarmed. "My people will need me desperately in four months, six at best."

"I am sorry," said Eira. "We are all sorry. We cannot afford the extravagance it would take to fund your journey."

"Even if I returned what I didn't use, should my journey fail?" Turesobei offered.

Tsuroko frowned and shook his head. "My boy, the chances of you reaching the Forbidden Library, much less returning from it ... that would be a poor deal for us. I'm sorry."

The fatigue he'd spent weeks recovering from rushed back into his soul. Turesobei sighed and hunched his shoulders. "I understand. And I can't blame you. Out of kindness, you have already given us much. Clothing and food. And we have given nothing in return."

"I wouldn't say nothing." Sun Priestess Oroki gestured toward a blank spot on the wall. "The story of you coming here, the boy from another world who was both a wizard and a dragon, shall be stitched upon cloth and hung here for all to see for centuries to come."

"To think that our modest village would host visitors from beyond the gate," said Earth Priestess Faika, "is beyond anything we could have imagined."

"Tsuroko and I will discuss the specifics of what your journey would cost," said Herd Chief Boronaru. "But keep in mind, you will be eating and living here. You must earn your keep beyond that. But we will be generous and not seek to make any profit from you, only to recoup our expenses."

"With your magic," said Eira, "I believe you can earn above your board and keep from us. But you will have to be patient. And you are fortunate, though we were not, that a plague three years ago cost us many lives, and there are plenty of rooms to house you and much work that is needed to be done."

"We have a shortage of able workers," said Boronaru.

"Then I will do what I can to pay you for what I need," said Turesobei dully, knowing the Chonda Clan would be finished by the time he even reached the library.

The Council stood, and War Chief Sudorga said, "You and your companions are welcome to stay here as long as you like, provided your adhere to our laws, simple as they are. We name you honorary members of Clan Aikora. And if you take the pledge, you can become members in full and be one with us."

Turesobei bowed. "Thank you, councilors."

After they exited, Narbenu patted Turesobei on the back of the head. "You okay, lad?"

"Yeah, I mean ... yeah."

"Their offer was fair."

"I know," Turesobei replied. "But life is not. I know this because it keeps proving it to me."

Turesobei gathered his companions in Motekeru's room and told them what the Council had said.

"I can't see any other way," he told them. "I'm sorry. I'm so incredibly sorry."

Enashoma wiped a few tears away and nodded. Zaiporo hugged her. Tears welled in his own eyes, but he bravely held them in check.

Iniru's face was perfectly expressionless. "At least we saved the world."

"Not that anyone will know," Turesobei said. "My people probably think I'm a coward, or worse, a traitor."

"Hasuferu went to your grandfather," Lu Bei said. "Kahenan will know. He will tell the others, if he must. And it doesn't matter what anyone else thinks you are — you saved all Okoro."

"Is this part of my grand destiny that you returned for, Lu Bei?"

"Master, I arrived too early. For what reason that happened, I do not know. I may never know. The things that happen now are not things I expected."

"We'll have to learn to live here," Turesobei said. "I mean, we knew we were probably stuck here. And we can save up for the trip. But I promise, we will get to the library eventually, and if there's a way, I will get us all home."

"You mustn't lose hope," Lu Bei said. "I believe you will all return to Okoro ... in time."

"I can do heavy labor to help earn our way," said Motekeru. "A lot of it. And I can stand guard for them. I do not tire. I will do whatever I can for you, master."

"Master?" said Turesobei. "Are you sure you wish to call me that still? You weren't too happy about being called back. And I forced you to obey me and got you trapped in everlasting winter. I mean ... you don't have to call me 'master' anymore. It's not necessary."

"I didn't like Chonda Lu much, and I'm not happy about being back or being trapped here. But I respect you, master. I like you better than him." Motekeru turned to Lu Bei. "I think we all do."

Lu Bei nodded. "I don't often agree with Motekeru, but I do on this."

After a few minutes of everyone sitting in depressed silence, Zaiporo said, "So we all need jobs? I've been a guard before. I can do that again. I can help with butchering too, maybe."

"I can sew," Enashoma said. "That seems important to their trade, though I'll have to learn how they do it."

"I can hunt, guard, and scout," Iniru said.

"When I'm well enough, I can cast spells and draw some sigils for them," said Turesobei. "There are things I can do that will more than earn our keep. We'll work hard. Hard enough that it won't take two years. Maybe a year. Maybe just six months. We'll do our best."

"What about Kurine?" said Iniru bitterly. "Won't she be a problem if we're stuck here? You can only put her off for so long."

"Oh, it would certainly be a problem," Turesobei muttered. "Her father is on the Council. He's enormous, intimidating, threatening, and he seems to like me and wants me to stay. Breaking her heart would be incredibly dangerous. I'm sure of that."

Chapter Twenty

Shaman Eira entered the room and sat across from Turesobei.

He lifted his still-broken arm. "I thought you might want to witness healing magic."

She bobbed her head. "Yes, please. While my eyes can still behold such a sight."

"I'm casting the *spell of winter healing*. With all the ice, wind, and water energy in this world, the effect will be powerful. Normally, I'd use the *spell of summer healing* instead."

"Because your world is warmer?"

"In part, but mostly because it requires less internal kenja to initiate. And the winter healing spell tends to be painful."

"So why know it at all?"

"You might want it for healing a burn victim or someone suffering with a high fever."

Turesobei removed the splint, and chanted the spell. His restored internal kenja pulsed into and through his kavaru. A white cloud formed over his broken arm. The energy penetrated like a cluster of thin needles stabbing all the way into the bone. He groaned and bit his lip until blood trickled down his chin. The arm went numb from the cold, an aching numb, but still far better than what he had experienced before the healing. He breathed a sigh of relief. Warmth returned slowly, and the pain faded away. He wriggled his fingers, flexed his elbow, and held the arm out.

Eira felt along it and gasped. "The bone was broken in three places but now it has healed back perfectly." She laughed. "That should've taken another six weeks to heal!"

"It doesn't always fix things back right like that. I was lucky. And if you hadn't set the bone first, it would be crooked now."

"It's amazing," she exclaimed. "Simply amazing. I wish I could learn magic."

"I wish you could, too," Turesobei said. "Most wizards would never say that, though."

"I think your magic could of much value to us here."

"Just remember, all I can do is accelerate natural healing. If injuries are too severe, especially internal injuries, there is nothing I can do. And if disease has set in, all I can do is delay the inevitable or reduce the symptoms. I cannot cure it."

Over the next several days, he healed four of Eira's patients who had lingering injuries that were causing them problems, plus one child with a disease. Eira hoped the healing would allow the child to recover enough that her immune system could fight off the disease. She was a sweet child who laughed through the healing, grimacing only once during the spell. Turesobei hoped it would work to save her.

A number of business arrangements swamped Tsuroko and his wife, which meant Turesobei was able to escape dinner with Kurine's parents ... at least until the birthday party. Enashoma was helping Kurine with all the preparations. Birthdays were a huge deal amongst the goronku.

Turesobei studied the *mark of relentless fire* in Chonda Lu's grimoire, combining some aspects of it with the *mark of warming* that was in his standard spell book. The goronku gave him a jar of sonoke blood for him to draw the marks with, since he lacked Zhura ink, which would've been the ideal substance to use. After three days of practice, he successfully drew a *mark of warming* that drew trace threads of fire kenja from the environment and focused them into the mark, radiating heat outward. Now he only needed to incorporate the *mark of renewal* to make it semi-permanent.

"Very good work, master," Lu Bei said. "Your skills are advancing rapidly."

Turesobei nodded. "They should. I'm battle-tested now. And Chonda Lu's grimoire is helping. I can't do much of what's in it, but I'm learning refinements I can apply to my standard spells. When I had those flashes of Chonda Lu's past, I picked up a little more understanding of his grimoire. Not enough to cast from it. I don't have the inherent power channels that would allow that. Just a better understanding."

While Turesobei worked on spells, Iniru and Zaiporo trained with Herd Chief Boronaru, learning to feed, ride, and care for the sonoke. Enashoma studied sewing with Kurine and her mother, when she didn't help with party-planning. Motekeru carried giant blocks of stone and stacked them, helping the goronku build a new outer building for storing supplies. Motekeru, once given the tasks they needed him to complete, worked tirelessly through the night. Turesobei introduced Rig and Ohma to the goronku community and told the wolfhounds to mingle and play. They were an incredible hit with not just the children, but the teens and adults, as well. The hounds rushed throughout the village, playing for hours at a time and delighting the residents. The goronku, who had nothing like dogs, were fascinated by them. The Ancient Cold and Deep did not produce pets.

Turesobei went into the staircase that led from the goronku common room up to the outside world. Halfway up, he sat down, and cut a slit on one of his fingertips.

"You know I don't approve of this, master. Using blood magic for something so common ... it's an unnecessary risk."

"There is little risk, Lu Bei. There are no entities to entangle with my essence. I'm not summoning anything, or attacking someone. It's a passive spell used to benefit others."

"You just recovered."

"I'm not drawing much."

Lu Bei placed his hands on his hips and stamped a foot. "Well, I don't like it one bit. If I could resign from my post, I would."

"That's a load of denekon poop, and you know it."

"Do not mock me, master. I take blood magic seriously."

Turesobei tapped the *Mark of the Storm Dragon* on his cheek. "So do I."

"Then you should know better!"

"It's not personal. There's no vendetta. There's ... I'm not going to discuss it any further. We have to do things to earn our keep faster. That's what I'm trying to do, and I don't have Zhura ink. I'm going to be facing worse dangers than this soon enough."

Lu Bei stuck out his tongue, went into the pack, and turned back into a book.

Turesobei completed the first *mark of warming*. A little bit of himself trickled into the spell as it activated. Some said blood magic was energy that never came back to the wizard, but Grandfather Kahenan didn't believe that was true, and neither did Turesobei. The energy came back, just slowly, sometimes over the course of a few years. And the energy he used on this was minor. He didn't need blood to activate or power the spell, just to bind it onto the wall. With the mark drawn, he now had to power and activate it through chanting and meditation. The process took him from dusk until dawn and left him so exhausted, he fell asleep on the stairs.

A tap on his shoulder woke him. He lurched forward, his entire body aching, several limbs asleep. He tried to stretch them out. One cheek was numb.

Narbenu stood over him. He glanced at the scarlet symbol with its twisting, interlocking lines incorporating odd glyphs and covering a space two hand-widths across. He held his palm near it and shook his head. "I can't feel any difference. Are you sure it worked?"

Turesobei rotated his shoulders. "Just needed a nap." He touched the mark and whispered the final activation command. Only a slight draw was required from inner kenja at this point. "Give it a few minutes."

Narbenu handed Turesobei a bowl of steaming sonoke milk. As Turesobei drank, Narbenu sat next to him. The goronku man reached his fingers out near the mark again.

"I can feel some warmth now."

"You can touch it," Turesobei said. "I made it as permanent as I could ... as permanent as paint. But it will wear down if touched too much."

Narbenu touched it and immediately drew his hand back. "Hot."

Turesobei nodded. "If you leave something touching it long enough, that something will catch fire. I made it as strong as I could, since the door at the top will let in cold air every time it opens. I'm going to make another one on the other side of the staircase. Fortunately, you are near enough to some fire energy currents for them to work. Probably from the hot springs at your lake and the thermal vents. I've never made runes this strong before."

"How long will it last?"

"A century, I'd guess, though the strength will fade over time."

"Anything we can do to keep them strong?"

"Nothing that your conscience would approve of, and nothing my conscience would let me tell you. Hopefully, this will make for less cold air getting into the common room. I'll do your chambers next."

Narbenu shook his head. "I'm a scout. I'm used to the cold. I don't want to get too used to the warmth. Do Shaman Eira's chambers. She's getting old. And the recovery room for her patients. Herd Chief Boronaru would appreciate warming runes in the pen for the calves and newborns. And I think you know it's most important that you impress him, above all others, with your contributions to the community."

Turesobei spent a week adding marks of warmth to all those places. As he did them, he got better at it, eventually managing two each day. By keeping busy and exhausting himself, he successfully avoided Kurine, having only to endure a few minutes of small talk each day. Once, he escaped her during her lunch break by darting outside, though he was woefully under clothed. So he hurried to the lake where it was a little warmer. Thankfully, no one was out tending the gardens. Lu Bei picked through the scraggly herbs and wildflowers trying to make a suitable tea blend.

"The pickings are slim, master," the fetch said as he tasted the herbs.

"You sure those aren't poisonous?"

"Why would they have poisonous herbs in their gardens, master?"

"They might be medicinal. Too much could harm us."

"One of my talents, master, is I can tell if an herb is poisonous or not."

"You never mentioned that before."

Lu Bei puffed himself up indignantly. "Well, master, you never asked."

Sun Priestess Oroki strolled out and joined them. Having never met her before, Lu Bei bowed and praised her.

"My lady, you are a vision of pure beauty, such that the sun must be ever so glad that you speak with him so often."

Oroki laughed with delight. "I'm not looking for a tiny, winged husband. You don't have to praise me so much."

"I speak only of truths," Lu Bei said, bending over to examine an herb. "I never lie."

Turesobei looked at her and shook his head no.

"My lady, I shall make you tea tonight. You shall be most impressed. I am a master of tea."

"That is true," Turesobei told her. "Though I think he uses some sort of subtle magic to enhance the flavors."

"My methods are proprietary," Lu Bei replied.

Oroki sat down beside Turesobei. "I sense you are uncomfortable with the marriage to Kurine."

"How did you know?" Turesobei asked.

"I saw you dart out when she appeared. I figured if you'd planned on going outside, you'd have worn your parka. You must be freezing."

"It's warmer here beside the lake, and I've added something to help me in this world." He stretched to show her his belt, which had a warming mark etched on it now, one much weaker than the ones on the walls. Its effect was similar to wearing an extra silk nightshirt — not much, but something. Of course, once they were away from the thermal energy below the village, the mark probably wouldn't help him anymore.

"It's okay," she said. "You can be honest with me. I know Kurine caught you unaware."

"I really had no idea. She knows that now. But ..."

"You can't break it without difficulty."

"If I leave this world or die ..."

"Kurine is quite the catch, you know: very pretty, highly skilled, the only child of a wealthy and respected family. Many boys are jealous of you, though they are all several years too young to marry her. The plague took many of the children that were Kurine's age. Not that it would have been a problem for her to wait if she wished, or take an older man, but the older ones ... well, they don't have mates yet for a reason, many of them, unless they've lost their wives. And then there's Kemsu. They were best friends for many years but had a falling out. And he's a slave and can't marry."

"Kurine is a wonderful girl," Turesobei said, honestly, "but my betrothed just died. And Iniru and I were ... I don't know. And I'm not an adult among my people."

"Kurine told me you would not be an adult among your people until eighteen. A curious custom. You are an adult here, though. And if you stay ..."

Lu Bei gagged on an herb, spat it out, and pranced around cursing. "Spicy spicy too spicy — bad bad!"

They laughed at Lu Bei, who scowled at them while scooping up ice and chewing on it.

"If you stay with us, you will be an adult," she continued. "And I hope you do stay. You and your friends have so incredibly much to offer our community. Skills and knowledge we've never encountered before. And this is a good place to live ... in this world, anyway."

"I won't argue that."

"You could all make families here and prosper. I sense your sister and Zaiporo are a couple."

"Maybe. Kind of. I don't think she's made up her mind. She's young still."

"And Iniru would have no trouble finding a husband if she should desire one."

Turesobei bit back a retort. He *would* be with Iniru. Somehow. "You should ask her how marriage works among her people. They can have multiple spouses and then declared friends who are almost like spouses but aren't and ... honestly, I'm not sure I understand it all. But if you'd like to learn about a culture more alien to yours than mine ..."

The priestess's eyes were wide. "That ... that really works?"

"She says it works for them, and they've done it for ages, but I can't even make things work with a single girlfriend, so I don't see how it could."

The priestess chuckled. "I was looking for you for a reason. The Council has discussed your situation. Since Motekeru does the work of eight men carrying blocks, night and day, and since your warming marks and healing are so useful, your debt will be paid to us in eight months. We will understand if you choose to set out then for the Forbidden Library. And if you fail and manage to return, you are welcome to live here all your days, and no one will think less of you for having tried to go home. Quite the opposite. You would be admired for your bravery and determination."

"Thank you, my lady, for understanding."

"I understand your situation is difficult. We all do, and we sympathize." Sun Priestess Oroki stood. "I will see you at the party tomorrow night."

The birthday party. His first ever. The Chonda frowned on the practice. At eighteen, he'd undergo a simple blessing from King Ugara and enjoy a lively tea. The zaboko had birthday parties. Most baojendari, though they'd never admit it, were jealous of their custom.

His first birthday party ... he should be excited. Among all the cool cultures, he was now an adult, having turned sixteen already. But there seemed to be so little worth celebrating. And Kurine ... he sighed. What a mess he'd gotten himself into.

Chapter Twenty-One

After Turesobei cast a healing spell on a herdsman who'd broken his hand in an accident, he returned to his room for some well-earned meditation time. But Kemsu and Zaiporo were waiting for him. They grabbed him by the arms and dragged him to the communal bathing room.

"We reserved time just for you," Zaiporo said.

"Got to get you cleaned up nice for your party," Kemsu added, smiling almost maliciously.

They shoved him into the room, and Kemsu tossed him an ivory comb engraved with swirling patterns. "A present, from your betrothed. And I'd say your hair could use some effort, my friend — it looks terrible. Oh, Narbenu wishes you a happy birthday, by the way. He's on scout duty this evening and won't be able to make it to the party. He apologizes."

Turesobei stripped down and sank into the tub, thankful he was here alone. The warm water was brought in by pipes from the hot springs. He figured the goronku could easily heat the entire village complex to a very comfortable temperature if they arranged the pipes correctly and dug further down to tap into the geothermal currents below, but there had to be a reason they hadn't done so already. He allowed himself to relax and tried not to think of anything serious.

Why shouldn't he allow himself some time for fun? Why shouldn't he celebrate his birthday? He always ended up just barely saving the day, and by the time he recovered, no one wanted to celebrate his accomplishments. They just wanted to put new burdens on him.

"I'm sixteen years old now," he muttered to no one. "Many cultures consider me a man. I'm alive. I saved my world. Two women love me ... I think. So tonight, I'm going to have fun for a change."

A nagging sense that he didn't know how to have fun danced through his mind, but he dismissed it as quickly as he could.

Lu Bei entered the bedroom and bowed in a most dignified manner. "Master, do you know what time it is?"

"No, what time is it?"

Lu Bei pumped his fists into the air, spun around, and shook his behind as if dancing. "It's party time!"

Laughing, Turesobei followed Lu Bei to the common room. He swept back a curtain that didn't usually hang there and stepped into — a giant, nearly empty room. Chairs and tables sat along the edges, clearing a large space in the center. Only half the star stones burned. A giant, flickering lantern hung from the center of the ceiling while colored ribbons draped from all over.

"Where is everyone?"

"Birthday madness!" Lu Bei cried, flying around the room and shooting sparks from his palms. "Happy sixteenth birthday, master!"

Drumming and piping erupted from the opposite hall, and a six-piece band — three drummers, two pipers, and a crooner — marched into the room and took up position in the corner. Cooks bustled out of the kitchen carrying plates of goronku delights: smoky meats, smoky vegetables, and smoky milk soups.

Zaiporo appeared behind Turesobei and shoved him forward. "Happy birthday, Sobei!"

Turesobei stumbled out into the common room. The Council entered. Each approached, patted him on each shoulder, and said, "Welcome to adulthood, Chonda Turesobei. Happy birthday."

Tsuroko's shoulder pats knocked Turesobei side-to-side.

Enashoma crashed into him. "Happy big one, big brother."

He squeezed her tight. "Yay! I'm an adult now."

"Yeah, only here, you know. Don't let it go to your head. Just imagine what Grandfather would say."

"I'd rather not!"

Iniru gave him a perfunctory hug and a peck on the cheek. He breathed in deep the smell of her. All the smoky meats in the world couldn't hide that scent from him.

She whispered into his ear. "Happy birthday, Turesobei. I'd give you a much bigger kiss ... if I could ... *if* I wasn't mad at you."

Before he could respond, she was shoved aside. Kurine stepped in, casting an evil sideways glance at Iniru. Kurine pulled him into a deep hug. "Happy birthday, my beloved." She moved in to kiss him full on the lips, but he turned his head just as she neared him. The kiss missed his mouth and slid across his cheek. An annoyed look crossed her face.

"My betrothed," he said as warmly as he could manage. "All this ... it's *wonderful*. I've never had a party before, and this is perfect."

She laughed. "Come, you must eat."

As Turesobei threaded through the crowd that had gathered, he received well-wishes from every goronku he'd gotten to know and many that he had not. The common room was big enough to fit all the goronku if necessary, but many had stayed home. Some were old and uninterested in parties. Some were on guard duty or out hunting. Others had early work shifts and were already asleep. The party was mostly made up of young people who would soon reach sixteen and those who had seen sixteen within the last twenty years.

Along with his companions and Kemsu, he piled his plate full of food. The goronku food was good, if all a bit the same. He reached a table of flagons filled with water and casks of what he would've guessed was mead or wine, except he knew neither of those was available here due to the climate. Two rows of tiny cups ringed the casks.

"What's this?" he asked Kemsu.

"Ikase. Fermented sonoke milk."

"That sounds disgusting," Enashoma said.

Kemsu filled a tiny cup with ikase and held it out for them to smell.

Enashoma flinched. "Ugh, it smells disgusting too. Why would you drink that?"

"You don't have spirits where you're from?" Kurine asked.

"Oh we do," Turesobei replied. "Wine from grapes and rice ... ale, mead, and others. But all of those smell good. None of them smell like milk that's turned sour three times over."

"It smells like that because that's more or less how you make it," Kemsu said. He took a sip, and then breathed out as if he'd swallowed a bit of fire. He offered the cup of ikase to Iniru. "Try some. I bet you can't drink more of it than I can."

Iniru snorted. "I probably can't. My senses are far more attuned than yours. I'll pass. Thanks."

Kurine filled a cup halfway and offered it to Turesobei. "For you, my love."

"I think I'll pass, too," he replied.

"But you can't," she replied. "It's tradition. You are old enough to drink ikase now. You must have some at your birthday feast, or else it's rotten luck."

"You won't survive more rotten luck," said Iniru, smirking.

He shot Iniru a dirty look and took the cup. "I'm already old enough to drink wine and mead where I come from."

Kurine put her arm around him. "You're not getting out of this. I suggest drinking it fast. One gulp. Get it over with."

With a lot of people watching, Turesobei downed the ikase. Immediately he regretted it. He doubled over as it scalded its way down his throat and burned into his gut. Coughing, his throat seemingly on fire, he begged for water. Enashoma passed him her flagon, and he drank all of it.

"More water, please."

"The burn fades," Kemsu said.

"What about the taste? It's the most disgusting thing ever."

"That takes a while," Kurine said. "There's a reason the only time I've ever had it was on my birthday."

"You get used to it," Kemsu said, taking a sip from his cup.

"You don't have many drunks here, do you?" Zaiporo asked.

"People who drink too much?" Kurine asked. "Oh, we have those. I guess some people —"

"Have no taste buds?" Turesobei said.

All of them sat together, their plates piled high with food, and they managed to have a pleasant conversation and laugh without any sniping or arguments for a change. Turesobei met many new goronku, but the names swirled through his mind. The ikase had made him fuzzy-headed and a little silly. He found himself laughing far more than he normally would've. He didn't like it. Not at all. A wizard didn't need addled wits, though he tried to tell himself that there was no danger here and he wasn't going to need to suddenly cast a spell tonight.

As they finished eating, Lu Bei landed on the table. He downed a cup of ikase and said, "To the skies again!"

Turesobei grabbed him by the arm before he could fly off. "Where have you been?"

"Mingling, master. Mingling. I also went to ask Motekeru if he wanted to join us. Surprisingly —" Lu Bei hiccupped "— he did not."

"How many of those have you had?" Enashoma said, poking him in the belly.

"No poke, Shoma Lady, no poke. I have fastest metabolism. I can handle many few of these."

Shaking his head, Turesobei let him go, and Lu Bei flew off.

"If he's really a book and doesn't have to eat," said Kurine, "then how is it he can drink tea and ikase? He doesn't ... you know, go to the bathroom, right?"

"No, he doesn't go to the bathroom," Turesobei said. "As to how he can drink tea and ikase ... we're not really sure. He's magical. Maybe he burns it off with his crazy antics."

"You've never asked?" Kurine said, surprised.

"Of course I have. But he won't say, and I've been nice enough not to order him to."

An impeccably dressed woman with a frame that was delicate, for a goronku, approached. "Chonda Turesobei," she said. "I am Ukiri ... Kurine's mother."

Turesobei stood and bowed. "I'm pleased to meet you at last, my lady."

She suppressed a giggle. "So well-mannered ... too well-mannered for here, I'm afraid. Kurine was right, you are handsome." She poked him in the ribs. "For such a scrawny thing. I apologize for not having met you already, but I have been busier than normal."

"The clothes you and Kurine made for us ... they are wonderful. Thank you."

"Of course. I'm glad, and I didn't mind, even if I have been working extra to catch back up to normal production. Come by tomorrow and have dinner with us, okay? I want to get to know you more. I think we'll likely be seeing a lot of one another for many years to come. Best to get off on the right foot, don't you think?"

"Um ... of course. Yes."

"I really am sorry it took so long for us to finally meet. Well, I am off to bed. Have fun tonight, children."

After her mother had vanished, Kurine grabbed his hand. "Come. It's time to dance." She dragged him a few steps along, then she turned to the others and said, "*Everyone*. Get moving now."

"I don't really know how to dance," he said. "I just know one dance. We use it at weddings. It's slow and formal and not suitable to this sort of music."

"Well, dancing's not hard if you don't care what you look like when you do it," Kurine said. "Just move your feet and your hips and your shoulders and bob your head. Here, take my hands and follow my lead."

Feeling awkward and looking, he suspected, as if he were about to go into a seizure as he flailed about *mostly* to the rhythm, Turesobei danced with Kurine for a long time, until Enashoma saved him. He danced with her for a while. Kurine danced with Zaiporo, and Iniru danced with Kemsu. That, Turesobei didn't like. He finally switched to dancing with Iniru, but that didn't last long before Kurine had them switch to a group dance where they passed from one partner to the next in time to the fast-paced music. She taught the dance to them as they went, and for people trained in various martial arts, and Enashoma, who knew how to dance already, it wasn't difficult to pick up. Turesobei messed up more than the others. He blamed it on the ikase.

At last, the music paused. The Council took over the center of the commons and danced a slow, stomping religious dance honoring the gods and blessing Turesobei. They said goodnight and departed.

Enashoma and Iniru went to the bathroom, while Zaiporo and Kemsu went to get more food. Lu Bei zipped crazily across the room, amusing the goronku as he crashed into many of them. He spotted Turesobei and zipped over to him. He didn't pull up soon enough and struck Kurine square in the chest.

"Oh good thanksness, madam," Lu Bei slurred, "for providing so much a soft landing spots."

"Little demon!" she said, slapping him playfully across the cheek. "You're scandalous."

Turesobei grabbed Lu Bei by the back of the neck and said, "Too scandalous. Apologize to Kurine and go to bed."

"I'm sorry, my dearest lady," he said, "future mistress of mine, though I must ... I must ... I must re — re — reiterate that I'm *not* a demon. I am a ... fetch."

"Bed," Turesobei insisted.

"No, master. The night yet lives on."

"Bed, or I call Motekeru to come get you."

"You w-wouldn't d-dare."

"Or, I could call Enashoma instead. Do you want her to take you to bed? She'd be most disappointed in you."

"You are play-play-playing me, master, like a zither with two and a half strings, and I do not like it. But fine, you win. I shall go. Happiest birthday and good-goodnight."

Turesobei released him. Lu Bei zoomed overhead three times, shouting good night to everyone, then flew down the hallway back toward the room, shooting sparks and crashing into the walls as he went. Laughing heavily, Turesobei leaned into Kurine. Then suddenly, he realized they were practically alone together with no one nearby.

"Have you enjoyed your birthday?" she murmured.

"I have," he replied earnestly. "I really have. This has been amazing. I've always been loaded down with responsibility. I've had very few chances ever for anything even resembling fun. I will *never* forget this."

"I can make it even better," she said, wrapping her arms around his neck and pulling him in close.

He muttered something that was supposed to be "back off" or "I can't" or "this is a bad idea" or "I love Iniru and you're a nice girl and I like you a lot but not like this." But what came out was just a jumble of random blurts and groans.

Kurine kissed him.

He made his first mistake then. He kissed her back. Because it was nice and she was very pretty and sweet and he still hadn't completely shaken that bit of ikase. Then he made an even bigger mistake. He made the mistake of enjoying it, and kept kissing her, for long enough that he lost track of time.

Something hit him in the back of the head. "*Ow!*" He spun around. A chunk of meat was lying on the floor. "What in the —"

Growling, Iniru stepped right up and grabbed him by the collar. "You — are — the — stupidest — boy — *ever*."

"Niru, I —"

"Don't *Niru* me. I can't *believe* you would —"

The doors from the stairway burst open. Narbenu and four goronku scouts entered. One limped in wearing tattered clothes and had a cut on his cheek that was bleeding. Turesobei didn't recognize him. But he recognized the look on Narbenu's face: fear.

The band and everyone in the room fell silent.

"Someone summon the Council," Narbenu called out. "Immediately. Turesobei?"

He stepped forward. "I'm here, Narbenu. What's wrong?"

"Sorry to interrupt your party. But we have a terrible problem — and not much time to deal with it."

Chapter Twenty-Two

On the one hand, Turesobei wasn't bothered by the interruption; it saved him from Iniru's retribution. On the other hand, the tremor in Narbenu's voice terrified him. It took a lot to rattle a goronku. Even worse was the look of recognition on the face of the strange, injured goronku as he gazed at Turesobei.

"You'd best come with me to meet the Council," Narbenu said to Turesobei. "Bring your companions."

"Party's over!" Narbenu called out, straining out a measured tone. "This is not an emergency. Don't be alarmed. But it is an early goodnight to everyone."

"Thank you," Turesobei called out to the guests as he headed toward the hallway that led to the meeting chamber.

Kurine grabbed his arm. "Is everything all right?"

"I'm sure it will be," he said, though he doubted it. "The party was great. I loved it."

She beamed a smile at him and started to follow, but Narbenu blocked her. "Sorry, Kurine. Official business."

As they marched after Narbenu, Iniru stepped right in behind Turesobei and jabbed him with a finger between his shoulder blades. "Don't think I'll ever forget," she whispered.

They gathered in the chamber, and several minutes later the councilors hurried in without ceremony and took their seats. Some looked bleary-eyed from having just been awoken. There were no cushions for Turesobei and his companions, so they had to stand.

"Narbenu, what's the matter?" asked War Chief Sudorga. "And who is this with you?"

The battered goronku bowed, and pulled out an amulet made from a giant tooth with a rune carved into it. "I am Hufu from Eastfall."

Earth Priestess Faika stepped forward. She touched the tooth, and then his forehead. "You are as you claim, ranger. Be welcome here. And tell us what you have seen, for you have traveled far if you came from Eastfall."

"Respected elders, I come bearing strange and terrible news. The yomon are on the march, heading in this direction. When I met Narbenu and told him the news, he bade me come here at once."

"You did the right thing," War Chief Sudorga said.

"I have seen the yomon myself," said Hufu, "as have several other rangers. We have been traveling, as swiftly as we can, to warn everyone in their path. The yomon are looking for a dragon made of storm clouds, a beast which many saw pass through the late afternoon skies five weeks ago. They are also looking for a wizard boy and his companions. Somehow, they are connected with this dragon." Hufu turned to Turesobei and his companions. "The yomon's descriptions are incredibly accurate."

"I am the Storm Dragon," Turesobei said. "Or I was, anyway. We battled the yomon and kept them from entering our world, but the Winter Gate closed again and trapped us here. I was hoping they would never search for me — that they'd be too afraid to do so and have nothing to gain by a confrontation."

"Afraid of you?" Hufu asked, confused.

"I killed at least a dozen of them."

"You — you killed a — a dozen?" Hufu stammered.

"When I was the Storm Dragon, yes."

"That explains why there are fewer of them," Hufu replied. "But there's more to it." He examined Turesobei, and then Enashoma. "They are led by a witch smeared with blood. She's ill-dressed for the cold, but it doesn't bother her — as if she were a reitsu. But she looks like the two of you, the same height, but with a powerful build for a woman and an almost ... well, I only saw her from far away, but I'd say she had a demonic cast about her."

"That — that *can't* be Awasa," Turesobei said. "She's only as tall as Enashoma, and she's dainty."

"Well," continued Hufu, "that's what she calls herself. I met with people from the village that they had just ravaged, having interrogated the populace for knowledge about you. The survivors said she called herself Ninefold Awasa, leader of the Eighty-Eight Yomon."

Turesobei staggered back and collapsed onto the floor, grabbing his head. "No, no, *no*," he muttered. "This is even worse."

"So you do know her?" Hufu said.

"Awasa is his betrothed," Iniru said. "Well, his other betrothed — the first one. It's a long story."

Turesobei groaned. Awasa was still alive but somehow bigger and demonic? And she was coming after him. He was doomed.

"You're betrothed to a witch?" Hufu asked, incredulously.

"She — she wasn't like that before," Enashoma said, distantly, almost in shock. "She was a normal aristocratic girl, about my size, not a monster ... well she wasn't *actually* demonic."

Turesobei gathered his composure and stood. "The short of it is, she became corrupted by a warlock named Barakaros. He was one of the Deadly Twelve. We prevented them from releasing the yomon and eternal winter onto our world, but when the gate closed, we ended up on the wrong side. Were her eyes purple? Was there an amulet around her neck?"

"Yes," Hufu replied. "She also had an eight-pointed star on her forehead."

"It's possible that Barakaros the Warlock yet lives ... inside of her," said Turesobei. "Or that an echo of his power has taken root and corrupted her soul. It makes sense that she would want to capture me, and probably kill my companions."

"She carries a strange sword, as well. The blade is almost white."

"Sumada," Turesobei replied. "My father's white-steel sword. Incredibly powerful, incredibly rare." Turesobei turned to the Council. "If Awasa is leading them in this direction, they *will* find us. My companions and I must leave. As soon as possible. We will leave with what we have and make the best of it we can. I won't risk any harm to your people."

Tsuroko glanced at his fellow councilors. "We could hide you here and lie when they come. We could tell them we saw you heading off. Then we could lock ourselves in. To fight their way in would be extraordinarily difficult, even for the yomon. They would soon give up and look elsewhere."

The other council members nodded.

"I am truly grateful for that offer," Turesobei said. "Honestly, you have no idea how warm it makes me feel for you to offer to defend us. But there's a strong chance that Awasa will be able to sense me once she arrives. Besides, my presence here is already known."

"Only by me," said Hufu. "I could stay here until they were gone, to keep your secret."

"No," said Iniru. "He means the reitsu. If the yomon reach the reitsu, they will surely tell them. They have reason to hate Turesobei."

"I must go," Turesobei repeated. "How much time do we have, Hufu?"

"They're moving fast, but they're having to meander from village to village to stop and interrogate people."

"How do they know he lies in this direction?" Herd Chief Boronaru asked.

"The flight trail of the dragon was seen by many people," said Hufu. "You have probably two weeks until they get here. Possibly less — especially if they get word from the reitsu."

Earth Priestess Faika stood. "The Council will recess for a few minutes to discuss this matter."

Turesobei leaned his back against a wall, and tried to shut out images of a blood-stained Awasa, taller and infused with more power from the warlock than before. Ninefold Awasa ... she must have learned how to use the amulet.

Enashoma fell into his arms. He hugged her tight.

"I'm so sorry," Shoma said. "This is terrible."

"It's my fault," he said.

"Let it go," Iniru said. "Even I don't blame you for this. Yes, you shouldn't have brought her along because of the danger — but no one could've imagined this happening."

Zaiporo started to say something, but then shook his head. He looked as shaken as Turesobei had ever seen him. Zaiporo may not have liked Awasa, but he had spent a lot of time around her, more than the rest of them had.

The Council returned to the chamber. Sun Priestess Oroki said, "We have discussed it amongst ourselves and agreed. The danger is too great for our people if you stay here. We hope that you understand."

"I do," he replied.

"However," said Tsuroko. "We shall give you the supplies and mounts you will need to escape here and take on the expedition you have planned on."

"I can't ask that of you," Turesobei said. "We haven't paid you."

"But you must take the supplies, or you won't make it," Tsuroko replied. "It's the only way."

"And you have done good work here," said Shaman Eira. "The machine man stacked stones night after night. You brought warmth to rooms with magic symbols. You healed injured people. You helped as much as you could. You made good on your promise."

"But we'd only just begun," Turesobei said.

"We know you would've followed through to pay us in full, faster than we could've imagined," said Earth Priestess Faika.

"I will personally share the largest part of the financial burden," said Tsuroko. If Turesobei wasn't mistaken, tears welled in the big grizzly goronku's eyes. "If you settle the matter and return safely, you can pay us back then. And live with us as long as you wish, my ... my son." Tsuroko restrained a sob.

Narbenu stepped forward. "They will have no chance without a guide. No chance at all. I would like the Council's approval to serve in this capacity."

"You are needed here, Narbenu," said War Chief Sudorga.

"There's nothing left here for me. I have friends, yes. And I may be of value to the community. But my heart is lost. My brother murdered ... a wife and two children lost to the plague ... too old to start a new family ..."

"You are not too old," Shaman Eira said. "You are just too depressed to try."

Narbenu shook his head and set his jaw. "With me guiding them, Turesobei has a chance at surviving, maybe even returning home to his clan. And the farther away he gets, the safer our people will be. Besides, it might be nice for me to see the wider world and have a bit of adventure."

"We can't ask this of you," Turesobei said. "It would be a death sentence."

"I insist," Narbenu told him.

"Perhaps Hufu can lead us away from here, taking us just far enough that it will be safe for your people," Enashoma said.

"Hufu has a sacred duty as a ranger," Narbenu replied.

"He's right," said Hufu. "I must go to warn other people. I can, however, see to it that word reaches the reitsu and the yomon that you have left here already. I can put them on a false trail."

"No," said Turesobei. "Put them on the correct trail. We'll be heading north, toward the Glass Sea. If they find out they've been misled, they might return here seeking retribution. I want them to stay far away from here, even if that puts us in greater danger."

"As you wish," said Hufu.

"Narbenu," said Turesobei, "you could lead us away from here for several days then double back."

"I want to help you find your way home. I insist. End of discussion." He turned to the Council. "Kemsu will come with me, of course, and we will return if we can."

"I'd rather you didn't doom Kemsu as well," Turesobei said.

"I go where my master wishes," said Kemsu. He glanced at Iniru. "And I wouldn't mind seeing more of the world. I might even earn my freedom through this."

Narbenu said in a doubtful voice, "You might."

Sun Priestess Oroki stood. "It is decided, then. Go and rest, all of you. We shall see to it that all the supplies you need will be ready by sunrise."

Turesobei gathered his companions in Motekeru's room.

"I could face the yomon and get this over with," he said. "As the Storm Dragon, I could save all of you and rid this land of the yomon. And maybe you could save Awasa. Afterward, I could roam the skies, and you could live here safely with the goronku. I doubt we can find a way back anyway, and we'll just get Narbenu and Kemsu killed."

"I don't like that plan, master," said Lu Bei. "You can't."

Motekeru nodded. "Only as a last resort. Stupid plan otherwise."

Zaiporo chimed in. "What they said."

"But this is the only way our safety is guaranteed," Turesobei argued.

Iniru slapped him. "Just stop. I'm sick of the *I can turn into a dragon and sacrifice myself* crap. If it's the last resort, the absolute *last* resort, like they're really about to kill us all, then you can do it. Otherwise, no."

"But, Niru, I —"

Iniru grabbed him and jerked him in close, face-to-face. "Look, I kind of hate you right now, but I don't want to lose you to the dragon." She kissed him on the lips, then shoved him back against the wall. "Got it?"

"Yes, Niru."

Shoma pointed at him. "That goes for me, too."

"And me," added Lu Bei. "But without that kiss. Gross."

Chapter Twenty-Three

At dawn, Turesobei and his companions gathered in the common room. Decorative ribbons still hung from the ceiling, and no one had shoved the tables back into their places. Turesobei smiled briefly and tried to burn the memory of the party into his brain. He'd barely slept, having stayed up worrying about the goronku and feeling guilty about what had happened to Awasa.

They sat down to eat a final hot meal before setting off. The goronku cooks had clearly been told, because they served a small feast made of leftovers from the night before. Narbenu, Kemsu, and War Chief Sudorga joined them and made small talk. As soon as they all finished, they put on their parkas and overboots.

Tsuroko, Ukiri, and Kurine entered the commons. Kurine was wearing full cold weather gear, as well. Turesobei expected her to run up to him and give him a deep embrace. But she didn't. Instead, she turned, with tears in her eyes, and gave her mother a tight hug. Tsuroko wrapped his arms around both of them, tears streaming down his cheeks.

"This doesn't look good," Zaiporo said.

"Turesobei," Iniru whispered, "tell me she's not coming with us. Tell me you didn't invite her."

"Of course I didn't."

"Kurine *has* to come along," Kemsu said. "She's your betrothed."

"But it's not safe," Turesobei replied.

"Doesn't matter," Kemsu said. "Betrothal is a sacred bond only one step short of marriage. You can't leave her behind."

"That's ridiculous," Turesobei said. "If I were on a trade expedition, would she follow along?"

"No, but that's different," Kemsu said. "If that were the case, you'd be expected to return. Doing this, you might never come back, whether from failure or success, so she must go with you."

"There's no way she can refuse?" Enashoma asked.

Kemsu shrugged. "Only if she could prove Turesobei was dishonorable and unfit. Then the marriage would be called off."

"So maybe if I suddenly ... I don't know ... made out with Iniru ... right here?" he suggested.

Kemsu scowled. "That'd just make her mad, very very mad. Look, no one here's going to believe you're unfit. They'd see right through it. And I don't think you'd want to use Iniru that way."

Judging from the dagger-stare Iniru was giving Kurine, Turesobei wasn't so certain she'd be opposed to doing whatever it would take to make Kurine stay behind.

Turesobei approached Kurine and her family. "I understand the betrothal is sacred, almost like marriage, and that we shouldn't risk being permanently separated ... but this is incredibly dangerous, Kurine. I care so much for you. I don't want to see you injured or killed."

Tsuroko rounded on him. "You'd dishonor my daughter by leaving her behind?!"

"I would *never* dishonor her. I just want to keep her safe."

"I know you'll do your best to keep her safe," Tsuroko said. "But all of us must face death someday. Dishonor, however, we do not have to face. And dishonor is worse than death."

"I won't be a drag on you," Kurine said. Her eyes were red from crying. "I have all the skills needed. I've been listening to Daddy tell me about how it's done all my life. I even went on one very short trade expedition two years ago. I have training in fighting. I'll be a ton of help."

Turesobei took her hands. What could he do? What could he say? "I know you will be helpful. I know. You'll be better out there than me. I just ... I don't want you getting hurt, is all."

"My daughter chose you," said Ukiri. "She must live with her choice. I think it was a fine choice made on good faith. I'm not happy that she must leave, knowing I might never see her again, but it is what it is. The decree of the gods does not change to suit our whims. To retain her honor, Kurine must go with you, or become a priestess, and that is not a suitable vocation for her."

Turesobei sighed. "I don't understand your culture. It's so different from mine. But if this is how it must be. If this is what you want, Kurine ..."

"It is." She hugged her parents one more time and kissed each on the cheek.

Tsuroko put his hands on their heads. "You have our blessing to marry at any point along the way. We understand you may never see us again, and that if you do, much time may have passed. Do not wait to marry just so we may be there to see it. Have the ceremony performed when it pleases you. Be with one another, and be happy, wherever you may end up."

"In my heart," said Ukiri, "I know that the two of you will always be happy together, and I will never believe otherwise. I shall never mourn this day."

Turesobei let Kurine spend a few minutes more with her family and returned to his friends. "I did all I could. Who knew one kiss could screw up so much ..."

"A single kiss can screw up a lot more than your tiny brain can comprehend," Iniru snapped.

Hufu entered from outside. "Thought you should know, there are two reitsu scouting the village. I didn't let them know I'd spotted them."

"I suspect one will return to report back to their village while the other follows us," said Narbenu.

"That's perfect," Turesobei said.

Hufu eyed Turesobei curiously. "I think most people, if I told them they were being stalked by a reitsu, would be terrified."

Turesobei shrugged. "Motekeru killed seven of them, and I defeated their champion in single combat, despite a broken arm." He felt a little guilty about bragging, but Narbenu nodded in appreciation. Hufu simply stared dumfounded at him.

The Council came and said their goodbyes. The priestesses both said prayers, beseeched the gods to protect them, and asked for their endeavor to be blessed. Goodbyes were said to all, including a last, tear-filled one between Kurine and her parents. Then they set off.

Outside, sturdy sonoke laden with supplies waited for them. Narbenu and Kemsu each rode a mount that carried extra supplies. Turesobei shared a mount with Zaiporo. Iniru and Enashoma rode together, as before. Kurine rode with the amber hounds, Rig and Ohma, who sat in a special saddle Herd Chief Boronaru had rigged up for them. Motekeru rode alone on the last mount, a particularly strong one that could easily take his weight.

When asked by a groom if he could guide the mount, Motekeru replied, "Just because I live simply and speak little does not mean I'm a simpleton."

Narbenu gazed at Aikora and sighed. "Let's ride slowly and make sure it's obvious we're leaving. Don't want those reitsu to miss it."

Once they were outside the village area, Turesobei cast the *spell of personal obscuration* on Lu Bei. The fetch flew up and circled several times.

"Good call," he said upon returning. "One wraith is following us, while the other has set off, back toward their village."

The group rode all day, stopping only for a midday break to stretch and eat. The travel was smooth and presented no problems. Kurine rode near Turesobei and asked him endless questions about his world. He figured her curiosity was mostly an attempt not to think about leaving everything she knew behind, something she hadn't even imagined twelve hours earlier. It was the most they'd ever talked. It concerned him that she'd wanted to marry him before ever having had such an opportunity. What had she expected out of him? Was he really the only decent choice around? Would she get bored with him and regret her choice? He *had* to get back to his world, where things mostly made sense.

By late afternoon, everyone was competent in guiding the sonoke. But they weren't skilled enough to ride them into danger. They'd have to work on that as they went. When they stopped at dusk, Narbenu and Kemsu instructed them in the proper art of cutting ice and compacted snow to make snow houses. Motekeru remembered it from before and began cutting immediately. He constructed one snow house with Kurine's help and settled the sonoke into a trench in the time it took the others to make half of a snow house.

At Narbenu's insistence, the girls again piled into one snow house with Motekeru and the hounds, while the boys went into the other. In the night, strange beasts howled in the distance. Even worse things hunted them. Turesobei curled up on the blanket, cold and miserable on the hard ice.

"This stinks," Zaiporo muttered.

"Get used to it," Kemsu replied. "We're going to have a lot of nights like this."

Chapter Twenty-Four

As they rode, Narbenu pointed out tracks of various creatures that could serve as game, though wild sonoke were preferable. "Starting tomorrow, we'll devote an hour each day to hunting. More, if we don't find enough game. We have to keep our stores up in case we get into trouble or get pinned by a blizzard. There are few places to stop for supplies along the way, and I have nothing to trade."

Kurine held up a tiny purse. "Father gave me ten jade and an ingot of iron." She smiled at Turesobei. "My dowry. Enough for a week of food for all of us."

"That's quite the dowry," Narbenu said appreciatively. Kemsu nodded in agreement.

"It was very generous of him," Turesobei said. He glanced at Zaiporo whose eyes were wide with surprise. In their world, Zaiporo had earned ten jade every month as a guard. Since he was a zaboko, he was considered by the ruling baojendari society to be a second-class citizen and wasn't paid nearly what he deserved. In addition to that, the Kobarai had fed him two meals each day, plus clothing and any equipment he needed.

"Are blizzards common?" Turesobei asked.

"Anything more than a light flurry is rare," Narbenu replied. "But blizzards do happen every few years. And you can't predict them. They'll come up out of nowhere."

"You do all know how to hunt, right?" Kemsu asked.

"I do," Iniru replied.

"I knew you would," Kemsu replied with a wink.

"Well, of course she can," Zaiporo replied. "Iniru is awesome like that."

Enashoma scowled at Zaiporo. Turesobei sighed.

"Zaiporo has hunted a little and is excellent at butchering kills," Turesobei said. "I've only hunted a few times. Once with magic."

"Cheater," Iniru said, almost playfully. She started to smile at him, but then she stopped and scowled.

"I can also detect the presence of any creatures nearby using a spell," Turesobei said. "Though I can't keep it up all the time."

Iniru snorted, and Narbenu stifled a cough. Turesobei glanced at them and shrugged. He almost asked what was so funny, but decided not to.

"I can use the spell periodically to make sure nothing's creeping up on us. Lu Bei can scout from above. We have the hounds, too, though I'm not sure of their footing on the ice.

I won't be able to sense exactly what's out there if I've never encountered it before. My range is normally limited to about two hundred paces, though it uses air kenja, which is strong here, so I can probably do three times that. I'll have to test it."

"I've gotten decent at cooking," Enashoma said.

"Unfortunately," Narbenu said. "We can't cook out here on the ice. No fuel for the fires. We can warm water to melt it with the star stones, but that's about it."

"You mean we have to eat the meat raw?" Enashoma asked. "That's gross."

"Only way to do it," Narbenu replied. "Cooking is a luxury. And you'll get used to the flavor. I prefer raw, personally."

"I've eaten raw as part of my qengai practice," Iniru said. "I didn't like it much, except for fish. Speaking of my training, the goronku may not have to worry about it with their fur and fat layer, but for all of us, you three more than me, we have to make sure we don't sweat. The moisture will freeze to your skin. Take off layers if you get hot. We have to avoid frostbite at all costs. Keep your circulation going. Watch your feet. Make sure they stay dry. Check them every night and rub them. You may not be able to feel frostbite setting in. If they do get frostbitten, don't warm them too fast and don't rub them."

"Where'd you learn all that?" Zaiporo asked.

"I had to learn cold weather survival in my qengai training, in case I ever had a mission to the mountains in winter. A qengai must prepare for all possibilities."

"We'll take an extra break each day to walk around," Narbenu said. "I forget you're not adapted to the cold like we are. Rotate your feet as you ride. It helps."

"If we have to take time every day to walk and hunt," said Enashoma, "won't the yomon catch up to us?"

"I think they'll have to hunt as well," said Kemsu.

"Maybe," said Turesobei, "but I'm certain they have much more endurance than us and can probably run through much of the night. I'll summon the moon mirrors so we can ride an extra hour or two. That's all we can do. Truthfully, I'm not even certain the yomon eat, since they're sort of like Kaiaru and sort of like demons."

"They eat," said Narbenu. "Though whether for pleasure or out of necessity, I don't know. I'm sure the witch must eat, though, right?"

Turesobei hoped so, but he wasn't sure what Awasa was capable of now. "At least we have mounts. We should be faster than them." That was all the comfort he could give.

The third morning passed without any sign of game. They crested a long, low hill, and before them stretched another expanse of endless ice in all directions, though to the northeast was a blotch that Narbenu claimed was the outer buildings of another goronku village.

As they traveled, Turesobei rode beside Iniru as much as he could. It wasn't that he was tired of Kurine. He was just tired of the endless questions about his life in Okoro. And he missed Iniru. Despite rescuing her, he still hadn't had a chance to spend much time with her. His excuse to Kurine was that he had to let Zaiporo talk to Enashoma, and that his sister would miss him. He doubted she bought it.

Whenever Iniru became relaxed or grew tired, she'd start to forget that she was mad at him and relax. She would tease him or exchange barbs with Lu Bei. They would talk about their adventure fighting the Storm Cult and trekking through the rainforest of Wakaro, and they would have long discussions about magic and fighting. But whenever Iniru remembered Kurine, she'd stop talking and cast dirty looks at him.

Kemsu, when he wasn't taking point, would ride nearby and try to butt into their conversations. Kurine never did that; he didn't think she was listening. When Turesobei wasn't nearby, she'd ride quietly, occasionally speaking to Motekeru or the hounds, who rode with her in their makeshift saddle. Turesobei felt guilty for cutting her out.

"Sobei," Enashoma asked late that afternoon, "do you think Aikonshi and Hakamoro are okay?"

"Tough as they are, I'm sure they got down from the mountain with no problem. They're survivors. And if I missed any yomon, I'm sure they'll track them down and find a way to get rid of them."

"I wish they were with us now," Enashoma said. "We sure could use their help."

"I'm *glad* they're not here," Turesobei replied. "They're where they belong. I just wish I could say that for all of you. I wish I hadn't dragged you in with me."

"You did what you had to," Zaiporo said. "It's not like you had a lot of control over the dragon."

"I barely had any control."

"Are you still having nightmares about the dragon?" Iniru asked.

"No," he responded.

She gave him a dubious look. "Liar."

"Well, they're not as bad now. They're back to the level they were at before we set off to rescue you."

Visions of the huge, shadowed monster with the flaming eyes had mostly replaced his nightmares of the Storm Dragon, but there was no way he was going to tell them about that. He didn't want to worry them.

Turesobei scanned their surroundings with the *spell of sensing presences* as soon as he woke up each morning and again at lunch, dusk, and just before going to bed. On the fourth morning, he got a hit — a feeling, a knowing that something was out there — and in this case, exactly what it was.

"I'm picking up a reitsu following us. He's at the edge of my range. His energy signature closely matches the ice. If I hadn't come into contact with one, I'd have never noticed him. He's keeping his distance. If there are others following, they are farther away."

"I don't get it," Zaiporo said. "What's he going to accomplish by tracking us? His comrades won't be able to catch up or find him."

"Could be an assassin," Iniru suggested.

"The reitsu have a weak psychic link with others of their kind, even over great distances," Narbenu said. "So they'll be able to follow him if they come in roughly the same direction and aren't too far behind. I know they want revenge, but as to what they're planning, I have no idea. They know they can't take out Motekeru easily."

They stopped a few leagues from a goronku village. Narbenu rode in to let the people know about the yomon heading this way. Kemsu invited Iniru to scout around with him to search for game.

"I don't know," Iniru said, "maybe we should all stick together."

Kurine grabbed Turesobei's arm. "Why don't we take a short walk? Just you and me."

"You know what?" Iniru said. "I think I *will* scout around with you, Kemsu. Right now. Let's go."

As the two of them rode off, Turesobei said, "Can you believe that? What does she see in him?"

"Who cares?" Kurine said, perplexed.

"I don't know what she sees," Zaiporo commented, "but I don't blame him."

Lu Bei, who had been flying around, zipped in front of Zaiporo. "Lady Shoma, do you want me to claw his eyes out?"

"What?!" Zaiporo said. He turned to Enashoma. "Did — did I do something wrong?"

"Did you do something *wrong*?" she asked. "You idiot — you've been hanging around Sobei too much."

"Hey!" Turesobei said.

"Don't claw his eyes out, Lu Bei," Enashoma said. "Not yet." She stalked over and played with the hounds, who seemed to enjoy running and sliding on the ice and snow.

Motekeru shook his head and said nothing. Lu Bei turned back into a book. Kurine tugged at Turesobei, so he hopped off his sonoke and walked with her, leaving Zaiporo on his own to figure out what he'd done wrong.

"Look," Kurine said, "I know you don't love me. No, shush. Let me finish. I know you don't love me. And you probably think I'm rash for choosing you without us really knowing each other ..."

"Yeah, honestly, I kinda do think that."

"Well, it was rash. I admit it. But you're cute and smart and ... different. You're the most exciting thing to happen here in ages. Goronku life ... it's pretty much the same, year in and year out, generation after generation. And then I saw you. And you flirted with me —"

"I did?"

"And so I knew you were interested in me."

"I was?"

"And so I went for it. I knew, suddenly, that my life could be special. That it didn't have to be predictable, and I could be someone special, too."

"You already *are* someone special, Kurine. You're incredibly talented."

"Just like my mother and my grandmother and my great-grandmother? I knew you could change everything for me, maybe even all the goronku people. And since I did find you attractive, it was worth the gamble. The only other boy I'd ever been interested in ... it just wasn't meant to be. It never can be. And I'm sorry about the kiss. I tried to be fair by asking you."

"I thought I'd embarrass you if I said no."

"You would've, but I'd have been okay — I'm tough. And it's not the end of the world if a kiss gets refused. It happens. I never stopped to think that in your culture, a public kiss might not mean the same thing. And now ..."

"We're stuck together because of your society and the rules. Hey, it's not my first time. My first betrothed, the witch chasing us ... my future marriage to her was arranged by our parents when I was only three years old. I had no choice."

"That's terrible."

"Your way is better than that, for certain."

"Iniru," Kurine said. "I know you like her ... maybe you love her. I watch you with her, riding beside her as much as you can, talking and laughing, enjoying each other's company. But tell me, what does she offer that I don't? I'm pretty, too."

"You are." And it was true.

"I'm witty. Maybe I don't have all her exciting skills — but she's a killer, a trained assassin. Doesn't that bother you?"

"Well ... I've never really thought about it that way." He had grown accustomed to not questioning how the Sacred Codex of the qengai worked, and it was easy to forget that Iniru was an assassin when she had never killed anyone except in self-defense — at least as far as he knew — and she hadn't been able to bring herself to kill the Winter Child. "What she does, it's to bring about a greater good."

Kurine cocked an eyebrow. "If you say so ..."

"Honest."

"Sobei, give me a chance. That's all I ask. Let me earn your love. I know I can make you happy." She stroked a finger along his lips. "Please." She stepped in until their bodies were touching. "Pretty please ..."

She kissed him.

Maybe Lu Bei should gouge *my* eyes out, he thought. He returned her kiss — but briefly. "I promise I'll give you a chance, Kurine. But Iniru is my friend. I risked everything to save her. You have to be nice to her. You must become friends with her."

Kurine frowned, pouted, then sighed. "If that's what it takes. Come on, we'd better head back."

A few minutes after they returned, Kemsu and Iniru rode in carrying four rabbit-like creatures they'd killed.

"Not much game around here," Kemsu said. "This area is over-hunted, being so close to a village. But we got dinner. The real way. Didn't even need magic."

Iniru snorted and dismounted.

Zaiporo skinned and butchered the creatures. Narbenu returned, carrying a block of cheese the village had given him in appreciation for the warning. They ate some of the cheese along with the raw meat. Turesobei hated the meat. The taste wasn't the worst, but it wasn't good either, and it was tough to chew, though the goronku and Iniru, with their sharper teeth, made quick work of it.

"You know," Iniru said to Enashoma, "your hair has really grown out. I like it."

Enashoma turned away from her. "I don't want to talk to you right now."

"What did I do?" Iniru asked.

"It's ... nothing," Enashoma said. "I'm just not in the mood for chatter."

Iniru turned to Turesobei. "Sobei?"

"What?" he snapped miserably.

"Oh fine," Iniru said. "Never mind."

"The cold," said Motekeru, and it was the first thing he'd said all day, "is getting to all of you. Maybe you should try silence for a while. You might learn to like it."

Three more days of riding, eating rations and some raw game, and three more nights spent in freezing snow houses flared everyone's tempers, except Motekeru and Narbenu. The goronku was so used to these conditions as a scout that they didn't faze him. They were now out in the true wilderness, far away from most settlements. It was an unusual route to take, and more dangerous, but it was the most direct route, and they didn't want to endanger any communities.

Having just finished a late afternoon stretch and walkabout, Turesobei cast the *spell of sensing presences*. Their reitsu stalker didn't appear, but Turesobei doubted he was gone. Probably he was just hanging further back. He did pick up something else.

"There's a beast northwest of us — two hundred paces. I think it's a sonoke."

"I don't see anything," Kemsu said. "Must be in a hollow, or maybe lying behind some rocks." Gullies and rocks had become increasingly common over the last day of riding. "But then it's hard to see anything right now."

The sky was deeply overcast, and a fine snow was misting down on them. The goronku considered this to be fairly heavy weather. Upon Kemsu announcing it as such, everyone from Okoro laughed, especially Iniru, who had grown up in a rainforest.

"Only one sonoke?" Narbenu asked Turesobei. "You sure?"

"He's on the outside of my range, but I think so. Why?"

"They're herd animals ... small herds, usually. It's not common to find one alone this time of the year, but it may have gotten lost or injured. Kemsu, you and Iniru go after it. We could use the meat. If we all go, we'll be more likely to scare it off."

"What about you?" Kemsu asked.

"I have ... business ... to attend to," Narbenu replied, eyeing a particularly tall boulder he could hide behind.

"Won't killing a wild sonoke disturb our mounts?" Enashoma asked.

"Never bothers them," Narbenu responded. "The wild ones are a different strain. Savage, too, so you have to be careful around them."

"Should I go and calm it with a spell?" Turesobei asked.

"I think Iniru and I can handle this," Kemsu said.

Kemsu and Iniru drew their spears and rode off. A lot of time passed ... enough that Turesobei grew concerned. When Narbenu began to fidget, Turesobei cast the spell again, putting more power into it than before.

"I think they must have just killed the sonoke. Its energy is fading. They're farther away than I expected, though. Must have had to chase — oh no!"

"What's wrong?" asked Narbenu.

"I'm sensing more sonoke coming toward them."

Narbenu drew his spear. "How many?"

"Hard to know exactly, but ... dozens. Thirty, maybe forty of them. Moving in on them fast."

Enashoma climbed up onto the saddle with Motekeru.

"We have to get to them and warn them." Narbenu kicked the flanks of his sonoke. "And fast."

Lu Bei popped out. "I'll fly as far ahead as I can, master, to warn them as soon as possible."

"I'll keep my spell up so I can judge their location."

"As soon as we alert them, we've got to get away from the sonoke herd," Narbenu said. "Packs that large are rare and incredibly deadly. If they smell the blood of one of their own, they'll go into a frenzy."

Chapter Twenty-Five

Having been alerted in advance by Lu Bei flying ahead screeching warnings, Iniru and Kemsu appeared over a ridge, racing their mounts at full speed. Wild sonoke were charging after them, and two ahead of the pack were closing in fast. As they joined Turesobei and the others, the two pack leaders surged forward, going much faster than their tame sonoke mounts could. Probably because the wild sonoke didn't have saddles, supplies, and riders to weigh them down.

The wild sonoke were different in appearance. Their fur was rust-tinged instead of gray. Their horns were larger, their fangs longer. Narbenu twisted in his saddle and jabbed at one with his spear, scoring a minor wound on its flank. The second beast tried to ram Kemsu, but his mount turned enough to dodge the blow. Iniru struck its tail with her spear, but that only angered it more. As it rounded on Kemsu again, Turesobei lunged with his spear, missing the beast entirely. But as his mount turned, Zaiporo got in a shot and stabbed the beast in the eye, causing it to fall back. The other wild sonoke nearby attacked Motekeru. He dodged his mount out of the way, then grabbed the wild sonoke by the horns and pulled it up off the ice far enough that he could reach in with the claws of his other hand and rip out its throat.

Narbenu and Kemsu gaped at Motekeru in awe, but only for a moment. Dozens more of the wild sonoke were closing in.

"We're not going to get away!" Kemsu yelled.

Turesobei tapped Zaiporo on the shoulder. "Switch places with me."

Carefully, while still riding, Zaiporo hopped ahead of Turesobei and took the reins of the mount. It was a maneuver they had practiced before on denekon, and it worked perfectly. Sitting backward in the saddle to face the enemy, Turesobei quickly cast the first powerful, non-storm spell he could think of that might affect an entire herd chasing after them, the *spell of the flame wall*. It was a poor choice in the Ancient Cold and Deep, but since the creatures would be unaccustomed to fire, he hoped it would terrify them.

A shroud of flame erupted between them and the wild sonoke. The beasts in the lead skidded to a halt, and then backed away in terror. But the flames flickered out, and Turesobei sagged in the saddle. He'd had to use a lot of internal kenja to pull that spell off with a quick-casting.

Lu Bei sped along beside him. "Didn't work long, master!"

"I knew the spell would fail quickly."

"I didn't mean that. Look."

The wild sonoke had conquered their fear and renewed the chase, their frenzy unabated. At least it had bought them a little time. Surely the wild sonoke would tire eventually.

"How good are their senses?" Turesobei asked. "If I magically summoned a cloud of fog, would it bother them much?"

"They can hear us and smell us well enough," Narbenu said. "I think we'd be at more of disadvantage than them."

They rode as fast as possible, but the wild sonoke gained on them steadily. Turesobei cast the *spell of dark-fire*. A crackling, black and purple globe of fire appeared in his hand. He tossed it at the lead sonoke. It struck the beast, melted its face, and sent it tumbling, slowing several others — but it didn't slow the herd.

"Wow," Kemsu said. "I didn't know you could do ... something like that."

"Turesobei ..." Kurine muttered in amazement "... how ..."

"The bloodlust is in them strong now," Narbenu said. "How many times can you do what you just did?"

Panting heavily, Turesobei said, "Unless I use storm energy, two ... maybe three more before I pass out."

"Doesn't sound like a good strategy," Iniru said.

"I could cast a wind spell to kick up loose snow to blind and disorient them. I have plenty of air energy to draw on here."

"Do it," Iniru said.

"Master, the *spell of the screaming wind-blast* from Chonda Lu's grimoire. That would surely knock them back and disorient them. It would be much more powerful than the *spell of heaven's breath*. Do you remember it?"

"Lu Bei, I can't do that spell."

"But you can draw on all the power of the air kenja here to make up for lacking the internal power and knowing the proper channels, just like you did with the storm spells using the *Mark of the Storm Dragon*."

"It's not scripted, and I haven't rehearsed it."

"But you do know it, yes?"

"You know I do." Turesobei rarely forgot a spell, even after studying one only once, but it was dangerous to recite one without having practiced it perfectly several times. One mistake could be fatal, or just lead to a lot of wasted energy. But then, this was a dangerous situation anyway.

"Master, imagine you are Chonda Lu, like you did before, and quick-cast the spell from memory. I think it will work. If it doesn't ..."

"All right. Everyone, clear away. Give me some room. The spell could backfire."

Zaiporo slowed their mount just enough that the others could pull ahead. With the wild sonoke nearly on top of them, Turesobei began chanting the spell. Since he'd only studied it once, he cast the spell slow and steady. As he did, he thought of the dream he'd had, of being Chonda Lu out on the plains battling Vôl Ultharma. He tried to feel exactly what Chonda Lu had felt then.

One sonoke got close to them while he was casting, but Motekeru dropped back and fended it off.

Turesobei fell into a trance where he became Chonda Lu, much like when he sometimes became the Storm Dragon. He was sitting over the grimoire, recording the *spell of the screaming wind-blast*, chuckling as he thought of the first time he'd cast it, in a contest against a short, dark-skinned Kaiaru rival. It had been a breezy day, and they were out on a hill, a kite flapping lazily overhead.

The spell went off, ripping Turesobei back into the present. A screaming, wailing, eardrum-assaulting blast of wind erupted behind Turesobei and his companions. Despite substituting air kenja, the spell drew on so much of his internal kenja that his eyes rolled back in his head as he slumped back against Zaiporo, but he stayed conscious, just barely. Air and ice energy poured into the spell, overpowering his intent. The energies far exceeded what the spell called for. And given that it was a Kaiaru spell he'd never practiced before, he had no control over it now that he'd cast it — like when he'd attempted the lightning spells at home the first time.

The wind blast struck the wild sonoke herd. Despite their forward momentum, some slid rapidly backward. Others flipped over and tumbled violently away. Even those that hunkered down were pushed back until they were out of sight.

The wind-blast kicked loose ice and snow up, forming a cloud behind them ... a cloud that began to spin up into the sky and kick snow back toward them, increasing the intensity of the flurries that had fallen all day. In minutes, a heavy snow began to fall over the area as a giant cloud billowed overhead, expanding out in all directions.

"It's rebounding," Turesobei said listlessly, his eyelids fluttering. It was all he could do to stay conscious. "The cloud, the magic. It's all rebounding. I've accidentally triggered a snowstorm. And it looks like the prevailing winds overhead are bringing it toward us while the lower winds I summoned are kicking snow up into the clouds."

"You can't stop it?" Kurine asked.

"It should've stopped on its own, once my connection to it was severed, but it didn't. And I can't take back control of a spell that powerful. We can take shelter, or we can try to outrace it. The magic will have to end eventually."

"Let's try to outrun it, then," said Narbenu. "We don't have time to take adequate shelter."

Turesobei doubted they could outrun it, but said nothing, because he was sure Narbenu knew that. Minutes later, a blizzard engulfed them. Visibility became poor ... and then nonexistent. None of them could see each other unless they were side-by-side. They tried to gather close, but then a howling wind struck them so hard it blew them apart from one another. Turesobei shouted to the others, but the responses he heard back were unintelligible. Turesobei couldn't see anyone. He thought he heard a shout from Narbenu.

"What we do?" Zaiporo shouted.

"I don't know!"

Turesobei and Zaiporo's sonoke crashed suddenly into the mount Iniru was riding. She must have stopped for some reason. As the two sonoke struck each other and recoiled, they plunged over a ridge, screeching, and slid down a steep incline. The sonoke tumbled, and they were thrown out of the saddle. Inadvertently, they triggered an avalanche of loose snow that had piled up on the slope and along the ridge.

Turesobei slid until he plunged into a deep snow bank. A wave of snow then crashed over him.

Chapter Twenty-Six

Buried under an avalanche of snow, unable to breathe or move, Turesobei fought back the urge to panic. He attempted a spell, but when he spoke, snow filled his mouth.

A clawed hand shot down, grabbed him by the collar, and yanked him free. "You okay, master?"

Gasping for breath, Turesobei gazed up into Motekeru's horrible, jagged bronze face, and nodded. He'd never before been so glad to see that ugly face. "The others?"

Motekeru nodded to where Enashoma and Iniru stood huddled together beside two sonoke. "Still looking for the rest."

A small section of snow nearby lit up and melted somewhat. With another burst of light, more snow melted. A spark fired upward, and Lu Bei burst free, shaking the snow from his wings. He zipped over and flew into Enashoma's arms.

Turesobei stumbled toward Iniru and Enashoma. Judging from their ruffled, snow-covered, somewhat battered appearance, they had gotten buried in the avalanche, too.

"You okay?" he asked.

"I'm okay," Iniru wheezed.

"Bruised," Enashoma panted. "Motekeru rolled over me. Zai ... we gotta find him."

Lu Bei zipped up into the sky immediately and began circling. Motekeru stomped around. Though the snow still rained down heavily, it wasn't as bad as it had been. Visibility had improved to the point where Turesobei could clearly see Motekeru from twenty paces away, probably because the snow was only falling down from overhead and not also blowing in from the side.

As he prepared to cast the *spell of sensing presences*, a sonoke squirmed free from the snow bank. Zaiporo came up along with it, one hand clutched to a saddle stirrup.

Enashoma ran to him, and gave him a hug which made him groan. "He's all right ... I think!"

Narbenu and Kemsu rode out of the blizzard — unharmed.

"We were worried you'd gotten buried in the avalanche," Narbenu said. "Kemsu thought he saw you go over the edge. Took us a while to carefully work our way down the slope."

"We collided," Iniru said. "Motekeru dug us out. Zaiporo and Lu Bei dug themselves out."

"Kurine's not with you?" Turesobei asked.

"Haven't seen her," Narbenu replied. "She's not with you?"

Iniru shook her head. "She wasn't in the collision."

"We've got to find her," Kemsu said. "Fast! If she's buried she'll suffocate soon."

"Lu Bei?" Turesobei shouted.

From where he was still circling above, Lu Bei called down, "No sign, master! I can't go any higher! Winds are too strong!"

"Kurine!" Kemsu shouted.

Turesobei cast the *spell of locating that which is hidden*. He thought of Kurine ... of kissing her, because he needed the best connection he could make in case she was far away or buried deep. Her presence popped into his mind instantly.

"That way!" Turesobei said, pointing. "She's not far."

"Hop on," Narbenu said.

Turesobei leapt into the saddle behind him. A few minutes later, they found Kurine. She was leaning against her mount, gasping, and clutching her knee. The amber hounds, Rig and Ohma, were nestled against her. They barked happily as Turesobei approached. Kemsu leapt down, and Turesobei followed him.

"Is anything broken?" Kemsu asked.

Kurine shook her head. "Just wrenched my knee. I'll be okay. My mount got free on its own, but I was buried. Not deep." She scratched Rig under the chin. "The hounds pulled me out."

Kurine took Turesobei's hand. "You found me with magic, didn't you?"

"Um ... yeah," Turesobei said. "How'd you know?"

"I just knew you would," she said. "We have a bond."

Kemsu sighed. "It's not like you were all that far away. We would've found you by searching."

Narbenu checked Kurine's mount. "He'll be fine with a little rest; sonoke are tough."

They helped Kurine into the saddle, and then rode back to the others. While Narbenu examined Turesobei's mount, Turesobei checked to see if any of their gear was missing. Zaiporo's spear was snapped in half. "We've got a broken spear, and one of our supply packs is gone." Motekeru dug around searching for it, but came up empty-handed.

Luckily, all the mounts were fine, having suffered no more than a few bruises and scrapes. The snow had cushioned the impact. Kurine's wrenched knee was the worst of their injuries.

The snow kept falling, showing no signs of letting up.

"We need cover," Kemsu said. "Maybe there's a cave or an overhang somewhere nearby."

"What about snow houses?" Turesobei said.

"Not an option," Narbenu replied. "We'd likely get buried inside. They'd be our tombs. Unless we can find shelter, we'll just have to keep riding. Do you have some sort of spell that can help us find shelter?"

"Nothing that I can manage," Turesobei replied.

There was a geographical spell in Chonda Lu's grimoire that gave the caster an impression of the area around them, in a way similar to the way the *spell of sensing presences* allowed one to detect other creatures or people nearby. But it was primarily an earth kenja spell, and the earth energy in the Ancient Cold and Deep was slightly depressed. Most of it was air and water kenja because of all the ice. There was no way he could do that spell.

"Let me try to study the kenja currents, see if I can get a feel for the terrain that way. That might help."

They rode slowly, with Turesobei concentrating. A solid cliff face that went straight up stopped them a few minutes later.

"Can't go this way," Narbenu said. "And the slope we came down is too steep for us to ride back up."

"We must be in a canyon then," Iniru said.

"Eew!" Kurine said to Turesobei. "Your eyes."

Enashoma chuckled. "They're supposed do that."

"It's creepy," Zaiporo said, "but you get used to it."

Turesobei's eyes turned a solid milky-white color when he studied the kenja currents. It hadn't occurred to him that the goronku had never seen this effect before.

With the snowstorm overhead, air and water currents swirled violently all around, making it difficult for him to get a feel for anything. He dismounted, knelt, and placed both hands on the ice. Slowly, he attuned himself to the flow of the earth kenja in the area. Once he got a good sense of it all, he climbed back into the saddle.

"We're definitely in a canyon, but I can't tell which way we should go. I can't feel the flow well enough for that. I'm guessing it's fairly steep on both sides, and the ends, whatever they're like, are far away from us."

"I've heard about this place," Narbenu said. "It is a canyon — a very long one, twenty leagues or more. I've heard the rangers talk about it. There's a way out on one end, but I can't remember which way that is or anything else about it. Don't even remember the name of it. Sorry."

"Twenty leagues?" Iniru said. "That's massive. We could be stuck in here for days, maybe weeks."

"Once the storm clears, I may be able to get a better sense of it," Turesobei said.

"Until then?" Kemsu asked.

Turesobei pointed to his right, the direction he thought was north. "That way seems as good as the other to me."

Narbenu shrugged. "Why not?"

They rode north, miserable, bruised, and cold. Visibility worsened again as the blizzard grew stronger. Tiny beads of moisture slicked Turesobei's skin under all his clothing

— the result of having been buried in the snow. He knew the moisture would freeze on his skin, and ultimately kill him, but there was nothing he could do about it until they got out of the storm; changing clothes with snow falling down on him wouldn't do any good.

The canyon narrowed, and the walls grew steep on both sides. Slowly, those sides closed in at the top, almost forming a cave. There was still an opening above and snow fell through it, but by riding to one side they were able to get out from under the snowfall. But what blocked out snow also blocked out light. Turesobei cast the *spell of the moon mirrors*.

"Should we continue?" he asked. "Looks like it's going to close up into a proper cave soon."

"Let's ride a little farther, then," Narbenu said.

And so they rode, until the two sides of the canyon merged above to form a ceiling.

"Well, it's not the way out," said Narbenu. "But we can wait out the storm here and rest. How long do you think the storm will rage?"

Turesobei shrugged. "I was going to ask you. My spell created a small but powerful storm. Unfortunately, I think that triggered a larger one from the snow that was already falling. The spell has almost certainly ended, but what it started is obviously still going."

"Blizzards rarely last more than a day," Narbenu said. "By daybreak, it should be over. We can rest up until then. But we need to be careful and not go any deeper. Large caves can hold ... well, you name it: sonoke herds, demons, beasts." He jumped down and started unloading the packs from his mount. "Everyone remove your saddles and check your mounts again, carefully. Make certain they're completely okay. Check the straps on your packs and saddles, be certain they're secure. They might have gotten damaged."

Turesobei and Zaiporo stripped their mount, and Narbenu and Kemsu checked it. There were no injuries worse than a scrape, so they strapped the beast back up, and then Narbenu inspected their work to make sure they'd done it correctly.

"If your clothes are wet inside, you're going to have to switch to dry gear," Kemsu said.

Everyone but Kemsu and Narbenu had wet clothes, so they had to switch. But the only extras they had were inner shirts and pants. Turesobei didn't really want to expose his bare skin to this cold. He reached for a star stone, then thought of how little warmth it could provide even at its maximum capacity.

"Could we risk a fire, for a short time?" he asked. "Enough to warm up and dry out our clothes a bit."

"A magic one?" Narbenu asked. "I guess it wouldn't be any more attention-getting than the mirrors. Go for it."

"I thought it was difficult to do fire spells here," Zaiporo said. "Your fire globes fizzled."

"It is hard, but I figure it's worth it. A quarter-hour is probably the best I can do."

"Don't overdo it," Enashoma said.

"I won't. Promise."

With a flat, ice-free rock as his target, he summoned a basic fire. The effort he put into it was enough to normally summon a small bonfire, but he expected the intensity of a flame suitable for slow-roasting a rabbit. What he got was a roaring campfire. The heat blasted out, causing everyone to back up a few steps.

"Wow," Kemsu commented. "Didn't expect that."

"Neither did I," Turesobei replied. "There's a lot more fire kenja here than I would've thought. Perhaps there's a hot spring deep inside the caverns." He motioned toward the fire. "Well, ladies first."

While standing near the fire, Iniru, Kurine, and Enashoma swiftly changed their inner layer of clothes and laid their outer layers out to dry. When they were done, Zaiporo and Turesobei changed. He felt like he'd been plunged into ice even while standing beside the fire.

The fire sputtered out after an hour. They put their outer layers back on, and brought out the star stones to give a little warmth. Because the space was large and airy, the cave wasn't going to be as warm as a snow house.

Lu Bei stood and twitched his nose and ears. He flicked his forked tongue out a few times and made a face, like he'd bitten into a lemon. He shot up and zipped around them several times, but didn't venture farther in.

"I don't like this place, master. Something's wrong."

"What is it?" Turesobei asked.

"Don't know, master. Just a bad feeling."

Turesobei remembered the stronger-than-anticipated fire energies. He activated his kenja-sight. "I'm seeing strong fire and earth kenja and — wow, didn't expect that. There's forest kenja here — and it's incredibly strong."

"Forest energy in a cave?" Kurine said. "How's that possible?"

"Don't know," Turesobei replied. "Based on what I'm detecting, I would guess that at the heart of this cave, there's an enormous hot spring that's exposed to a *lot* of sunlight and surrounded by a *large* forest. Naturally, that doesn't make sense. And ... and there's something else about the energies ... something that's just not right."

"Like what?" Narbenu asked. "Demons? Beasts?"

Turesobei shrugged.

Motekeru peered deeper into the cave. "I can take the hounds and explore deeper, master."

Lu Bei plunged down and landed on Turesobei's back. He leaned over and whispered, loudly. "Trouble and trouble, master. We're not alone."

Turesobei reached for the sword that wasn't on his belt. Zaiporo backed up to the mount and drew a spear.

Iniru lifted her head. "I smell ... a tree ... coming toward us." Her ears twitched. "Maybe a whole forest worth of trees ... somehow."

Everyone drew weapons and backed up together toward their mounts.

Tiny emerald eyes sparkled at the edge of the darkness, reflecting the light from the moon mirrors. Dozens and dozens of eyes sparkled from deep within and from the walls and ceiling, too.

Chapter Twenty-Seven

Hundreds of knee-high, human-like creatures with knobby wooden bodies, stunted heads, stumpy legs, and spindly arms rushed toward them. The creatures scurried along the walls, the ceiling, and the floor.

Turesobei jumped into the saddle behind Zaiporo. "Take the reins."

"Do you know what they are?" Zaiporo asked.

"Not sure," Turesobei replied. "Narbenu?"

"No clue," the goronku responded.

"Maybe we should talk to them," Turesobei said as they backed their mounts away. "Some spirit creatures are friendly."

"Nothing in our world is friendly," Narbenu said.

The creatures began chanting in clicking, rasping voices. "Knob knob knob. We the knob, they the bad. Get them, get them. Bring them in."

The knobs launched toward them.

"Ride!" Iniru shouted.

The group spun their sonoke around and rode toward the open canyon. Lu Bei soared above them. Turesobei turned around in the saddle so he could face the knobs. With adequate fire kenja available, Turesobei cast the *spell of the curtain of flame* and held it in his mind, ready to release it should they need it. While he'd never been good with the flame curtain and this would be a weak and brief one, causing the knobs to pause, even for a few moments, could save their lives. But he didn't think it would be necessary. The sonoke were outpacing their pursuers easily.

"Master!" Lu Bei cried. "Look out!"

Something struck Turesobei in the head and landed on the back of his shoulders. Something solid, heavy, and grasping. He tumbled off the mount, and struck the icy cavern floor. The spell vanished from his mind, along with the breath from his lungs. A knob clutched at his throat. Dozens closed in on him. Lu Bei zapped the knob on Turesobei's back. The creature's grip loosened, and Turesobei slung it off him, turned, and ran toward his companions.

Knobs poured from a hole in the top of the cavern, falling onto Turesobei's companions. Shoma, Kurine, and the hounds were on the ground fighting off knobs, trying to get back to their mounts. Narbenu elbowed one off his mount, speared at another, then fell as two landed on top of him. Kemsu struck one with his spear. The point glanced off the knob's body. Two knobs grabbed Kemsu by the leg and pulled him from the mount. Iniru vaulted off her mount and landed beside Enashoma.

A knob slammed into the small of Turesobei's back, and knocked him down. He squirmed free, only to be tackled around the waist by a second one. Motekeru jumped down from his mount and plowed toward Turesobei, swatting the creatures aside.

"Motekeru!" Turesobei yelled. "Protect Shoma!"

A knob wrapped his arms around Zaiporo's neck, choking him, but Lu Bei zapped it in the face, and it dropped off, clicking and chattering. With a knob clutching her leg, Kurine limped back to her mount, and drew an iron war hammer from her saddle. She spun around and smacked the knob in the head. A sharp crack like wood splintering resounded. The knob fell dead.

Turesobei shoved free of one, but others leapt in, clawing and hitting him. Lu Bei landed on Turesobei's shoulders, shooting sparks to ward them away. Though no more fell from the ceiling, the mass that had first pursued them closed in. Turesobei was surrounded and too far away from his companions. Catching a moment's break, he quick-cast the *spell of prodigious leaping*, spending far more internal kenja than it normally called for to make it work immediately. He leapt over a dozen knobs, and landed between Kurine and Kemsu.

Nearby, Iniru dodged, spun, kicked, and jabbed with her spear. Narbenu shattered his spear against a knob, and then drew his mace, swinging it back and forth in wide arcs to keep the creatures at bay. Motekeru clawed the head off a knob, and then shattered the chest of another with a kick. The hounds zipped around Enashoma, biting at the knobs. There wasn't much they could do to them, but getting in the way helped. The knob bodies were solid and heavy, almost as hard as petrified wood.

"Regroup!" Iniru shouted. "To me!"

Slowly, they all backed up together, forming a circle. Why was Iniru gathering them here? Why not with the mounts? Turesobei swatted a knob away and looked to the sonoke. Attacked by the knobs and without their riders, the sonoke had turned wild. Spitting and hissing, the sonoke thrashed with their tails and butted knobs with their horns.

Hundreds of knobs closed in. While no one was seriously hurt yet, since the knobs were tougher than they were vicious, they couldn't keep this up. Motekeru was the only one who could injure them reliably.

"We've got to break free," Iniru said.

Turesobei backed into the center of the circle. "Shield me so I can cast a spell!"

Kurine winked at him. "Whatever you need, lover." She turned and cracked a knob in the head with the war hammer, shattering its jaw. Iniru flicked her eyes angrily at Turesobei, and then, appreciatively, at Kurine before resuming the fight.

Turesobei again quick-cast the *spell of the curtain of flame*, aiming it at the center of the knob mass. It was a tiring spell, one of the newer ones he'd learned after returning from Wakaro. He hoped fire would frighten these kagi, since they were made of wood.

A sheet of flame no thicker than a rope strand but a dozen paces in length and height erupted amidst the knobs. With a force of will that caused him to cry out and buckle at the knees, Turesobei threw the flame curtain over on its side, as if casting it across the ground like a blanket.

The knobs touched by the flames screamed and flailed and ran wildly about, their limbs and heads singed and smoking, but not on fire. It wasn't the effect Turesobei had hoped for. The rest of the knobs didn't panic. Instead, they entered a maddened frenzy and charged with such abandon that the faster knobs leapt and crawled over the slower ones.

The flames flickered out. Turesobei cast the *spell of compelling obedience*. "Stop fighting!" he shouted, his voice echoing through the cavern, filled with power and deeper than normal in resonance. "Stop fighting, and leave us be!"

Unfazed by the spell, the knobs crashed against them like waves against rocks on the coast. For each one they knocked away, two more took its place.

A knob leapt over Enashoma and crashed into Turesobei. He chucked it over his shoulder and cast the *spell of banishing lesser entities* which was used to send demons back into the netherworld. He had used it with some success against the kagi that had ambushed them on their way to the Monolith of Sooku.

The spell went off. The knobs nearest them paused and staggered back momentarily, but dozens more rushed through and over them.

He staggered. "Too many ... of them ... nothing I can do ..."

One of the hounds, Rig, yelped desperately. Two knobs had captured it and were running away with it. Ohma charged after her companion, but was likewise taken and carried off.

A knob tackled Zaiporo, and as he went down, a second elbowed him in the jaw. Zaiporo fell limp.

"Zai!" Enashoma shouted. "Are you —"

Blood sprayed into the air as a knob leapt feet first into Enashoma and smacked her in the face. She slumped. Lu Bei zoomed in, firing sparks so they couldn't capture her. Turesobei stepped toward her, but a leaping knob crashed into him. By the time he fought it off, five knobs had dragged Kurine to the ground, and Kemsu was staggering, swinging wildly, with a knot swelling on his forehead. Before Iniru could step in to help, the knobs took Kemsu down. Narbenu fell a moment later. Kurine and Iniru fought, back-to-back, desperately. Motekeru began to sag under the weight of the knobs that were piling onto him. A blow brought Iniru to her knees. No longer shielded by his companions, Turesobei faced the onslaught of knobs.

It was over; they couldn't win.

But the knobs weren't killing anyone, just disabling them, and they had carried the hounds away ... Turesobei held his hands up.

"Wait! We surrender!" He fell to his knees. "We surrender. We won't fight anymore." The knobs paused, peering at him with their sparkling emerald eyes, their tongues clicking maliciously. A huge knob, as big as Motekeru, waded forward.

He spoke with a voice like the groan of an old oak in a storm wind. "Wise it is. Most very wise." His lips parted in a smile showing teeth of amber. "You can't get away from my brothers. We are many, too many for you."

Motekeru stopped fighting, and Iniru set down her spear. Turesobei crawled over to Enashoma. She held a hand to her nose; blood was gushing out; tears streamed down her cheeks. "It's broken, I think. Zal?"

"I'm okay," he responded in a slur of words. "Just ... a bit ... wonky is ... all."

"Kurine?" Turesobei asked. "Iniru?"

"I'll be okay," Kurine replied.

"Just hacked off," Iniru responded.

"I'm going to be hurting tomorrow," Kemsu said, "if I'm still alive."

"Me, too, lad," Narbenu added.

"Get your mounts and follow me," the big knob commanded.

The mounts were still hissing, but they weren't thrashing now that the knobs had backed away. Narbenu approached them with soothing words, and they calmed down enough that they could grab the reins. Knobs had lined up between the mounts and the entrance. There would be no sudden attempt to mount up and break through.

"What do you want with us?" Turesobei asked.

"It is not us who want," the big knob replied. "It is Master who wants."

Hundreds of the knobs surrounded them and escorted them deeper into the cave.

"Oak and leaf, root and knob," the creatures chanted. "Knob knob, cavern clan. Outsiders for the master. Outsiders feed the tree. Knob knob, cavern clan."

This was bad. If only he'd had a full supply of spell strips. And Sumada — especially Sumada. Slicing through dozens of them might have struck fear into them. He was going to have to call on the Storm Dragon. The only question was whether to do it now or wait.

Iniru tapped him on the shoulder and shook her head. He got the message and nodded in response. He'd wait; maybe there'd be some other way out of this.

The knobs led them deeper and deeper into the canyon. "Oak and leaf, root and knob. Knob. Knob."

Chapter Twenty-Eight

The cave narrowed until they were crammed hip-to-shoulder with the chanting knobs, while the ceiling lowered to the point that Motekeru had to hunch over. But then abruptly, the passage opened into an enormous, brightly-lit cavern. Turesobei stopped to gaze in wonder at the sight before him. A pool of water lay in the center of the cavern, and a brilliant golden light shone out from the pool, emanating from a glowing orb like a miniature sun that sat at the pool's bottom. Hanging from the ceiling above the pool, upside down, was a giant oak tree with sprawling branches that stretched all the way out to brush the pebbles along the pool's shore. Roots as thick as a sonoke threaded the cavern roof, anchoring the oak.

The knobs shoved Turesobei forward. A wave of vertigo briefly washed over him. Suddenly, he was walking through the sky, upside down, the miniature sun in the pool above him, the tree on the ceiling below. Kurine stumbled, and Kemsu grabbed her arm to support her, but he was lurching, as well.

Enashoma muttered, "I'm going to be sick."

Zaiporo fell to his knees and vomited. Iniru closed her eyes and swayed. Narbenu fell. Lu Bei did barrel rolls as he flew. Motekeru stomped on as if nothing had changed.

Swaying, Turesobei cast the relatively simple *spell of dream breaking,* and the illusion ceased. Their perception of everything returned to normal. They were walking across the cavern floor. The tree was hanging up above, with the pool below it. The knobs didn't seem to care that he'd cast the spell. Perhaps they hadn't even noticed.

"What — what was that?" Kurine said.

"An illusion. I dispelled it."

"And the big tree ... the yellow sun in the water?" Enashoma asked.

"Those are real," Turesobei said.

"I've never seen a tree like this before," Kurine said. "It's amazing."

"We have trees like that everywhere in our world," Turesobei said, "though few are as magnificent as this one."

The knobs herded them into a section marked by knee-high boundary stones near the shore on the far side of the cavern. The amber hounds were waiting there already. They rushed up to Turesobei, and he patted their heads to comfort them.

The big knob walked in front of them and fell to his knees at the shore.

"Great Master, we have brought fresh sacrifices. Many of them. Some of them ... they are unique."

Leaves rustled. Branches bounced and creaked.

A figure stepped out and walked along a limb all the way to the edge, his steps so light that the increasingly small branch bounced only lightly. He stepped onto the tip of the branch that brushed the shore, and even this delicate section held him up. The figure's tall but thin build suggested a baojendari man. His features were refined. He had long, brown hair and tanned skin. An emerald kavaru stone embedded in his forehead matched his eyes and his pale green robes.

"Breaking my illusion was not polite," he said in a whispery voice like wind through spring leaves.

"You are not a Kaiaru," Turesobei replied with certainty, though how he could know so surely and so quickly, he had no idea.

"And why," the being asked, strolling toward them, "do you think that I am not a Kaiaru? For I certainly am."

Visions flashed through Turesobei's mind. "You have the form of the Kaiaru Ysashu, who disappeared four millennia ago. His kavaru was lost. You are not he."

"Master?" Lu Bei asked. "How do ... how do you know that?"

"I just ..." Turesobei shrugged. "I just do."

The being from the oak scowled. "I do not like you at all, boy. And you are wrong — I am Kaiaru."

"No, what you are," Turesobei said, "is an eidakami-ga, one who has lived many centuries and acquired enormous power. These knobs are your children."

The ga sneered. "You are not easily deceived, are you?"

"Not when it comes to this. I am descended from a Kaiaru. I carry the stone of one. And, unlike you, I have bonded with the stone and know how to use it. Why do you pretend to be a Kaiaru?"

The eidakami-ga shrugged. "I like the form."

"How did you come across the kavaru?"

"I found it."

Turesobei smirked. "I'm sure you did."

"May we go, please?" Enashoma begged. "My brother doesn't mean to insult you."

A smile spread across the eidakami-ga's face. "Of course your brother intends to insult me. His kind would naturally take offense toward a pretender."

"My kind?" Turesobei said.

"Is it your turn now to pretend you are something else? What is your name, Kaiaru?"

"I am not a Kaiaru. I'm merely descended from one. My name is Chonda Turesobei."

The eidakami-ga waved a hand flippantly. "This stone does not remember anything anymore, so I will take your word for it, Kaiaru."

Turesobei sighed. "I'm not Kaiaru."

"Then how did you know that I wasn't? You even know whose stone this is."

"Look," Turesobei snapped, growing frustrated. "Are you going to let us go?"

"Hardly." He grinned malevolently. "You have not asked my name ... it is Satsupan." He cast his eyes up and down Motekeru. "I like this one. The work is intricate, mostly wood." He made a half-bow to Motekeru. "You, sir, I shall not harm. You may go if you like."

"What I shall do," Motekeru said, "is rip you limb from limb."

"Oh, do please tell me you intended the pun," said Satsupan. He frowned at Lu Bei. "What is your power, winged one?"

"My power is to blast my master's enemies," Lu Bei spat.

"Well, your posturing does not impress me. If you could not beat my knobs, then you cannot defeat me. This is not your complete form. Show me."

"Humor him," Turesobei said to Lu Bei. The fetch turned into a book and fell into Turesobei's hands. Then he returned to fetch form.

"Brilliant! Simply marvelous." Satsupan sighed with delight. "You, too, may go if you wish. I mean you no harm."

"I must stay near Master always. I am his fetch."

"Pity." Satsupan examined the others. "You three," he said, pointing to Kurine, Narbenu, and Kemsu, "are boring." He spent an extra moment looking at Iniru. "You're too much like them, and I remember your kind well enough. Boring." He pointed at Enashoma and Zaiporo. "It has been many ages since I've seen baojendari and zaboko as well. But again, boring. Especially zaboko. So many, for so long."

"How long have you been here, in this place?" Turesobei asked.

"I have been here since before this was the Ancient Cold and Deep. When it was a larger, more prosperous land. Before it was split off from the normal world."

"Split off?" Turesobei said.

"Indeed. I have no clue who did it or why, but a portion of Okoro was copied and split off and tossed into ... whatever this truly is. In the Ancient Cold and Deep time passes, but the world does not evolve. It does not change. And it is an old world. You've seen the red sun ... dying ... casting the world in eternal winter."

Satsupan bent down and strummed his fingers through the water, sending bright ripples through the room. "All my brethren died. Only those trees that could grow along the hot springs survived. But I had something special: a taiotsu."

Turesobei craned his neck to peer down into the water. "A sun stone?"

"A fragment of the sun in its brighter days, fallen from the heavens, as with lumps of white or black ore from the moons, but so rare, so incredibly rare, that you'd think white ore was nothing more than copper. The taiotsu gives me warmth eternal. The knobs brought it down into the cavern and then, to survive, I reversed my growth. And believe me, that was not easy. But nutrients ... alas, I have drained the soil these many years. I require nutrients, and my knobs cannot go far into the world because they cannot easily endure the cold beyond the caverns. So when something comes along ... something of physical worth ... well, it must be sacrificed so that I may continue. That means all of you, naturally, except the machine and the book."

"That's not acceptable," Turesobei said.

"Do you wish to bargain with me?"

"No," Turesobei said.

"That is too bad."

"We won't give up easily," Iniru said.

"Ah, she speaks. How delightful." He spun to look at them all derisively. "I never thought you would give up easily. But I also don't think that you can win. You cannot overpower two hundred knobs. And if you think my power is not significant, then you are in for quite a rude surprise. I do have a proposal, however." He jabbed a finger toward Turesobei, Lu Bei, and Motekeru. "If the three of you will perform a minor quest for me, I will let these others go without eating them. Not the sonoke, though. I simply must eat. No one has wandered in here in over a decade."

"What quest?" Turesobei asked.

"Long ago, I fell in love with a nozakami. We can still sometimes communicate through dreams. She is out there, but she is bound to a statue in her old vine grove, deep in a cave. She has faded to almost nothing, but here she could thrive. Retrieve her and the statue, and bring them here. Then I will free you and your companions. However, if you do not return within two weeks, I shall assume that you failed or that you have betrayed your companions, whom I shall begin to consume — one by one, day by day — starting with the sonoke."

"What's the catch?" Iniru asked.

"Ah, clever, aren't you? I have sent many after her before, and none have returned, no matter the enticement. I have no idea why. I presume the trek there is dangerous."

Chapter Twenty-Nine

"I need more than Motekeru and Lu Bei," Turesobei said. "I need the goronku to guide me. I don't know this land or how to survive in it. We came through the Winter Gate, from Okoro and —"

"Oh, very well and fine. You may take the younger male goronku with you as a guide — but not the other two."

"I need two mounts to ride there, and I need Iniru as well. She has great skill at sneaking and thieving."

Iniru shot him a look, but said nothing.

Satsupan tapped his chin thoughtfully. "I think you are trying to save as many as possible and thus reduce your losses."

"The two amber hounds are bound to my kavaru. Enashoma is my sister. Kurine is ... my betrothed. If you do not think that I care for them ..."

"Fine. You may take the k'chasan with you."

"You will not harm any of them for three weeks."

"Two was what I offered. And you have my word."

Turesobei pointed at him. "Say it again, and recite the Vow of the Ga."

Satsupan stamped his foot. "I will not!" The limbs of the tree creaked and groaned; leaves shivered and rattled.

Turesobei strained a smile. The eidakami-ga was not just bound to the tree. He *was* the tree. What they saw before them was a manifestation of energy made to appear human. This was possible for some ga, but impossible for a normal eidakami. Satsupan had probably spent centuries mastering the form he now took.

"Then I will not seek the statue for you," Turesobei said. "I will stay here, and you can kill me."

Satsupan stalked over and stared him in the eyes. "I would not regret that."

"I would not regret fighting and killing more of your knobs, of unleashing Motekeru's full power against them — or unleashing mine. You have no idea what you are dealing with. See this sigil on my cheek? If I become desperate enough, I can become the Storm Dragon."

"Like Naruwakiru?"

"I ate Naruwakiru's heart. Her power resides in me."

"That — that is impossible."

"Touch the mark on my cheek and see."

Satsupan tentatively touched the mark with his forefinger. He drew back and stepped away. "Why have you not become the dragon already? You could have stopped the knobs from bringing you here."

"I did become the Storm Dragon once, and I nearly became the dragon permanently. I don't wish to do it again, but I will if I have to, to save my companions. You will wait three weeks. Take the vow."

His face ashen, Satsupan spun around and faced his tree. Long moments passed without him saying anything.

"You do remember how to make the vow, don't you?" Turesobei asked.

Satsupan spun and cursed at him. Tears welled in his eyes. "You are the most insolent creature I have ever met." Satsupan stuck his fingers in his mouth and drew forth a golden cord of energy which he wrapped around his neck. "I hereby vow by Kaiwen Earth-Mother to not harm anyone here present nor allow the knobs to harm them, until three weeks have passed or the statue I desire is brought here to me. I reserve the right to harm in self-defense. I swear this on my life."

Turesobei half-bowed. "Thank you."

"Leave now!" the eidakami-ga shouted. "Leave the way you entered. A thousand paces past the cavern entrance, you will find a blind in the canyon wall. If you take it, you will find a path that climbs up out of the canyon. It is much faster than taking the long way out. Travel due north for two days until you reach the crumbled tower, turn east and travel for a day. You will come to a stone formation the shape of a fan. A thousand paces further north, there is a cave entrance behind a stone door. Enter and retrieve the statue."

Turesobei looked at Enashoma, holding a hand over her broken, bleeding nose. "I must rest a while and see to my friends' injuries."

"I want you gone," Satsupan said. "I can heal them. I swear that I will. Just go."

Tears streaked down Kurine's face as they prepared to leave. Turesobei hugged her. "We'll be back."

She squeezed hard and sobbed. "Promise?"

"I promise." He peeled himself free, and kissed Shoma on the cheek. "You'll be safe, Little Blossom."

"I know," she said. "I've heard Grandfather talking about the vow before. I'm more worried about you."

He whispered in her ear. "I know it's a trap, so I'll be okay. Did you see his face? He's afraid I might actually succeed. Explain this to the others. Be brave."

The knobs escorted them to the edge of the cave. It was nearly midnight. Only a light, fine snow was falling now. At least his storm had diminished.

"You certainly were antagonistic back there," Iniru said as Turesobei cast the *spell of the moon mirrors.*

"I know how to deal with a kami-ga, especially one that old and proud. He hasn't been challenged in ages."

"Maybe, but I also think that the storm sigil on your cheek is giving you a lot of confidence," she added.

"Is that a bad thing?" he asked.

"Not yet," Iniru replied.

"I just wish I could've done more. If I'd had a prepared strip for banishing spirits, I could've gotten us out of the cavern ..."

"No spell strips, no white-steel sword, too many enemies," Motekeru said flatly. "You did the best you could."

"So this is a trap, right?" Kemsu said.

"There's a reason no one comes back," Lu Bei said. He was in fetch form, but only had his head sticking out of Turesobei's pack. He was wearing his knitted hat. "What I don't understand is why we're being sent at all. What purpose does it serve?"

"You don't think there's a chance that he's sincere?" Iniru asked. "Maybe he really does want the statue and is in love with the girl, only it's guarded."

"Love can make someone do strange things," Kemsu said distantly, like he was thinking of something entirely different.

"I guess it's possible," Turesobei said. "But then why not keep just Enashoma and send all the rest of us? Why not let us go and offer a reward? Maybe he's sending us to someone who has control over him ... as tribute. We'll find out."

"Why didn't you just threaten him with the Storm Dragon to begin with?" Kemsu said.

"He would've called his bluff," Motekeru answered.

"How do you know?" Kemsu asked.

"Like Master said, he's a proud old ga, and all his knobs were watching. Bad enough he had to make the vow in front of them."

"That's what I was thinking," Turesobei said. "I knew if I could get him to make the vow, we'd have a chance of getting through this without me turning into the Storm Dragon." He looked to Iniru. "I promised I would try to avoid doing that."

It wasn't easy in the dark, but Iniru spotted the blind. The slope up the steep canyon wall had clearly been cut into it long ago, when people still lived here.

"Master," said Lu Bei, "about you recognizing which Kaiaru's stone he wore and all that ... were you actually offended by it?"

Turesobei glanced back at the fetch. "I honestly don't know what came over me, or how I knew. I don't really want to talk about it, because I suspect if I did I'd just end up passing out."

Chapter Thirty

After they had traveled a league beyond the canyon, Turesobei pulled on his reins.

"We need to stop. We have three weeks to do this. There's no reason to run ourselves into the ground. My mount seems irritated to be moving at all. Let's camp early and get plenty of rest."

"How can you be so calm about all this?" Kemsu asked as they dismounted and prepared to set up camp. "I'm too nerve-wracked to sleep."

Turesobei gave him a half-smile. "This isn't my first time rushing off to save someone I love with little assurance of how much time I had or whether I could get past the dangers I'd face. But this time it's easier."

"How so?" Kemsu asked.

"The eidakami-ga cannot violate his vow. So I know they'll still be alive, if we can return. When I went to rescue Iniru ... well, we figured she would be dead by the time we got there."

Iniru kissed him on the cheek. "But you came anyway." He started to smile, but then she shot him a look. "Don't think that I've forgiven you for picking up another betrothed to replace the last one."

"At least this one's much nicer," he said, though he immediately regretted saying it.

Lu Bei slapped Turesobei on the back of the head, and turned back into a book. Kemsu shook his head in wonderment.

Iniru sighed. "Sometimes you make me feel so ... oh, never mind. Let's build the snow house." She looked at both of them. "And if either of you think I'm sleeping in a snow house by myself to meet some moral code the people of this land have, you can forget it."

Motekeru set the final block in place. "I would stay with you, my lady."

"My lady?" She snorted. "Just call me Iniru. Please."

"No. It would not be proper to do so."

Turesobei chuckled silently. Iniru didn't give up a fight easily, but Motekeru wasn't easy to argue with. The lack of facial expressions was worse than his intimidating build. He didn't inflect his voice much, either. It was hard to judge his moods.

Iniru eyed Motekeru cautiously, and then shrugged. "Oh ... okay. Thank you for the offer, but I'd rather snuggle up for warmth."

"As you wish," Motekeru said.

Turesobei smiled, until he noticed Kemsu was smiling, too. Then they both frowned at one another.

With the snow house finished, they climbed in. As they did, Turesobei noticed Iniru wince.

"You're injured," he said.

"I was about to say," she replied. "Honestly. Do you have the strength to heal me?"

"I always have strength enough for you," he said.

Iniru slapped him lightly on the cheek. "Aw, is that why you're trying to marry another girl?"

They stretched the sleeping furs across the floor of the snow house. With the wind blocked out, the star stones glowing, and their body heat trapped, the warmth inside grew steadily. By morning, it would be an almost tolerable cool. Narbenu claimed a proper snow house carefully made was almost as warm as their village underground, but Turesobei found that difficult to believe. After a small meal of cheese and dried sonoke strips, Turesobei meditated for an hour, blocking out his worries and drawing in kenja to replenish himself.

"Okay, I'm ready. Who has injuries?"

"Take care of yourself first," Iniru said. "If there's one thing I've learned, it's that you're indispensable. You can do things no one else can do."

"Out here," Turesobei replied, "Kemsu is the indispensable one. I don't know this land well enough to survive on my own. Not yet, anyway."

Kemsu bowed his head. "Thank you, but I'm fine. Banged up, some deep bruises ... exhausted ... think they jarred a tooth loose. No big problem."

Turesobei frowned. "I can fix all of that with a simple spell, but if you were to somehow get seriously injured in the next few days, I wouldn't be able to help you again."

"I'll suffer through it then," Kemsu said. "I've been attacked by a snow bear cub before. That was a lot worse than this."

Iniru snorted. "A cub?"

"Don't laugh," Kemsu told her. "The cub was nearly as big as Motekeru."

She twitched an eyebrow dubiously, then shrugged. "If you say so ... Sobei, I'll take the healing. Those knobs cracked three of my ribs. That could take weeks to heal on its own, and I'd like to be full strength when we face ... whatever it is we'll face this time."

Turesobei nodded. "I figured as much the way you winced, and I can tell you're struggling to breathe."

Kemsu shook his head. "How do you do that, Iniru? When you were fighting and walking and riding, I couldn't even tell something was wrong with you. It's amazing."

"It's really not all that amazing," she said. "I've been training since I was a little girl. One of the first lessons I learned was how to block out pain. And you really don't want to know how they train kids to do that."

"Sounds terrible," Kemsu replied.

"I had a choice. I didn't have to be a qengai."

"I kind of doubt that," Turesobei told her.

"You think I'm lying?"

"No. It's just that I was given a choice to be a wizard. But it was a formality. It's not like I could really say no."

"Oh, I had more choice than that. It would have been a big disappointment for my family, but if I didn't want to or couldn't handle it once the training started, they would have shipped me off to a peaceful maka centered on farming."

"What's a maka?" Kemsu asked.

"A k'chasan tribal village," Iniru said.

Motekeru groaned.

"Something wrong?" Turesobei asked him.

The jagged face stared at him. "I do not like discussing choices. I am going to shut down for a while."

The fires in his eyes dimmed, and his head sank until his chin touched his chest.

"What was that about?" Kemsu asked.

Turesobei shrugged. He had no idea.

"Have you ever seen him do that before?" Iniru asked.

"No," Turesobei said. "But look at him. He's taken a lot of damage since he came back. He's tough, but the yomon and the Deadly Twelve, the reitsu, the knobs ... he deserves a good rest, I think. Lu Bei, have you ever seen him rest before?" The fetch didn't answer. Turesobei felt the spine of the diary, then breathed a sigh of relief. He could feel Lu Bei's kenja heartbeat. "I think he's exhausted, too."

"Well, let's get to healing me," Iniru said.

She grabbed the bottom of her shirt and lifted it up slowly, revealing the downy fur that rippled across her muscled abs. She pulled the shirt up further. A deep splotch of purple showed, even through the fur on her ribs. She pulled farther, bringing the shirt right up to her small breasts.

"Whoa!" Turesobei spun around. He slapped Kemsu on the shoulder, but it wasn't necessary. He had turned around, too. Of course, Turesobei didn't want to be turned around. But he should do the right thing. Although, was it the right thing if he was an adult here? And Iniru was considered an adult by her people. No one was here to stop him from looking ... she didn't mind ... surely that made it okay ... but still ... he couldn't ... could he?

"Turesobei, I'm waiting."

"You ... you didn't have to ... you know ... remove your shirt," he replied.

Iniru sighed. "You're such prudes. Both of you. You can turn around."

"But, Iniru, I —"

"I didn't take my shirt off, dummy."

Turesobei turned back. Iniru had rolled her shirt up so that it fit tightly under her small breasts, leaving her stomach exposed.

"For starters," she said, "it's still way too cold in here for stripping down. For seconds, I know your cultures are weird about topless girls. I only rolled my shirt up because I remembered you saying that healing magic worked better on bare skin ... or fur, in my case."

"Well, it does, but it's not a huge difference."

"I'll take what I can get. Now heal me. This hurts really bad, and I'm not in the mood for your silliness."

Nervously, Turesobei slid over to her. "I have to warn you, this healing spell ... it's not pleasant like the other one. Lean back a bit ... please."

Still kneeling, she bent backward, far enough that it made Turesobei's spine itch. He was certain he'd break if he tried doing that. He chanted the *spell of winter healing*. A silvery fog formed just under his hands, drifted down onto her fur, and seeped in. Her ribcage glowed. Her eyes turned to saucers, and she surged up.

"Kaiwen Earth-Mother!" she shouted. She stuck her claws into his neck, seizing him tight. "That hurts!"

"Ow! So does that," he said.

She retracted her claws and released him. "Sorry."

Turesobei, his palms still glowing with some of the magic, slid his hands up along her ribcage. He'd forgotten how soft her fur was. They hadn't been this close since they'd crowded into a tiny tent in Batsakun while a storm raged over them. He slid his hands up a little further. He caught himself and pulled back.

"Sorry," he said.

"Don't be," she purred. "Ah ... finally ... the pain's stopped. It's just cold now." She leaned forward, took his head into her hands, and pulled him into a deep, passionate kiss. He squirmed, feeling overly self-conscious — Kemsu was right there.

She pulled back and shook her head. "Feeling a bit dizzy."

"It's the spell," Turesobei lamented. "As the cold spreads, you start to relax and become groggy, maybe even a bit disoriented ..."

"Well ... that just stinks," she replied.

Turesobei, despite his excitement, was relieved. This wasn't the time for ... he didn't know what it wasn't the time for, just that it wasn't.

Iniru spotted Kemsu, who was fidgeting and looking highly uncomfortable and highly disgruntled.

"Aw, poor, poor Kemsu," Iniru cooed. She leaned over and patted his face. "Don't be jealous."

Kemsu shifted and tried to look away. "I — I — I'm not."

"Yes, you are." She scooted up and kissed him on the lips.

She lingered!

Turesobei's heart thundered. His head throbbed. Time slowed to a standstill. What — what in Torment was that?

Iniru ruffled Kemsu's hair. "That better?"

"I — I mean ... um ..." Kemsu couldn't think of anything to say.

Turesobei wanted to shout at Kemsu. Maybe hit him. And Iniru ... he wanted to tell her that she might lose out to Kurine, that he might choose *her* instead because that would ... make her jealous? Would that even work? Or would she just get incredibly mad at him for being mean? He didn't understand what was going on, and dealing with Iniru ... it was like casting a dangerous spell that he could never understand.

Iniru smiled, self-satisfied, grabbed up the blanket and snuggled up with her back against Kemsu. She motioned to Turesobei. "Come on, scoot over. Don't let all the body heat go to waste."

She held out her arms, and he snuggled into her embrace. He started to say something, anything, but she put a finger to his lips and shook her head. Then she fell asleep instantly, snoring or purring — it was hard to tell. Turesobei craned his head back and shared a brief, incredibly awkward look with Kemsu.

Turesobei was so incredibly tired. He wanted to sleep. But his head swam with confusion, and his heart pounded. He stared, open-eyed into the darkness. She had kissed Kemsu. Why? Because of his engagement to Kurine? Because she liked Kemsu, too? The k'chasans did have weird rules about marriages with multiple partners. He'd read a little about it, and Iniru had tried to explain it to him. It never sank in. He just could never wrap his head around it.

After an hour of worry, exhaustion finally overtook him.

They ate breakfast at noon and pretended everything was normal. Or at least, he and Kemsu pretended everything was normal.

"I'm going out to hunt," Kemsu said. "I won't go far."

Turesobei cast the *spell of sensing presences*. "I'm picking up some small creatures not far off to the east. No sign of the reitsu. Is it too much to hope the wraiths stumbled into the knobs?"

"Probably," Kemsu said. "You coming with me, Iniru?"

She patted her ribs. "I should probably avoid doing anything unnecessary today."

"Right," Kemsu replied. He hovered, reluctant to leave, then finally stepped out.

Motekeru followed him outside to check on the sonoke and keep watch in case Kemsu ran into trouble.

"What was that?" Turesobei said to Iniru, now that they were alone.

"What was what?" Iniru asked.

"Last night."

"Oh, that. It was nothing."

"It was a lot more than nothing," Turesobei said. "It was most definitely ... well ... something."

Iniru kissed a finger, and then touched it to his nose. "You're so cute when you're flustered."

"I've been flustered all night! I don't get it. Do you like Kemsu?"

"Don't you?"

"Not really. He's okay. I mean ..."

"What *do* you mean?" she asked.

"You know what I mean."

"No, I don't, or I wouldn't ask you."

"You do know, and you're having fun at my expense, and I'm tired of it." He stood, but she grabbed his hand and tugged him back down.

"I'm sorry," she said. "Last night ... that wasn't okay with you?"

"No, it wasn't."

"Well, it wasn't okay with me when you kissed Kurine. Twice. It was just twice, right?"

"Well ... it was ... three times ... I think."

"You think?" she asked. "Three times, you think? I'm really not sure that you do think. If you can kiss other girls while you're in love with me, and then betroth yourself to them, then I get to kiss any boys I like. That's only fair, don't you think?"

"I guess — wait, no, it's not fair. I just want to be with you, and I didn't intend all that with Kurine. It's not my fault. I mean, the second kiss ... and the third ... sure, those were my fault. I was stupid, but —"

"Yep, you are stupid. But also ... you do like her."

"She's okay," he replied.

"I'm not clueless, Sobei. Whether you admit to it or not, you like Kurine ... *a lot*. Maybe not as much as you like me, but a lot."

"I'd walk into Torment for you."

"I know that. But if you want this to be about just you and me, well you should have said so."

"I would have, but we haven't really had time to talk about us. I don't even know what our relationship is."

"We're just friends," she said sadly. "We are nothing more than that, Sobei."

"You don't love me?!"

"Oh, of course I do. Why else would I be jealous of Kurine? I come from a culture that would accept you having two girlfriends, and I still don't like it, because I want only you."

"I think of you as my girlfriend."

"That's great, really. But just don't get any grand ideas. Remember after the Storm Dragon's Heart, how you and I just couldn't be together no matter what? I thought you understood. Your people will never accept me, and my culture is very different from yours. If you're going back home, we're never going to be a proper couple. No matter how much we love one another. And this thing with Kurine, I know it won't last either, not if you return to Ekaran. It will end just like it did with me."

"I risked everything for you, Iniru."

"Do you really think that will change anything when you get back? That suddenly you'll be able to say, 'Hey everyone, guess what, I've decided I'm going to marry the k'chasan qengai after all, and we'll live together happily ever after and I won't have an aristo-cratic baojendari wife, and you will all just have to deal with it?'"

"I could make them change," he said, half-heartedly. "Make them accept you."

"No, you can't. If anything, it will be worse when you get back. They won't ever take their eyes off you, and you'll be forced into a marriage. Look, I just figured that we'd have a bit of fun until you got back. I never expected Kurine and the betrothal. But it is what it is, and we know what will happen when we return. I figure we just keeping loving one another, and let's just have fun whenever we can and not worry about having any rules. You like Kurine. That's fine. Just say so. And I think Kemsu is cute, and he's fun. Nothing special. But that's okay, too."

"But that's not what I want, Niru."

"You can't have what you want. You don't even really know what you want. And even if you figured it out, it wouldn't last."

Kemsu returned, shaking his head. "Whatever you detected, Turesobei, it was gone by the time I got out there. We'll have to stick to rations. One good thing, though. The snow has nearly stopped falling."

Chapter Thirty-One

Five days later, under a languid, crimson sun, Turesobei, Iniru, Kemsu, and Motekeru stood outside the entrance to the cave Satsupan's directions had led them to. The stone door blocking the cave entrance was engraved with strange markings that none of them could read. It seemed more like a burial mound than a nozakami's cave. The hill the entrance led into was a small, solitary rise amidst miles of flat plain.

Despite terrible screeching noises echoing across the ice during the last several days and nights, they had avoided nasty encounters with beasts or demons. But that was only because Turesobei had used his magic to detect where the kagi were so they could navigate around them.

Lu Bei fluttered down from having scouted above. "This hill has been here for centuries, but I don't think it's natural."

"So you think it is a tomb then?" Iniru asked.

Turesobei shrugged. "Perhaps. Or maybe it's an abandoned shrine. This is a dangerous world. Long lost worshipers may have shut the cave off to protect their goddess."

Turesobei knelt in front of the door and opened his kenja-sight. Strong earth and plant kenja flowed up to the cave door but went no further. He cast the *spell of sensing presences.*

"I'm detecting four kagi, not that far within. One is a lot closer to us than the others, but it's not right inside the door ... I'd say forty paces within. These are pretty nasty beasts, judging by the strength of their signatures." He stood. "Let's prepare ourselves."

"What do you have in mind?" Iniru said.

"Without spell strips, it's pretty hard to cast spells fast enough to do much good, especially here. The air magic is so strong that I have to be careful using it, while fire kenja is poor and earth kenja is diminished, though not in this case. And I need to avoid anything resembling storm kenja, for obvious reasons."

"So ..." prompted Iniru.

"So I'd like to use all my magical efforts before we go in. I'm going to place some spells on you, Iniru. They will feel ... tingly. You might find them uncomfortable, like your skin is burning. Most people do. I've grown used to it, barely even notice now. You're tough — I think you can handle it just fine. Once the magic is active, it won't last long. So we need to push forward quickly, but carefully."

Turesobei stepped up to Iniru, took her hands, and cast low-powered, short-lived versions of the *spell of the strength of three men* and the *spell of prodigious leaping* on her.

She took in a deep breath and stumbled back. "Yikes. My skin is burning ... all over. Like a bad rash. A really, really bad rash."

"Are you going to be okay?" he asked.

"I can manage it."

"Pick up Motekeru," Turesobei said.

Reluctantly, she grabbed the machine man by the waist and lifted him, only straining a little. "Wow!" She flexed her muscles. "This is awesome."

"Try a few jumps. Be careful."

Iniru leapt ten feet straight up with a cautious jump. When she landed, her eyes were wide. On the next, she pushed it and reached twenty.

"Moshinga of the Mountains!" she exclaimed. "That was awesome. You have fun spells! And we've never used them before!"

Her next leap, however, only took her only five feet up.

"What gives?" Iniru asked.

"It's a weak version. I wanted you to get a feel for it first."

"That was the weak one? So, will the regular version sting more? Because that felt like I'd fallen into an ant bed without bothering to get up."

"Yeah ... sorry. You must be sensitive. Maybe because you're k'chasan. When I put the big one on you, the magic will remain dormant for up to a quarter-hour, if we're lucky. I will activate it when we need it."

She scratched thoughtfully behind her ear. "So why haven't you let me do that before?"

"Never had a chance, really."

"On the trip back from Wakaro," she suggested.

"I guess so. Enashoma got mad at me in Sooku because I had never cast a spell to let her levitate before, so —"

"You could make me levitate?!" she said, flustered. "I just assumed that was all stuff that only you could do. I didn't know you were holding out on me."

"It's a lot easier to cast spells on myself, and they last longer. Like I told Shoma, I never thought about magic being something that could be fun. It was just another thing I did, like you would do a fighting maneuver. It wasn't fun when I did my first levitation spell because it was so much work. I was exhausted, and Grandfather scolded me for not having done it just right. And if I ever tried to play while under a spell I got punished."

Iniru sighed. "I can understand that ... I guess. But if we get out of all this alive and ever have some quiet peaceful time, you're going to cast spells on us and we're going to have fun with magic for a change."

"You're on," he said. "Though ... peaceful time ... what is that exactly?"

They all looked at one another, and surprisingly, it was Motekeru who laughed first: a rumbling, clanking bellow that Turesobei could feel as much as hear. Lu Bei rolled on the ice, cackling, and then everyone laughed until Turesobei cried tears. Not that it was that funny, but they were so stressed and were always in danger, to the point where it really had become ridiculous.

Turesobei put his hands on Iniru's shoulders. "You ready?"

She took a few deep breaths, then nodded. He cast the spells on her again, and stumbled afterward from the huge drain it took to put them on someone else and then place them into stasis.

"You'll feel when they wear off," he said.

She clutched her arms close to her and fell to her knees. Her eyes clenched tight, she breathed and muttered a mantra.

"What about me?" Kemsu asked.

"Sorry," Turesobei replied. "Takes too much energy for me to boost everyone without using spell strips." Kemsu scowled. "Iniru is our best fighter, so she should be the best equipped. And I've got to save some energy for the spells I'm about to cast and hold for myself, and for anything unexpected that might come up."

Turesobei summoned the moon mirrors then cast the *spell of compelling obedience* and interlaced it with the *spell of calming beasts,* and then he put the linked spells into stasis. The draw on his internal kenja was enough to send a sharp pain through his gut, but the pain abated. He was going to need a lot of rest if he survived this. The effort now was mostly mental: it was like holding and remembering a string of thirty numbers in his head. As long as he kept the spells there without letting any parts of them out of his memory, he'd be fine.

Iniru stood. "I'm ready. Sobei, what about your obscuration spell?"

"Won't help against a spirit creature," he replied. "Everyone ready? Good. Motekeru, would you please do the honors?"

Chapter Thirty-Two

Motekeru pushed the door open, stepped forward, and hunkered down, ready to be charged by an enemy. Nothing came. Turesobei sent the moon mirrors ahead, but dimmed them so that they could see what was ahead while not being as likely to alert anyone that they were coming. Motekeru eased forward. Lu Bei landed on his shoulders and peered around his bronze head. His batwings were poised so he could take flight in an instant. Spear held ready, Iniru crept along the wall, almost even with Motekeru. Kemsu followed along the other side. Turesobei hung back behind them, keeping the layered spell held in his mind.

A beast roared and barreled around a bend in the cave tunnel. It was massive, like a fat denekon, but with moldy blue skin and giant horns. Motekeru charged, lowered his shoulder, and struck it head-on. The beast knocked Motekeru down and ran over him. Lu Bei blasted it in the face and darted past it. The creature didn't even seem to notice the blast. Kemsu stabbed at it with his spear but missed. Iniru struck it hard in the flank. Her spear point went only a few inches in. The beast kept charging, and the spear snapped off at the end.

The beast lowered its horns to strike Turesobei.

Turesobei didn't move. He unleashed the intertwined spells of compelling obedience and beast calming. He put everything he could afford to give into them. The beast skidded to a halt, kicking up dust and ice in the cave. Its horns stopped an inch from Turesobei's chest. He drew in a deep breath but maintained eye contact with the kagi. He was lucky that the *spell of compelling obedience* depended largely on air energy, or he would never have managed that.

Maintaining eye contact, he stepped sideways and went around the creature. The creature rotated to maintain their eye contact.

"Everyone okay?" Turesobei asked.

Motekeru groaned as Iniru helped him up. "Motekeru's got some new dents," Iniru said, "but he's alive."

"I've gone through worse," Motekeru said, his voice fainter than normal. He flexed. "I don't seem to be compromised in any way."

"Let's keep going," Turesobei said. "And be careful, there are at least three more nasties ahead, and they may be worse than this one."

"You sure you've got him under control, master?" Lu Bei asked.

Turesobei handed his spear to Iniru. "As sure as I can be."

The others advanced as before, but Turesobei walked backward. He held his hand up. "Stay," he told the creature. It did as he commanded. They rounded a corner, and he lost eye contact with it. He paused, worried ... but the creature didn't follow. He breathed a sigh of relief.

The tunnel opened into a domed room, large by any normal standards, but not even half as large as Satsupan's cavern. The room gleamed as if illuminated by Avida, and was bright enough that it drowned out the moon mirrors. Turesobei let them go to reduce the drain on his kenja. Like with the eidakami-ga's cavern, this place had a pool in the center, and the light was coming up from the bottom of the pool. Along the ceiling hung thick tangles of moon-blossom vines heavy in white blooms. Their scent was cloying and aggressive, as if they were invading Turesobei's nostrils.

A statue of a beautiful female nozakami-ga stood at the edge of the pool. Sapphires gleamed in the eyes of the statue.

Something was wrong here.

"I don't see the other beasts," Lu Bei said as he circled through the cavern. "Are you sure you detected more, master?"

"I'm sure."

Kemsu reached toward the statue.

"Wait!" Turesobei said, but too late.

Kemsu's fingertips touched the statue, and he instantly collapsed, unconscious ... or worse.

Strands of webbing, like those from the sea spider demons Turesobei had fought on the way to Wakaro, shot out from amongst the vines. Two sets of webbing, from two different beasts. The webs engulfed Motekeru, one set entangling his legs and the other locking his arms against his side.

A beautiful woman, identical to the statue, leapt down from the vines and landed on the shore. She looked like a counterpart to Satsupan, except where he appeared to be baojendari, she possessed zaboko features. Turesobei activated the strength and leaping spells on Iniru. She charged the nozakami-ga. Two spider kagi crept out of the vines and blasted webs at Iniru, but she leapt over the shots. She stabbed downward. The nozakami-ga dodged, but Iniru knocked her down and landed on her.

Lu Bei attempted to spark the webs off Motekeru, but webs struck him and took him down. A blast of webs came for Turesobei. He dodged to the side. He tried to cast a spell, but as he did, he could feel himself begin to lose control of the creature in the tunnel. He couldn't let that happen. They were in bad enough shape as it was.

The nozakami-ga wrestled out from under Iniru. With her increased strength and jumping ability, Iniru leapt over the ga's head, spinning in midair and attempting to land behind her. But she never even hit the ground. A mass of the nozakami-ga's vines shot down and caught her. Turesobei watched Iniru for too long. A strand of webbing pinned his arms and knocked him flat.

Iniru couldn't break free of the vines, despite the strength boost he'd given her, and Turesobei couldn't even budge his arms. The nozakami-ga planted a foot on his chest and smiled.

"You're mine now," she said. "And what a delectable catch you are."

Chapter Thirty-Three

The spider-kagi hung them from the ceiling above the pool; all except Iniru, who was already hanging from the vines. Kemsu hung limply, but his chest heaved with breath. Turesobei kept his focus invested in the kagi beast he'd charmed in the tunnel. The nozakami-ga hadn't said anything about the creature yet.

The nozakami-ga paced the pool's edge. Turesobei studied the white orb in the bottom of the pool.

Iniru whispered to him, "Is that a moon —"

He shook his head.

"So, my love has sent me a lot this time," the ga said at last. "Though I confess, I do not know what to do with the machine man. I cannot eat him. Maybe I can dominate him and replace my slain beast."

So she thought they'd killed it — that was perfect.

"We don't even know your name," Turesobei said.

"Is it important?" she replied.

"I would prefer," said Lu Bei, "to know the name of the one who eats me, lady."

Her lips curled into a self-satisfied smile. "Utotsu. Now, you can be happy when I eat you."

"It's a nice game you have worked out between you and Satsupan," Turesobei said. "But what does he get out of it?"

"Nothing, save my everlasting love. There was a time when I could visit him ... millennia ago. The world was different then. But alas, we have only shared dreams now. And gifts between us."

Turesobei mentally commanded the beast in the hallway to come to him and attack Utotsu at full speed. If the beast didn't attack immediately, she'd be able to reassert her dominance over it.

"Ah, I can see that you are about to ask me another question, but unlike my love, I find talking to my food tedious. I mean, what question could possibly matter when I'm about to eat —"

The beast charged into the room. Utotsu spun, but too late. The beast slammed into her, and with its horns tossed her to the other side of the pool where she struck the cave wall and slumped ... dazed, but not dead.

"Motekeru!" Turesobei said. "Her heart's the glowing orb at the bottom of the pool. She's my enemy. You know what to do."

He cast the *spell of unbinding the bound*. The webbing peeled off Motekeru, who dropped into the water and plunged underneath before the spider-kagi could hit him with new webs.

Lu Bei turned into a book and fell into the pool. Amidst a column of bubbles, he transformed back into a fetch and shot upward, firing sparks at the spider-kagi and drawing their fire as he darted around the room.

Motekeru grabbed onto the orb with his claws.

"No!" Utotsu screamed, climbing to her feet and reaching out. "I'll let you go. I'll give you anything you want. I swear."

Gazing up at Turesobei, Motekeru paused. Apparently he could hear them through the water.

"Banish your kagi," Turesobei said. "Then we can bargain."

Utotsu scowled at him. Motekeru scraped his claws against the orb.

"Aaaaaa!" She fell to her knees. "Fine. I'll do it."

She chanted. The spider-kagi disappeared. The lizard-ram-beast melted into the floor. Turesobei scanned with his kenja-sight, putting as much internal kenja into it as he could muster. Four fine threads of energy flowed out from the nozakami-ga and into the either. The creatures weren't completely banished back into the nether reaches of the Shadowland from whence they had come. She had only pushed them into the first layer of the Shadowland. She could easily pull them back as soon as she wished.

"Take what you want from the bottom of the pool," Utotsu said. "There are riches: copper, jade, pearl. Take the treasure, but please, leave my heart alone."

Turesobei shook his head. "How many you must have eaten over the years ..."

"I did what I had to do to stay alive," she replied. "Just as you must kill to eat, so do I ..."

"There was a better choice. You could have faded away like the others of your kind. You didn't have to murder innocent people. And I know you're going to attack us as soon as we let down our guard. Motekeru, end her."

Motekeru swallowed the white, glowing stone. The nozakami-ga screamed. Her body shattered into tiny pieces. Some of these kenja pieces dispersed; others flowed down into the water and into Motekeru. The vines released them, and they fell into the pool of icy water.

The chamber went dark as the energies flowed into Motekeru, leaving only his dimly glowing eyes to light the room. Turesobei swam to the shore fast, terrified by the nearly pitch-black room and the icy water that sucked the air from his lungs.

He scrambled onto the shore, shivering violently, and cast the *spell of the moon mirrors*. The spell failed. He focused harder, and the second cast summoned half as many mirrors as normal, dim ones at that, but it was enough light to manage.

"That ... was ... cold," Iniru said, crawling over to collapse beside him, shivering violently like he was.

"It's ice water," Lu Bei said. "What did you expect?" He had pulled Kemsu to the surface and was dragging him to the shore. The cold had woken Kemsu, but he was confused.

Iniru scowled at Lu Bei. "I meant killing the nozakami-ga."

Turesobei replied, "She could bring those creatures back whenever she wanted. She would've betrayed us. And she got what she deserved. Besides, Motekeru looked like he could use a meal."

"I'm not saying you didn't do the right thing," Iniru said. "Just that it seemed cold."

"This coming from an assassin," Lu Bei said.

Iniru frowned, but made no reply. Turesobei felt certain Iniru had never assassinated anyone before. He was fairly certain the Winter Child was only her second mission ever, and she hadn't been able to bring herself to kill the girl. It turned out that killing her hadn't even been possible. Which meant either the Sacred Codex of the qengai had been wrong, or it had known this would happen but didn't want Iniru to know beforehand. That was the thing about prophecy: you could never really know for certain.

Kemsu crawled along the shore and joined them. He looked around, still dazed. "I'm guessing we won."

"Yes," Iniru replied, "though I think we're going to freeze to death now."

Turesobei tried a fire spell, but as cold as he was and with the energies available to him, he couldn't manage anything.

Motekeru stalked out of the pool with strong, heavy steps that didn't lend to the least bit of creaking in his joints. His body gleamed as if newly polished. The injuries that had piled up on him were healed. The nicks in the wood of his frame had disappeared. The dents were gone from his bronze head, and his flattened nose had been restored. The fire in his eyes burned brighter. Even his claws looked refreshed, as if they'd been sharpened.

Lu Bei hovered in front of him. "I haven't seen you looking this strong in … five centuries. Good to see you back to your old self. Actually, I've never seen you look this good."

Motekeru flexed. "That was the best meal I've ever had." He pointed at Lu Bei. "You just said something nice, and you have not snarked at me in weeks. We understand one another now, yes?"

Lu Bei looked at Turesobei and said, "We are good, Motekeru. Because everything is different now."

Motekeru nodded. "Yes, I like him … I like the way things are now. And I do *not* wish to see *anything* change."

"I don't really know what you two are discussing," Turesobei said, teeth chattering, "but it doesn't matter, because we are going to freeze to death soon."

Motekeru drew a ball of fire from his mouth as he'd done in the Lair of the Deadly Twelve. "Use this. I have more than enough now."

Motekeru placed the flaming orb on the floor, and Turesobei cast the fire spell onto it with the barest whisper. Almost instantly, they had a roaring fire to heat and light the room. Motekeru went outside and brought their sonoke in.

Lu Bei examined Kemsu. He held up a finger and asked him to track it with his eyes.

Kemsu managed that. Lu Bei sparked him.

"Ow! What'd you do that for?"

"Reflexes are normal," Lu Bei pronounced. He turned to Turesobei. "He's fine, master. Just a sleep spell. Doesn't seem to have improved him, though. Unfortunate, that. I'm going to take a rest now."

Turesobei sighed. Apparently, Lu Bei didn't like Kemsu now, probably because his master didn't anymore. Lu Bei placed himself near the fire and turned into a book. Not that he was close enough that Turesobei was worried about it, but could Lu Bei catch fire? He was waterproof, so maybe he was fireproof, too. Turesobei would have to ask him later.

"Why doesn't he like me?" Kemsu asked, still shivering.

"The fetch hates everyone," Iniru said, "except his master and Enashoma."

Smiling, Turesobei told Iniru to take the first turn stripping down to warm herself and dry out her clothes.

She drew her spare shirt from the pack on her sonoke. "That's a lame idea." She pulled out one of the blankets. "We strip down and lay on the blankets, on opposite sides of the fire from one another. You two can face away from the fire while I face it, then we'll switch. Once we're dry, we can wrap up in the furs while our clothes dry."

"Good plan," Turesobei said.

"Our clothes are water-resistant, and we were only in a short time," Kemsu said. "They'll dry pretty fast with all this heat."

"We can spend the night here," Motekeru said. "It's safe. The clothes will be dry by morning, then we can return."

Iniru let them face the fire first, since Kemsu was the coldest. A few more minutes, and he might have died. Turesobei stared longingly at the supple muscles and ripples of fur on her back, the smooth curve of her spine. Her hair fanned out across her shoulders. It was only when they rotated and faced the wall that he could think straight again.

"I have a plan," he announced.

"I was hoping you would," Iniru said.

"It's risky, but I'm pretty sure it'll work. Motekeru and I will need to coordinate our actions over a distance, but I think it can be done."

Motekeru climbed out of the pool with his large hands full of copper, jade, and ivory coins, as well as rubies and emeralds. He piled them on the bank with the rest that he had brought up. It was an incredible fortune. Whatever money they didn't need along their way, they would send back to the goronku tribe if possible, to repay them for what they had done.

"I am ready for anything now, master," Motekeru said.

Chapter Thirty-Four

As they rode back toward the canyon, bitterly cold winds battered them. Wild sonoke and demon-beasts chased them, but they managed to avoid getting attacked. On one afternoon, with Lu Bei as a high-flying spotter, they hunted a pack of kotooto beasts: blubbery, blue-furred creatures with five legs, antenna, and non-functional wings. Turesobei hated wasting valuable time, but if they didn't replenish their food stores, they would starve. Of course, the raw kotooto meat from their two kills smelled like a chamber pot and made him contemplate starvation. Surely, rotting sonoke meat would taste better. After a few bites, they vowed to dump the kotooto meat as soon as they found better tasting game.

When they reached the edge of the canyon, they didn't ride down into it. Instead, Turesobei led them to a spot that, by Iniru's estimation, was roughly located above the eidakami-ga's cavern. Turesobei knelt on the ice and activated his kenja-sight. Traces of forest, earth, and fire energy seeped up from the ground around him. Focusing, he tapped his internal kenja and boosted his kenja-sight. Deep in the ground beneath him, below the layer of snow and ice and below the permafrost, stretched a network of roots pulsing with viridian forest kenja. The roots here were thin. Crawling on the ice, he followed them inward until he reached a mass of entangled roots and kenja so bright he had to dim his kenja-sight.

"This is it," Turesobei announced. "Directly below me lies the root-cluster of Satsupan's tree."

"His heart?" Iniru asked.

"Based on my reading of the currents, the heart itself is locked within the tree's root ball, which is buried deep within to keep it safe. It would take a lot of time and effort to reach it."

"So we can't kill him?" Kemsu asked.

Turesobei shrugged. "We might be able to, if we damaged enough roots and left them exposed to the cold, but that would take weeks, months, maybe years. And his knobs would live on after him, for as long as the sun stone remained."

"Motekeru could eat the sun stone and take away his light source," Kemsu said. "He couldn't survive without it."

"Too much energy," Motekeru replied. "I would melt. Doubt I could even hold it."

Turesobei nodded. "Satsupan wasn't bluffing. That *is* a shard of the sun itself."

"So what do we do?" Iniru asked.

"We cause him enough pain that he'll agree to our demands," Turesobei said. "We'll have to dig down far enough to expose some of the dense root mass. Motekeru, I'll need you to do that. Sorry, but I never learned the *spell of the shoveling ghost.*"

"My pleasure," Motekeru said. "Tell me where to start."

Turesobei pointed, and Motekeru immediately plunged his clawed hands into the ice, cutting out blocks as if building a snow house.

"What, you don't have *all* the spells memorized?" Kemsu said, testily.

"It's harder than you think," Turesobei said.

Kemsu shrugged. "Just seems like you usually have a spell to do everything for you."

"Learning a complicated spell is like memorizing an epic poem with several thousand lines," Lu Bei explained. "And there are many more things than that which go into it." Lu Bei crossed his arms and stared at Kemsu. "Now, would you like to continue being snarky about stuff that can save your life?"

Kemsu looked down at his feet. "Sorry."

"Don't you think Satsupan's going to notice when you start tearing through his smaller roots near the top?" Iniru asked.

"I'm counting on it," Turesobei replied. "I need him to already know we mean business when we get there. Motekeru, I will need you to do a lot of damage to the roots when we begin bargaining with him."

"Not a problem." Motekeru bent his head back to the sky and belched out a blast of crackling flames.

Everyone, Turesobei included, stumbled back in awe. Lu Bei yipped and clapped and danced with glee.

"Since when could you do that?!" Turesobei said.

"Yeah, that would've been useful against the Twelve," Iniru added.

"I was built to do it," Motekeru replied, "but I can only manage it when I'm at full strength with a surplus of fire within me. It runs out if I don't eat, and I had not eaten in a very long time. The nozakami's heart held a lot of power. I think I could probably take out several yomon now."

"Good to know." Turesobei patted him on the back. "I'm going to link you to me with a simple signal spell that uses two responses: stop and go. When we start to bargain with Satsupan, I will signal you to do some serious damage to get his attention."

"Can you make the signal go that far, through earth and rock?" Motekeru asked.

"Bound as we are by the kavaru, I think so. It's an air kenja spell, so I shouldn't have much trouble here, and I'm keeping it simple with just two responses."

After two hours of digging, Motekeru reached a knot of thick roots. "If I keep ripping, I'm betting he's really going to start to feel it."

"That's deep enough, then," Turesobei said. "Expand the hole across to expose more of the roots to the cold air."

"You can't make Satsupan feel too desperate," Iniru cautioned. "If he thinks he's going

153

to die, he'll lash out and kill us for revenge."

That should've occurred to Turesobei, but it hadn't. "We'll have to play it carefully, then. It's all we've got."

The big knob, rocking side-to-side nervously, and dozens of small knobs met them at the start of the cave and escorted them to the cavern — this time without chanting. Instead, the little knobs chittered amongst themselves. Once in the cavern, the knobs led them to the shoreline and massed around them, waiting. Satsupan was nowhere to be seen.

As soon as Turesobei dismounted, Enashoma nearly tackled him. Kurine was a step behind her, and she lifted him into a deep, rib-crushing hug. Turesobei retreated, looked them over, and saw no sign of injuries. Satsupan had kept his word about healing them.

"Told you I'd be back," Turesobei said. "You okay?"

"Peachy," Shoma replied. "Better than Satsupan."

"I'll bet."

"Until this morning he was a lot of taunting and bluster," Narbenu said, thumping Kemsu on the shoulder approvingly.

Kurine smiled at him and hugged him again. "About time," she said. "I was getting bored listening to the tree prattle on about himself hour after hour."

Turesobei had to admit he was happy to see Kurine. She always cheered him up, but then she also made him uncomfortable. Of course, all girls made him uncomfortable. Kurine planted a big kiss on his lips. He could feel Iniru's gaze burning holes in his back, so he squirmed out of the embrace as fast as possible.

Satsupan emerged and walked slowly and carefully down a branch, as if afraid he might miss a step. The muscles in his face trembled as he restrained himself from showing any expression.

"So, you have returned," he said pompously, but with a tremor in his voice.

Turesobei reached into his pack, pulled out the now-inert nozakami statue, and tossed it onto the shore. "Brought it back, just like you asked. Our agreement is fulfilled. Though I don't think you were entirely honest with me ..."

Satsupan's eyes flared in shock as he looked at the statue, then his eyes narrowed. "How dare you! What happened to Utotsu?! Why can't I visit her in the dreamtime?"

"Oh, that," Turesobei replied. "You can't visit with her because Motekeru ate her heart. Sorry, you only said to bring the statue. I know, a technicality, but you did fail to mention that she was going to eat us."

"How dare you, mortal!" Satsupan marched toward them, and the knobs closed in, chattering angrily. "Kaiaru dog, I am going to enjoy killing you. Slowly. You will suffer for years."

Turesobei shook his head. "Yeah, I don't think so. How are you feeling, by the way? Under that anger ... you look a little bit afraid. Something the matter with ... oh, I don't know, your roots, maybe?"

"How dare you?!"

"Master dares," Lu Bei replied. "You should ask yourself, where is Motekeru? What is he up to? Is he, perhaps, directly above you, digging into your roots, exposing them to the cold?"

"You would never," Satsupan hissed.

"But I would," Turesobei replied. "In fact, you know that I have already. Would you like for me to order Motekeru to do a little more digging ... a little more clawing?"

Satsupan grew long wooden claws out from his fingertips. "I will crush you before the machine man does enough damage to harm me."

Turesobei smiled and snapped his fingers, activating the spell to signal Motekeru. Satsupan collapsed, screaming and grabbing at his body. Turesobei sent the stop signal, and stood over Satsupan.

"On my signal, he will attack your roots again with claws and flame. And if I die, he will know immediately, and he will dig, slash, and burn until you are no more. Are we clear?"

"Even if your machine could kill me, my knobs would destroy you all."

"I realize that," Turesobei said. "That's why I returned here for my friends instead of killing you first. I figured we could work something out. You let us go, and Motekeru won't keep hurting you."

Satsupan lunged at Turesobei. Before he could reach him, the two amber hounds pounced onto Satsupan and knocked him off course. As he started to get back up, Turesobei clicked his fingers. Satsupan started writhing on the ground again as Motekeru burned his roots. The knobs hesitated, not knowing what to do.

"Everyone, mount up," Turesobei said. "Start moving toward the entrance. Push through the knobs if you must."

Turesobei walked backward behind his friends as they shoved through the knobs toward the entrance to the cave. He clicked his fingers again to make Motekeru stop. Satsupan lay gasping for air. The anger was gone from him ... for the moment. The big knob rallied the horde, and they started rushing in. Iniru and the others began to fight them off.

Turesobei yelled with his fingers above his head. "Back off or your master suffers and dies!"

Some of the knobs backed off, but others did not. With Lu Bei and the hounds shielding him, Turesobei cast the *spell of the sun-fire globe*, drawing on the sun stone's power. A giant, glowing orb appeared in the top of the cavern. While the orb crackled and flamed, it couldn't burn anything. It merely gave off light. It was nothing more than an impressive bluff, or so he hoped. Half the knobs backed away in fear, but that still wasn't enough.

"Call them off or die, Satsupan!"

"Your word?" Satsupan yelled.

"My word!" Turesobei returned.

Satsupan ordered the knobs to stand down, but many of them disobeyed him. With dozens chasing them, Turesobei leapt up onto the mount behind Zaiporo, and they raced out through the tunnel, outpacing the knobs. When they reached the outside and the endless ice and deep drifts of recently fallen snow, the knobs slowed as they began to slip and tire. They couldn't handle the cold, nor walk well on the ice.

Once the last of the knobs quit chasing them, Turesobei and his companions stopped to catch their breath. Luckily, no one had gotten any serious injuries fighting off the knobs this time. Turesobei stared back toward the tunnels, deep in thought.

"Going to get rid of him, master?" Lu Bei asked.

Turesobei sighed. "No, I can't go back on my word."

"He could kill more people," Zaiporo said.

"True," Turesobei replied, "but I don't think many people wander into this canyon anymore. He's suffered, that'll have to be enough."

As Kemsu and Narbenu nodded, approving of his honor in keeping his word, Kurine beamed at him with pride.

"Let's get as far away from here as fast as we can," Iniru said. "Those knobs are determined. They may keep coming."

As they rode toward the blind with the shortcut path leading up out of the canyon, a strange feeling struck Turesobei — a disturbance in the kenja currents. He turned and looked to his left. His heart plunged into his stomach, and bile rose into his throat.

On the edge of the sloping side of the canyon, the side they had slid down in the snowstorm, stood a long line of yomon. Eighty-eight of them, he suspected. At their center, scantily clad in ripped traveling clothes — blood-smeared — taller — filled out with hips and breasts and corded muscle — a pentagram on her forehead — was Awasa. She stood with one hip cocked and her head turned almost coyly to the side. The familiar pose made her new form look even more twisted and monstrous.

Her purple eyes locked onto him. He thought he saw a grin. Then she pointed Sumada toward them and bellowed, "Charge!"

Chapter Thirty-Five

Awasa ran madly down the slope, somehow managing not to fall and slide down. The yomon poured down behind her.

"Oh gods!" Enashoma cried out. "That's not —"

"It's her," Lu Bei said. He had the sharpest eyes out of all of them.

"We've got to get out of here and fast," Iniru said.

Turesobei opened his kenja-sight and peered up at Awasa; he had to see. "The blood ... she's painted herself with the blood of the Winter Child. That's why she's safe from the cold."

"Sobei," Iniru urged. "We have to get out of here. Now!"

"Right." He took a deep breath. "When I give the signal, ride hard for the blind. I'm going to cover us."

He chanted the *spell of the fog cloud*. Normally, it would cover only a small area at best, but the spell used air and water kenja, the two most abundant energies in the Ancient Cold and Deep, and he planned on putting everything he had into it.

"Hurry," Shoma urged.

The yomon and Awasa were halfway down into the canyon when he finished chanting the long spell. Almost instantly, a mist rose from the ground and clouds fell from the sky, filling the canyon with a fog so thick that Turesobei couldn't even see the tail end of the sonoke he was riding.

"I can't see anything," Kemsu said. "How's this supposed to help us?"

Turesobei spoke a command, and a bubble within the fog cloud formed around them so that they could see each other and just ahead of themselves.

"Ride to the blind," he said.

"Master, what if the yomon or Awasa can follow our trail magically?" Lu Bei asked.

"Do you think they can?"

"I'm not sure. I would assume that Awasa's powers are similar to those of Barakaros the Warlock. I'm certain that he could've tracked us. Of course, you have stirred up a lot of energy here, and she hasn't had time to get used to her powers — or had any magical training for that matter."

"We'll just have to ride and hope she can't," Turesobei said. "It's the only choice we've got."

"You say that a lot," Kemsu said.

"That's how I live my life," Turesobei replied. "I never seem to have any good options. I just work with what fate gives me."

"They could physically track us once the fog clears," Iniru said.

"The fog will last in the canyon for days, maybe weeks."

"It's not going to spread, is it?" Narbenu asked.

"I localized it as best as I could," Turesobei said. "If it spreads, it will do so slowly. We should be able to stay well ahead of it. Meanwhile, they can flail around blindly and take the long way out of the canyon."

"I hope they run into the cave and face all those angry knobs and what's left of Satsupan," Zaiporo said. "That would be justice."

As they rode up the blind, a frustrated, shrieking howl pierced the fog and echoed through the canyon. Turesobei knew the voice behind it.

"Sounds like we've thwarted them for now, master," Lu Bei said.

Kurine pulled alongside Turesobei and stared at him. "So that ... that was ..."

"My other betrothed," he replied dully.

As they rode, Turesobei stared blindly into the distance and thought of the time he'd run into Awasa with his shirt stuck over his head. That was the day Lu Bei had come to him. He thought of the tea they'd had with their mothers before the note from Iniru had changed their lives. He thought of the dance he'd offered to take her to — a dance he would've attended. Without that note, she would still be the same old Awasa: not the good person she had started to become and not the nightmare she was now. But even without that note, the Deadly Twelve would have come after him, and Awasa would probably be dead. Although that would be a better fate than being turned into what she was now.

When they reached Motekeru an hour later, he was meditating near the destruction he'd wrought. He nodded tersely, and then climbed into the saddle of his mount. But they didn't go on immediately. They gave their mounts a few minutes to rest, since they'd be riding them nonstop for the rest of the day and part of the night.

"You okay?" Iniru asked.

Turesobei shrugged. "It's my fault."

"It is, but what's done is done. I'm sorry it happened."

"The trip was making her a better person. She was trying so hard. She'd turned the corner."

"She really had," Shoma said. "She was becoming almost tolerable. She worked so hard to earn Sobei's respect and now ..."

"The magic has brought out all the worst in her," Turesobei said. "If not for all those yomon, I'd do anything I could to help her, though I'm not sure what I actually could do."

"I haven't seen many things like this before," Lu Bei said, solemnly, "obviously, but my experience and instincts tell me there's probably no way to cure her of this."

Chapter Thirty-Six

For the next several days, they pushed on as hard as they dared, over increasingly rough terrain with jagged rocks, sudden gullies, and sloping hills. But with no sign of Awasa and the yomon, they eventually slowed to a more reasonable pace that wouldn't kill the sonoke. The only good thing about this region was how sparsely populated it was, so they didn't have to worry about the yomon tearing through any villages. This also meant game was plentiful. Unfortunately, most of it was able to fight back. Periodically, Turesobei would cast the *spell of the baby's breath* to blow snow and debris over their tracks. It was the first wind spell an apprentice learned and was normally sufficient only for blowing out a candle across a room. Here, its effect was considerable.

Turesobei was settling down for the night in the snow house with the others when Iniru appeared at the entrance.

"I'm coming in." By the time Narbenu could start to complain about the impropriety of it, she was already inside. "Turesobei is needed in our snow house."

"He can't go," Narbenu said, "and you can't stay here any longer."

"His sister needs him," Iniru said in her screw-you voice.

Narbenu frowned. "I don't think —"

"Motekeru is there, so is his sister," Iniru said irritably. "We're not going to do anything improper."

"I'm going to check on my sister," Turesobei told Narbenu authoritatively. "I'll be back."

"Sobei," Zaiporo said. "Tell Shoma ... tell her ... tell her I said ... hi."

"Um ... okay," Turesobei said, and he stepped outside, following Iniru.

"What's wrong with Shoma?" Turesobei asked.

"She's cracking under all the pressure. She's exhausted, and seeing Awasa, I think it really shook her up. I tried to comfort her, but she's mad at me."

"What? Why?"

"Because I flirted a bit with Zaiporo a few times. Several, maybe ... I think."

"You flirt with a lot of people; it doesn't necessarily mean anything."

"Yeah, but he flirted back and ... it's just ... you know how it is." She cocked an eyebrow at him. "Well, *you* probably don't."

"I feel like I don't know what's going on between us all anymore."

"Well, if we could share the same snow house, we'd all communicate better, and you'd get to see Shoma more. That would help. If Narbenu wasn't such a prude. I'm really not fond of him."

"Narbenu's a good man, Niru. He saved my life and took me in. He risked his neck to help rescue you, too. He's just trying to do what he thinks is right. He feels responsible for us."

"Maybe so," Iniru said, "but I don't think he's that simple. He has a slave. Good men don't keep slaves."

"And you're an assassin. Good people don't kill other people."

Iniru spun on him. "Oh, yeah?"

Turesobei shrugged. "I'm not holding it against you. Just saying the world isn't that simple. And things are different here. Just like they're different for k'chasan qengai and k'chasan families. Kemsu's paying a blood debt, and if he's okay with that, then so am I."

"Well, I can see Kurine is good for one thing."

"Wait ... what? What does she have to do with anything?"

"You were a lot easier to manage when you had less backbone," Iniru said with a sigh. "Still, it has to be a good thing in the end."

"What makes you think Kurine has anything to do with me having more backbone? I've always had backbone!"

"Before her, you never thought of me as anything but wonderful. I was magical ... perfect. It was a good feeling. Now, I'm an assassin ... though an excusable one, at least." She gave him a kiss on the cheek and stroked her hand down his neck. "Reality had to set in eventually, I suppose."

With that, she ducked inside the girls' snow house, leaving him to stand in the cold, utterly bewildered. Kurine had given him backbone? He thought of all the times he'd stood up to people, dared the unknown, faced dangers deemed insurmountable, done things his way. He'd faced down the Storm Dragon and was still himself. How, by the love of Kaiwen Earth-Mother, could he not have backbone already? It just didn't make any sense.

He shook his head. No sense in pondering it. If Shoma, Kurine, and Awasa didn't make sense to him, there was no way he'd ever understand Iniru. He entered their snow house. Motekeru sat in the corner with Enashoma cradled in his bronze-jointed, wooden arms. Enashoma was sobbing, her head against his chest. Turesobei paused, overwhelmed by the absurdity of that image.

Kurine popped up from the side and gave him a smile and a quick peck on the cheek. She gave Iniru a seething glance then said, "Enashoma's been crying for an hour now. I did what I could ... but she doesn't really know me and ..."

"It's okay," he responded. "Thank you for trying." He turned to Iniru. "Thank you both."

He knelt beside Enashoma. She spun into his arms. Motekeru nodded to him, and Turesobei nodded back.

"Shoma, Shoma, what's wrong? Are you okay?"

"I'm ... I'm fine," she sobbed.

"You don't sound fine."

"I don't want to trouble you, Sobei. You've been through so much. And seeing Awasa ... you must be —"

"I'm fine," he said.

"You're lying."

"I'm trying not to think about it." That was a lie. He thought about Awasa all the time while riding, even more now that he'd seen her. That was the problem with riding in the cold all day long as fast as you could, bundled in thick furs with your face covered: there wasn't much chance for conversation. He and Zaiporo had long ago run out of things to talk about, and talking between mounts was difficult. Even Kurine had largely given up, now that the terrain was rough.

"Awasa ... is that what's bothering you?" he asked.

"Yes ... no. It's everything. This isn't what I set out for. Freedom, a little adventure — that's what I wanted. I miss our world. I miss warmth. I miss home. I miss Grandfather ... hot meals ... tea ... even Mother. Life was easy at home ... Home was okay, I just wanted to be myself ... to marry who I wanted ... see a little of the world."

"I know. I failed you. I'm sorry. I wish I'd made you stay."

"I don't want to end up like Awasa. I'm okay with dying, but not that. Never that. If something like that happens to me, kill me, okay? Don't hesitate. Don't wait because you're going to try to save me. Just end it."

"Shoma —"

"Promise me."

"I'll do better than that. I promise I won't ever let it happen." He held her for a while, letting her cry. Then he kissed her tenderly on the nose. "I love you, Little Blossom. Be strong. I'll get you home yet." He sat back and smiled at her. "Now, I have just the thing to cheer you up. Lu Bei!"

A few moments later, the fetch flew into the snow house, circled the room three times, sticking his tongue out at Iniru and Kurine with each pass, and landed before Enashoma. He swept one hand out and bowed before her.

"My lady," Lu Bei said. "Most Wondrous Blossom, Fairest of All. I have come to bring happiness. Which, of course, means that I have come to serve you tea." In his other hand, he held a tin bowl.

"We don't have any tea," she muttered through sobs. "And no fire."

"Tut. Tut." Lu Bei shook a finger at her. "Such negative thinking." He held the bowl out. "Water, please."

Kurine grabbed a canteen and poured clean water into the bowl. The water was nearly frozen. The only way they could keep it liquid was by storing it with the star stones. Lu Bei flicked his hand out, and suddenly, between his fingers, he held a sachet filled with herbs. He dropped the sachet into the tin bowl. Jasmine — Turesobei picked out the scent immediately, along with ...

"Tea buds!" he said. "You have white tea buds. You were holding out."

Enashoma clapped and laughed.

"Desperate times call for special teas," Lu Bei said. "I've always got something good stashed away, for just the right moment."

"Where do you stash anything away?" Kurine said. "You're naked."

"Madam!" Lu Bei said, folding his wings around to cover himself. His amber cheeks darkened. "We do not point out such things. We also do not question the magic of tea storage. Are we clear?"

"Um ... okay ... sure," she responded.

"Good." He stuck his tongue out at her. "Now, master, if you would so kindly warm the tea. Friend Motekeru, I think master could benefit from a bit of assistance."

"For Enashoma," Motekeru said. "Of course."

Turesobei cast a fire-wielding spell and held a hand out toward Motekeru, who spat a small flame into it. Turesobei held his hand under the tin bowl until steam began to rise from it.

"You can hold fire!" Kurine said.

"It's a simple trick. Just a minor talent and a bit of focus. I couldn't walk through fire, just to be clear. That would require serious magic."

Lu Bei dipped a finger into the bowl. "Ahhh ... perfection." He passed the bowl to Enashoma, but she handed it to Turesobei, wiped away her tears, and took Lu Bei into a hug, squeezing him tightly.

"Oh my, I cannot breathe, my lady. Cannot breathe. I shall perish!"

Laughing, she let him go and took the bowl. She drank from it and sighed with pleasure. "Oh, it's like a bit of home. It's perfect." After a while, she handed it to Turesobei. "Have a sip. But just one. A small one. The tea is mine."

He took a sip, and it *was* like tasting home. Enashoma let Iniru take a sip next, and she too sighed with pleasure. Enashoma took the bowl to Kurine. "Try some."

"Are you sure?" Kurine said, almost blushing. "It's your tea."

"You are my friend now. We're almost sisters now, I guess. I want you to try it."

Nervously, Kurine tasted the tea. "It's ... it's sort of bitter and tangy. The herb is nice. Sorry, I didn't mean to — it is tasty. We don't have anything like that."

"I know," Enashoma moaned.

"I am reminded," said Lu Bei, "of the *Ballad of the Man Who Could Not Taste Tea*. Have you heard that one?"

None of them had heard it, of course. Lu Bei recited the tale, delighting everyone, especially Shoma. Turesobei suspected the fetch was making up the tale as he went. But that didn't matter. All that mattered was that Enashoma was a little bit better.

Chapter Thirty-Seven

As they continued on, the land ceased to be barren, and they were forced to bypass a region of hot springs that hosted dozens of villages. After that, the terrain leveled out again, and they picked up speed, soon returning to wild, unpopulated areas. They encountered few problems, and the yomon remained out of sight, as did their reitsu pursuer, if he still followed them. Turesobei hadn't detected him since the blizzard. Lu Bei and Narbenu were both certain the yomon needed little if any sleep, and their stride was long, which would allow them to cover much distance. So if the yomon picked up the trail, they would close in fast.

As they crested a hill, sunlight sparkled along lines on a flat plain in the distance.

"What is that?" Turesobei asked.

"The Glass Sea," Narbenu replied.

"What are those lines?" Zaiporo asked.

"The lines," said Narbenu, "are the result of sailing ships traveling across the ice, pushing aside the snow that has fallen onto the smooth surface."

An hour later, they stood on the shore. The sea was solid, glassy on top, with a dark gray color underneath. And it was wrong, all wrong. Turesobei was standing on the edge of a sea, and there was only the faintest scent of salt in the air, as if he were yet leagues away from the shore.

Zaiporo walked out onto the sea and began to slide around, despite the treads on his overboots. "Whoa, it's slick."

"That's how come ships can sail on it," Narbenu said. "The sails catch the wind, and the skates glide along the surface."

"Sailing on ships with skates underneath, that I would like to see," said Lu Bei.

"The ice isn't going to break beneath us, is it?" Enashoma asked.

Narbenu shook his head. "They say that even the thinnest patch of ice on the sea could hold the weight of ten goronku. I've never heard of ice cracking or breaking on the sea. Never heard of anyone falling in. Many people fish the sea, despite the dangers out here. They drill holes through the ice to do so. I've heard they have to drill ten feet in most places to reach water."

While everyone took a short lunch break, Narbenu scanned their surroundings, searching for some marker to get their bearings. It was hard with a plain of barren ice behind them and a frozen, barren sea ahead. And he had never been here before.

"With the treasure you took from the pool in the cave, we could afford a ship to transport us there," Narbenu said. "If we could find a port."

"I didn't think we needed a ship," Turesobei said.

"It's not necessary, since our mounts can handle the ice," Narbenu replied. "But there's less traction, and they will travel much more slowly across it. A ship would be a lot faster. I never mentioned it before because we couldn't afford one. We could also use some precise directions on where the Forbidden Library is on the sea."

Turesobei knelt. "I'll see if I can detect any presences nearby, anyone that might help us." He extended the spell out as far as he possibly could, but didn't pick up any signs of people or beasts. "So what now? Skirt the coast and look for a port, or just take off across the Glass Sea?"

"It's your call," Iniru said, "but I think we should try to find a port first. We just can't take too long doing so."

"Are there many ports?" Turesobei asked Narbenu.

"I've heard that there are a number of tiny villages, and ships visit them regularly, but there aren't many ports."

Turesobei considered their options. The ice should inhibit the yomon as much as them, if not more. But a ship would let them outrace the yomon completely. "Let's ride along the coast and try to find a village, at least to get more info about the Forbidden Library. Anyone have a problem with that decision?" No one did. "All right then, east or west?"

"How about east?" Kurine said. "The rising sun always brings hope."

"How is that?" Turesobei asked.

"Our sun has faded," Kurine said. "We always fear that one day it will go out and never rise again."

They struck out east, riding along the shore, and found nothing that day. They made camp fifty paces away from the shore as the sun set. Turesobei decided they'd try one more day before giving up and riding out onto sea.

As they did every night, Turesobei, Lu Bei, and Motekeru stayed outside for one final check before tucking in. Darkness had set in completely, and the night sky overhead was moonless. Thousands of stars twinkled. Turesobei stared up at them, steamy puffs of breaths coming from his mouth.

"They're all a bit wrong, the stars," Turesobei said. "Like ours but a little out of place."

"The stars change over time," Lu Bei replied. "Like the planets and the moons. They just move very, very slowly. I don't think Satsupan was lying. I think this very well may be a version of our world that's in the far future. Though I can't explain the whole crossing the barrier into oblivion aspect, or how a copy of one section of our world could be moved and put into another place."

Motekeru stomped away, making a big circuit around the camp. Lu Bei circled overhead. His eyes were good in the dark. Turesobei knelt and cast the sensing spell one more time. He was doing it so much, three or four times every day, that it was becoming routine. Several dozen presences immediately sparked in his mind: coming up from the sea and heading toward them fast. He leapt to his feet.

"We've got incoming! Motekeru, guard the mounts. Lu Bei, they're coming from the sea. Keep watch."

Turesobei turned to warn the others, but they were already rushing out of the snow houses.

"What is it?" Iniru asked.

"Kagi of some sort. Haven't encountered them before. Should we crowd into a snow house and block the entrance? Or should we run? They're moving fast."

"If we block ourselves in, we'll lose our sonoke," Narbenu replied.

"I can guard them, master," Motekeru called out.

"Risky," Iniru said. "You're not invulnerable, big guy."

"My flames will scare off whatever they are."

Turesobei still had his sensing active. He focused and searched out for the creatures again, so he could count how many there were, but the creatures were gone.

"They've vanished! Lu Bei, do you see anything?"

As he continued to circle overhead, Lu Bei shouted down. "Nothing, master."

"How could they vanish?" Enashoma said.

Narbenu glanced everywhere. "I can't think of anything. We should stay on our guard. Better yet, let's move on. Can you do the mirrors?"

"I'll do them gladly. Everyone get your gear and mounts. Let's get out of here."

Kemsu darted into the boys' snow house. "I'll get the blankets and pack our supplies while you all get the mounts ready."

"I'll do the same," Kurine offered, and she ducked inside the girls' snow house.

Turesobei pushed the sensing spell back, reducing its strength temporarily, while he cast the *spell of the moon mirrors*. As soon as the mirrors were active, he picked up the kagi again. Coming in fast, and they were almost right on top of them. But that didn't make any sense, because they hadn't spotted them. Were the kagi invisible? The beasts had disappeared from his sensing, and then —

He looked down at his feet.

"They're coming up from underneath us!" he shouted. "They went too deep for me to detect, and now they're —"

From inside the girls' snow house, Kurine screamed.

Chapter Thirty-Eight

Rig and Ohma charged into the snow house. Turesobei dove in after them. As he stood, hunched over due to the low ceiling, a wave of revulsion hit him, and he nearly retched. A kagi no bigger than the hounds had pounced onto Kurine and wrapped six suckered tentacles around her arms and two around her waist. An ichor that stank of sulfur and rotting flesh oozed from its pulsing, fanged maw. Each drop that touched the floor melted the ice. Each drop that touched Kurine's arms melted through her parka and burned her skin. The kagi tried to pull Kurine's head to its mouth, but she had latched her hands around the beast's head and was holding it back. Kurine's arms were shaking as they weakened under its grip. Two of its seven eyestalks whipped around and glared at Turesobei. Another two eyestalks flashed at the hounds.

Turesobei recognized the creature from the *Manual of Demon Beasts Most Uncommon* — an orugukagi. Information flashed through his conscious mind: fast swimmers — voracious hunger — sensitive to light — tentacles like an octopus — flippers and the long body of a seal — spikes on their suckers causing temporary, localized paralysis — acidic saliva — its bite —

Turesobei drew his knife. "Kurine! Its bite is deadly!"

Tentacles whipped up from a hole in the floor at the back of the snow house, as another beast pulled itself in. The hounds intercepted that beast, while Turesobei lunged toward the one latched onto Kurine. He stabbed the orugukagi in the body, pulled the blade free, and slashed off the two eyestalks that glared at him. But the demon-beast didn't release Kurine. It gripped her tighter. The beast knew its wounds were temporary, that its eyestalks would grow back. This was why Turesobei so desperately needed his white-steel sword. One slash, and this fiend would have been dead.

Turesobei drew back to stab it again, but another demon-beast burst out from the hole and launched itself through the air, hurtling toward him. He ducked, and the beast flew over his head. But as it passed, a tentacle lashed him across the cheek, scratching deep enough to draw blood.

Kurine screamed. Her arms fell limp. She jerked her head to the side. The orugukagi missed her neck, but bit deep into her shoulder. She moaned and slumped to the ground. The creature that had flown over Turesobei's head surged toward him, but Lu Bei zipped in through the entrance and sparked it in the face, disorienting it. Turesobei plunged his knife into the head of the orugukagi biting Kurine.

One of the hounds yelped in pain. Lu Bei flashed by Turesobei and sparked the second orugukagi again. Two more beasts crawled out of the hole. Turesobei repeatedly plunged the knife into the head of the beast that had bitten Kurine. Finally, it loosened its grip and relaxed its tentacles, falling away, wounded and confused.

The scuttling and barking of more demons echoed up through the hole. The tunnel wasn't newly made. It must've lain there unused, sealed over by only a thin layer of ice, and they just hadn't noticed when they'd made the snow house.

The hounds couldn't fend off three of the beasts. An orugukagi engulfed Rig in its tentacles and bit deep into the hound's flank. As Rig sank with a whimper, Ohma tore at the beast on her brother, but another orugukagi caught Ohma, as well. That left Turesobei and Lu Bei to face two of them, with more on the way. Lu Bei shot sparks from each hand, trying to keep the orugukagi back. That slowed them only a little.

Turesobei hooked Kurine's arm over his shoulder and started dragging her away. Tapping a heavy amount of internal kenja, Turesobei chanted the *spell of the moon mirrors*, hoping to blind the orugukagi. But the poison from the tentacle that had struck him had numbed his cheek. He slurred his words, and the spell failed.

Two more beasts slithered up out of the hole. It was hopeless.

A tentacle latched onto Lu Bei, grabbing him by a wing. Lu Bei hit the ground and shrieked. Lu Bei sparked the creature, but it didn't let go. Turesobei started toward him.

"Go, master!" Lu Bei yelled. "Get out of here!"

Motekeru burst suddenly into the snow house. With his claws, he tore through the beast grasping Lu Bei. Then he turned his bronze head toward the hounds and the five more orugukagi charging toward them. His hideous, jagged mouth opened, and a gout of flame burst out, engulfing the hounds and the demon-beasts. The heat was so great, Turesobei had to throw up his hand to shield his face. The hounds ... the poor hounds ...

The ice began to melt around them. Iniru crawled through the snow house entrance. "Do you need —"

Turesobei shoved Kurine toward her. "Pull her out. Fast!"

Iniru took Kurine and pulled her out. Flames still poured from Motekeru's mouth. With the one wing he could still move shielding him from the heat of the flames, Lu Bei limped toward Turesobei. He grabbed up the fetch and scurried out of the entrance.

With Lu Bei turning into a book in his hands, Turesobei said to the others, "What in Torment took you all so long to ..."

Narbenu lay on the ice clutching a limp arm. Blood oozed through a hole in his clothes. Zaiporo sat gasping for air, unharmed. Enashoma knelt beside him, splattered by orugukagi guts. Two orugukagi lay dead, their bodies rent in half by Motekeru's claws. A giant block of ice, ripped free from the boys' snow house, plugged a second hole in the ice.

"Oh," Turesobei responded.

"Kurine!" Kemsu yelled. He slid down next to her and took her hand. "She's not conscious."

Iniru pulled Kurine's hair back, revealing the wound on her shoulder. "Ugh. That's not good."

"One of the orugukagi bit her," Turesobei said, slurring his words. "Their bite ..."

"Do something for her," Kemsu said.

"I can't. Not now."

"Sobei," Enashoma said. "What's wrong with your voice? You sound drunk."

He touched the deep scratch that trailed across his cheek from his ear lobe to the edge of his lips. "Paralyzed my cheek. I can't cast any spells until it wears off. I've already tried. We have to get out of here. There are more on the way. Motekeru can't fight them all. Iniru, Shoma, Kemsu, get the mounts."

"But Kurine," Kemsu said.

"I know," Turesobei told him. "Get the mounts. I'll stay with her."

As the others went to get the sonoke, the snow house behind Turesobei collapsed. Melting ice blocks tumbled away as Motekeru surged free, a hound tucked under each arm. Miraculously, they were still alive. And somehow completely unharmed by the flames.

Turesobei helped Narbenu get in the saddle.

"I'll be fine, lad," the goronku said. "As soon as I can move my arm again."

"Hand Kurine up to me," Kemsu said. "I'll hold onto her. I can guide the sonoke with my knees well enough."

Turesobei and Iniru lifted Kurine up and placed her in front of Kemsu, who leaned back as far as he could to make her comfortable and then wrapped his hands around her waist.

"I'll keep the hounds," Motekeru said.

Turesobei took Kurine's mount.

The block of ice plugging the hole outside shifted and resettled. Turesobei tried to cast the *spell of the moon mirrors,* but again his words slurred, and the spell didn't go off.

"Sorry, we're going to have to ride by moonlight." Unfortunately, there wasn't much of that.

Zaiporo and Enashoma both took out star stones and tapped them to full strength, holding them out with one hand, protected from their heat by their gloves. Those stones and a dim, waning Zhura was all the light they had. The group raced blindly along the coast. Turesobei kept glancing back toward their former camp with his kenja-sight open. Now that he'd encountered the beasts, he felt certain he could see them coming based solely on the energy currents. He didn't see anything, but he still thought it best to keep riding.

"I don't think they're following, but let's ride a little further inland to set up camp."

A half-hour later, they stopped on a small rise.

Iniru took charge. "We make one big snow house, and we all get in it and block the entrance. Just in case those things are persistent."

Narbenu started to complain, but Turesobei interrupted him. "I don't care about your rules. Not tonight. If you like, we can … hang some blankets to make separate sections. Good enough?"

Narbenu grumbled but nodded. "Given the circumstances."

Motekeru dismounted and set down the wolfhounds. Both were conscious, but groaning in pain. Turesobei knelt over them. Not a strand of fur was singed. The bites from the orugukagi were puckered and oozing pus but already showed signs of healing.

"Motekeru, are the hounds indestructible?"

"They seem almost like spirit beasts themselves, master. Impervious to many things. I don't know the full extent of their powers. Chonda Lu hid them away before my time."

Lu Bei nodded. "Those hounds predate both of us by centuries. Chonda Lu only spoke of them once or twice."

"Maybe we'll figure it out one day," Turesobei said. "Motekeru, when the snow house is finished, you will block us in and guard the mounts."

Motekeru plunged his claws into the ice to begin cutting a block. "It will be done, master."

Turesobei checked on Kurine. Kemsu had taken her from the mount and laid her atop some blankets. Turesobei bent down and placed his lips on her forehead.

"Fever has set in," he lamented.

"How … how long does she have?" Kemsu asked.

Turesobei tried to recall every detail he'd studied about the orugukagi. It turned out that Grandfather Kahenan's instance on him memorizing beast after beast hadn't been pointless. "Complete paralysis first, then fever sets in, followed by a coma. Then …" The words choked in his throat. "A day … at the most." Not again. He couldn't lose another. "But I can cast spells as soon as my voice returns properly."

"You can heal her?" Kemsu said with hope.

Turesobei shook his head. "I can delay the poison and counter the effects. There's no spell that can heal her. All I can do is delay the inevitable for a week … maybe two." He touched Kurine's cheek tenderly. "Unless we find a cure somewhere …"

Kemsu shoved him. "This is your fault!"

"How is this my fault?" Turesobei replied. "Did I ask for demons to attack us?"

"She's your betrothed," Kemsu snapped. "She's your responsibility."

"There was nothing I could do. The beasts popped out from a hole in the ground. I can't predict the future."

Kemsu stepped up and got in his face. "Everything you touch gets ruined. I've seen it. You dragged your sister to our bleak world and nearly got her and your — girlfriend, whatever Iniru is to you — killed. And your former betrothed is some sort of demon-witch. You come here, and you expect to have Kurine along with Iniru. You accepted Kurine's kiss without warning her about what being around you means. You came to our village, and you ruined everything. Now you've gotten Kurine killed."

"I think you need to calm down," Turesobei said.

Kemsu shoved him back again, and threw a punch. With a solid thump, his fist struck

Turesobei in the jaw. Turesobei fell hard on the ice, stunned for a moment. As Turesobei stood, Kemsu threw another punch. His fist never reached Turesobei.

A clawed hand caught Kemsu by the forearm. Eyes blazing bright, Motekeru lifted Kemsu off the ground and held him up in the air by his arm. He twisted Kemsu so they could see one another eye-to-eye.

"I can break you, boy," Motekeru said menacingly.

"You wouldn't," Kemsu said, wincing as Motekeru's grip crushed into his forearm. "And I'm no boy."

"I have killed hundreds, thousands maybe. What's one more boy? And you are a boy. I know, because you act like one. And soon, you may be a broken boy."

The others gathered around, but no one dared say anything. Not even Narbenu would speak up. Lu Bei crawled out of Turesobei's pack, limping and fussy.

"Do it," the fetch said. "Mutinous brat deserves it."

"Master," Motekeru said, "shall I break him? I would delight in eating the heart out of his chest."

Everyone looked to Turesobei. Heart pounding, anger searing, he glared at Kemsu. Turesobei wiped the blood from his lip. The storm sigil on his cheek was burning.

Chapter Thirty-Nine

"Let him go," Turesobei said.

Motekeru threw Kemsu at Turesobei's feet.

Clenching and unclenching his fists, Turesobei loomed over Kemsu. "You have *no idea* the sacrifices I've made for those I love. You have no idea what all of us had to endure to save our world and my people. Do you think that was easy? Do you think such a thing comes without a price?"

Kemsu, shaking, got up. Turesobei grabbed him by the collar. The storm sigil burned even hotter on his cheek now. "Do you really understand what I'm capable of? I don't need Motekeru. I can consume you myself anytime I wish."

Enashoma threw herself between them.

"Time to calm down, big brother. We don't need you to turn into a dragon just to teach Kemsu a lesson." Turesobei glared at her until she touched his cheek, the one without the *Mark of the Storm Dragon*. "Sobei, none of what happened was your fault. Kemsu ... he's just upset about Kurine, and he's a long way from home now, just like we are. We're all under a lot of pressure. Let it go."

"Sobei, Kemsu," Iniru said. "Drop it. You're not helping anyone. We have to stick together."

"Fine," Turesobei sighed. "It's over. It's done."

"I'll start on the snow house," Kemsu muttered, and he stalked over to his mount, drew a knife, and knelt on the ice. But he shook so badly that he couldn't even manage a simple cut. Anger drained out Turesobei. He went over to Kemsu and apologized.

"I'm sorry," he said simply. What more could he say? It took all he could do to manage that.

"Kurine ..." Kemsu whispered. "She's my ... my oldest ... friend and ... whatever. It's over."

"Are we okay now?" Turesobei asked.

"Sure," Kemsu replied dully. "Whatever."

Turesobei approached Narbenu. "I'm sorry about that. It was uncalled for."

"What Kemsu did was uncalled for, as well." Narbenu shot Kemsu an angry glance. "He did start it, after all. But thank you for apologizing, and for your restraint. The dragon ... I saw it, remember? I can't imagine what you must be holding in."

"Thank you for understanding," Turesobei responded.

He sat down beside Kurine. He was thankful she'd hadn't seen any of that. He'd keep his dignity with someone, at least. She was Kemsu's oldest friend ... when had they stopped being close? When he became a slave? When the goronku rules started making it hard for boys and girls to spend any time together? He had a feeling they'd had a major falling out, but neither of them spoke about it.

Enashoma scolded Lu Bei. "I don't care if you are hurt and miserable, you should not have encouraged him. Sobei nearly dragoned-out on us."

"I didn't encourage Master, my lady," Lu Bei whined. "I encouraged Motekeru."

"You needed to defuse the situation," Enashoma continued. "But you made it worse. Don't do that again."

"I'm sorry, Lady Shoma." Lu Bei bowed. "Forgive me. I'm very protective of Master, is all."

Enashoma wasn't finished. She marched over to Motekeru, who was cutting ice, and thumped him on the chest with her forefinger. He stood up, and she faced him, staring into his eyes. "We do not break our companions — or eat their hearts. Even when they do stupid things. You got that?"

The two of them stood face-to-face for several tense moments. Turesobei was prepared to give Motekeru an order immediately, if necessary. Motekeru moved forward ... and took Enashoma into a hug.

"You have a good soul," Motekeru told Enashoma.

She laughed. "Thank you, Motekeru."

The machine man leaned down and whispered something to her that Turesobei couldn't hear. Whatever it was it delighted Enashoma. She kissed him on his bronze cheek.

"We lost some supplies and blankets in our snow house," Iniru said as she sorted through the gear on the mounts. "Not a lot, but out here, every little thing counts."

As Turesobei and Narbenu sat with Kurine while everyone else worked on the double-sized snow house, he began to feel embarrassed about what he'd said and done. He sighed and shook his head.

"I really am sorry, Narbenu. I feel like an idiot now. I hope you won't think less of me."

Narbenu chuckled. "Aside from Motekeru and the dragon in you, it really wasn't a big deal."

"It wasn't?" Turesobei asked in surprise.

"Hardly the first time two boys got in a fight over a girl," Narbenu said. "Well, in this case a fight over two girls. These things happen, even when people aren't under stress. You're a good lad. Kemsu's a good lad. Don't worry about it."

"I guess ... I guess you're right."

Turesobei noticed then that his voice was a lot clearer. Adrenaline from the encounter with Kemsu had driven the toxin out of his system. He cast the *spell of the moon mirrors* successfully, and that made finishing the snow house go a lot faster. Once inside, to placate Narbenu's rigid standards, they strung two blankets through the middle. But Turesobei started out on the girls' side so he could tend to Kurine.

"We've got to get some of these clothes off her," he said. "She's sweating."

Enashoma removed all but Kurine's inner shirt and pants. The wound on her shoulder had turned purple and oozed pus that already smelled of decay. Acid had burned the skin all around it, and she had several burns on her arms as well, though those would heal without any problems.

"What do we do now?" Enashoma asked.

"We need to clean the wound and draw out as much poison as we can," Iniru said. She dipped a cloth in ice water and began washing the wound, holding her head away due to the smell.

Enashoma sponged Kurine's forehead, then she combed out Kurine's hair and braided it to the side away from the wound. "Are you sure there's not a cure?"

"There is one," Turesobei said, "in our world. But the plants I'd need only grow in the hotter regions of the rainforest. They'd never survive in this cold."

Enashoma choked back a sob. "So she ... she's going to —"

"We're not giving up hope," Turesobei said. "I can keep her alive long enough for us to reach the Forbidden Library. Hopefully, there we can find a way to cure her."

Turesobei meditated and tried to tame his emotions. Healing spells should never be done in anger or distress, or they wouldn't work well. And he needed this to work, or Kurine would die. But he was having a lot of trouble calming down. The attack and the fight with Kemsu had riled him up too much.

"Sobei, we're changing her shirt out for a dry one," Shoma said. "Close your eyes. No peeking."

As they changed Kurine's shirt, he thought back to his first meeting with her and how she wanted to see him naked and kept teasing him and even tried to sneak in a look. He could return the gesture now. He had the advantage. Not that he would, even if she were well. Of course, he was fairly certain she would've peeked at him, provided he wasn't dying. He smiled, and the anger left him.

"Okay," Iniru said. She frowned at him. "Why are you smiling like that?"

"Sobei," Shoma challenged. "You didn't peek, did you?"

"Of course not! I was just thinking about when I met Kurine. I was getting myself into a happier place mentally, so I can do a healing spell."

He chanted the *spell of poison drawing*, putting everything he could muster into it. A pulse of energy left his palms and formed a bubble over the wound on her shoulder. The tiny bubble filled up with all the toxin it could get out of her system. With something less deadly, especially if the spell had been cast immediately, that's all it would've taken. But this stuff raced into the system far too quickly to be completely drawn out, and in Kurine's case, it had had far too long to set in. With the bubble hovering over his hands, he went outside and tossed it away. Motekeru sealed them inside the snow house after that.

Turesobei caught his breath and cast the *spell of winter healing* on Kurine. He sagged at the end, but Iniru caught him.

Kurine's eyelids fluttered and opened. "Sobei," she whispered, grabbing his hand weakly.

"I'm here."

"You're ... okay?"

"I'm fine. We're all safe. We got away. The kagi poisoned you, but I'll get you cured."

"I know ... you will ... I know ... because ... you're amazing and ... you love ..."

Kurine drifted off into sleep.

Chapter Forty

A sumptuous feast of berries, goat cheese, and honeyed rice cakes lay spread out on a table beneath a cedar gazebo. Tea steamed in two bowls on opposite sides of the table, and in the center sat an iron kettle and a bowl of loose tea leaves. Sunlight sparkled on the stream that splashed over a rock fall and into the pond surrounding the tiny island on which the gazebo stood. A warm breeze carried the scents of jasmine and mimosa.

Dressed in his finest emerald robes, his hair tied neatly into a braid, his skin clean, his body rested and injury-free, Turesobei knelt at the table. He bit into a fresh strawberry, and as the sweet juice flowed over his tongue, he sighed contentedly. He'd never been so happy before ... so relaxed. He didn't have a single worry in his life.

Footsteps crunched delicately along a gravel path. Awasa, carrying an umbrella, her face lost in the shadows beneath it, stepped onto the bridge that led across the pond to the island. She wore robes of lilac, matching her deep, plum-colored eyes, over inner robes of palest pink. Ivory pins held her blue-black hair in a bun, save for two locks that framed her heart-shaped face. She stepped into the gazebo, folded up her umbrella, and set it to the side. She was taller than he had remembered. Her hips had widened; her breasts had grown larger. Funny, how on earth could he have forgotten those details? He had just seen her yesterday.

Turesobei stood and bowed. Awasa turned her pale face up toward him. Enticing, extraordinarily crimson lips peeled into a smile revealing sharp, bright teeth. She met his eyes and suppressed a giggle.

"May I?" she said, gesturing toward the table.

"Please."

She knelt across from him and bit, daintily, into a strawberry. The juice dribbled down her chin. She wiped it away with a laugh.

"Wasa, you are the most beautiful thing in all the world," he said.

"Silly," she replied, delightfully. "I am so happy, Sobei. Just think. This time tomorrow, we shall be married. And tomorrow night ..." Blushing, she took up her tea bowl and glanced coyly away.

"Married ..." he said, sipping a strong, almost bitter, black tea. "Tomorrow?"

"Tell me you haven't forgotten, Sobei ... how could you?"

"I — I don't know. Probably I ..."

"You've been working too hard?"

"Probably."

"Remember, you promised me you won't work as hard once we are married. Not the first year or two. Kahenan is still strong. He can manage without you there all the time."

Turesobei nodded and bit into a honeyed rice cake. It was almost heaven. "Oh, I've missed good food so much."

"Missed it? How could you miss it? What do you two eat in the tower?"

"Well ... I guess ... I guess if I've been eating poorly then I *have* been busy. Though I can't remember what we're working on." He was starting to feel disoriented. Why was he so forgetful? Had he overdone a spell and dazed himself?

"You know what I think?" Awasa said. "I think you have wedding jitters."

"Really?" He wasn't about to tell her, but that didn't make sense. He couldn't even recall having set a date for their wedding.

"Shoma told me so when we had tea this morning."

"You two are getting along?" he said with surprise.

"Of course we are. We're going to be sisters soon. Sobei, you know I love you, even if you are spacey sometimes."

Awasa finished her tea. She leaned forward to scoop fresh tea leaves into her bowl. Her robes fell open far enough to reveal a mark on her chest — a raised tattoo of an eight-pointed star the color of a dark bruise, a shade that matched her lilac robes and her deep plum eyes.

But since when had her eyes been that shade of purple? Why did she have a tattoo? That was hardly acceptable. How could she have gotten one?

Awasa sat back and gave him a curious stare. "Turesobei, are you all right?"

Now that he focused on her harder, he felt, like a whisper across his skin, a pulse of magic ... violent, chaotic. Awasa's skin was not the creamy pale he had first thought, but the pale of one lost forever in night, or one returned from the dead. And on her forehead, faint but growing more noticeable, was a tattoo that matched the one on her chest. Thick veins rose along her temples and forehead. Her features sharpened. Were those — were those specks of blood in her hair?

He opened his kenja-sight.

"Sobei!" she exclaimed as his eyes turned milky-white. "Don't! Please, don't."

Awasa blazed with sinister magic — magic that he knew, that he had fought — the magic of Barakaros the Warlock, leader of the Deadly Twelve. He chanted the *spell of dream breaking*, and Ninefold Awasa, the blood-smeared, terrifying witch that used to be his betrothed appeared across the table from him.

Turesobei staggered back as the full truth rushed back. Though how he'd come here and where this was, he had no idea. Smeared with blood and wearing torn clothes, Awasa snarled and leapt over the table. She tackled him and pinned him to the ground, squeezing her legs over his hips. He struggled to break free, but she was stronger than him. She licked her lips and fangs and ran claw-like fingernails along his check.

"Oh Sobei, I didn't want to have to do it this way, but if this how you'd like it ..."

"Like what?" he muttered.

"Why, being my thrall, of course. You are *mine*. You were mine *first*, long before that k'chasan slut. And now you will *always* be mine."

The gazebo within the elaborate garden faded away, leaving only crumbling ruins tucked into a vast wasteland beneath an empty, twilit sky. All was dust and shadow with not a single sign of life, except for himself and Awasa. The Shadowland ... a realm between Death and Life, Torment and Paradise, Oblivion and Existence — many-layered, infinite, inscrutable. The abode of nightmares and demons and stranger things still. This was the layer nearest the real world, draped over it like a burial shroud, accessible by ritual or dream. If he was in the Shadowland, he was trapped in a nightmare, though how he had been brought here, he had no idea.

Turesobei cast the simple *spell of waking*. Nothing happened.

"You cannot leave here until I let you," Awasa said, sneering. "And I won't let you until I've broken you."

"How did you do this?"

She pulled back her shirt to reveal a fresh cut over her heart. She drew her finger along it and bit her lip. "Our bond was never broken. I used it against you."

How utterly simple and devious. She had exploited their betrothal as a connection, and then strengthened it with — "Blood magic."

"You cannot break free," she said. "I know because Barakaros tells me it is so."

"The Warlock? He's possessing you?"

She slapped him hard across the face and busted his lip. "Don't insult me like that! I am my own self. The Warlock's ghost merely resides within me, whispering secrets, teaching me all the sorceries he knew."

If she had stolen into his dreams with blood magic, exploiting the bond between them, how could he break free? Banishing her wouldn't work, and waking himself had failed. Dream-breaking had already done all it could by destroying the illusion. Maybe if he hadn't shared tea with her in the dream ... that had given her more power here. He tried again to throw her off again, but it was no use. He could only think of one thing that might work, although it might just take him from the frying pan and into the fire.

"I am Chonda Turesobei!" he cried out at the top of his lungs. He didn't know what had summoned her before, so he continued on. "The heir of Chonda Lu! I bear the power of the Storm Dragon! I'm trapped in the Shadowland! Please, by Kaiwen Earth-Mother, I beg of you to help me."

"No one can help you here, no matter the name you use or who you call on." Awasa put a finger to his lips, lowered herself down, and bit his earlobe. "Anything you attract here will be as bad, or worse, than me."

"I know," he muttered.

And then she arrived, rolling in from the horizon like a night-black cloud — punctuated by eyes of searing flame, slowly filling the sky, darkening even the Shadowland. The shadow spoke, as it had before, with a voice both feminine and primal.

"You will let the Storm Dragon go, foolish girl."

"Never!" Awasa screamed at the flaming eyes above them. "He's mine alone!"

"You cannot have Naruwakiru. His fate lies with me. I have waited centuries ... millennia ... for our day of reckoning, here at last at the end of the world."

So this — whatever she was — was after the Storm Dragon? It had nothing to do with him *or* Chonda Lu. It thought he was Naruwakiru returned.

The flaming eyes plunged toward them. Awasa recoiled and reached toward her scabbard. But there was nothing there. A white-steel blade couldn't enter the Shadow-land. Awasa grabbed Turesobei by the collar and pulled him close. "I have touched your soul. You can never hide from me again."

Then, a moment before the eyes fell upon them, Awasa released him and disappeared.

Turesobei shot up, wide awake within the snow house. Everyone was kneeling around him with concern etched on their faces.

"Master, you've been screaming," Lu Bei said. "We couldn't wake you. I thought perhaps you were —"

"Everyone pack your things." Turesobei stood, shaking. "We have to go. Now!"

"But it's not dawn yet," Kemsu said. "And the sonoke —"

"Now!" Turesobei shouted.

Everyone looked at him, amazed, no doubt wondering if he'd lost it. But Lu Bei said, "Everyone do as Master says. Quickly."

Under light from the *spell of the moon mirrors*, they gathered their things and ran out to the sonoke. Motekeru wrapped Kurine in a blanket and held her in his arms as he climbed into the saddle. They rode with abandon along the coast, trusting that the sonoke would spot any dangers in the terrain and adjust in time. The sun rose. A strange feeling tweaked Turesobei's senses. He whipped around. On an inland rise loomed eighty-nine terrible shadows. The smallest one in the center bellowed a screeching war cry and charged. Light glinted off the white blade in her hand. The rest of the shadows followed her.

Chapter Forty-One

Ninefold Awasa and her eighty-eight yomon fell out of sight as the sonoke outpaced them, but the yomon were tireless. They would catch up.

"What do we do?" Zaiporo asked. "We can't outrun them. They'll catch us by nightfall."

Narbenu stroked the back of his sonoke's neck. "Sooner. The mounts will be dead by noon if we keep this pace. We've ridden them hard for two days with little rest between."

"Maybe we can find a cave and hide," Iniru said.

"Awasa touched my soul in the dream," Turesobei told her. "She found something to exploit ... a nice moment we once shared. An afternoon tea, the last one we had together before I left Ekaran, only this time without Shoma or our mothers there. Awasa used that and our bond of betrothal, and blood magic, to get to me in my dreams, pulling me into the Shadowland. Fortunately, she won't try that again. Unfortunately, she can now track me wherever I go. There's no escaping her. We're going to have to face them. So just ... just keep an eye out for any terrain that might give us an advantage."

But all the terrain was the same: barren coastline and low, rolling, inland hills. One by one, the sonoke tired out, slowing to a leisurely pace. Forcing another hour of sprinting would kill them. Turesobei closed his eyes and meditated, preparing himself to change into the Storm Dragon. Because maybe if he had his mind ready, he'd have more control and a chance at turning back into himself ... maybe ... eventually.

"Master!" Lu Bei shouted from where he soared above them. "There's a ship on the horizon!"

"Can we reach it?" Turesobei asked.

"Its sails are furled." Lu Bei looked behind them. "Oh demon droppings! I can see the yomon now, too. But I think we can reach the ship before them."

Two masts, taller than any Turesobei had ever seen on such a small vessel, towered over the flat-bottomed ship. Three skates, each made of a single piece of bone or ivory, stretched the length of the ship and were held in place with wood beams and rope. The skate-booms lifted the ship up off the ice, high enough that it could easily pass over a sonoke.

"What's the ship made of?" Turesobei asked. "I can tell it's not wood."

"The frame and the booms for the skates are wood," said Narbenu. "That's what makes ships so incredibly expensive. The rest is processed hide. The skates are made from the ribs of ice behemoths, and the hides come from their treated skins."

"The creatures would have to be huge!" Zaiporo said. "I hope we don't run into any."

"We won't," Narbenu said. "The ice behemoths roam the lands of the Northeast. The yomon are the ones who kill them, mostly for sport. Goronku scavengers follow behind them, bravely, and gather up the bones and hides to sell."

Fifteen men worked on the two-decked ship. It looked as if they were preparing to set sail. A sixteenth man up in the crow's nest spotted Turesobei and his companions and yelled out a warning. Immediately, half the crew gathered javelins, while the other half worked frantically to pull up the ship's two anchors and lower the square, battened sails.

"We're not going to reach them in time," Iniru said.

"I'll race ahead and talk to them," Narbenu said, "I think my mount's got a little burst left. The rest of you slow down. We need to earn their trust."

"Be careful." Turesobei glanced behind him and saw the faint outlines of the yomon. "And hurry. Lu Bei, pop into my pack. Let's keep you a secret and not alarm them with anything more unusual ..." Turesobei glanced at Motekeru "... than we already must."

Narbenu sprinted his mount, guiding it with his knees, his hands raised above his head. Luckily, the sailors didn't hurl any javelins at him. When he reached the ship, he began talking with one of them. Whatever he said must have worked, because they allowed Turesobei and his companions to close without attacking, though they still held javelins at the ready and looked nervous, especially when they spotted Motekeru, who sent a wave of murmurs amongst them. Turesobei twice heard someone utter the word *demon*. The skin around the human sailors' eyes was baojendari pale — the rest of their faces were covered with gray scarves — but they had physical builds like zaboko. Or it seemed so, anyway. It was impossible to accurately judge their sizes when they wore just as much clothing as Turesobei did.

Narbenu was bargaining with the lone, crimson-clad, incredibly rotund goronku who stood amongst the sailors.

"Captain Boki of the Falcon's Cry," Narbenu announced. "I have persuaded him not to kill us, nor leave just yet."

The ship groaned as the winds pulled at the half-lowered sails. The large stone anchors were beside the ship and were now one good tug from being lifted off the ice.

"Captain Boki," Turesobei said, bowing. "It's a pleasure to meet you."

"I won't say the same to you," Boki replied with a gruff lisp. He was about to say something else, but he spotted Motekeru. "Who — what — are you people?"

"We come from the land beyond the Winter Gate," Turesobei said. "Please, we are in a desperate hurry."

"There are too many of you," the captain replied. "It would weigh the ship down."

"I can pay you," Turesobei said. "Handsomely."

"We're already laden with cargo," the captain said. "We can't —" The captain's eyes widened, and he stammered unintelligible words.

"Yomon!" the sailor in the crow's nest shouted, having spotted them too. He must've been distracted by Motekeru to not have noticed the yomon sooner.

One man dropped to his knees and began praying to the Crimson Sun. Another cursed his fate. Most of them clutched to their weapons and trembled, murmuring amongst themselves. Tears rolled from the corners of a few sailors' eyes.

"We need to get out of here fast," Turesobei said.

"You — you have angered the yomon," Captain Boki stammered.

"Please. We must get to the Forbidden Library."

"If we help you, the yomon will hunt us as well," the captain said.

"Your ship could easily outpace them," Narbenu said.

The captain barked orders, and his men finished lowering the sails. "The Forbidden Library won't allow you in."

"You know how to reach it though, right?" Iniru said.

"Of course I do."

Turesobei pulled out a large bag filled with ivory, copper, jade, and pearls. He had three more bags like it, hidden. He opened the bag. "This is yours — all of it — if you take us."

Eyes narrowing, Captain Boki rubbed his hands together. "You understand I'm not responsible for the library taking you in?"

"I understand." Turesobei glanced back to see the yomon closing to within half a league. "We don't have much time."

The captain gestured toward Motekeru. "That thing safe?"

"He's my servant," Turesobei responded.

Boki closed his eyes and took in a deep breath. "Lower the gangplank! Make ready to sail!"

Moments later, the gangplank thumped onto the ice, and they rode their sonoke, one at a time, up the gangplank. The yomon were now a quarter-league away. Awasa rode on the shoulders of one. About a dozen of the yomon, who were faster than their brethren, raced ahead of the pack. The yomon carrying Awasa was not one of those.

"Who in Torment is that girl?" Boki said.

"Oh, that's my betrothed," Turesobei replied. "It's a long story."

"I should think so. Don't try to double-cross me, boy, or you'll regret it."

"I won't," Turesobei replied.

Narbenu whispered in Turesobei's ear. "Be on your guard. They'll try to rob us as soon as they get a chance. The only difference between a pirate and a trader out here is that a trader already has his hull full of goods to sell."

Once Turesobei and Narbenu rode onboard, Motekeru raised the gangplank by himself, a feat which greatly impressed the five sailors who were standing nearby, probably having intended to do that themselves.

The yomon charged down the beach. The sails puffed with a strong breeze. The sailors raised the anchors. The ship lurched forward on the ice ... and stopped. Then it jerked forward again ... and continued inching along.

"Sobei!" Iniru shouted, readying a spear. "The yomon!"

Snarling and brandishing their onyx-bladed weapons, the dozen yomon running ahead of the others neared the ship. Some were closer than others.

"Battle stations!" Boki cried.

All the sailors not working the sails gathered their javelins or drew out hand-axes. Boki gripped the wheel and bowed his head. "My greed's killed me. The winds are too weak, the ship's weighed down, and there's no time to dump the lot of you. It's over for me."

"Captain," Turesobei said. "Keep your hands on the wheel. You're about to get a big boost of speed. Be ready."

Turesobei began to chant a low-powered version of the *spell of spring's first gust,* a medium-level wind spell he'd had no need for since he'd learned more powerful ones at age twelve. Good thing he still remembered it.

Narbenu thumped the puzzled captain on the shoulder. "He's not kidding about being ready. He's a wizard. He's casting a wind spell."

"Sobei!" Awasa screeched, her voice shrill like fingernails scraped against a writing board. "Sobei, you're mine!"

While casting the spell, Turesobei watched as the first yomon came within range. Three sailors attacked it — two javelins struck one of the vermillion-skinned savages in the chest. The points barely punctured the skin, and the yomon swatted them away. The other eleven closed within range. The sailors unleashed a barrage of javelins, and it did almost nothing but annoy the yomon. Their skin was too thick for a normal weapon to damage them. One yomon got struck in the eye by a javelin, and the point went deep. It fell to its knees, howling mad, and ripped the javelin out. Then it picked itself up and staggered forward as if drunk.

Motekeru shoved sailors aside and stepped to the edge.

A yomon leapt toward the ship. Motekeru opened his mouth and spewed searing flames that engulfed the yomon but didn't stop its momentum. The scorched yomon crashed into him, its brush-like mustache on fire, its eyes melting. The two fell onto the deck. Motekeru raked the yomon with his claws, hit it with another burst of fire, and tossed it aside. The yomon turned into a pile of ash. A second yomon jumped on board, and with his axe, chopped the head off a sailor. Motekeru belched a sustained burst of flames and melted the yomon into oblivion. But then a third yomon barreled into Motekeru and pinned him.

Iniru stabbed a fourth yomon with her spear. The point slid in between its ribs ineffectively. She darted back as it swiped at her with a spiked club. A sailor then struck it in the back with an iron sword. The yomon spun, and smashed the sailor's head into a red mist. Narbenu charged in and chopped hard with his hafted axe, the blade slicing deep into the yomon's neck. It didn't kill the yomon, but the brute sagged to its knees, dropped its club, and grasped at its neck.

A fifth yomon climbed onboard, ignored three javelin strikes, and a sword-strike, and shouldered into Narbenu, knocking him across the ship. Kemsu stabbed it in the stomach, but the yomon grabbed the spear, ripped it from Kemsu's hand, and clubbed him with it, knocking him flat. It raised its club to attack Kemsu, but Iniru darted in and struck it with her spear, nicking it on the chin, which was just enough to distract it into turning away from Kemsu and toward her.

Motekeru incinerated the yomon who had tackled him. He turned toward the fifth yomon and burned it to ashes before it could hit Iniru. But this time, the flame spluttered a bit at the end. Motekeru was using the most heat he could manage, Turesobei could feel it all the way across the ship. It was fortunate the ship wasn't on fire. He feared Motekeru wasn't going to be able to manage many more bursts like that.

Six more yomon were only paces away from the ship, and the other seventy-six yomon and Awasa weren't all that far behind. A sixth yomon jumped up and tore into three sailors, wounding them and knocking them back. As soon as they were clear, Motekeru hit the yomon with a weakened spurt of fire and shouldered into it, knocking it back onto the ice, where it writhed in agony, grasping at its face.

At last, Turesobei completed the spell.

Blasted directly by the wind, the sails popped taut. The masts creaked under the strain.

A seventh yomon leapt toward the ship as it rocketed forward, skates screaming on the ice. Everyone onboard staggered backward. The savage demon missed the ship, and fell belly-first onto the ice.

Chapter Forty-Two

The keening skates sliced across the ice as the ship zoomed along, powered by Turesobei's wind spell. In the distance, Awasa howled with rage, but her voice soon faded away.

"We've got two dead, Captain!" a sailor shouted. "Three injured, one's in bad shape."

Captain Boki shut his eyes and sighed. "Patch up the wounded, first mate. Patch them up. It's all we can do."

"And the dead, sir?"

"We can't stop now. Store the bodies for later burial. Mop the deck."

"Yes, Captain."

Bile rose into Turesobei's throat as he stared trancelike at the two headless bodies. Sticky crimson droplets were freezing onto the deck as the lifeless eyes from one severed head stared accusatorily at him. The other head was nothing but a splatter of crimson gore and white matter splattered across the deck and many of the sailors. Motekeru was wiping the mess off his body.

Enashoma buried her head in Zaiporo's chest, turning away from the dead men. Turesobei wished he could turn away, but he couldn't. He choked back a sob, and then nearly vomited. Those two men were dead because of him. Men who probably had families who loved them and depended on them. This was his fault. If he hadn't come to this ship, those two sailors would still be alive. This wasn't their fight. He should never have endangered these innocent people. Kemsu was right. Everyone he encountered was in danger; everyone one around him suffered.

Iniru knelt beside Kemsu and put her fingers on his neck to check his pulse, while Motekeru helped Narbenu to his feet.

The goronku scout groaned miserably. "I'll be okay. Just feel like I've been run over by a sonoke ... or three. I've never been hit that hard in my life. Surprised it didn't just punch right through me. Kemsu? How is he?"

"Knocked out," Iniru said. "His pulse is good. I think he's going to be all right." She looked up at Turesobei. "You okay?"

He didn't respond. He merely stared, blankly, as the healthy sailors bandaged their wounded brethren and pulled the two bodies together, side-by-side.

"Sobei?" Zaiporo said. "Something wrong?"

The ship began to slow.

Captain Boki slapped Turesobei on the shoulder. "Hey, is the wind supposed to be giving out on us already?"

Turesobei snapped out of his trance. "What? No. Sorry. I let my focus go. My mind was too far from the spell." This wasn't a spell he could cast and let work on its own. Like most spells of its nature, it had to be maintained. The only way for it to be otherwise would be to let the surrounding air kenja rush into it uncontrolled, which wasn't an option in the Ancient Cold and Deep. As he restored a bit of focus to the magic, the winds picked up again and the ship's speed increased.

Captain Boki followed Turesobei's stare. "Never seen a dead man before, eh?"

"I have. My father and our bodyguards, as well as bandits and others ... I've even killed three men myself." He thought of the charred Gawo scouts he'd blasted with the *spell of heaven's wrath*. "But I did that in self-defense. These men ... their deaths are on me. I got you involved in my troubles. This wasn't their fight. It was mine alone. They had nothing to do with it, and now —"

"Let it go," Captain Boki said. "Just let it go."

"But if I hadn't asked you for help ..."

"You would've died on that beach. That's life. You took a risk, and so did I. Don't forget the part my greed played in this. My greed cost me two men — two good men. And I'll toast their names when I get to port and mourn them as I should. But this is a violent world. People die. There's no preventing that. You move on. And this ain't the first two men the yomon have ever killed, you know." He nodded toward Motekeru. "Your beast there killed several yomon. I didn't even know they could be killed. Any fight that rids this world of a few yomon is a good fight, no matter the cost. I'd have been okay myself, dying in a fight where a few yomon got what's owed them. Don't mourn the dead, just worry about the living."

Turesobei nodded and said dully, "I can heal the three wounded men with magic, though I won't be able to do it until I take a break from the wind spell."

Motekeru stomped over to join them. "They died nobly. Honor their deaths. That is all we can do."

"I'll try." He'd try not to let it affect him, though like with Awasa, what happened here would continue to haunt him. But he had to control his emotions; the others needed him. "You did well, Motekeru. I noticed your fire sputtering there at the end, though. All used up?"

"Not entirely, master. I can do maybe a few dozen more short bursts that could hurt a yomon, but not any strong enough to kill one."

Once the wounded sailors were bandaged, Turesobei dropped the wind spell and healed each of them, as well as Kemsu, who was concussed, and Narbenu, who had suffered several cracked ribs and had a dark bruise expanding beneath the fur on his belly. The ship had slowed to a crawl, so once he was done healing the injured, he cast the wind spell again.

Enashoma, Zaiporo, and Iniru sat in the prow. Shoma didn't want to see the bodies or the blood being swept from the deck. Motekeru helped the sailors lead the sonoke below deck into the cargo hold.

The Glass Sea proved smooth with few obstacles to impede their path. From time to time, the captain steered to avoid tall rocks or large snowdrifts, but that seemed easy enough and uncommon.

"That spell, can you teach me to do that?" Captain Boki asked.

"Sorry." Exhausted from lack of sleep, running, and casting too many spells, Turesobei plopped, groaning, onto a nearby canvas sack full of what he guessed were furs. "You have to be of the same descent that I am and have studied for years."

"That's too bad. Sure would be useful. How long can you keep this up?"

"It's a simple spell, and on your world there's plenty of energy to draw on. Normally, I could keep it going all day, but I had a rough night."

"I can see that," the captain said. "You all look terrible."

"Will I need to keep the ship going with the spell the whole time?"

"When the winds are at normal strength for this season, we will move," said Captain Boki, "but slowly. Not much faster than your mounts could go. The ship really is overburdened now. The winds are usually stronger than this, though. They'll pick up soon."

"In that case, I'll try to keep the spell active for three more hours to give us a lead over the yomon, then I'll get some rest. After that, I'll keep doing the spell as much as I can to keep us well ahead of the yomon."

"What's wrong with the goronku girl?" Captain Boki asked, peering at Kurine, whom they had lain out on top of some blankets alongside Narbenu and Kemsu. During the battle, she and the still-recovering hounds had remained strapped into the saddles.

"An orugukagi bit her," Turesobei replied, "day before yesterday."

Boki shook his head and tut-tutted. "Poor thing. You know she's going to die, right? Honestly, I can't believe she's still alive."

"I cast a healing spell on her to slow the advance of the poison."

"But there's no cure," Captain Boki responded.

"There is on my world," Turesobei said.

"You think she'll last long enough for you to make it back there?"

"I'm not sure we can get back," Turesobei replied. "I'm hoping I can find a cure at the Forbidden Library. I think I've slowed it enough that she'll live for a week. That should give us time to get there, right?"

"We can reach the Forbidden Library in four days, maybe less with that wind spell of yours. But I don't see any way they'll let you in. They don't let anyone in. It's ... well ... forbidden."

"I'm hoping that since we're so unusual they'll let us in."

The captain nodded, but said nothing else about it. "First Mate, the deck's too crowded. Make room in the cargo hold to fit these people and their gear. The mounts too, if you can manage."

"How, captain?"

"I don't know. Cram everything in, stack it high as it'll go. Throw the cheap hides overboard. Whatever it takes."

While Turesobei focused on maintaining the spell, letting himself drift off into a state that was almost meditative, the sailors cleared space and tossed some of the hides overboard. Then they escorted his companions and their sonoke below, except Motekeru who stayed above.

"You're going to have clean up after your beasts," Boki said. "I'm not scooping sonoke crap. I want it spotless down there."

Iniru returned to the deck and tapped Turesobei on the shoulder. "Scoot over and give me some of that sack. The deck's wet and cold."

"We just scraped it this morning," Boki said. "Ices over, you know."

Turesobei shifted to share the canvas bag with her. "Is it warm down below?"

"Relatively. There's no wind. We stretched out the furs, and we're fit snugly in there. But it's not as nice as a snow house."

Turesobei chuckled. "Never thought I'd think of a house made of blocks of ice as a luxury."

"Kurine's fever's down for now. Kemsu's watching her. He's still pretty upset. I told Shoma and Zaiporo to get some rest."

"Do you think Kemsu's in love with Kurine?" Turesobei asked.

Iniru shrugged. "They were best friends as children, and then they couldn't be together anymore. I think maybe they were both in love, or close to it, at one time. Given their ages and history, they probably thought they'd end up together when they were growing up. But then Kemsu —"

"Became a slave," Turesobei said. "I'm going to make sure Narbenu gives Kemsu his freedom when we're done."

Iniru laughed. "You're funny, you know. Always fighting battles to help other people."

"I don't see what's funny about it. He should be free."

"I agree completely, but you don't even like Kemsu."

"He's ... he's ... okay."

"I bet Kemsu does still love her. No wonder you two don't get along."

"Maybe, and he's also jealous of me because he likes you, too."

Iniru nodded. "You have everything he doesn't. Freedom, Kurine, me ... well, maybe me."

"If I don't screw it up some more. Why don't you get some rest, Niru?"

"I'll stay up with you," she said. "You had a rough night. And besides, we really haven't gotten to spend much time alone together."

"I know! I braved unimaginable dangers to rescue you. And now, I hardly get to see you. It really isn't fair."

"And don't forget how you got engaged to another girl. Seriously, how do you manage to get into so much trouble?"

"I don't know. My life used to be exceedingly boring and then ... I'll tell you what

187

happened. Lu Bei showed up. Nonstop chaos since then." He expected a response from the fetch, but then remembered he'd told Lu Bei to stay out of sight.

"He *is* a troublemaker," Iniru said. "And you're really, really bad with girls."

"I'm not bad at trying to marry them! Just all that other stuff. Imagine how hard it'd be for you to cast a spell."

"Okay ..."

"Well, that's girls for me."

"But it can't be that bad."

"Oh yes it can. I don't understand any of you. Not one bit."

For a long time, they sat together quietly, just being together. Every so often, he'd smile at her, and she'd smile back. Eventually, Captain Boki started talking, perhaps because he thought they were bored.

"You seem unused to the ship," he said. "You don't have ships on your side of the gate?"

"We don't have all this ice," Turesobei said. "But we have ships, without skates. They sail on water."

"Water?" the captain said, astonished. "Melted ice? Unbelievable."

"What I find unbelievable is a creature with such big bones that you could use them as skates," Turesobei said. "It's amazing."

"The skates have to be honed and lacquered first," the captain said. "And they work best if we stop every three days to oil and polish them, though you can go a lot longer than that. We'd just finished the procedure when you came upon us."

"What's your cargo?" Turesobei said.

"Most of it's preserved meat and furs. We have a little wood and iron to trade, rope and bone knives. We're taking it to the Far West. It's faster to sail there than travel by land. Safer too ... but that's only because we're moving faster."

Turesobei tapped his foot against the stretched hide that covered the deck, overlaying the wood frame. The hide was pulled so taut that it felt almost as solid as wood and a bit like walking over a reed mat, only with a little bounce to it.

"In our world ships are made entirely from wood," Turesobei said. "This ship looks like half of it is made from hides."

Captain Boki's hands dropped from the wheel. "Entirely of wood? The expense!"

"We have huge forests of trees that stretch for miles and miles."

Iniru sighed, probably thinking of home.

"And these ships of wood aren't slow, and they don't sink in the water?"

"If they weren't wood, they *would* sink," Turesobei said, "and ships of comparable size are faster than your ship."

Boki fell silent, though every now and then he would murmur in astonishment and shake his head.

An hour later, Turesobei grew tired at last. "I've got to get some rest." He released the spell, and the ship slowed dramatically, but it did keep moving under the breeze, at about the same speed as a sonoke, like Boki said.

Following Iniru, Turesobei went down a ladder into the hold and squeezed past the sonoke and into a tiny, cramped space. Sacks filled with goods were piled high all around. Turesobei sank down beside Enashoma and the hounds and was asleep before Iniru could even sit.

Thankfully, no further nightmares of Awasa or the shadowy demon plagued him. Not meaning to, he slept nearly twelve hours. At first, he was mad that no one woke him, but with a surge of natural strong winds, the ship had moved steadily, and he was forced to admit that without the rest, he'd be in no shape to help out with magic in a pinch.

Lu Bei woke up as well. "Should I remain out of sight, master?"

"I think it's still wise. We don't know these people."

"Master, the men who died ... I know how that makes you feel. You can't afford to blame yourself. You didn't mean for that to happen. We won, and only two were lost."

"I know. It's just ... those two won't be the last. I fear more innocents like them and Kurine will die. And if we survive ourselves and make it back, I'll be a weapon. The clan will use me to kill enemy soldiers. Innocents will die, too. I don't want this. I don't want *any* of it."

Lu Bei patted him on the hand. "I know, master. I know. You're a good man."

"You think I'm a man and not a boy?"

"Master, from the moment you took in the Storm Dragon energy, willingly sacrificing yourself to save tens of thousands of people, I have considered you a man."

"I'm going to go up and get some fresh air."

Turesobei walked out alone onto the deck. It was night. Avida, the bright moon, was nearly full, though it was only a little more than half as bright in this world as it was at home.

"No clouds," Captain Boki said, having noticed him looking up at the moon. "Lucky break for us. We couldn't have sailed this fast in the dark otherwise. Too dangerous."

"Do you need more light? I have a spell that can give you that."

"You're full of surprises, aren't you?"

"You have no idea," Turesobei said. I'm even full of surprises that I have trouble thinking about or knowing at all.

The captain chewed on his lip. "Why are the yomon after you? Those jewels you got stolen from them or something?"

"Oh, I wish it were that simple. I told you the witch girl leading them was my betrothed, right? She's angry at me, and I stopped the yomon from invading my world."

"You did mention the witch girl was betrothed to you ..." Captain Boki jerked his head toward the cargo hold. "But someone else told me the dying girl was your intended."

"Well, yeah. She's my second one."

"And the girl what was out here with you earlier? She your intended too?"

"Oh no," Turesobei said, chuckling. "That's my girlfriend. Sort of. I think."

The captain shook his head. "You sure I can't learn magic? Because it really seems to be working for you."

189

Over the next three days, they stayed watchful, in case Captain Boki attempted to rob them, but he didn't make a move. Even if he'd originally planned to, seeing Motekeru in action had probably scared him off that course of action. When they weren't keeping watch, they rested as much as possible, huddling together in the cramped cargo hold. Even though it was colder, after weeks of riding and adventure, it was nice to lie around and avoid the saddle. Narbenu didn't even worry about them mingling much, though he had placed sacks of furs in a line to make a section for the boys and a section for the girls.

Turesobei knelt over Kurine and stroked her feverish brow. "Hang in there. Just a few more days."

The hounds, their injuries now healed, slept nestled beside her.

Kemsu joined him. "Is she going to make it?"

"If they have a cure at the Forbidden Library, then yes, I think so."

"And if they don't?" Kemsu said.

"They will have a cure. I'm sure of it."

"I'm worried she won't make it that long," Kemsu said.

"I can cast another healing on her tomorrow. It will buy her more time. She's very strong. I think most people would've died already."

"She's always been strong," Kemsu said.

"You love her, don't you?" Turesobei asked, the words spewing suddenly out of his mouth.

"Yeah ... I mean, I used to." Kemsu surprised him by answering honestly. "Now ... I don't know. I'd hoped to win my freedom somehow before she found someone else. I can't really blame her for moving on. It's just hard because ..." He sighed, his shoulders slumping dejectedly. "Kurine and I had been friends — more than friends — for a very long time. When we were kids, we'd talk about getting married someday. You know how you do."

"I don't, actually. I was betrothed to Awasa when I was three years old and she was two. She hated me until a few months ago. It's a lot like slavery, really. Women in my society don't have much freedom, not like they do here."

"That's why your sister left with Zaiporo, isn't it?"

"Basically. I think they chose the wrong traveling companion, though. Look, I'm sorry about me and Kurine. Honestly."

"Well, you didn't intend it. And I *am* a slave. Like I said, what could she do? I don't think she ever forgave me for becoming a slave."

"You had a choice?"

"The alternative was that I could forfeit everything my father owned and be exiled from my people. So it wasn't much of a choice. But I think she had this dream that she'd run away with me when I was exiled. Like your sister and Zaiporo." Kemsu looked away, nervously. "Look, if Kurine survives and you and her ... I mean ... about Iniru ... you can't marry two women, so if I —"

"If you're about to ask me if I would be okay with you pursuing Iniru, the answer is no. Besides, it doesn't really matter."

"Why is that?"

"Because she's the one that gets to pick, not you or me."

Chapter Forty-Three

A sailor opened the hatch leading down to the hold and poked his head in. "Captain Boki says you'll want to come up now."

All of them were asleep except Motekeru and Turesobei. He was sitting with Kurine, holding her hand, hoping it would bring her comfort. Her fever was getting worse, even though he'd just given her another healing spell. She'd be dead before he could give her another.

"Are we there?" Turesobei asked.

"Nearly," the sailor replied as the others were sitting up, rubbing their eyes, and yawning. "You'll want to see."

Motekeru knelt beside Kurine. "I will watch the girl."

Turesobei woke his companions, and they all climbed the ladder and joined Captain Boki on the foredeck. He shouted an order to trim the sails. The ship slowed.

In the distance appeared the faint outline of what looked like a fortress on an island rising up out of the Glass Sea. From this far away, it was hard to tell how big it was, but Turesobei thought it must be nearly as large as the Palace of the High King in Batsa, the capital of Batsakun, his homeland. To the starboard side, a ship appeared. From its mast flew a crimson flag that at first Turesobei thought sparkled in the sun, but as the ship drew closer, he could tell the flag actually glowed. It was a subtle magic in a world in which he had not seen any magic so far.

"What does the glowing flag mean?" he asked.

"They have a license to trade with the Forbidden Library," said Boki wistfully. "Unlike me, they can sail to the island and make port. Very few captains have such a commission, but those who do are famously wealthy. The Forbidden Library pays well for the finest cargo, and not even the most desperate pirates will attack a ship flying that banner. Those that did in the past ... it was said that strange beings hunted them down and killed them, leaving a messy warning to all others."

"And no one in this world can fake the glowing flag," said Turesobei, "which is convenient."

"Indeed," Boki replied. "I applied once through an intermediary for a trading permit but was turned down."

The trade ship, traveling at full speed away from the library, passed them.

The Forbidden Library came into full view: three dome-capped buildings linked together, sitting atop a flattened hill on a tiny island. A massive, cylindrical building was in the middle, taking up most of the hilltop. The thinnest building towered over it to one side, while on the other side was a short building a little bigger around. The domes appeared to be made of a shiny black stone, obsidian perhaps, while the rest of the buildings were made of a common gray stone etched with patterns Turesobei couldn't make out from this distance.

Sailors rolled up the last of the sails and tossed the anchors overboard. The ship groaned to a halt. Turesobei handed the bag of pearls, gems, and coins to the captain. Boki immediately divided jade coins amongst his crew and promised more wealth after he could evaluate the gems.

"Can't have a mutiny," he muttered to Turesobei. "Sorry I couldn't take you all the way in, but I'd like to avoid execution today."

Turesobei bowed. "Thank you for taking us as far as you could, Captain Boki. I am deeply sorry for the two men killed by the yomon. The fault was mine."

"We live in a dangerous world," Boki responded. "All my men know that."

"Nevertheless, please give a share of the money I paid you to their families."

"I always do."

Turesobei pulled out the pouch of coins Kurine's father had given her as a dowry. He'd added as many gems as it could hold to it. "And split this between their families as well. I hold it on your honor that you do so."

"On my honor," the captain replied solemnly. Turesobei trusted him to do so. This gesture was the best he could do.

"Farewell, Captain Boki."

"I fear you are marching to your death," Captain Boki said, "but I wish you well and hope you find a way back to your world."

And with that, Turesobei and his companions led their sonoke down the gangplank and out onto the ice. They strapped Kurine into one of the saddles. She woke halfway for a moment.

"Sobei ... are we ... in your world?"

"Not yet," he replied. He hoped she wouldn't have to go back to Okoro to be cured. He was already afraid she planned on going back with him no matter what. She needed to stay in her world with her own people. She didn't deserve to be the only goronku in Okoro.

"That's ... that's too ..."

She fell back into her coma. Iniru climbed into the saddle behind Kurine. Turesobei waved to the Falcon's Cry as it pulled away. Then they turned and rode toward the Forbidden Library.

Chapter Forty-Four

As they neared the island, Turesobei realized that from a distance he had underestimated the size of the Forbidden Library. The main building dwarfed the High King's Palace in Batsa and was easily three times bigger. The thin tower soared higher than Chonda Tower, the Monolith of Sooku, and the High Wizard's Tower combined. Even the smallest library building dwarfed everything back home in Ekaran.

A tiny village hugged the eastern coastline, as if its presence were barely allowed. A ship flying a glowing banner docked there. Steep cliffs blocked in the western side of the island. The southern end sloped upward to the library, intersecting a long staircase that climbed to a set of massive doors. Unfortunately, the climb was too steep for the sonoke.

Since the southern end was closest, that's where they headed, intending to ride along the coast to the village. The sonoke would get better traction on the frozen beach than on the slick ice of the Glass Sea.

Lu Bei flew overhead and announced that he didn't see anyone, but when they reached the island, a tall figure suddenly appeared out of nowhere. The being, whoever or whatever it was, wore a charcoal-colored cloak with a deep hood that entirely hid its features. The tips of blue-and-white feathers poked out from under the hooded cloak. Turesobei guessed the figure wore a second, feathered cloak like Shaman Eira's underneath. A steel rod no longer than Turesobei's forearm hung in a sheath from the being's belt. What purpose could that serve? It was too short to be a club, and it didn't have a blade.

Turesobei stopped his sonoke and started to speak a greeting, but the being held up a hand and said in a lyrical yet powerful voice:

"You do not have permission to step foot on the Great Isle. We do not allow visitors ..." he said, glancing at Motekeru and Lu Bei "... of any kind. You must leave at —" He paused, and with his hooded head cocked to one side, he stared long and hard at Turesobei. "You wear a kavaru."

"Yes, I do." Turesobei bowed. "I am Chonda Turesobei. Except for the three goronku with us, my companions and I come from Okoro, the world beyond the Winter Gate. We have come seeking a way back to our world. Your library is our only hope. And Kurine, my betrothed, she was poisoned. She needs help. Soon."

The cloaked figure stepped forward and peered at Turesobei's kavaru. "Chonda

Turesobei?"

"This is the kavaru of my ancestor Chonda Lu."

"Master speaks the truth," Lu Bei said.

"The Winter Child opened the gate for us," Turesobei explained, "but she died on this side, and the gate closed on us. We were fighting to stop the yomon from coming into our world and unleashing destruction and eternal winter. The yomon pursue us even now. They're probably not far behind."

"The yomon are of no concern to us," the being said. "Our protocol normally forbids me from allowing you in. However, this is a highly unique and unforeseen situation. I will allow you an audience with the Great Librarian. If she accepts your cause on merit, she will argue your case before the Gathering. If they do not decide in your favor, you will be allowed to leave here. But I must warn you, if the Great Librarian will not take up your cause and argue your case, death will be meted out upon you for trespassing. This *is* the most likely result."

Turesobei gulped as several of his companions breathed in sharply.

"If you are not willing to take that risk ..."

"Our alternative is to face the yomon," Turesobei said, "and to have no chance at returning to our world. We accept."

Iniru urged her mount forward a few paces. "Wait. I think Turesobei may be getting ahead of himself. Before we put our lives on the line, could you tell us if such a way back exists?"

The figure nodded. "There is a way ... of sorts. But that doesn't mean you'll be allowed to take it. And if you are given the chance, I highly doubt you'll succeed."

"You'd be surprised what we can do," Iniru said.

"We accept," Turesobei said.

"What's your name?" Enashoma asked. "You never said."

"I have two names," the being replied. "One that you cannot pronounce and one that I would never share with a stranger. You may call me by my title. I am the Keeper of the Shores."

The guardian walked toward the warehouse. "Follow me."

He led them to the edge of the village where a group of men in heavy winter clothing met them. The men bowed before the guardian.

"These men will see that your mounts are cared for," said the Keeper of the Shores. "Your effects will be brought up if the Great Librarian allows you to stay. No harm will come to your things, and nothing will be stolen. If your cause is not accepted and you are executed, your things shall be donated to the villagers."

Turesobei and his companions dismounted, and the men silently took the mounts.

"What about our weapons?" Iniru asked. "Should we leave them behind?"

"I have no concern for any weapons you carry," the guardian told her. "None here will. But the Great Librarian and my brethren might consider the presence of weapons to be impolite."

And so, they also handed over their weapons to the villagers.

"Thank you," Turesobei told the men. The men nodded in acknowledgement, but said nothing as they left with the mounts.

"The humans who live in the village," said Turesobei, "are they allowed in the library?"

"No one has been allowed inside except those of us who guard it in seven centuries. And the last three people we did allow in, we executed within a day."

"Did they try to steal something?" Zaiporo ventured.

"No," the guardian replied casually. "After reflection, the Great Librarian decided their causes lacked sufficient merit."

Everyone tensed; worry knotted in Turesobei's stomach. The Keeper of the Shores wasn't the least concerned about the yomon. If the Great Librarian rejected their cause and they had to fight their way out, would even the Storm Dragon be enough?

Motekeru lifted Kurine and cradled her in his arms.

"We are ready," Turesobei said.

Enashoma tugged his sleeve. "Sobei, don't you think you maybe should ask Narbenu and Kemsu if they want to risk their lives by entering the library? It might be better for them to buy passage out on one of the trade ships. They could make their way past the yomon safely. The yomon wouldn't even know, and they wouldn't care about them. Awasa only wants you."

"Could these two goronku leave the island on one of the ships?" Turesobei asked the guardian. "It's not too late for them to leave, is it?"

"The commitment is made once you step foot in the library. There will be no going back after that point."

"I'm not turning back now," Kemsu said. "I didn't come this far for nothing."

"And what if I say otherwise?" Narbenu asked.

"Say otherwise all you want," Kemsu replied, facing his master. "I'm going forward. Turesobei will see us through this, right? That's what everyone always says anyway. Besides, I'm not leaving Kurine. She's my oldest friend, and they might have to take her to their world. I'm not going to let her be the only goronku there."

Lips pinched tightly together, Narbenu nodded. "I can respect that, even if I don't like your insolence. Do not forget you belong to me still." With a sigh, Narbenu relaxed his posture. "But it doesn't matter, because I'm coming too."

"You really don't have to go on, either of you," Turesobei said. "We can manage without you now. You've done your part. You got us this far and risked your lives for us. We are honored and indebted to you and cannot ask for more. In fact, I can give you most of the money we got from the nozakami-ga's cave to repay your people when you return."

"No," Kemsu said flatly. "I'm staying with you. At least until Kurine's well and you return home."

"I've faced death before," Narbenu said. "Quite a lot since I met you, Turesobei. I battled a yomon and survived. I've seen a magic tree growing upside down and escaped its guardians. And now I've reached the legendary Forbidden Library. I can go in and see

196

wonders none of my people have ever seen. I may even live to return and tell the tale. No, I'm going on. I'm finishing my grand adventure. I think it's well worth the risk."

"If that's what you want," Turesobei said, sadly. He'd seen enough adventure and wonder to not think it was worth trading the comforts of a simple life without danger. Maybe he wasn't much like his father, after all.

"Follow me," the Keeper of the Shores said, and he led them up a winding path toward the Forbidden Library.

A narrow staircase with steps dusted by snow and coated with ice rose before them. Only the single handrail to one side made Turesobei think they stood a chance of climbing up it successfully.

Suddenly, his vision darkened. The pinkish afternoon sky deepened to blood-red. Shadows lengthened unnaturally, and the island turned a deep gray like the terrain within the Shadowland. Turesobei looked to his companions, but they were nowhere to be seen.

A cloud like a shadow cast by the moon appeared, coiling around the library like an enormous snake. Blazing eyes opened within the shadow as it stretched down toward him.

"I knew you would come to me one day," said a voice, rumbling like thunder within the cloud. "You and I shall have our reckoning, Storm Dragon."

Turesobei collapsed to his knees as the shadow and the blazing eyes crashed in on him. A hand clutched his shoulder. The world returned to normal. The shadow was gone. His companions once again stood around him.

The Keeper of the Shores released his grip from Turesobei's shoulder. "The nightmare cannot hurt you. And it will not visit you again. You are under my protection."

"Thank you," Turesobei said. "What was it?"

"Your doom, should the Gathering grant your wish." The guardian stepped onto the staircase and offered no further explanation. Turesobei didn't even bother to ask. He'd find out soon enough.

"Are you okay?" Enashoma asked.

"I'm fine. Don't worry about it."

"What was it?" Zaiporo asked.

"I don't want to talk about it right now."

Iniru sighed. "You've been hiding something from us, haven't you?"

"Just a nightmare I've had a few times since we came here. I didn't think it was anything more than that until ... now." He decided not to explain about calling on the shadow in the nightmare Awasa had lured him into.

Enashoma slapped him on the arm. "Jerk. Stop lying, and stop hiding things."

"It's not something you could've helped me with."

"What if something happened and we needed to know?" Iniru demanded.

"Then Lu Bei could tell you," Turesobei replied.

Everyone turned toward Lu Bei, and he held his hands up. "Don't look at me like that! I can't tell you private things unless Master allows it."

"Since when has that ever stopped you unless you were given a direct order?" Iniru said.

Lu Bei ducked his head. "Well ... I mean ... you know ... I ... I can't win here."

"Let it go," Motekeru said. "Arguing accomplishes nothing."

No one wanted to disagree with Motekeru, for which Turesobei was thankful. He didn't feel bad about not telling them. What was the point of worrying them any further, especially about something he still didn't understand?

Turesobei stepped onto the staircase, and his foot immediately slipped across the smooth, ice-slicked stone, despite the treads on his boots. He stepped again, planting his foot firmly and grabbing the rail. The treads crunched against the ice and only barely held. The Keeper stepped lightly, completely unaffected by the ice.

"Careful everyone," Narbenu said, slipping as he stepped up beside Turesobei, who reached out a hand to steady him. "We'd better go up single-file and use the handrail."

"Rig, Ohma," Turesobei said, and the two amber wolfhounds rushed forward. "Climb up." The hounds started onto the stairs and slid around, completely unable to gain purchase. "That's enough, and what I figured. Stop, both of you. Someone will have to carry them."

Everyone looked at one another and then at the stretch of what was surely a thousand steps or more going up, winding treacherously. Motekeru could have done it, but he already had Kurine.

"We'll have to fashion some sort of device to carry them," Narbenu said. "But for that we would need our packs."

From where he stood waiting, a dozen steps up, the Keeper of the Shores made a strange sound, almost like a disgruntled crow cawing. He walked down, picked up the wolfhounds, tucked one under each arm, and continued up without a word. Turesobei restrained a smile and avoided looking at the others. He could feel Enashoma about to burst with a giggle and didn't want to set her off.

Thighs burning and feet sliding, they climbed the staircase. Fortunately, Motekeru didn't have any trouble, despite carrying Kurine. He had spikes on the toes and heels of his feet, and his weight jammed them deep into the ice. The rest of them were not so lucky, and they treaded slowly. Lu Bei darted between them all, catching anyone who started to slip by their sleeves to make sure they didn't lose their handhold.

An hour later, they reached the flattened top of the island. A flagstone path led to an enormous doorway. Standing in front of the stone double doors were two more hooded beings like the Keeper of the Shores, their faces entirely hidden. They also carried rods at their waists. Turesobei opened his kenja-sight for just a moment. The rods emanated a strong combination of storm and fire kenja. It was unlike anything he'd ever seen. And from the library beyond them flowed every sort of kenja imaginable. Yet under it all, deep within, lay shadow. He dropped the kenja-sight.

"I have granted them an audience," the Keeper of the Shores announced to his comrades.

Turesobei and his companions bowed. In response, the guards at the door cocked their heads strangely, as if considering them. Then they turned and pulled open the great doors as if they weighed nothing.

Chapter Forty-Five

Turesobei followed the Keeper of the Shores into the library's cool, pervasive silence. The scents of decaying paper and lacquered wood hung heavy in the air. Only a few lanterns flickered overhead. Each strike of Turesobei's boots against the polished marble floor reverberated through the short hallway and echoed into the cavernous central chamber ahead, and as his companions entered behind him, the noise increased to a rattling thunder. The Keeper snapped his head around and pointed at a set of shelves intended for storing shoes.

"Quiet," the guardian ordered.

They removed their boots and stored them on the shelves lining the wall. They started forward, but Motekeru's clawed toes and heels still clanked against the marble. The Keeper stopped, his spine erect, but before he could turn around, Turesobei whispered: "I'll take care of it ... unless you have a rule against me using magic here."

"No one here shall stop you from using benign magic."

Turesobei cast the *spell of the silent footfall* and targeted Motekeru's feet. The simple spell used air kenja, so he could make it last for hours, especially since he was focusing it on such a small target. Motekeru took a few muffled footsteps, and nodded. They continued into the main chamber of the Forbidden Library. Above them soared twenty floors built around a wide rotunda ringed by a spiraling staircase. The top of this center section ended not in the dome that was visible from the outside, but with a glass mosaic ceiling depicting abstract shapes.

Each gallery-style level contained floor-to-ceiling rows of mahogany shelves packed with books and scrolls. Vermillion columns held the floors aloft. Thousands of flickering lanterns hung throughout, though only half were lit, leaving the library surprisingly dim for a place intended for reading. Of course, that didn't really matter, since no one but the library's guardians were allowed inside.

Looking upward, Turesobei spun around. "Wow, this is ... this is Paradise."

"It's pretty," Iniru mocked. "Pretty but boring."

"Don't tease him now," Enashoma said. "You know this is amazing. Imagine what it's like for him."

"I don't read much," Zaiporo said, "but I think I could probably spend a year in here before I got bored."

"Just imagine what all this library must contain," said Narbenu.

"A lot of books," Kemsu muttered. "Books I can't read."

"I think it would be worth learning how to read if one could stay here for a while," Narbenu added.

"I could stay here forever," Motekeru said.

"You can read?" Kemsu said.

"I am *not* a savage," Motekeru replied.

Kemsu started to respond but dropped it.

"Feels like ... *home*," said Lu Bei.

Enashoma poked him in the belly. "That's because you're a book."

Lu Bei giggled, then said, "No, that's not what I mean. It reminds me of the Grand Eternal Imperial Library of Tengba Ren, only it's about twice the size. Master went there frequently for volumes he didn't already own."

The bottom level was free of shelves. An array of tables, each with its own lantern and kneeling cushions, lined the edges. Near the far side was a freestanding stone cabinet, built like an outhouse, with a single door that lacked any sort of opening mechanism Turesobei could see. Beside the cabinet was a pedestal on which lay a tremendous codex bound with copper wire.

The Keeper of the Shores turned toward them and dropped his cowl. Turesobei took a step back, while several of the others stumbled back and gasped. The guardian — the Keeper — he was ... Turesobei didn't know *what* the Keeper was. Certainly not human in the sense of the baojendari, zaboko, k'chasan, or goronku peoples. While his body was that of a brown-skinned human male, leanly muscled, his neck and head matched those of a falcon, with beady black eyes, a sharp pointed beak, and downy, blue-gray feathers.

"No, I am not human like all of you, even though I resemble you in a few ways," the Keeper said. "I am eirsenda by birth. My people are older even than the Kaiaru, though we came to this world after them. We are no longer a living race. We few carry on in our sacred role as Keepers, immortal guardians of important places and powerful artifacts. Yes, I have wings. Yes, I can fly. Do you have any other questions?"

"We hadn't asked any," Iniru blurted out.

He flicked his beady eyes at them. Was that a smile? It was impossible to tell for certain.

"Are those not the questions you wanted to ask of me?"

Wings beat above them, and two more Keepers spiraled down from the top level. When they landed, they folded back their brightly colored wings. One had feathers of blue and purple, while the other had feathers of orange, vermillion, and scarlet. Neither wore cloaks. Instead, they wore simple tunics belted at the waist. From their belts dangled those same mysterious metal rods.

Turesobei bowed. "I am Chonda Turesobei."

"We know," said the Keeper with vermillion wings. "I am the Keeper of Scrolls. Welcome to the Forbidden Library. I am in charge, and I will see that your needs are met, and that our rules are followed."

"You're in charge?" said Turesobei. "What about the Great Librarian?"

"The Great Librarian manages the collections and interviews petitioners allowed in by the Keeper of the Shores, arguing their cases on the rare occasions she deems them worthy. Ultimately, however, she must answer to me and the Gathering of Keepers, and our lord, the Keeper of Destiny. It is our responsibility to protect the knowledge and artifacts stored here. Your chances with the Great Librarian are slim, and your chances of winning over the Gathering dire, but that is how the system works. You may think it is unfair, but the system is not to my liking, either."

"You would help us?" Turesobei said.

"No, I would kill you the moment you stepped foot into my library," he said nonchalantly, his eyes locked onto the Keeper of the Shores, "regardless of need, unless your coming had been foretold by the Keeper of Destiny. This I would do even to you, Chonda Turesobei, heir of the great Chonda Lu."

Anger flared within Turesobei, and with it the sigil on his cheek grew hot. The Keeper of Scrolls focused his eyes on the mark, but showed no further reaction. Taking deep breaths, Turesobei restrained his anger. He gestured toward Kurine who lay quiet in Motekeru's arms, missing the splendor of the library.

"Kurine, my betrothed, she's dying. She was poisoned by an orugukagi. I don't have the resources to cure her in this world. I was hoping you could help her here."

The Keeper of Scrolls shrugged. "If she is dying and you cannot stop it, then that is her fate. There is nothing I can, nor would, do for her."

Turesobei stepped toward him, but Iniru caught his sleeve and tugged him back, shaking her head. Clenching his eyes shut, he sighed. She was right. There was no point growing angry. The cirsendan Keepers were clearly alien, and he would gain nothing by trying to argue with them, especially if he needed their support later. Maybe the Great Librarian could help her. Maybe home and a cure was only a day away. He could hope ...

The Keeper of Scrolls ruffled his feathers and took a deep breath. His voice became friendlier. "Now, as for your stay, it is warm here in the Library, especially once the cold air you allowed in heats up. We will provide you with a change of clothes, rooms with baths to wash the filth away, and a brief time to rest before meeting with the Great Librarian.

"You must at all times follow the rules of the library. First, you cannot take anything from the library, should you be allowed to leave." He gestured toward the outhouse-sized box to the left with the pedestal beside the door. "Second, you cannot enter the Lower Stacks. Any attempt to open that door will result in death. Third, you are free to read any of the books in the Main Library, but handle them with care and replace them on the shelves properly when you are done. Fourth, if you speak amongst the Upper Stacks, even so much as a whisper, the punishment is death."

What was the point of the rules if they never let anyone in? Who would they interrupt by speaking? Turesobei was beginning to think the Keepers were short on good nature and even more lacking in sanity.

The Keeper of the Shores bowed to them. "I shall return to my duties now. Should you have the chance to face the Gathering, you will have at least one vote in your favor. Mine. It was given automatically when I allowed you in. I do not think we shall meet again, but one never knows for certain. It was a pleasure to meet you all."

With the purple-winged eirsenda following silently behind, the Keeper of Scrolls led them to a door on the west side of the library, which opened into a tunnel that took them into the squat, smaller domed building. It was styled in the same manner as the Main Library, with each level a gallery and the center open all the way up, except in this building the dome did open above to the lower levels, all ten of them. But there were no stairs nor any other methods for reaching the different levels. On each of the levels there were many doors, all of them closed. The dome above was not obsidian as he'd expected, but some sort of thick glass that was clear from the inside but dark on the outside. The last rays of the setting sun added an ominous crimson glow to the lantern light.

"The first floor contains our guest rooms. There is a free room for each of you. Baths have already been drawn. Tunics of appropriate size will soon be brought to you. We ask that you remain quiet and respectful. My brothers sleep on the level above you. Remember, it is we who will vote on and decide your fate if the Great Librarian looks upon you favorably."

Enashoma volunteered to share a room with Kurine and take care of her. Iniru offered to come help her, though she took a different room.

"I will stay outside with the hounds," said Motekeru, "and guard you all."

"I assure you that we will not harm you," said the Keeper of Scrolls. "The Keeper of the Hearth —" he gestured to the purple-winged one "— shall see to your needs."

"You have your duty," Motekeru said. "I have mine."

The Keeper of Scrolls nodded solemnly, and then departed.

"I will remain out here at all times, should you need anything," said the Keeper of the Hearth.

Turesobei walked into a warm room lined with reed mats on the floor and heavy tapestries on the walls. A single lantern blazed on the far wall. A copper bathtub sat on one side of the room, while a plush sleeping mat was rolled out on the other. There was a desk for writing and a few empty shelves for storing books and clothes. Heat poured into the room through vents in the wall, which was probably why Turesobei was sweating under his clothes already. This was the warmest place he'd been in since he'd arrived in the Ancient Cold and Deep.

"Wow, this is nicer than my room back home."

"But the neighbors are stinky mean," Lu Bei whispered. "And weird. But Keepers are like that."

"You know about them?"

"From long ago. Never expected that's what guarded this place. Master disliked the lot of them."

"Why?"

"Because they would never give him what he wanted," Lu Bei replied. "Only if the Keeper of Destiny ordains it can you gain access to anything they guard, even if all you want is to examine it. Master found this inconvenient, for they guarded many treasures he would have liked to have, or at least study."

"Chonda Lu wouldn't just take what he wanted from them?"

"Do not underestimate the Keepers. A Keeper is nearly a match against a Kaiaru. And just because he didn't like them or their methods, don't think that Master didn't respect the Keepers' mission to protect things that shouldn't fall into the wrong hands. And the cirsenda and the Kaiaru had a long-standing agreement not to fight against one another."

Turesobei peeled off his many layers of clothing and climbed into the steaming water. He felt as if he'd formed an outer skin of ice and that it was now melting away.

"Ohhhh, I have missed baths and heat so much. This *might* just be Paradise. Warm baths, warm rooms, millions of books."

He pushed all the worries he had from his mind — Kurine, getting home, the great shadow, the Keepers — all of it. He needed to rest and relax, or he'd never get through this.

Lu Bei sat on the edge of the tub and dipped his feet in with a sigh. "I wish they'd give us a week — a whole week to rest."

"I know, but Kurine won't last that long."

"You'll convince them to help us and get her cured, master. I know you will."

"I don't know. This time ... this time may be different. I wish this was something I could solve with a spell or a daring plan, but it's not. And the shadow from my nightmares ... I think it's a dragon. And it's here ... somewhere."

Chapter Forty-Six

A tap sounded on the door. Startled awake, Turesobei sloshed water out of the bathtub as he nearly jumped.

"Come in!"

Lu Bei popped back into fetch form — he had been lying on the sleeping mat — and rubbed his eyes. Lu Bei only needed sleep when injured, but he enjoyed napping.

Motekeru stepped into the room carrying a second towel and a saffron-colored tunic.

"Oh, it's you," Lu Bei said, and he turned back into a book.

"I offered to distribute the clothes," said Motekeru, "so that I could check on everyone."

"Thank you, Motekeru. That was ... that was incredibly thoughtful."

Motekeru nodded. "Of course, master."

"You know, when I first met you, I thought you'd be nothing but a killing machine, since that's what you were made to be."

"Master ... Chonda Lu ... he did not like for me to be anything else."

"Because you were once an enemy and he wanted to keep punishing you?"

"Yes, master."

"What did you do?" Turesobei asked.

"I killed one of his lovers, an assassin named Shi-Kun. Chonda Lu sent her after my liege. She was supposed to be unbeatable, but I stopped her. After he found out, Chonda Lu unleashed his full might against us. Once we were defeated, he made me into what I am now, so that I could always guard him."

"That's awful, truly awful." Sometimes Turesobei was completely embarrassed to be Chonda Lu's heir. "I'm so sorry that he did that to you."

"That is why I gladly serve you, master. Because you are everything a liege should be."

"I am honored, Motekeru. But you don't have to serve me. You can be free once we return. You can do whatever you wish."

"What would I do? In this form, there will never be joy for me. Before, I wanted to be left in limbo. Now, I choose to help you. I trust you to always do what's right."

Motekeru bowed and left. Turesobei said to Lu Bei, "You two didn't get along because of Chonda Lu?"

Lu Bei returned to fetch form, and sighed. "That was part of it."

"And the rest?"

"We are very different beings, Motekeru and I. He wasn't always this casual, carefree, lighthearted, and friendly, you know. And the bigger reason is that by the time I came along, Master had tired of giving the orders to Motekeru himself. It no longer brought him the same old pleasure it once had. So ..."

"You were the one who had to deliver the orders?"

"No one likes the messenger that brings bad news. Motekeru doesn't like killing, not humans anyway, even if he's made for it. He hated me because he couldn't refuse the orders. There must be at least a dozen spells inside Motekeru binding him to Chonda Lu. Master bragged to me once that not even he could break the spells and free Motekeru."

Turesobei got out of the bath and dressed in the saffron silk tunic, belting it at the waist. The tunic went down to his knees. He drew the sandals Motekeru had brought him onto his feet, and wound the cross-gartered straps up his calves.

"After all those thick clothes for weeks, I feel absolutely naked in this. Honestly, it's way too little for decorum. No one in our world wears anything this skimpy, except to bed. Are they going to make the girls wear these, as well? Even I don't think that would be decent — Narbenu's going to lose his mind."

"I think he might be too exhausted to — no, you're right. He's going to throw a fit."

Turesobei went to Kurine and Shoma's room and tapped on the door. Iniru opened it. She wore a burgundy tunic that was no longer than Turesobei's. He'd seen her in less: her shorts and shirt that she wore under her uniform. But he wasn't supposed to have seen her in so little, even though it wasn't truly revealing.

She was stunning. He'd seen so little of her on the ice, except when he'd healed her that night, that he'd forgotten how beautiful her red-brown fur was, how supple her muscled limbs were.

A hint of playfulness danced in her eyes, and she started to smile — but then stopped. "Gonna stare at me all day long?" she whispered. It took him a moment to shake his head. "Good, because it wouldn't be right to do that in here with your betrothed."

"How is she?" Turesobei asked.

"Getting worse."

Enashoma joined them. Her tunic was solid black.

"You look beautiful, Little Blossom."

"I feel —"

"Naked?"

She nodded.

"I know."

"You baojendari!" Iniru said.

"You've got to admit," Turesobei said, "that after all that cold weather gear ..."

"That even I feel naked?" Iniru asked. "No, I feel free at last. That was torture."

"Enjoy it while you can," Lu Bei said. He landed beside Kurine and looked her over. "This doesn't look good, master."

"I'm going to do one more poison delay spell on her," Turesobei said, kneeling beside Lu Bei. "Diminished returns, I know. I can't heal her anymore. I've done all I can."

"Master, her fevers have been high. The longer this takes ... a cure may not be enough. She may die anyway ... or ... or be irreparably damaged."

"I know." Turesobei cast the spell on her. He kissed her on the forehead. "I'm doing all I can for you. Hang in there."

Motekeru entered. "Master, you are needed."

The Keeper of Scrolls waited for him outside. "The Great Librarian will see you now. You and your fetch. The others should wait here. Their presence is unnecessary."

"She doesn't want to interview us all?" Turesobei asked.

"You are the only one who matters to her," the Keeper of Scrolls replied.

Motekeru stepped forward, but Turesobei raised a hand. "I'll be fine. We are at their mercy anyway. Stay here with the others. Tell them where I've gone."

Turesobei followed the Keeper of Scrolls back into the library and up the spiraling staircase. He suspected the Keeper was merely climbing the stairs now for Turesobei's benefit. It was strange, because even though no one used these stairs, they were polished and entirely free from dust. The guest rooms, which could not have been used in centuries, were in perfect condition. Nothing here had deteriorated, and everything was kept spotless. But maybe that was what the Keepers did to occupy their time.

At the final level, the Keeper walked through the stacks to a place where a ladder led up to a trapdoor. "Go up. The door will open for you. She will be occupied. You must wait for her to acknowledge you."

Turesobei climbed the ladder. He reached the top and was about to push on the trapdoor, but it flipped open on its own. He climbed into a room capped by a glass dome. In the center of the room stood a tall woman with a baojendari frame but incredibly angular features: a sharp jaw, high cheekbones, deep-set eyes. Living tattoos in silvery blue ink danced across her pale, parchment-colored skin. She was naked, so he could see that the tattoos covered nearly every inch of her body. Blue-black hair cascaded down her back, all the way onto the floor, like a cape. Her eyes were a solid scarlet that matched the kavaru embedded into her navel.

The moment he saw the channeling stone and felt its power, Turesobei and Lu Bei whispered her name at the same time.

"Ooloolarra."

Chapter Forty-Seven

Turesobei and Lu Bei glanced sharply at one another. Yet again, he had recognized a Kaiaru instinctively. But unlike the eidakami-ga, this was a *real* Kaiaru, the first he had ever met, or at least the first who hadn't become a dragon.

Ooloolarra, the Great Librarian, didn't give any sign that she'd noticed their entrance. She was observing a section of the glass interior of the dome. The entire surface was *alive* with text in all sorts of languages and sizes constantly scrolling and shifting.

Turesobei bowed and knelt on a cushion that sat nearby, he assumed for this purpose. Lu Bei flew around examining the text. Turesobei gestured for Lu Bei to kneel beside him, but Lu Bei gave him his "whatever" look and carried on. Turesobei tried to read the text while he waited. Every now and then, he spotted characters from a language he knew, but it would scroll away too fast for him to read any of it.

He tried hard not to stare at Ooloolarra. He failed. Not because she was naked ... not *just* because she was naked ... but because the shifting tattoos mesmerized him. Like most Kaiaru, her form was unique. Chonda Lu had been one of the few who'd taken on an almost entirely normal human appearance.

Over an hour had passed when suddenly she turned and said, "Chonda Lu, my old friend. I never expected you to come here seeking my help."

"I am not Chonda Lu," he said, bowing. "I am Chonda Turesobei."

Her eyes darted to Lu Bei. "I suppose you are ... Chonda Turesobei." She made a gesture, and then peered at a specific spot on the glass dome. Her eyes widened, then narrowed as she bit her lip. Turesobei followed her gaze to the section of now-frozen text, but he couldn't read it.

"You are Lu Bei, yes?"

"I am, Madam Ooloolarra. Don't you remember? We have met before, on numerous occasions."

"Oh, I remember," she said. "But I just wanted to be sure. You were much smaller then, and didn't have the *Mark of the Storm Dragon* on your chest."

"Some of the energies Master took in when he absorbed the Storm Dragon's Heart bled into me. I grew and gained a little power."

"You can turn into a book," she said with a spark in her eyes. Her lips curled into a smile. "I never knew that before."

Lu Bei frowned with worry. "Master wished me to hide that from you."

"Oh, I am certain he did. But now I know." She nodded toward the dome. "Now I know ... well, almost everything. Everything written throughout history is here on my screen. There is a lot to read through. Stand please, my brother. We are all siblings, the Kaiaru." After Turesobei stood, Ooloolarra stepped in close ... and stroked a hand across his cheek. Her breasts lightly brushed against him. He averted his eyes and tried to keep his focus. "You even look a lot like him. You know, we were always friends, Lu and I."

"Friends?" Lu Bei said. "That's a bit of a stretch, don't you think?"

"Well, we were not enemies. We helped each other on many occasions. For a Kaiaru, that amounts to friendship, wouldn't you say?"

Lu Bei shrugged. "It's true that you weren't enemies."

"I hear some of the other members of Chonda Lu's ... menagerie ... are with you. Though Rig and Ohma were before your time, as I recall."

"Indeed, madam."

"And Motekeru is here." She shuddered.

"I summoned them by accident before we came through the gate," Turesobei said.

"Child, nothing in your brief life has been by accident. Everything has been to Chonda Lu's design. I am sure of that."

"The big destiny I can't understand," Turesobei said. "I know. But Lu Bei returned too soon."

"That's true," Lu Bei said.

"Is it?" Ooloolarra asked. "I wonder. Just because you returned before Lu said you would doesn't mean it's earlier than he desired." She gestured and another cushion appeared from nowhere. "I have stood a long time. Too long. Perhaps a week, I think. Come, let us sit and talk for a while. You are no doubt full of questions. I am guessing you do not understand the nature of the Ancient Cold and Deep, is that correct?"

He nodded as she sat lotus-style across from him. She was terribly close. He shifted uncomfortably, and mostly kept his eyes averted.

"My nakedness bothers you?"

"All of this bothers me," he replied. "But yes, especially that."

She delicately touched her cheek and batted her eyes. "You don't think I'm beautiful?"

"You are — very much so." He kept trying to look away. "It's just that ... um ..."

"Master is confused by everything here," Lu Bei said, coming to the rescue.

"Is that so?" Ooloolarra said.

Turesobei nodded. "I'm in a strange place, and I've never encountered a Kaiaru before, and yes, you are naked and I'm ... unused to that. It's not proper in my society." He had actually never seen a woman naked before. "I'm sorry."

"Do not be, then." Chuckling, she scooted a little farther away and placed her hands in her lap. He realized then that she had been toying with him.

"What is this place, really?" he asked. "The Ancient Cold and Deep ... it's not exactly what I expected."

"This realm is a duplicate of the part of Okoro you call Zangaiden and some of the ocean beyond it. This perfect copy was placed in a pocket dimension separated out from the normal world. Every snowflake in that portion of Okoro, every book, every living being ... duplicated and placed in this little dimension with its finite boundaries leading off into nothingness. And yet despite that, the world functions just as you would expect. The sun and moons rise, the wind blows, and life goes on. The original Zangaiden and all its inhabitants went on living their normal lives in their normal world, completely unaware of what had been done. They experienced nothing more than a mild earthquake and a wave of vertigo."

Turesobei shook his head. "But that's ... that's just ..."

"Ridiculous?" she suggested.

"I was going to say impossible."

"Clearly it's not, even if you and I cannot fathom it."

"But the goronku don't exist in the Zangaiden I know. How can this be a copy when so much is different?"

"This copy was made over a dozen millennia past your time, after the sun began to fade."

"So we're in the future now ... the far future?" She nodded. Satsupan hadn't been lying; not that Turesobei had doubted him, but it had seemed too far-fetched to believe. Turesobei glanced at the text scrolling on the inside of the dome. "That means you know everything that will happen to me and my companions, right? My future is your past."

"Well, I know of one specific past that involved you, yes. My past. But your future will be different from what I know."

"How?" Turesobei asked.

"That's simple. In my past, Chonda Turesobei never came to the Winter Realm. There are most likely thousands of other, smaller differences as well. The short of it is that your venturing here did not happen in the time-stream from which this land was taken. From the moment you entered the Ancient Cold and Deep, the history of the world which I possess here will be different from what occurs in your world. Suffice it to say that anything I tell you about your future or the future of your world is largely irrelevant."

"Why was this place copied into a pocket dimension? And how?"

"The Ancient Cold and Deep," Ooloolarra said, "was created by the Blood King. He created all nine realms."

"Wait, I thought there were only four realms!"

"There are only four whose existence were known and remembered in your day. But there are actually eight gates that each take you from Okoro to one of the realms. And in each of those eight realms, you will find a gate that takes you to the ninth realm, the Nexus."

Turesobei's head began to swim. "So who's this Blood King?"

"Bad news," Lu Bei said.

"You know something about him?" Turesobei asked.

"Only a few legends Master was trying to track down before he died. But that's not how I know he's bad news. Blood King, hello? No one going by that name's gonna be friendly."

Ooloolarra grinned. "Lu Bei is right. The Blood King was a mad tyrant who conquered Okoro millennia before your time. Only with the help of the Earth Dragon were the Kaiaru of Okoro able to defeat him and imprison him in the Nexus of the Realms, where he sleeps for eternity. Of the twenty-one Kaiaru brave and powerful enough to oppose the Blood King, just nine survived. They absorbed his power and that of the realms. From that moment forward, the zaboko, and even your people, have worshiped or honored them as the Shogakami."

"That's the origin of the Shogakami?!" Turesobei said.

"Indeed, as much of it as I know."

"And you don't know why the Blood King did it?"

She swept her hand out toward her screens. "All this knowledge, so many secrets, and yet so very little about the Blood King. You might as well search for a record of Vôl Ul-tharma. The only thing I know for certain is that he was mad." She sighed. "I think the purpose of the Ancient Cold and Deep was to preserve this library. I was here the day this realm was made. When I was copied into this place."

She closed her eyes and shuddered. "A day I can only describe as pure torment, when it felt like my insides were being shredded and my brain melted. You cannot imagine the chaos and confusion, especially along the boundaries. People and homes were severed. Loved ones lost beyond the boundary. The many who walked unknowingly into oblivion for days and years afterward. And I tell you, the sight of a hundred panicked Keepers is not one you will ever forget.

"That morning, before everything started, a tall man with baojendari features came to the library. He was clad in black leather and wore a cloak of scarlet. The Keepers, if you can believe this, let him walk in without consulting me, without challenging him. They abandoned all their protocols. I went down to meet him and ... the rest is lost to me."

"You think that was the Blood King?" Turesobei asked.

"I do, and I wish I recalled more. The Keepers don't remember seeing him at all. Or they claim not to, anyway." She turned to Lu Bei. "So Chonda Lu knew nothing more than that about the Blood King?"

Lu Bei shook his head. "I don't know that he knew even that much. Master began re-searching the gates soon after he discovered Okoro and met the Shogakami. He often tried to pry secrets from them, but the Shogakami resisted him. I think he had pieced some se-crets about the realms together but was far from understanding all of it. Unfortunately, he forbade me from recording any of what he learned. That wasn't something he normally did, so he must have thought the knowledge dangerous. Perhaps he knew as much as you, but if so ..." Lu Bei shrugged.

"So why are the gates lost?" Turesobei asked.

"The Shogakami wanted them forgotten."

Turesobei rubbed the palms of his hands across his face and took a deep breath, trying to absorb all the information. "So if all this knowledge is important for me to know, that means —"

"There is no way to open the Winter Gate from this side," said Ooloolarra.

"I'm going to have to enter the Nexus of the Realms, aren't I, since it connects all the realms together?"

"Yes. From the Nexus you should be able to venture into other realms and seek a way home. Perhaps some of the other realms will have a means to be opened on their side."

"You mean you don't know? I could travel through the realms in vain searching for a way home?"

"I don't know everything for a reason. The Shogakami didn't want people passing between Okoro and the realms. But just as the Winter Child was a key, there are bound to be others. The Ancient Cold and Deep once had a key on this side that corresponded to the Winter Child, the Winter Crone, but the Shogakami removed her when they imprisoned the yomon here."

He began to piece all the information together. His heart stopped. His hopes crashed. "The Shogakami used the Nexus as a prison for the Blood King. I can't go there. I can't risk waking him and giving him a way to escape."

"You must go there to have a chance at returning home," she said.

Lu Bei scratched his chin. "If he's asleep, perhaps we can pass through without waking him. And his power was absorbed by the Shogakami, right? So maybe he's a pushover now."

"That assumes the scraps of information we have are correct," Turesobei said. "And that might be relative. He might still be too powerful for us to deal with. Even weakened, he would probably be amazingly powerful."

"I think that even if you entered and left the Nexus," Ooloolarra said, "the Blood King would be unable to follow."

"But the risk," Turesobei said, shaking his head. "What if I unleashed the Blood King on the world again? The Shogakami disappeared centuries ago, and we have only one known Kaiaru in Okoro now. There would be no one who could stop him."

"We can't stay here, master," Lu Bei said. "You have to go back. And poor Lady Shoma."

"Worry about the risks later," Ooloolarra said. "Now that you are here, you must continue moving forward, or the Keepers will execute you. Don't even pretend you can escape them. Win their approval and get the sword you need to enter the Nexus. You can decide if it's worth the risk after you leave the library."

She frowned as if she pitied him, and perhaps she did. "I do not want to get your hopes up. Just acquiring the sword will be next to impossible. First, I must convince the Gathering of Keepers to accept your bid. Then you must persuade them that your cause is worthy. The Keepers are peculiar and difficult to reason with, and you must understand that they don't like dealing with situations not foretold by the Keeper of Destiny."

"The Keeper of Destiny knows what will happen in the future?"

"Not exactly. It's not simply that Keepers prevent powerful objects from falling into the wrong hands. Their mission is also to put those objects into the right hands, hands that will lead the world to the destiny they wish to bring about."

"So it's like the k'chasan Sacred Codex."

She nodded. "Well, there is a lot more power involved with further-reaching consequences, but yes, it is like Jujuriki Notasami's childish book."

Lu Bei giggled, and Turesobei filed that comment away in things he should never mention to Iniru. "So this sword I need to open the Nexus Gate ..."

"It is an ancient sword buried halfway up to the hilt in a stone block lying at the heart of the library. Its name is Fangthorn. When the sun faded, all the Keepers who yet remained, across the world, converged here at my Grand Library of Okoro, which was built on top of the shrine that housed the sword in its stone. You see, this place is more than a library. It is a treasure vault and a museum. Every item stored here has already played its part and awaits the end of the world. The Keepers must allow you to have the sword, but your having it was not foretold. So they must wake their lord and get his permission."

"But if they are guided by destiny, wouldn't they already know if I'm to have it or not?"

"No Keeper was ever appointed to guard this sword, and yet here it is. When the Keeper of Destiny took over the library and allowed me to stay on, I asked him what he wanted to do with the sword, and he told me to leave it be. If the Keepers decided someone deserved the item, he should be awakened and presented with that person. He would then make the final decision."

"So I have to convince you, all the Keepers, and then their lord?"

Ooloolarra nodded. "And it gets worse. The Keepers have no control over Fangthorn, and unfortunately, the dragon bound into the sword hates you."

"Dragon ..." Turesobei winced. "The terrible shadow I saw in my nightmares! That's why it knew I'd come to her. Because I'd want to get out of the Ancient Cold and Deep. She *thinks* I'm Naruwakiru."

Ooloolarra gestured toward the storm sigil. "I cannot imagine why."

"My life stinks."

"So a sword with a dragon bound inside is the key to the Nexus?" Lu Bei asked. "That's a really weird key."

"Well, it is not a key exactly," she said. "The Shogakami didn't create a key to open the Nexus. They did not intend for it to ever be opened again. Perhaps you have noticed that the Shogakami prefer imprisonment to killing? Though it's possible the Blood King could not be killed."

"Then how can the sword get me in?" Turesobei asked.

"There is always a loophole in an imprisonment spell, yes?"

Turesobei didn't have much experience with imprisonment spells, especially any that would have been cast by a Kaiaru, but he had studied the theory behind the common variety. "An imprisonment spell can be interrupted or broken by the one who casts it."

Ooloolarra nodded. "The dragon within the sword helped the Shogakami cast the spell that locked the Blood King within the Nexus. That is why you need her cooperation. It is not enough to merely wield the sword. The dragon must be *willing* to help you. She can open the gate to the Nexus."

"But the dragon hates me."

"Because she thinks you're Naruwakiru, master. It shouldn't be hard to convince her otherwise. Once she sees you in person, all will be fine."

"You are infused with the power of the Storm Dragon, though," said Ooloolarra, "and this dragon ... she has gone mad from millennia of captivity and isolation. I'm not sure she will understand the difference. She may not even care."

Turesobei slumped. "Great, more good news."

Eyes narrowing, Lu Bei asked, "So who is this shadow dragon?"

"Not a shadow dragon," Ooloolarra replied with a pitying sigh. "The Earth Dragon."

Turesobei gulped. "The Earth Dragon?!"

"Lady Hannya of the Caverns, powered by the depths of the earth, rivaled only by Mekazi Keshuno the Shadow Dragon and Naruwakiru the Storm Dragon."

"No, no, no." Lu Bei fluttered his wings nervously. "It can't be Hannya. The Earth Dragon vanished ages ... oh." Lu Bei scratched his chin. "But wait a second, lady, who could possibly bind the Earth Dragon into a sword? And what kind of sword could hold her?"

"Hannya was bound into the sword by Tepebono."

"The hero who killed the Storm Dragon centuries ago?" Turesobei asked. "But he was just a zaboko man. How could he bind something as powerful as the Earth Dragon?"

Ooloolarra chuckled. "He may have looked zaboko, just as you look baojendari, but he was Kaiaru. Did you think a normal human could slay the Storm Dragon on his own?"

"Well, no, I guess not. But none of the tales mentioned it."

"I didn't know, either," Lu Bei added.

"Perhaps the tales are wrong because the people of Okoro forgot about the Kaiaru until the baojendari invaded. The Shogakami were more than Kaiaru by that point, just as the dragons were."

"So he bound Hannya after he killed Naruwakiru?" Turesobei asked.

"Before. He bound Hannya into the sword and used it to kill Naruwakiru. That is the only way he could rescue his lover, Lady Amasan, whom Naruwakiru had kidnapped. Remember, by that point Naruwakiru had more than a dragon's kavaru heart. She had merged her kavaru with the jade heart made by her priests with blood magic. Her power had tripled and was growing steadily."

"How could he bind her into a sword?"

"It wasn't just any sword. This blade was forged of dark-steel."

"Dark-steel? That's impossible ... right?" Dark iron was temperamental, and it supposedly couldn't be forged into steel, unlike the equally rare white iron.

"Fangthorn is a unique sword. Only its forger ever knew how it was made."

"Even still, I don't get how he could bind the Earth Dragon so easily."

"Tepebono was a master of binding spells, and in this case, he prepared them in advance using blood magic, which centuries later killed him so thoroughly he couldn't be resurrected through his kavaru."

"Why not use the sword directly against Naruwakiru?"

"She was too powerful for him to kill by that point."

"Okay, I understand why Hannya would hate me if she thought I were Tepebono, but she thinks I'm Naruwakiru. As a sword, she was used to defeat Naruwakiru. Why would she hate the Storm Dragon so much?"

"Yeah, I don't get it either," Lu Bei said.

Ooloolarra shrugged. "That is the great mystery. I know they were rivals long, long ago, before Hannya and Naruwakiru became dragons. Obviously, something happened between them. What, I couldn't even guess. But Hannya has had millennia to nurse this grudge."

Turesobei started to speak, but she put a finger to her lips and shook her head. Then, smiling sympathetically, she leaned forward and touched his arm. "I know you have dozens more questions in you still, but let us not delve into more mysteries. I have told you everything you must know to move forward."

"I'm *never* going to get home."

"No," she replied, "I do not think you will. But nevertheless, I will aid you as I can, and wish you the best. Tomorrow morning, I will formally present you to the Keepers and speak well of you."

"Thank you, Ooloolarra. I'm indebted to you."

"Of that, I am certain." Her lips peeled back into a broad smile, revealing razor-sharp teeth. "My services have a price, though."

Turesobei sighed. Of course. None of this could be easy. "What's your price?"

"Here it comes," Lu Bei muttered dejectedly.

"You have something I want." Her eyes fell upon Lu Bei. "You must leave the fetch with me."

Chapter Forty-Eight

"Yep, just as I expected," Lu Bei said. "There's a good reason Master kept my book form secret from you."

"No!" Turesobei clenched his fists. "I can't leave him behind! I *need* Lu Bei. He's bound to me — and he's my friend."

"I am, above all, a collector of books and information," Ooloolarra said. "And he is the most unique book I have ever seen. You know, you might be better off without him. If you understood your destiny well enough, I think you would agree."

"I don't care about my destiny," Turesobei replied. "I *love* Lu Bei, and he's mine. I won't leave him here."

"I'm sorry, but that is my price." She twirled her hair through her fingers.

"Once he's more than two hundred paces away from me, he won't even be a fetch anymore!"

"I'll find a way to work around that," she replied. "And if not, so be it."

"I can't agree to this deal."

"Without me to plead your case to the Keepers, you have no hope of returning home," Ooloolarra said. "And you will die here."

"Do as she says, master. If my staying here is the price, then so be it. You *must* return home with the others."

As he glared at Ooloolarra, the storm mark on Turesobei's cheek started to burn — but he reined it in. Freeing Lu Bei from this deal would just be one more problem to solve, one there was no point in worrying over yet, since he might not even live that long.

Turesobei gritted his teeth. "Fine. I agree." He stood to leave. "If you speak on my behalf, you may keep Lu Bei."

"Go now and rest. The Keepers will gather at dawn."

The Keeper of Scrolls met him on the staircase.

"She will represent me tomorrow," Turesobei told him.

"So be it," the Keeper replied.

"I can find my own way back."

The Keeper stepped to the edge of the gallery, jumped off, flew several levels down, and disappeared. To where, Turesobei didn't care.

Stoically, he walked down the staircase, crossed the library, pausing for a moment to look at the door that led to the Lower Stacks, and returned to the building that housed the guest rooms. Lu Bei fluttered along silently behind him.

Motekeru bowed and opened the door to his room for him. He didn't ask anything.

"Lu Bei, stay out here with Motekeru. Do not record anything that happens inside. When they ask, tell the others what they should know."

Lu Bei bit his lip and frowned, then he sighed and bowed. "Yes, master. I will do so."

Turesobei entered his room and locked the door behind him. He sat on the bedroll and stared at the wall absentmindedly. His brain was numb; his heart overwhelmed.

A tap sounded on the door.

"Sobei!" Shoma called. "Are you okay?"

"I'm fine," Turesobei replied. "I just need to rest and prepare for tomorrow."

He could sense her hovering at the door.

He cast the *spell of pervasive silence*, placing it over the room. Then, by its silver chain, he held his kavaru up before him and stared into its amber depths, watching its kenja pulse like a heartbeat. If he could've taken it off, he would have. He didn't want it anymore. He didn't want *any* of this. He wanted to be a normal sixteen-year-old. Heck, a normal sixteen-year-old wizard would be fine. He didn't want grand destinies or ancient enemies threatening to destroy his clan or kill his friends. He didn't want all this pain, all this responsibility. And he especially didn't want to be the Storm Dragon.

With a wave of his hand, he turned the lantern off, plunging the room into complete darkness. For a moment, he thought he heard the whisper of a laugh.

Turesobei brought his knees to his chest and rested his head on them, wrapping his arms around his legs.

He cried.

An hour before dawn, the Keeper of the Hearth woke them all. Turesobei opened his door, and Shoma rushed in and threw herself into his arms, nearly tackling him.

"Lu Bei told us everything," she muttered. "Sobei ... I ..."

He stroked her hair. "It'll all be okay, Little Blossom. I always find a way, don't I?"

She looked into his eyes. "You're starting to crack."

"That just makes me more dangerous for my enemies."

Frowning, Iniru leaned against the doorframe. "Get some food in you, and then give the Keepers hell."

Motekeru brought in a plate heaped with food that the Keeper of the Hearth had provided.

"Let's all eat together in Shoma's room," Turesobei said.

Because it might be their last meal together.

With Lu Bei at his side, Turesobei left his companions on the bottom floor of the Main Library. The Keepers were allowing them to watch the proceedings from there. The Keeper of Scrolls led him back up to the observatory where Ooloolarra beckoned him to the center of the room.

"Stand here beside me."

The circular portion of floor they stood on sank downward, descending through the ceiling of the Main Library. On this levitating disc, they floated halfway down, fifteen levels. There, the disc paused and rotated slowly.

His eyes went wide with amazement. Gathered along the edge of each floor of the library were Keepers, dozens of them, with feathers in every imaginable hue. Aside from that, they all looked strangely the same — identical heights, builds, eyes, and even the same white tunics. He'd only seen five of the Keepers before now. Did the rest sleep all the time?

"Ninety-eight of them," Ooloolarra whispered. "You have one vote already, from the Keeper of the Shores. You need forty-nine more, plus a volunteer who will present you to the Keeper of Destiny. That will be the hardest part for you."

"Why is that?" he asked, but Ooloolarra didn't get a chance to answer.

The Keeper of Scrolls, perched on the highest level, swept his wings out. "We are gathered! Our proceedings shall now begin! Let all who should be heard be easily heard."

A flicker of kenja passed through the library.

"A voice-boosting spell," Ooloolarra whispered. "So we won't have to yell at one another."

"Present your case, Great Librarian," the Keeper of Scrolls said pompously.

"Most gracious lords ... my dear eirsendan friends ... thank you for hearing me," Ooloolarra said silkily, her voice echoing throughout the library. "Long have we known each other, and few claimants have I presented to you. Four, if I recall correctly, and long has it been since the last. Today, I present to you Chonda Turesobei, and I ask you to hear his plea and grant his wish. His cause is great and just. I say this not because he is the ... descendant of my Kaiaru brother and friend of old. I say it not because I have pity on him for his youth and his friends. I say it because he is a good person, with good intentions. I say it because of everything he meant to our world, because of everything, both good and bad, that he has yet to become.

"Can we deny his timeline the impact he had on ours? Because that is what we will do by not giving him a chance to return. I know he must first draw Fangthorn from the stone and his chances of doing so are slim. But if he succeeds, he will remove from below us the darkness that ever haunts this place and our hearts. My lords, I beg you, as I have never done before, let him meet with your lord."

A ripple of murmurs spread amongst the gathered Keepers.

"Now you," Ooloolarra whispered.

Turesobei fell to his knees and bowed. His palms were sweaty. His body trembled no matter how he tried to still it, as did his voice.

"My lords, I beg your help in returning to my world. We came here by accident while saving my world ... your world of old. The Deadly Twelve, assassins from the Shadowland, used the Winter Child to unleash the yomon and eternal winter on Okoro. I had to become the Storm Dragon to stop them, but unfortunately my friends, and members of my family, got dragged through the gate with me. They are innocent, and if I cannot get them home, they will die. My betrothed, Kurine, who is from this world, is already dying. My clan, back home, they need me desperately. I am their future. Please. My cause is good and just. I only ask for a chance."

Many of them were shaking their heads, clearly unimpressed. He had to do better. But what could he say? What else was there to do but explain why he did what he did and hope that they would understand?

"Surely you remember fighting for what you believe in?" he said. "Surely you remember being willing to give everything to save those you love? I have never done anything but give all of myself to save the ones who matter to me. I believe that is the noblest thing a person can do, and I would gladly die for any one of my companions, man or beast or book. I am not claiming to be perfect or flawless; far from it. I have made many mistakes, but my love for my family and friends is perfect in its intent. Give me a chance to see them home, back to where they belong."

Turesobei shrugged. He wanted to say more, but what could he say? Either they would care or they would not. "I rest my case, humbly begging for your support, my lords. I will respect your decision, and I shall not fight it."

"It is put to a vote, then!" the Keeper of Scrolls declared. "All those in favor, unfurl your wings."

Chapter Forty-Nine

While most of the Keepers eyed one another indecisively, an emerald-feathered Keeper immediately stepped to the edge, stood on his toes, and dramatically flared out his wings revealing their golden underside. Seeing him, another loosed his wings to vote in favor of Turesobei. Then another and another. Many, however, did not budge.

The flutter of movement stopped. Turesobei counted frantically. The vote was close. Ooloolarra could scan fast. She put an arm around his shoulders. "That's something I have never seen before," she whispered. "You are almost there."

"By a margin of fifty-two to forty-seven, the Gathering supports the claimant," announced the Keeper of Scrolls. "However, for the measure to pass, one of us must volunteer to represent him to our beloved lord, our Keeper of Destiny. You all know what a great and terrible honor that is."

The first Keeper to have voted, the one with emerald and gold feathers said, "I shall."

A few Keepers gasped, while others stared at him dumbfounded, their beady eyes unblinking. The rest chattered to one another in amazed tones. Turesobei choked back a sob, and breathed a deep sigh of relief. The tension in his muscles released.

"Then so shall it be," the Keeper of Scrolls pronounced. "Present him, brother, with our blessing and love. The Gathering is now over."

The Keeper of Scrolls stepped away from the edge and disappeared, but the rest of the Keepers continued to speak rapidly amongst themselves in their language of clicks and chirps, which the magic of this world did not interpret for Turesobei as it did with the goronku. Turesobei met the eyes of the emerald-winged Keeper and nodded in thanks. The Keeper nodded back, and then retreated into the stacks.

Lu Bei landed on Turesobei's shoulders and hugged him. Turesobei allowed, for a moment, a smile to cross his face.

"Congratulations," Ooloolarra said. "You did something no one else has ever done. And now you shall do something else few others have done. You will meet the Keeper of Destiny. They will retrieve you just before midnight."

"Will I be in danger?"

"The Keeper of Destiny will not harm you. Even if he chooses not to grant you your wish to draw Fangthorn, he will grant you a favor. If it were me, I would ask to live out the rest of my days here in the library, where it is warm and safe."

Turesobei spent an almost festive afternoon with his friends. They'd crossed one of the biggest hurdles. And he wouldn't think, for now, about their chances of passing the ones still ahead. They ate and talked of the most frivolous things they could think of. No one mentioned Kurine's deteriorating condition or the possibility that Turesobei could fail to draw the sword. Instead, they took a couple of hours to browse the library, looking in wonder at the beautifully illuminated texts all written in strange languages that meant nothing to them.

A half-hour before midnight, the Keeper of the Hearth came for Turesobei. They walked silently to the Main Library, Lu Bei fluttering behind. From there, the Keeper led them through one of the connecting passages to the tall, narrow tower.

The emerald-and-gold Keeper was waiting for them. Some sort of unspoken message passed between the two Keepers. Then the Keeper of the Hearth nodded slowly and deeply, almost bowing, to the emerald one and left. Turesobei's representative stood for a long moment before shoving the door open and leading him inside.

"What's your name?" Turesobei asked. His voice shook nervously, and he realized he was terrified, which was strange considering all the demons and monsters he'd faced. But normal Keepers were intimidating enough, and they all held their lord, the Keeper of Destiny, in awe.

"I am the Keeper of the Forested Isles," he said in almost longing voice.

"I can't thank you enough for what you did for me, being the first to vote, and so dramatically. I think without you the vote would not have passed."

"You are welcome," the Keeper replied.

"What happened to your islands? I mean, why aren't you with them still?"

The Keeper let loose a sigh. "The isles now lie beneath the ocean."

"Oh, I'm sorry."

The Keeper of the Forested Isles locked his beady eyes on him. "Time undoes everything, good and bad. It is the way of life."

The Keeper placed a hand on a second door and chanted. A few moments later, it swung open. The Keeper spoke a word, and a few anemic lanterns on the walls sputtered to life. The building wasn't what Turesobei had expected. It was full of cobwebs and dust and entirely empty. High, high above, he spotted a trapdoor in the ceiling.

The Keeper spread his wings. "I shall have to carry you."

"I can levitate up there, if you like."

The Keeper of the Forested Isles nodded. "That would be more dignified for both of us, I should think."

Turesobei noticed the Keeper's hands were trembling. "Are you nervous to see your lord, too?"

Was that a smile? It was hard to judge their expressions. "I have never met the Keeper of Destiny before."

"Never?" Lu Bei asked. "Wow. That seems strange."

"More than half of us have not. The Keeper of Destiny was ancient even when I was young. He sleeps and dreams almost all the time. When last he walked among us, it was to summon us here, but by the time I arrived, he was already in hibernation. So it is an extreme honor for me to finally meet him."

"Ooloolarra made it sound like getting a representative would be difficult. If it's such an honor to meet him, why wouldn't all of you want to volunteer?"

The Keeper made no reply. Turesobei exchanged a look with Lu Bei; the fetch shrugged. Turesobei positioned himself directly under the trapdoor and chanted the *spell of levitation*. He rose slowly up into the air, Lu Bei circling around him, and the Keeper of the Forested Isles met him when he reached the top. The Keeper grabbed onto a handhold and chanted again to unlock the door.

"After me," said the Keeper of the Forested Isles.

The Keeper climbed in through the trapdoor, and Turesobei followed him up. A single room, much like Ooloolarra's, took up the top of the tower. But this dome was crystal clear, and it magnified one's sight so that everything beyond looked closer. Avida, hanging full above them, was enormous — easily four times its normal size. Gray blemishes and pock-marks scarred the moon's surface that, until now, Turesobei had believed to be purely white and smooth. Only a few stars could peek through Avida's dominating, magnified light.

"Wowza!" Lu Bei said, and Turesobei nodded.

The Keeper of the Forested Isles sunk down onto one knee and placed his hands on the floor. He tucked his head down and spoke in a strangely lyrical alien language of clicks and whistles and grunts.

The chamber was bare, except for a figure standing at the other end of the room. Stooped and frail, though clearly he had once been a head taller than all the others, the Keeper of Destiny stood, statue-like, staring up through the dome. Gossamer webs draped from his hoary, emaciated frame. His wings hung limp and pale, with almost translucent feathers that looked as if they might fall off. His hands and limbs were gnarled and scarred, as if he had fought mighty beasts in the distant past. But his eyes, focused on the sky above — unblinking, clear, and sharp — sparkled under Avida's light.

Turesobei dropped to his knees and bowed his head. Lu Bei mirrored him this time. Now that he'd taken in the sight of the Keeper of Destiny, something bothered Turesobei. Something here was wrong.

The moon! Shaking his head in confusion, he gazed at Avida.

"You are wondering," said a deep, deep voice, "why Avida is full above when it should be crescent now and lying, at this time of night, on the horizon."

The eyes of the Keeper of Destiny lowered onto Turesobei.

"I just realized it, your majesty," Turesobei replied, bowing low.

"Do you long to return home?" the Keeper of Destiny asked.

"I do, your majesty."

"So do I."

With a groan and the cracking of stiff joints, the Keeper of Destiny rolled his head, relaxed his shoulders, and swept the cobwebs from his chest and arms. Looking as if he might tumble forward, he took creaking steps on his frail legs. He crossed the room and stopped in front of the Keeper of the Forested Isles, who kept his head tucked down and said nothing. The Keeper of Destiny grabbed the hands of the Keeper of the Forested Isles and brought him up to his feet.

"Rise, my brave child, and face me."

The Keeper of the Forested Isles did so. "I am yours, Lord Keeper."

"It has been a long, long time since any of you visited me ..."

"We have had no reason to disturb you, my lord."

"You were all afraid."

Trembling, the emerald-winged Keeper nodded. "Yes."

"It is difficult to be alone. And soon, all too soon, you will understand that. I am sorry."

"It is the highest honor to serve you, my lord."

"An honor that I am sorry I must bestow. Are you ready?"

"One moment." The Keeper of the Forested Isles turned to Turesobei. "Thank you, Chonda Turesobei, for reminding this ancient soul what it was like to live and love, even at the peril of one's own life. I had forgotten. And now, I wish you success on your noble efforts, and honor you with this: my second secret name, the one that humans can speak, is Inatiasharra. I am, in your world and time, still on the islands. They lie between Okoro and Tengba Ren, but a little south. If you should ever have the chance ..."

"I don't understand," Turesobei said.

The Keeper of the Forested Isles nodded. "I am ready now, my lord."

"Fix your gaze on our beloved homeland."

The Keeper of the Forested Isles turned ... and gazed up at Avida. Then the Keeper of Destiny, like lightning, struck and bit deeply into Inatiasharra's neck, his sharp beak tearing through the throat.

Turesobei jumped to his feet and screamed, "No!"

Chapter Fifty

There was a spray of blood, but none of it ever touched the ground. Inatiasharra's body, tunic and wings and all, burst into a cloud of white mist. The Keeper of Destiny inhaled deeply, and the cloud poured into him. As Turesobei watched helplessly, the Keeper of Destiny was rejuvenated. Muscle returned to his frail limbs. His feathers turned from translucent white to deep gold and shining silver. His wings stretched out. His back straightened. His skin went from gray to light bronze. He bent his head back and cawed deeply, his voice reverberating through the dome.

Then he turned.

Turesobei backed up a step, and Lu Bei flew in front of him, with his hands spread out, sparks falling from his palms.

"Watch out, master!"

"I am not going to hurt either of you," the Keeper lord replied with a hint of mirth in his voice.

"Why — why did you do that?" Turesobei asked.

"Because there is a price to pay for all magic, that which grants immortality most of all. I am not Kaiaru like you."

"I'm — I'm not Kaiaru."

"How odd that you should not know what you are," the Keeper of Destiny said. "Inatiasharra was given the greatest of honors. He died so that his lord might live, just as others of our people gave of themselves to make Inatiasharra immortal, in those days when our strength failed and war had nearly ruined us. We could save only some of our people, but we saved those few most brilliantly. It is our way. I do not expect you to understand. You reminded Inatiasharra what it was like to live, and thus, he was ready to die. It is as simple as that. And it was necessary. My own life-force is far too precious to spend on events like this that have not been foreseen."

The Keeper of Destiny once more gazed up toward Avida, and after a few minutes during which Turesobei didn't dare move or speak, the Keeper said, "I will allow you to take Fangthorn from the Lower Stacks, if that is your wish. Do you know what you will be facing?"

"The Earth Dragon Hannya," Turesobei replied. "Ooloolarra explained it all to me."

"I would not blame you for choosing another blessing, Chonda Turesobei. I could give you access to another item. Or allow you and your friends to go free, or to live here at the Library for as long as you wished."

Turesobei thought of years of warmth and peace with those he loved, with a million books to study. It was a nice thought. He savored it a moment then shook his head. "I must return to my world. Or die trying."

"So be it." The Keeper of Destiny put his empty hands together and drew them apart. He held an amulet in one hand, and in the other a cord bound to it. "Show this to my children, and they will know that you have my blessing to go into the Lower Stacks to retrieve Fangthorn. Follow the instructions of the Keeper of Scrolls. You will not like the requirements, but they are necessary. And let me, in advance, apologize. Magic always has a price."

"I understand. Once I have the sword and have convinced Hannya to aid me, how do I get to the Nexus?"

"It lies due north of here, at the edge of the world. Hannya can pinpoint the precise location for you."

The Keeper pointed outside his dome. "Your enemies have arrived."

Turesobei stepped up the glass and saw the yomon led by Awasa approaching, illuminated somehow by an Avida that wasn't really there.

"They will not harm us, of course," said the Keeper of Destiny.

"How will I get away from the yomon when I leave here?"

"I leave that up to you," the Keeper said. "We will not fight them for you."

"Why not help me? Why not rid the world of them?"

"Because it is not in our destiny to do so."

"What happens to my companions, if I should fail in retrieving the sword?"

"I will allow them to leave the Forbidden Library unharmed, or remain if they wish."

Turesobei breathed a sigh of relief. At least the others could live on, even if he failed. Perhaps Awasa would leave them be once he was dead.

"My fetch, Lu Bei —"

"You had to bargain him to Ooloolarra? And you are wondering if I can help you? I cannot." The Keeper gazed at Lu Bei. "You need the fetch to fulfill your own destiny. I think you should take him with you. Whatever way you find to do so will not offend me."

"There is one other thing. My betrothed, Kurine, she is dying from poison ..."

"I cannot heal her. The poison is too advanced for any magic I possess. There are items in the Lower Stacks that could heal her, but you can take only one item. The rules are the rules. What I can do for her, if you wish, is give you a spell that will place her in perfect stasis. It would halt the spread of the venom's effects. If you can then get her to another world, perhaps there you can find a cure."

"Thank you," Turesobei said, relieved he wouldn't have to decide between a cure for Kurine or the sword that could get them all home.

The Keeper of Destiny kissed the amulet and spoke the words of a spell. Violet flames burst around the amulet, then faded away. "Place this on her chest after you show it to my children. It will need a few drops of your blood to activate. No other command is needed. To wake her, merely ask her to do so, again using a drop of your blood."

He held out the amulet. "You should go now. I wish you good fortune, Chonda Turesobei."

Chapter Fifty-One

Turesobei rapped on the door, and the Keeper of Scrolls opened it. Turesobei stepped through, and the Keeper quickly closed the door behind him.

Turesobei held up the amulet. "The Keeper of the Forested Isles died well. He was brave and true."

"I am glad to hear that," said the Keeper of Scrolls.

"Your lord is well, and he gave me permission to go to the Lower Stacks."

The Keeper of Scrolls examined the amulet. "Then so shall it be."

"Can I get some rest first?"

"No, it must be done now. Go to the catalogue beside the door to the Lower Stacks and select the item you wish to retrieve."

"I would like to see my companions before I go."

"As you wish."

"Tell them to bring Kurine, as well."

The Keeper of Scrolls nodded to the nearby Keeper of the Hearth, who hurried off. Turesobei went to the catalogue beside the closet-like structure, and opened the cover. Each page held listing after listing of wondrous objects, named and illustrated. The book was thousands of pages long, but he knew where the item he wanted would be listed. Taking sections between his hands, he flipped until he reached the last page, which showed a dark sword amidst a shadow with flaming eyes. He remembered the nightmares and considered what lay ahead: Hannya, the Earth Dragon, Queen of Flame and Shadow.

"I have found the item I want. What now?"

At that moment, his companions shuffled in, rubbing their tired eyes. Motekeru carried Kurine in his arms. One by one, Keepers then stepped out onto the edges of the library's levels and gazed down.

"Sobei," Shoma said with worry. "Does it have to be now?"

"Apparently so." He kissed her on the forehead. "Don't worry. If I die below, you will all be allowed to remain here or leave safely."

Zaiporo clapped him on the shoulder. "Good luck."

"Thanks, Zai. Look after Shoma if ... well, you know."

Iniru kissed him full on the lips, warm, eager, and trembling. He tried to savor the moment, to soak it all in to the deepest part of his being. She leaned her head on his shoulder for a few moments, then pushed him away, her face tense as she tried to smile. "Try not to turn into a dragon, okay? Only if you have to."

"Only if I have to."

"After we get home," Shoma said, "I forbid you to do anything dangerous again. *Ever.* I'm sick of watching you almost kill yourself for the rest of us."

He chuckled. "I'll try."

Motekeru sat Kurine down carefully, stepped back, and shook his head. "She should not have been moved."

"I had you bring her here for a reason," Turesobei said.

Kemsu leaned his head down to Kurine's chest. "She's barely breathing."

Narbenu felt her forehead. "The fever's gone too far."

Turesobei clenched his jaw. "I promised her she'd be well again. I will see it done. I just need to —"

The Keeper of Scrolls approached and interrupted him. "There is a price to pay before you can enter the Lower Stacks."

Turesobei whispered to Iniru, "Bet you a string of pearls that it's blood."

"You must first pay with blood," the Keeper of Scrolls announced.

"I win," he said.

"I never took the bet," she whispered back, trying to sound upbeat. "I'm not dumb, you know."

The Keeper of Scrolls drew a knife and cut Turesobei's palm. Relief flooded through Turesobei as the Keeper turned Turesobei's hand over, allowing the blood to drip. Compared to all that Turesobei had suffered over the last month, that was nothing more than a cat scratch.

This was actually convenient, in a way. He needed blood to put Kurine in stasis. He knelt beside Kurine, kissed her on the forehead, and placed the amulet on her chest. He squeezed his hand into a fist and let a few drops of blood drip onto the amulet. A golden light shone around her and was absorbed into her skin. She took in one sharp breath, convulsed, and then stopped breathing. Her face looked peaceful, angelic. He opened his kenja-sight. The magic was active. She was preserved.

"You've killed her!" Kemsu snapped.

"I've preserved her. She will remain like this and neither age nor die nor truly live. I will wake her when I have the cure."

"And now you must pay with pain," the Keeper of Scrolls announced impatiently. "You must enter the stacks wounded, humble, and alone."

His stomach wrenching, Turesobei stared at him. "You're joking ... right?"

The Keeper shook his head. "I am sorry, but that is the way the magic of the stacks works. It can be no other way."

Turning to his friends, Turesobei said, "Whatever happens, stay calm. Don't interfere. I'll be okay."

Turesobei followed the Keeper of Scrolls as he went to the codex and dripped

Turesobei's blood from the knife onto the Fangthorn entry. The Keeper placed his palm onto the page, chanted, then turned back to Turesobei, watching him, expectantly.

"Okay," Turesobei said, "what do I do n —"

A burst of flame erupted on Turesobei's chest, just above his sternum. He screamed and fell to his knees as the flame seared his skin and burned into the bone. The flame went out, but the pain continued, beyond his chest and into every fiber of his body. He fell onto the floor, gasping for breath.

"You may open the door and go inside now," the Keeper of Scrolls said.

Turesobei realized he was crying. Shoma was crying, too. "I'm okay," he said, but the words tumbled out on instinct. He didn't want to worry them, but he was anything but okay.

Heavy footsteps thudded toward him. Motekeru knelt beside him. "Let me help you up, master."

Turesobei grabbed onto Motekeru's arm and stood. He regulated his breathing, trying to reduce the pain.

Lu Bei threw jabs and hooks as if shadow-boxing. "Go get her, master! Show that dragon who's boss!"

The others voiced encouragement, too. But he couldn't respond. He didn't have the energy. But he felt their love. That was all that mattered, all that he needed to keep going. To face his death.

Turesobei limped on his own to the door to the Lower Stacks, his chest afire, his mind and body throbbing with pain. He pushed the door open.

Chapter Fifty-Two

Turesobei stepped down onto a staircase barely illuminated by a single, no doubt magical, lantern hanging near the door. The door boomed shut behind him with the finality of the closing of a burial tomb. Head spinning, he slumped down onto a step. On his chest was a perfect circle of charred flesh with a glowing rune in the center. This was the worst library ever.

Turesobei shivered uncontrollably, from shock and from the icy cold within the staircase. He gathered his composure. Sitting on the steps hurting and freezing ... he was only going to get weaker. No choice but to move on. He lifted the lantern off its hook and held it up to light his way.

Turesobei trudged, and stumbled, down perhaps a hundred steps ... until the staircase ended with a simple door engraved with a black circle punctuated by a crimson eye — shadow and flame — the *Mark of the Earth Dragon*.

How did one reach the other artifacts? Some sort of magic, obviously. Perhaps a tunneling spell to pocket dimensions. Ooloolarra had said she built her library on top of the original shrine. This was the only artifact that had to be physically present. While such magic was incredibly powerful, it probably wasn't beyond what the Keepers were capable of, or a powerful Kaiaru given enough time and knowledge.

He touched the handle and drew in a breath. Weaponless, no spell strips, his chest scorched, down even into his soul — and he had to face one of the most powerful dragons ever to haunt Okoro. A dragon that believed him to be her nemesis reborn. Sure, Hannya was bound to a sword. But Ooloolarra had said that he'd need to convince Hannya to help him. She had to be willing. Based on his nightmare encounters, Hannya clearly thought she could defeat him when they met. And unfortunately, he was no Kaiaru, even when he was at full strength and prepared for battle.

He pushed the door open and lifted the lantern.

The chamber, only slightly larger than Turesobei's workshop at home, was walled in black granite and littered with the debris of collapsed ornamental cedar beams and rotting mats and tapestries. A polished block of white marble, etched with hundreds of runes, sat on the far side of the chamber. Embedded halfway into the block was an old-fashioned, two-handed longsword with a blade as dark as wrought iron. Runes carved into the blade writhed as if aflame. The pommel held a ruby so dark a crimson that it was nearly black.

The dank room smelled faintly of salt, and beyond the weeping, rough-hewn walls, the sea below the ice whispered.

Hannya herself was nowhere to be seen.

He stepped inside and set the lantern down. The runes on the blade continued to flicker on their own. He bowed, wincing in pain as the skin and muscles of his chest stretched.

"My Lady, I, Chonda Turesobei, come before you with a humble heart and ask —"

A great shadow billowed out from the sword and expanded to fill the entire room, save for a small space around Turesobei. Flaming eyes illuminated a slender snout capped with twin horns. Her breath struck him like fire and ice.

"Naruwakiru," said the deep, feminine voice he'd heard in his nightmares. Here, her voice had regal textures and undertones he'd not heard through the Shadowland.

This was not what he had expected. This was far, far worse. Why hadn't Ooloolarra told him the Earth Dragon could leave the sword?!

"I'm not Naruwakiru," he said quickly. "I'm Chonda Turesobei, a male baojendari wizard who absorbed her power."

"You are the Storm Dragon. You are Kaiaru. You are Naruwakiru."

"I have her power, yes. And a kavaru, but —"

"I know why you have come here, but I would never help you return to him. Do you think I'm a fool? No, no, not a fool am I. Do you know what I will do for you? I will teach you a lesson."

He wasn't getting anywhere. Perhaps he should play along. "What am I supposed to learn?"

"Suffering," she replied. "You shall know my suffering. You shall know it, and it will ruin you."

"I'm sorry for anything Naruwakiru did to you, but I'm not her. I am Chonda Turesobei."

Hannya opened wide her gaping jaws, and fell upon him. Not knowing the binding runes on the blade, there was nothing he could do to stop her. She swallowed him whole, and he fell into a pure cold of desolation ... of nothingness. His sense of self eroded ... until he was all but unmade. Only a sliver of his consciousness remained.

He was not Chonda Turesobei anymore. He was a slender Kaiaru woman with fangs and claws, steel-black hair, shadow-blue skin, and a ruby kavaru at the navel.

He was Hannya.

Before him ... before her ... stood a naked man with skin the color of fog and sea-dark hair. His eyes sparkled with madness, shifting from color to color, one moment gold and another moment crimson and another moment black. Nine kavaru, each a different color, were embedded on his forehead, chest, navel, both hands, both feet, and both thighs. The man lifted a wooden bowl. Blood sloshed within it. He offered it to her.

"My Queen of the Earth, drink with me," he said in a voice that rattled within Hannya's brain.

"No," she replied, with a tremor of fear. "I will not."

The Blood King's eyes narrowed. His voice lowered to a whisper. "Do you not love me?"

She loved him so intensely she thought her heart would burst. "I do love you, and I would *die* for you. But this ... this I *cannot* do. I think you should give up now."

"I cannot stop, Hannya. I cannot stop until I get what I desire."

The Blood King had courted madness and lost his way, and she had followed, not because she still believed in his quest, but because she loved him. But she would not drink this blood for anything.

"If you will not drink," he said, "then you are no longer of any use to me."

"My love, surely —"

"I will choose a new queen. Your old rival Naruwakiru will share her power with me and drink the blood. She has told me so. Unlike you, she has fully embraced the kenja within her. She has become a dragon. And we are lovers already."

"*Lovers?*" Hannya whispered. Her knees thudded into the earth as betrayal stabbed deep into her soul.

"Lovers as you and I once were," he said. "Leave me now. You are nothing to me. She is more beautiful and more willing than ever you have been."

Hannya stumbled away. She trudged a hundred leagues, every step a step of torment and sorrow, and crawled into a cave. Down and down she crawled, into the deepest cave in the Central Mountains of Okoro. And there, in the womb of the deep earth, at last she fully embraced the powers she had mastered, blackest shadow and volcanic flame. She gave herself over completely. Her human form dissipated, and her body shifted into a dense cloud veined with thin trails of lava. And suspended in her midst was her ruby kavaru.

Hannya stood now in front of a gate with a shimmering portal. Alongside her stood nine other Kaiaru with wild forms and appearances, looking as if they'd spent far too long alone in the wilderness. Their newfound power emanated from them in waves. They were the only Kaiaru left from the dozens who had fought the Blood King.

Hannya burned with a rage so hot she thought she'd burst into flames, and yet deep within, she was cold and empty. She loved him still, not the Blood King he had become in the end, but the passionate, inquisitive Kaiaru he had been when first they had met. But she could never forgive him for what he had done to her and Okoro.

In chorus with the other Kaiaru, Hannya chanted a spell and locked the gate to the Nexus, imprisoning the Blood King in case he ever awoke from his slumber. Killing him would have been easier, but he had become a god. Slumber and a prison were the best that even they could manage.

Hannya turned back into her Earth Dragon form. "Speak to me no more," she told the others. "Look not for me again. This is your land to rule now. Do so wisely."

Only yearly feedings, primarily on demon-beasts, punctuated the centuries that Hannya haunted the deepest bowels of the earth, free from human contact, free to dream of better days long gone.

Until a Kaiaru she had never before met ventured into her lair. "I am Tepebono, Consort of Lady Amasan of the Winds," he declared. "And I am deeply sorry for this."

Before she could even respond, he drew forth a two-handed longsword of dark-steel engraved with lifeless runes and with an empty hole in the pommel. The blade was ancient ... legendary ... unseen for millennia.

"Fangthorn," she hissed. "No!"

She struck at him, but he plunged the blade into her and spoke the first rune of binding. Howling, she fell back — unable to attack — unable to flee. Again he thrust the blade into her, speaking the second rune of binding. Over and over, he plunged the blade into her body and uttered runes of binding. Until at last, her billowy form snapped into the blade, and her entire being was crammed within. Her ruby kavaru fell to the floor with a clink and rolled to his feet. Tepebono picked up the stone and fitted into the hole in Fangthorn's pommel.

"Why?!" she shouted, her voice vibrating from the blade. "Why have you done this to me?!"

"Because I have to stop the Storm Dragon," he said.

"She has returned? How?"

"I don't know," Tepebono said, "but she's back, far stronger than ever, and her power is growing. Soon, she will rule the land. The Shogakami won't stand up to her, even now that she's kidnapped one of their own."

"If you had asked, I would gladly have helped you fight her," Hannya said bitterly.

"I know, but you are not strong enough."

"Then how does having me bound within this sword make anything better? If I'm not strong enough in my dragon form, then I'm certainly not strong enough bound." He didn't answer, but she could feel his fear, his desperate hope that he was doing the right thing. "Oh, I see. You're not using me to attack Naruwakiru. You are giving me to Naruwakiru. She wants to open the Nexus and restore the Blood King, and she cannot force the Shogakami to obey her. So that just leaves me, because a dragon *can* be compelled."

"Given the right magic." Tepebono hefted the dark-steel sword and gazed upon it sadly. "I went to great lengths to find Fangthorn — the only blade in existence that could contain your power. I swear, I'm only doing this because I must."

"You're a fool! Do you know who the Blood King is? What he will do if you free him?"

"I know what he is. I'm aware of the risks."

"Then why take them? The Shogakami aren't powerful enough to stop him once he's free, especially if Naruwakiru is stronger than before."

"I have to take the chance. I have to save Amasan. No matter the cost."

"Amasan doesn't even know you're doing this, does she?"

He shook his head. "I love her. I don't expect you to understand."

"I understand love, you fool. But I also understand that what is best for all is some times more important."

Tepebono brushed her off. "I have a plan. I can make everything right."

Hannya tried, over and over to escape, but each time, pain lashed her like a bladed whip. Being in the sword was a torment of suffocation, and even worse, he was taking her to the one being she hated above all others.

High in the Orichomo Mountains they met. Tepebono stood before the Winter Gate and lifted Fangthorn. An hour earlier, he had stopped and placed an arrow made entirely of white-steel on the floor of a cave deep within the mountain. White-steel was incredibly rare in Okoro.

"I am here!" Tepebono shouted.

From the violent storm raging above, a lightning bolt struck, and on the blast mark appeared Naruwakiru in her human form. Beside her, in binding chains, slumped the Lady Amasan.

Tepebono handed over the sword, and Naruwakiru shoved Amasan into his arms.

"The binding on those chains will release once I'm gone," Naruwakiru said, smiling. She trailed a sparking finger along Fangthorn's blade. Hannya cried out in pain. "My revenge and the key to our lord's rebirth, all at once. Did you miss me, little Earth Dragon?"

"Hannya, attack!" Tepebono ordered unexpectedly.

Forced by his command, she instantly billowed forth from the sword, and in her dragon form struck Naruwakiru, knocking her back against the gate's arch. Flame and shadow met wind and lightning, and for a few moments, their battle raged. But Tepebono had been right. Even in her human form, Naruwakiru was now more powerful than Hannya had ever been. Naruwakiru drew down power from the storm above and smote Hannya.

Tepebono chanted a spell and broke the binding on Lady Amasan's chains. But they were too late to help. While Hannya was reeling, Naruwakiru locked her palm against the blade and shouted a command that burned a new binding rune onto the hilt of the sword: the *Mark of the Storm Dragon*.

"You are mine forever, Earth Dragon," Naruwakiru said as Hannya seeped harmlessly back into the blade. "Now, shall we —" Naruwakiru spotted Amasan, and Hannya saw it through her eyes. The Shogakami of the Winds was pointing at the storm cloud above, which had ceased to rage when Naruwakiru struck Hannya. "What are you —"

The white-steel arrow shot out from the cave and flew into the storm cloud. There was a sharp bang — followed by a single, deafening peal of thunder. Naruwakiru vanished. The storm dissipated. And down fell the Storm Dragon's jade heart. It fell into Amasan's hand. The white-steel had only cracked the surface.

"It will heal over in time," she said, "but it would take powerful magic to resurrect her."

"We must lock her heart away," said Tepebono. "I know the perfect place."

Tepebono spoke spell after spell for days on end, but nothing worked. At last, he gave up.

"I can break the binding I put on you, Lady Hannya, but I can't break the *Mark of the Storm Dragon*. Only Naruwakiru could do that. I'm sorry, I didn't mean for this to happen."

"So I'm trapped in this blade ... forever ..."

"I'm sorry."

"You're *sorry*?!" Hannya shouted. Her voice coming from the sword shook the earth and cracked the walls in Tepebono's workshop. "You took away my freedom!"

"It was the only way we could defeat her. And I knew you'd want to see Naruwakiru stopped."

"The plan was idiotic, and you know it! You traded my freedom for Amasan's!"

"If ever I find a way to release you, I swear that I will do so."

"I hope you rot in Torment, Tepebono. I wish now that you'd freed the Blood King, so I could see him slowly tear you and your precious Amasan to shreds."

Tepebono started to say something else, but Hannya howled incoherently at him, until the blade started to smoke. Tepebono set it down, and Amasan pulled him off to the side.

"We must hide her away," she said. "Bound like this, Hannya is too dangerous. Someone else might one day find a way to use her and free the Blood King."

"I know a place where we can hide her," Tepebono muttered. "An island no one knows about. Bound by sea, the Earth Dragon will be hidden away, her power reduced."

Sea air whipped against Hannya as Lady Amasan and Tepebono took Fangthorn to a shrine on an uninhabited island thirty leagues off the coast of Zangaiden. Few ships would ever be able to sail here through the reefs. They plunged the blade into a white marble slab and departed.

The sea sloshed outside. Gulls cried, zipped through spindrift, and plunged after prey. Seals barked on the shore. Storms rolled over. No one ever came. Days passed ... years passed … centuries passed. A few people came at last and built a tiny shrine and worshiped her. The *Mark of the Storm Dragon* had weakened, and Hannya won enough freedom that she could billow forth from the blade, but only so far. She was anchored to the blade and the ruby kavaru in the pommel.

Still, she emerged rarely. Only enough that the worshipers would remain and she wouldn't be alone. But even that was a lie, she told herself. She was utterly alone, always.

She missed freedom. She even longed for war and heartbreak, and for the days before she became the dragon. She wished now that she had sipped from the bowl offered to her by the Blood King, for her soul had fallen into Torment all the same.

Millennia passed. The sun turned red. The world grew cold. Then someone of power came to the island, a Kaiaru she had known in the distant past: Ooloolarra. She took pity and tried to free Hannya from the blade, but she too failed, even with the mark now diminished.

"I wish to build my Grand Library here," Ooloolarra said.

"Do whatever you wish," Hannya replied. "I do not care."

Her existence became nothing but darkness and suffocation and the endless awareness of both. And yet, she could feel the world, whispering to her as a dream, as it aged and iced over. The sea stopped crashing against the shore. The gulls stopped crying. Time ceased to have any meaning to her. The Keepers came, and they did nothing for her, never even making an attempt.

And then one day, Naruwakiru called on Kaiwen Earth-Mother, and her … now *his* … cries resonated through the earth and even into the Shadowland. And Hannya heard them like a trumpet blaring a note of hope. She awakened from her stupor. And she knew, beyond any doubt, that Naruwakiru would come to the blade again. How the Storm Dragon had returned, she did not know and did not care. He was back. He would come to her. She would kill him. She would have her revenge. That was all that mattered. Not freedom. That had lost all meaning to her. Only a single death mattered: Naruwakiru's. And she was *certain* that she could manage it, despite the binding. She'd prepared herself, imagining what she'd do a million times, should this day ever come.

Turesobei became himself again, his awareness slamming back into his brain, as if pounded in by a hammer. Panting … overwhelmed … he laughed … he screamed … he burst into tears … he sang … he whimpered … he curled up into a tiny ball, muttering, rocking himself.

Hannya loomed over him, laughing.

"And to think, we have only just begun, Naruwakiru, and already you are breaking."

He became aware of himself again. Darkness spread through his mind. Pain through his body. How much time had passed? Minutes? Hours? He faded in and out of himself. At times, he saw himself through her eyes, as if he'd already left the world and his spirit had drifted into her. Tendrils of her shadows wrapped around his throat, squeezing ever so gently. A fourth trip through Hannya's worst moments would kill him. The last time, though he remembered little of it, she had taken him deep into her past, before she came to Okoro.

He was dying. He thought of all the ones he'd loved. He wished he could see them one last time. He thought of Iniru's last words to him.

There was only one choice left to him: the Storm Dragon.

He opened the channel.

Chapter Fifty-Three

As the *Mark of the Storm Dragon* blazed bright on Turesobei's cheek, the power of Naruwakiru poured into him. The tendril of shadow around his neck snapped away. Lightning fired up from the floor and through his spine. Thunder boomed in the chamber. The walls shook; the floor cracked. The last of the cedar beams fell from the ceiling.

Turesobei's eyes blazed with electric fire. Wings of mist unfurled from his back. His body began to change: flesh became compressed storm cloud, bones turned into ice. As he stood, howling winds circled him. Sparks danced along his limbs. He was still human, but that would end in a few more moments.

He snarled at Hannya, and she cackled with joy.

"Oh, this is so much better," the Earth Dragon said, her veins of volcanic energy pulsing. "The wait has almost been worth it. I can defeat you in your dragon form."

Turesobei heaved a bolt of lightning. The shadows that made up Hannya's body parted, and the bolt passed through harmlessly. Then, unexpectedly, the lightning diverted its course. Hannya screamed as the bolt struck the storm mark on Fangthorn's hilt and was absorbed into the blade. "Nooo!"

Though he was changing rapidly, Turesobei wasn't the dragon, not yet. And now he had a plan to avoid that fate — but he had to move fast. In a few more moments, he would fully expand into his dragon form. Possibly forever, since he wasn't a Kaiaru like Hannya who'd spent years mastering the power within herself.

Hannya rocketed toward him, but Turesobei fired another bolt through her. When the bolt contacted the sword, Hannya cried out and drew away. Body shifting, face elongating, Turesobei charged forward and dove onto the marble block. He grabbed the sword, placing his hand directly onto the *Mark of the Storm Dragon*, and unleashed, through his palm, the most intense burst of storm energy he could muster.

"Return to the blade!" he commanded.

With a tremendous thunderclap and a flash of blinding light, Hannya's form dissipated. The blast cracked the floor, the walls, and the ceiling.

Dust rained down on him.

Dust ... onto his human body.

He was free from the Storm Dragon. He gasped in pain. He wasn't free from the wound on his chest, though, and the vigor given to him by the storm energy was fading fast.

The blade vibrated and hummed like a tuning fork, but Hannya was silent ... for now, at least. The dark-steel sword had soaked up the excess storm energy, just as it had once drawn in Hannya's earth energy. The blade had saved him from becoming the Storm Dragon.

Shaking, he drew the black blade from the stone as easily as if he were drawing it from a sheath. He flipped the sword to view both sides of the broad, symmetrical blade. No one made two-handed longswords like this anymore, not from *any* material. It was an ancient Tengba Ren design he'd seen only in pictures. The Chonda Clan's white-steel swords, over a thousand years old, were of a newer, smaller design than this one.

The binding runes blazed with blue-white fire, and suddenly he realized something. In the visions, he had watched Tepebono repeatedly fail to break them because he had to first undo the powerful *Mark of the Storm Dragon* on the hilt. Only the Storm Dragon could do that, which meant Turesobei could do it. And though he had no idea how to cast bindings this complex and powerful, thanks to Tepebono he knew the commands to break them. Turesobei could free Hannya; he could trade her freedom for cooperation.

Though he wasn't certain why that was necessary. She was bound and could be commanded, yet Ooloolarra had told him he needed Hannya's willing cooperation. That meant there was something else to this. Did Ooloolarra think he couldn't command Hannya because he wasn't Kaiaru? Or that he'd have to become the Storm Dragon to make the commands work? Or was it because the binding had weakened over the years? Hannya could free herself partly from the sword on her own now. Maybe commanding her to do something she strongly resisted could no longer be managed.

The blade stopped vibrating. And then he felt Hannya clouding his thoughts, trying to influence him through the blade, through the connections they had made in his Shadowland nightmare, and through the visions she had just imposed on him. She was going to attack him with the visions of her torment again; she wasn't through fighting him in any way she could. The power he'd blasted her with and the command he'd spoken had restrained her physical manifestation, though that probably would not work for much longer.

"Do we have to do this?" he asked. "If I have to command you to cooperate, I will."

Her voice entered his mind through the sword. "Go ahead and try. Do you think Amasan hid me here for no reason? You were always so arrogant, Naruwakiru. Even at your strongest, you would have had to fight me for control every moment you wielded me. And these bindings have grown weak over the last thirteen millennia."

"I don't want to make you do anything." He had to reason with her. He couldn't constantly call on enough kenja to control her. He'd end up tapping the storm sigil, and then he'd end up being the Storm Dragon for good. Or he'd go to sleep one night and get eaten by a dragon. "Look, we can work together. We are *not* enemies."

"You are Naruwakiru reborn. And I will have my revenge!"

"I'm *not* Naruwakiru!"

"I am not a fool. You are Kaiaru, and you have the Storm Dragon's power. I will not fall for your tricks."

Turesobei sighed. "I am Chonda Lu's ... heir ... in some special way that makes people think I'm actually a Kaiaru. But I'm not. And I am definitely not Naruwakiru. She was my enemy, too. She tried to take control of me. I split her heart with a white-steel sword, something Amasan and Tepebono couldn't do, or were unwilling to do. When the power was released, I absorbed most of it ... and survived, somehow. I *prevented* Naruwakiru from returning. So you could show a little appreciation for that."

"*Lies.* I know what you are, and I know why you came here. You want to enter the Nexus."

"Yes, but not because I want to free the Blood King. In fact, I'm scared to go there. I'm scared that I might accidentally free him. Even more so now that I've seen him in action. But going to the Nexus is the only way for me to get my companions back home and to save my clan. Look, I'm sorry your life stunk, but it wasn't my fault. And for the record, Naruwakiru is the cause of most of my troubles these days."

Hannya started to disagree again, but he stopped her and said, "You know what? I'm sick of arguing with you. You've been steeping in bitterness and rage so long that I think you've gone half mad. So let's solve this once and for all. I'm going to let you into my mind. I'm going to give you access to my thoughts, and to my memories. That way you can see who I really am. Go on. Merge your mind with mine. Have a taste of *my* suffering."

The sword hummed for a few moments, and then she said, "You would risk a another direct connection to me?"

"I'm willing to take that risk, because once you know who I am, we won't be enemies anymore."

Boy, he really hoped he knew what he was doing. He'd barely broken free of the visions she'd imposed on him. If he let her into his mind, and she decided to take over ... he'd likely never get her out.

Turesobei sat down on the slab and, taking his hand off the storm mark on the hilt, placed the blade in his lap. He let go of any sense of command he had over her, took deep breaths, and opened his mind.

"Enter and see who I really am."

Two thin tendrils of shadow emerged from the blade, latched onto his hands, climbed up his arms and neck, and then attached themselves to his temples. Hannya's consciousness flowed into his mind, probing tentatively. He didn't even try to keep her out of his most intimate thoughts. It was all or nothing if he wanted this to work.

His eyes rolled back into his head, and vertigo swamped him. Everything went dark as she raced through his thoughts and memories so fast he couldn't follow. And then suddenly, she was out, and he had a throbbing headache.

"You ... didn't ... take ... long," he gasped.

"I didn't need to know everything about you," she said. "I don't care about the spells you studied when you were eight or how you like your tea."

"So ... did you learn anything ... useful? Like maybe ... I'm not your enemy?"

"You are not Naruwakiru reborn," Hannya replied. "And you are not exactly Chonda Lu, either."

"Told you."

"You are his Inheritant."

His brain started to go a little fuzzy. "I'm his what?"

"A Kaiaru Inheritant. That means ..."

He slumped back, but kept the sword in his hand, not daring to let go. Not a word of the rest of what she said made it through to him.

"It is interesting how the magic works on you," she said.

"Yeah, fascinating." He'd caught his breath, the headache had calmed somewhat, and he only now noticed that the shadow tendrils had withdrawn back into Fangthorn. "So, you also learned that I'm a boy who has a girlfriend and two fiancées, one of them dying and the other maddened with dark power ... that I love my family, my friends, and my clan, and I'm always throwing myself into terrible situations to sacrifice myself to help them."

"I did learn all that ... and more."

"Great, so I hope you're finished torturing me, because we can help each other." He took a deep breath and braced himself. "Once you get me into my world, I will free you."

"You must free me when you reach the Nexus, or we do not have a deal."

He sighed. One problem at a time. "Fine. We will do it then."

"Are you certain you can?"

He nodded. "I'm going to let you back out of the sword now, freely. Though I'd prefer to face your human form."

Turesobei bravely spoke a command. Shadows poured out from the sword and swirled into the form of a slender zaboko woman with night-black skin, prominent cheekbones, a gossamer dress of smoke that hid very little, and the ghost of a ruby kavaru below her navel. The real kavaru was on the pommel of the sword in his hands. Her deep-set eyes, long nails, and sharp teeth were fiery red, and sparkling vermillion hair cascaded wildly down her back.

Hannya looked at herself and ran her hands along her body. "I have not taken this form in so long I'd nearly forgotten it. Why did you want to face me this way?"

Because he thought it might make her more human, but he wasn't about to tell her that. "Because this way we can meet sort of as equals. I cannot face you in my dragon form."

"Because you would permanently become the Storm Dragon if you did. You have had the dreams, you have become the dragon, and yet you will not embrace it."

"You've seen my memories. You must understand why."

"I understand why you do not want to lose yourself, yes. But I do not understand why you have not tried to master the Storm Dragon. You do not have to make the dragon form primary. I didn't do that for centuries."

"I haven't had time."

"Time is not your problem. Fear is your problem."

"Yeah, I guess."

"You fear what you do not understand."

"I faced the Storm Dragon in my dreams before I came here."

"You may have seen the power, and accepted its presence, but that is not enough. If you understood the Storm Dragon, and I mean *truly* understood it, in the way you understand that the sky is blue and water is wet and that you are who you are, then you could learn to wield the energy. But perhaps you do not know who you are yet. You are still a child."

"I'm not a child. I'm ..." Was he really an adult? He should be. For all the responsibilities he bore, he deserved to be. But he also felt like he hadn't yet become who he was supposed to be. Like he was unfinished ... a half-carved statue.

"The sooner you figure it out," she said, "the better for you and your companions."

"So," he said, wanting to move on to more urgent things. "I will free you in exchange for you getting me into the Nexus and helping me get back home. Do we have a deal?"

"We have a deal."

"You can return with me to Okoro, if you wish, though I guess we have a Hannya already in my world, bound into the sword."

"I do not think it is a good idea to have two identical beings in the same world. I will find another realm, one where another me does not exist. That seems safest."

"I will free you once we're in the Nexus, and I'll free the version of you in my world from the sword. As soon as I get the chance. I swear."

"I would be grateful for that, but you may find it difficult. Amasan and Tepebono placed spells on the island to make it nearly impossible to find, even for one such as you. Those spells are still active in your time."

Hannya stared at him with her flaming eyes. "Despite everything I just put you through, you don't bear the slightest drop of anger toward me. I expected to find it in you, but it was not there."

"I'm not happy about it, no. But why would I be angry at you? You lashed out. It's understandable, given what you endured. I would've done the same."

"No, Chonda Turesobei, you would not have. And that is why I am trusting you. I will get you into the Nexus."

Chapter Fifty-Four

Adrenaline depleted, Turesobei slumped down and put his back against the slab. His head was swimming and pounding. The wound on his chest — it was like the flame was still burning. The pain was becoming unbearable. He had nothing left in him. He was never going to make it back up those steps.

"Perhaps you should heal yourself," Hannya suggested.

"I can't," he said. "The last traces of the storm energy I summoned have left me. I'm wounded and exhausted, and the Keeper of Scrolls burned me with his stupid magic fire. And you nearly killed me, you know."

She knelt beside him. "If you will allow me, then ..."

"You can cast a healing spell?"

"I *am* a Kaiaru," she replied indignantly. "Becoming a dragon doesn't take that away from you."

"When did you last use a spell?"

"Ages ago. The binding prevented me from casting. But I assure you I know how. Kaiaru have nearly perfect memory. All you have to do is give me permission."

"I'd rather not have a healing spell go bad on me."

"As you wish," Hannya replied. "If you prefer, you could draw energy from me, using the blade, and then do the spell yourself. You could substitute my power for your internal kenja to trigger the spell."

Turesobei swooned, his eyes fluttering.

"If you can manage not to collapse before then ..."

Turesobei gripped the hilt. "I can. I've done it before using the *Mark of the Storm Dragon*."

Nodding, he gripped the blade by the hilt and opened a channel, tapping the power within the blade to supplant his own internal kenja. Hannya was strong, and her kenja was a roiling mix of earth, shadow, and fire kenja. Her power emanated from the depths of the earth, so that made sense. For a moment, he feared he would become like her, but of course that wouldn't happen. She was right: he *was* scared of the dragon.

Along with raw power, darkness and rage flowed into him. To cast a healing spell, he needed calm, positive energy. This wouldn't do. A voice pressed against his mind. He allowed her to speak to him telepathically.

"I am not merely anger," Hannya whispered into his mind. "You must draw on something else. You know that I am more than that. Remember the cold emptiness I felt? That is the place of my calm, in the darkest cavern where all is quiet and empty, deep within the earth."

Turesobei released the anger and thought of the dark emptiness Hannya had always retreated to in the deep caves whenever she felt alone and rejected. Then a strange calm flowed into him, bringing a different character of kenja. It was warm, but not inviting. It wasn't ideal, not for him, but he could work with it. He could have done the *spell of summer healing* for a change, too, but because of the burn on his chest he decided to stick with the *spell of winter healing*.

He cast the spell. The searing mark the Keeper of Scrolls had burned onto his chest remained unchanged. And it still burned like a thousand beestings. But the pain it had caused beyond the burn mark faded. His headache and dizziness went away, and some strength returned to him — enough for him to get by.

"Thank you, Lady Hannya. Now, are you ready to face the world again?"

"I am."

"And the Nexus ... and the Blood King?"

She stared into his eyes. It was hard to meet them they were so intense, but he did. Just like with a cat, he didn't want to look away and let her think she was dominant over him.

"I am ready for that, too. I put him there. I can handle it."

"Good, now we just need to reach the Nexus. And to do that, I need to figure out a way to get out of the Forbidden Library without having to fight the eighty yomon waiting for me outside. I feel certain the Keepers won't help me escape them."

"It is not in their nature to do anything more than what is foretold," Hannya replied. "The eirsenda are alien to even the Kaiaru. And these last of the eirsenda with their mission of destiny ... they are fanatics. And like me, they have probably lived far too long. But do not worry about bypassing the yomon. I can get you out of here using powers unique to me. I can take you through the Shadowland."

"I am not taking my physical body through the Shadowland, nor the bodies of my companions."

"It is the only way," she replied. "I can guide you. I can safeguard you. You need only do it long enough to get past the yomon. Then you can try to outrace them."

"How long can we travel safely through the Shadowland?" Turesobei asked. "Maximum safety."

"I can get you two leagues from here. That should be far enough that you will be out of their sight, if you are careful."

"But Awasa, the one you met in the Shadowland, she can track me now. She will know we are leaving."

"Though young, you have already led an interesting life, Chonda Turesobei. And I do not envy you being in love with three women, two of them dangerous."

Turesobei shook his head. "I care about all of them, deeply. I do. But I only love Iniru."

243

"If that is what you would like to tell yourself, then by all means do so. But what do I know? I have only lived for twenty thousand years." Hannya chuckled. "Now, if you wish to escape Ninefold Awasa's notice as we travel through the Shadowland, I suggest the *ritual of the simulacrum*."

"That's a great idea."

The ritual would form a mirror for his energy signature, and he could leave that mirror behind in the Forbidden Library. Awasa would think that he was still in the library. The ritual was difficult, but if he maintained it long enough, he could get a good lead on her and the yomon.

"Can you give me the strength I need to do the ritual and maintain it from the Shadowland?"

"I can help you some, but it will take most of my energy to get you through the Shadowland with your companions and mounts. We dragons may be godlike, with power to rival a half-dozen Kaiaru combined, but we are not limitless deities — especially when we are old and no longer feared."

Turesobei nodded in understanding. "Now I just have one final problem: Lu Bei."

"Rescuing your fetch won't be difficult, as long as you can manipulate Ooloolarra properly and get the timing right."

Chapter Fifty-Five

Turesobei threw open the door and strolled defiantly back into the Forbidden Library, Fangthorn in hand. "It's done."

Lu Bei pumped his fists and spiraled up through the air. "Master, you did it!"

The rest of his companions were waiting with smiles of relief, and stepped toward him. They didn't seem nearly as relieved as he had expected. Turesobei eyed Lu Bei and chuckled.

"You all knew I was okay before I got back up here, didn't you?"

Lu Bei chewed on his lip and looked away. "I might have kept them informed, master."

"Well, I didn't tell you not to."

Enashoma took his hand. "We were so worried. Lu Bei kept us updated as best as he could, until the shadow engulfed you. Then we didn't know what was happening for a long time. Lu Bei couldn't tell. And then Lu Bei became a little dragon, and thunder shook the entire library. The Keepers didn't like that much and —"

"Take a breath," he said. "Relax. I'm all right."

"Of course you are," she said, seriously. "I never doubted."

He grinned. "Liar."

Iniru gave him a kiss on the cheek. "I really didn't think you'd make it back from being a dragon."

"Did Lu Bei tell you how I did it?"

"I did, master. I did. And I told them all about your deal with Lady Hannya."

"Good, because I don't want to have to explain it all right now."

Zaiporo patted him on the back and congratulated him, as did Narbenu and Kemsu. Motekeru gave him a single, declarative nod. Turesobei looked to Kurine, lying there peacefully in stasis. He wished he could share his success with her, too. A motion caught his eye. High above, Ooloolarra was leaning over a gallery rail. He met her eyes, and she bowed to him.

"So you have succeeded," said the Keeper of Scrolls, stating the obvious. "Congratulations."

"Yeah, thanks."

The Keeper reached out and touched the burned spot on Turesobei's chest. The wound faded away, along with the pain it caused, leaving no sign that it had been there at all. Turesobei sighed with relief. He wasn't sure how he had blocked it out for so long. Maybe he was getting used to pain.

"You must leave no later than two hours after dawn tomorrow," the Keeper of Scrolls said, turning away.

"Wait a second!" Turesobei said. "I could use some rest. A few days at least."

"You and your companions have already rested here, and you obviously healed yourself down in the stacks. It is time for you to go. You have what you came here for."

Turesobei stepped deliberately in front of the Keeper of Scrolls to block his way. The Keeper scowled at him.

Turesobei clutched Fangthorn tight. "You could have warned us of that beforehand. This is unacceptable. I demand you let us stay another day."

"You demand?" the Keeper of Scrolls said. "Do you really wish to demand anything of me?"

Turesobei sighed with frustration. "I'm not trying to insult you. I'm just asking for a little more time."

"Our rules are our rules. You were granted a tremendous boon in being allowed to stay here at all. You should feel honored. And you are getting to stay one more night. I think that is exceedingly generous. Too generous, in my opinion."

"Please, at least let my two goronku companions stay after we leave. Just until the yomon pursue the rest of us. Then they can go back to their people."

"No, I allowed them inside only because they accompanied you. The goronku must leave with you tomorrow morning, or their lives are forfeit."

"I'm sorry," Turesobei said to Narbenu and Kemsu. "But maybe we could buy you passage on a ship leaving the port."

"No ships are here right now," said the Keeper of Scrolls. The next one won't arrive for two weeks. And they cannot wait in the village."

"Why?" Turesobei demanded.

"Because they cannot!" the Keeper of Scrolls almost shouted.

Turesobei turned to Narbenu and Kemsu and shrugged helplessly. "Sorry."

Kemsu glanced furtively at Iniru. "I'm enjoying the adventure. I'd like to continue on."

"We agreed to see you on your way," Narbenu said, "and that's what we'll keep on doing. You may still need our help."

"I was really hoping they'd let you stay, though. That way I'd know for certain you could make it back to your people ... alive."

"There's no guarantee in that," Narbenu replied. "You saw how dangerous it was for all of us to get here."

"You realize, though," said Iniru, "that seeing us to the end could mean leaving your world and coming to ours."

"Sounds exciting," Kemsu replied.

Iniru rubbed the grayish fur on his shoulder. "You might be a bit overdressed."

246

Narbenu sighed. "I'd miss my home, but how many people get to go to another world, especially one that's better than this one?"

"Well, it's not perfect," Zaiporo cautioned, "not to those who don't look like Turesobei. But it *is* a lot warmer and safer."

"And we have tea!" Lu Bei said.

"And if the two of them come along, Kurine wouldn't be the only one of her kind," Enashoma said.

"Tea," Lu Bei said wistfully, "something I shall never again experience, for I shall be trapped here ... forever. Woe is me." He winked at Turesobei who had a hard time restraining a laugh.

"Sobei," Enashoma said, frowning toward Lu Bei. "What are you going to —"

Turesobei shook his head. "Nothing I can do. I made a deal. I will honor it. I have no other choice."

While the others slept after eating dinner, Turesobei worked on his simulacrum ritual. Before starting it, he spent two hours reviewing how it worked, until the text on the pages of his spell book began to blur. Then Lady Hannya gave him advice and a little power throughout the actual ritual. He was absolutely exhausted, but he had no choice. He'd always heard that there was no rest for the wicked, but he was discovering that reality was quite the opposite. After midnight, he finished. Having placed the magic on the amulet, he stepped outside and spoke with the Keeper of the Hearth.

"Could you give this to the Keeper of Destiny ... the next time someone goes to him?"

"You can keep the amulet," the Keeper of the Hearth replied. "Returning it is not necessary. It is powerless now."

"I insist."

The Keeper eyed it carefully. "There is a spell on this. A powerful one."

"It will have faded long before you give it back. And it won't harm anyone. I promise."

The Keeper continued to study the amulet. "A simulacrum spell?"

"A spirit mirror, so Awasa and the yomon will still think I'm here for a short while. It should give us a few days head start on them."

"You cannot leave an item with such magic on it here."

"It won't harm anyone."

The Keeper of the Hearth sighed. "I will take it up with the Keeper of Scrolls, but he will not allow it, I can assure you of that."

"Then don't tell him. Just hold onto this for a few days. Hide it if you must. Please. Otherwise, Inatiasharra's sacrifice was all for nothing."

"Inatiasharra ... how do you know that name?"

"He told me before he died."

The Keeper of the Hearth studied him contemplatively. Turesobei had learned to wait them out. Minutes passed, then at last he said, "I shall do this in honor of my friend, who represented you so bravely."

Turesobei handed him the amulet. "Thank you."

"Is there anything else you require?"

"Can you have our mounts prepared and ready to go in the morning, but without taking them out of the stables? Just line them up inside and have them ready."

"It is a good plan," the Keeper of the Hearth said. "A risky one, but clever."

"I didn't tell you what my plan was."

"It is obvious, is it not, given who your new ally is? And the simulacrum does no good if they see you leave. I will see that the arrangements are made. And I will hide the amulet for as long as I can."

Chapter Fifty Six

Bundled once again in their many layers of sonoke fur, Turesobei and his companions left the Forbidden Library. The Keeper of the Hearth and Ooloolarra, who was now dressed in a silk robe and sandals, escorted them out. None of the other Keepers saw them off, not even the Keeper of Scrolls. Once outside, the Keeper of the Hearth turned them over to the Keeper of the Shores, who bowed his head in greeting.

"I am glad that you succeeded, Chonda Turesobei. I did not think that you would."

"Thank you for letting us in and giving me the chance," Turesobei said.

"You are welcome. Now, follow me. Everything has been made ready for your departure, exactly to your specifications."

When they reached the steep, ice-covered stairs, Turesobei cringed and groaned.

"Oh gods, I'd forgotten the steps," Enashoma said.

Ooloolarra cast a spell and waved a hand. The ice on the stairs melted, and the water poured off to the sides where it refroze, leaving the steps dry and ice-free.

"You melted it without using fire kenja," Turesobei said with surprise.

Ooloolarra winked. "You don't live for millennia in a world coated by ice without learning a trick or two."

Once they reached the stable in the tiny village, the Keeper of the Shores said a curt goodbye and departed. Their mounts awaited them, saddled and loaded with gear, and lined up inside the main hallway. They strapped Kurine into the saddle behind Motekeru, and then everyone else mounted up.

"It was my pleasure to represent you," Ooloolarra said to Turesobei. "I have not had the company of another Kaiaru in so long." Turesobei let the Kaiaru comment slide. "And goodbye to you as well, Lady Hannya. I wish you well on your journey."

Hannya, remaining within the sword, made no reply.

Lu Bei gave Turesobei a hug. "Goodbye, master. Take care. Eat your vegetables. Do well with your magic. Get everyone home safe and sound, please. Do it for me! And drink lots of warm tea ... in my name."

Turesobei worked hard to keep a straight face. "I will, Lu Bei. I promise. And I will never forget you."

"Can't you please change your mind about Lu Bei," Enashoma begged Ooloolarra.

"The fetch comes with me," Ooloolarra said. "That was the deal. It was a fair one. And

I have agreed to leave the library for the first time in seven centuries so that Lu Bei may see you off. I think that is exceedingly kind."

Lu Bei flew into Enashoma's arms, faking huge sobs. Turesobei was worried the ridiculous dramatics would give their plan away. "Oh, do not cry, dear Lady Shoma, my most cherished friend. You will know many happy years, even without me. I shall live on, and ever shall I think upon you."

Turesobei spoke the command phrase for his simulacrum ritual. The energies activated. A wave of dizziness swamped him. He stumbled a few steps, but recovered.

Ooloolarra cocked a silvery eyebrow. "That was an impressive piece of magic you just did."

"Thank you for sponsoring me," Turesobei said, bowing. "I will be forever thankful to you."

"It was my pleasure," Ooloolarra replied. "Come to me, fetch."

Lu Bei drifted over to her. "Of course, my new together-forever friend."

"Now for another piece of impressive magic." Turesobei drew Fangthorn from a sheathe the Keeper of the Hearth had brought him, which he had strapped onto his back. "Lady Hannya, if you would, please." He spoke another activation command. "Everyone, remain calm."

The world around them darkened, as if a veil had fallen over them. Ooloolarra screamed and lunged as Lu Bei zipped away from her. The fetch landed in Turesobei's lap and waved to her.

"Bye-bye, usually-naked, crazy book lady! Sorry I lied about the together-forever thing. In a few hundred years, you'll recover from this jilting. I promise."

Ooloolarra reached out to grab him, and her hand passed through Lu Bei. Then she faded away from their view ... along with the stables, the village, and the library. The sun overhead was so dim its light could barely penetrate the clouds. The ground was not ice anymore but dust and rock. Eerie mists drifted over the barren terrain around them.

"That was perfect, master." Lu Bei laughed. "Can't believe she fell for it."

"Do you really think you fooled her?" said Hannya, her deep voice vibrating from the sword — surprising everyone except Turesobei.

"You think she was just playing along?" Turesobei asked.

"She was giving you a chance to best her," Hannya replied. "Otherwise, why not demand you leave Lu Bei with her in the library? She could have done so."

"You're probably right," Turesobei said.

"I know I am right," Lady Hannya replied. "Kaiaru such as her love to play these games."

Lu Bei nodded as he flew over to Enashoma. "Master and she used to do these sorts of things all the time with one another. It was a sign of respect, I think."

Enashoma planted a big kiss on Lu Bei's cheek. "I don't care why or how, I'm just glad you're sticking with us. Though Turesobei could've said something."

"I didn't want her to find out by accident," Turesobei said. "Thought it best to keep it just between Lady Hannya, Lu Bei, and myself."

"Too bad she didn't find out," Iniru replied with an over-the-top, fake scowl. "I'd rather we had left the little jerk."

Lu Bei stuck his tongue out and blew a raspberry at her.

"Is it just me," Zaiporo said, shivering, "or is it actually colder here?"

"It's a mystical cold," Turesobei said. "Caused by the absence of life and love. No amount of clothing can shield you from it."

Lu Bei popped up in front of everyone. "My lords and ladies, and you two." He pointed at Iniru and Kemsu. "Welcome to the Shadowland. Remain calm and stick together. Do not stray, or you will become lost, and never find your way again. We need only be here for a short while, which is good, because otherwise, we would die."

Lu Bei's speech wasn't really necessary. Turesobei had already explained it to them all that morning. Having never been to the Shadowland before, it clearly unnerved them, though they were putting on brave faces. It *should* unnerve them. He'd been here through astral projection several times along with Grandfather Kahenan, and in the nightmare with Awasa, but being here physically was another matter altogether. It felt terrible, like half his life had been sucked out of him.

"So this ... this is where people go when they die?" Kemsu asked.

"They pass through the deeper layers," Lady Hannya explained, her voice vibrating from the blade. "Most souls quickly head on to Paradise or Oblivion or Torment, after only a few moments in the Shadowland, though a few do linger for days, sometimes years. Do not think too much on it. I find it is best that way. We are only in the first layer of the Shadowland. It gets less pleasant and more dangerous the farther in you go. You should all get moving."

As they rode, they tried talking to one another to calm their nerves, but that failed. Their voices were weak, and silence dominated the Shadowland. Even Lu Bei's chatter trailed off eventually. Turesobei worried about Kurine because she was closest to death, but the stasis seemed to be preserving her well enough.

After an hour of riding at top speed, Zaiporo said, "I really don't see the point in going back ... to the real world, I mean. It's fine here. I thought it was bad at first, but it's really not. You get used to all the gray."

Enashoma sighed. "We could ride toward Paradise, you and I."

It was the sort of statement that might have made Zaiporo dance with glee any other time. Instead his response was flat. "Yeah, I'd like that."

"I'd be okay with Oblivion," Narbenu said.

Kemsu began to stray out of the line, heading toward some random spot in the distance.

"Oblivion, Paradise ... all that sounds like too much trouble," Iniru said. "I'd be happy if we just stopped and took a nap."

"It's time to go back, master," Motekeru said.

Turesobei snapped out of the trancelike state he'd fallen into and noticed his disinterested mount was slithering along at half-speed.

"Oh, right. Lady Hannya ..."

Adding in his own power, to the point it nearly knocked him out, he helped Hannya tug them back into reality. He was a little disturbed that she'd been willing to keep them here longer, but he didn't say anything about it.

With what seemed like a crack of thunder, they returned to the real world. Even the Glass Sea had a vibrancy and life to it that was breathtaking. The snow and ice sparkled a thousand shades of pink and white under the crimson sun. The sky was many shades of deep blue and purple overhead. The sonoke snorted and sped up, playfully racing one another.

Narbenu took in a deep breath and exhaled a laugh of relief. "Really gives you an appreciation of life, doesn't it?"

"That it does," Turesobei said.

"No difference to me," Motekeru said. "But the hounds didn't like it." The hounds had, indeed, whimpered throughout their Shadowland journey.

"I can't believe I wanted to stay," Enashoma said.

"Worry not, fair lady," Lu Bei said. "It was the Shadowland tempting you. We all would have fallen to it eventually."

"Even you?" Zaiporo said.

"Even me, though I would not have died. I would have wandered the Shadowland for ages ... until I turned into a demon."

"He is not joking," said Hannya. "That is what happens to those who never pass on. When you die and find yourself here, do not hold on. Head toward the Gates and pass on."

As sunset approached, Turesobei stopped them.

"Let's go ahead and make camp."

"Shouldn't we keep riding a few more hours under the moon mirrors?" Iniru said. "Avida is rising, and the sea is free of obstructions."

"Another hour of riding and my simulacrum ritual will start fading, because we'll be too far away from the amulet. Once we are out of range, Awasa will know, and they will pursue us. So we might as well get a good night of sleep before the magic fades out."

"Oh, that makes sense then," Iniru replied. "Assuming it worked and it fooled her."

Turesobei closed his eyes and concentrated. "I can't feel her pursuing us, so I assume so."

"You're that connected to her?" Iniru said, with a hint of worry in her voice. "I knew she could track you, but I didn't know you could sense her."

"It's not a strong connection. I wouldn't want to rely on it."

Motekeru began cutting blocks out of the ice, and the others stacked the blocks to build a giant snow house. Narbenu was back to his old insistence on separate snow houses, but

Turesobei managed to talk him into a single snow house with blankets hung down the middle.

"If you end up in my world," Turesobei told him, "at least your moral standards won't be a problem."

Narbenu laughed. "Assuming people accept that we look different?"

"You're not that different from Iniru," Turesobei replied.

"The Chonda will accept you well enough because of Turesobei," Zaiporo replied, "but I don't think you'd feel at home or welcome. I'm heading to Zangaiden. Hopefully, Shoma will go there with me. But I'm not sure how well you'd fit in even there."

Zaiporo glanced toward Enashoma, but she said nothing and pretended to not have heard him.

"You'd probably do best among my people," Iniru said. "The k'chasa would accept you. The city of Dogo Daiyen in the far west would definitely welcome you, too. But something tells me a city of a million people would be overwhelming for you."

"A million people?" Kemsu shook his head. "I find it hard to imagine your world. Leagues and leagues of trees and fields. Millions of people crammed into one location. Even ten thousand in one spot would amaze me. It sounds wondrous. And ..."

"A bit frightening," Narbenu added.

Turesobei cast the *spell of sensing presences* to make his regular check before they turned in. As he scanned, he picked up something, but only for a moment. It had seemed almost human, but it was gone. His brow furrowed in concentration, he knelt and placed his palms on the ice.

"What is it, master?" Lu Bei whispered.

Even after doubling the spell's energy, he couldn't sense anything. Turesobei shook his head. "Nothing. I thought for a moment that I had picked something up, but it's gone now, if it was ever there at all."

"The yomon?" Iniru asked.

"Definitely not one of them," he replied.

"A reitsu?" Lu Bei said. "We haven't seen them in a long while."

"I don't think so. I'm pretty sure they gave up after the blizzard in the canyon. Haven't detected one since. And I don't think they would've kept after us on the sea or waited outside the library. I'm not sure what it was. A beast of some sort ... or maybe just a mistake. The spell's not perfect. Hannya, did you sense anything?"

She replied telepathically, "I'm not sensing anything powerful or demonic."

"Probably nothing then," Turesobei said. "But I'll check again before I go to sleep, just to be safe."

With the snow house finished and the sonoke resting in the trench, they went inside. As the others tapped a couple of star stones to life, Turesobei removed the sheathed darksteel sword from his back and placed it onto his blanket beside him.

The others glanced at the blade, nervously. None of them had asked him anything about it. They wanted probably to but were terrified. He was carrying around a sword containing the legendary Earth Dragon Hannya. In a way, this was the most ridiculous thing he had ever done. It was almost as bad as turning into a dragon himself.

"Why are you smiling?" Zaiporo asked.

Turesobei touched the ruby kavaru in the sword's hilt. "The Earth Dragon. Amazing, huh? Would you like to meet her?"

"I'm good," Zaiporo said. "No offense to you, my lady."

Turesobei could feel a vibration in the blade that he thought was laughter.

Over the next three days, they rode until the mounts couldn't go any longer. Late on the third night, as they set up camp, Hannya spoke to Turesobei.

"You are getting close. We are less than a day's ride away. You should make it there by midmorning."

Turesobei relayed the news to the others.

"Good, because our food supply's nearly gone," said Narbenu. "Hope we can find food in this Nexus we're going to."

There was little game out on the ice of the sea, and they didn't have time to hunt. They certainly didn't have enough time to dig holes ten feet deep through the ice for fishing.

Turesobei gazed south, back toward the Forbidden Library. "I can feel Awasa getting close. She's not far away now."

"I can sense her, too," Hannya said telepathically.

"Do we need to keep moving?" Iniru said.

"The mounts have got to have some rest now, or we'll kill them within an hour or two," Narbenu said.

Turesobei frowned. "I think we have enough of a lead. We'll get up as early as we can and head out."

Turesobei woke. The snow house was barely lit. Kemsu was pulling on his parka and his overboots.

"Narbenu went outside to get the mounts ready," Kemsu whispered. "Thought I'd go help him. I couldn't sleep either. And I do need to repair a strap on one of the saddles."

"Worried about leaving your world?"

"Yeah," Kemsu whispered. "Narbenu and I both are, but we'll be all right. I just want to keep busy so I don't think about it too much, you know."

Turesobei yawned and tried to pry his eyes open. "You need me to help?"

"No, you rest. You've got about another hour before the sky starts to lighten. I'll wake you when it's time."

"I'll send Motekeru out with you."

Kemsu drew a hanging blanket back, revealing Motekeru in the corner on the girls' side. He was cradling Kurine, with Enashoma and the hounds curled up against him. Since he'd eaten the vine spirit's heart, Motekeru's body generated more heat than anyone else's by far. Without a blanket under him, he would have melted the ice overnight.

"I don't want to disturb them."

Drifting off, Turesobei nodded in understanding.

He slept until Hannya, in her human form, appeared to him within a dream and yelled, "Turesobei, wake up! Now!"

Chapter Fifty-Seven

Hannya's shout thundered through his brain.

Turesobei snapped awake.

A tall, slender form shot toward him. A dagger flashed in the wan light of a star stone — white-steel!

"Twist left!" Hannya warned.

Turesobei wrenched his body to the left. The white-steel dagger missed his heart and sliced across his ribs. He grabbed the hilt of Fangthorn.

"The other way!" Hannya said.

Turesobei twisted back to the right. The second strike also missed his heart, but stabbed deep into his shoulder. The assailant didn't draw the blade out. Instead, she twisted the blade and grabbed him by the neck with her free hand.

Warmth drained out of him.

His eyes locked onto the face of his opponent.

"Lady Umora," he gasped.

An orange paint that reeked of decay was smeared onto her face and body.

"Took me weeks to track you down," she sneered. "Figured out a way to stay hidden from your magic using togokagi egg yolks. And whatever spell you used to trick the yomon at the library, it didn't work on me."

His companions woke. Motekeru and Iniru launched into action, but another yolk-painted reitsu dove into the snow house and intercepted them. For the agile reitsu, fighting in the close confines of the snow house wasn't a hindrance, but Motekeru was limited since he couldn't even stand up straight, except in the center of the room.

Turesobei thought about opening the connection to the storm mark, to kill Umora the way he'd killed her brother, but he was groggy, wounded, and unprepared. He wasn't sure he could keep the storm energy in check this time.

"Unleash your dragon energy on me, if you dare," Lady Umora said, sensing his thoughts. "Doesn't matter. I've got nothing left to live for. You can kill me easily enough, but I've already had my revenge. I've made sure the yomon will catch up to you."

He was losing vital warmth rapidly. There had to ... be another ... way.

Hannya whispered telepathically, "Let me out. I can take care of her."

"Hannya," he said. "Strike."

Shadows poured from the blade and wrapped around Umora, who released her grip on Turesobei and stumbled back, screaming. Umora swung the white-steel dagger and cut through the shadows, piercing a fiery vein. Hannya screeched and drew away. Staggering, Lady Umora smiled and brandished the white-steel dagger.

It was the last thing she ever did.

Motekeru's claws ripped through Umora's neck, and her head bounced across the floor, trailing blood on the ice.

Zaiporo, Iniru, Lu Bei, and the hounds had cornered the other reitsu, who was fighting like mad. Iniru and Zaiporo had both been wounded several times. Shoma was backed into a corner, unable to do anything to help. The hounds were shielding her and seemed to be looking for a way they could dart in to help, but there just wasn't enough space. Hannya's flaming eyes opened within the shadow. She zipped over Iniru's head and, like a viper, struck the reitsu, swallowing him whole. When she peeled away moments later, the reitsu was cold and silent. Still, Motekeru cut the reitsu's throat for good measure.

"Kemsu and Narbenu," Turesobei said, placing his palm over the wound in his shoulder to stop the bleeding. "They were getting the mounts ready."

Lu Bei zipped outside, followed by Motekeru and Iniru.

Zaiporo clutched his arm. Blood seeped out from between his fingers. "I'll stay here with the hounds and guard Shoma and Kurine. Be careful."

"You okay?"

"I'll bind his wound," Shoma said. "What about you?"

Turesobei pulled his palm away. Blood was flowing freely through all the layers of fur. He looked at his ribs but didn't see any blood yet. "I can manage."

Turesobei could endure the pain. He was getting used to it, and this wasn't as bad as the mark the Keeper of Scrolls had burned into his chest.

Fangthorn in hand, Turesobei crawled, slowly, out through the entrance, with Hannya flowing after him. No other reitsu were in sight. Lu Bei flew up and circled around as Motekeru and Iniru leapt down into the trench where they kept the mounts. Hannya spread out from the sword into her full shadow form.

"I will keep a look out as well," she said. "And do my best to intimidate any further attackers."

Turesobei rushed over to the edge and looked down.

"Oh no." He fell to his knees. "This — this can't be."

Chapter Fifty-Eight

Narbenu ... blood flowed from his throat and pooled on the ice. His head was bent back at an awkward angle, and his eyes were as cold and lifeless as the Glass Sea. Kemsu lay nearby. Bloodstains were spreading across his parka in three different places. A deep blue bruise stained his neck, rising up onto his cheeks.

"Niru," Kemsu gasped hoarsely as she took his hand. "Reitsu ... ambushed us ... out of ... nowhere."

"Rest," she told him.

"Narbenu ... threw himself in front ... to save me." He winced in pain. "Kurine ..."

"Everyone else is okay," she said. "Just a few cuts is all."

"Let's get him inside," Turesobei said.

Motekeru lifted Kemsu and carried him into the snow house. Iniru held Kemsu's hand as they went.

Only then did the full weight of what had happened register for Turesobei.

A deep pool of blood filled the other end of the trench. The reitsu had slit the throats of the sonoke — all of them. That's why Lady Umora had been certain of her revenge. With no mounts, there was no way to outrace the yomon.

Turesobei marshaled his emotions. He had to keep calm and lead everyone, and he had to heal Kemsu. "Lu Bei?"

"I don't see anything, master, but I'll keep circling."

Palm placed against his shoulder, he moved toward the snow house. But Hannya took on her human form and stopped him.

"Why are you blocking me?"

"You are wounded," she replied. "You cannot heal him while you are injured and losing so much blood yourself." She drew his hand away. "Will you allow me this time?"

Turesobei nodded. "Do it fast."

With her hand hovering over the wound, Hannya chanted the *spell of summer healing*. The casting was perfect. A soothing warmth flowed into the wounds and into his bones. The wound sealed over, and the pain dulled. It would take some time to recover fully from the wounds, since they hadn't taken the time to bind or clean them first, but he could function, and that was all he cared about now.

"First spell I have cast in an age," she said, proudly. "I think it went well."

"Perfect. When we get inside, could you heal Zaiporo and Iniru?"

"Of course."

Turesobei crawled inside. Shoma met him at the entrance.

"Sobei ... Narbenu?"

Turesobei shook his head.

She put her hand to her mouth and stifled a sob. He grabbed her by the shoulders. "Shoma, be strong and brave. We have much to do. I need you and Motekeru to go outside and get the gear off the sonoke. Only the essentials."

Shoma shook her head in confusion. "Why ... why would we need to ... oh no."

Turesobei nodded. "Get only what we can carry on foot."

Enashoma took a step toward the entrance and then stopped, her eyes wide. She gasped and stumbled backward. Zaiporo almost screamed, and Iniru flinched. Turesobei spun around, worried, but then relaxed. They hadn't yet seen Lady Hannya in her human form, with her fangs and claws, her black skin and vermilion hair, and the ghost of a ruby kavaru at her navel, visible through her gossamer dress.

"Do not be alarmed," Hannya said. "I am your friend."

"Zaiporo," said Turesobei, "Lady Hannya is going to heal your wound while I tend Kemsu, okay?"

Zaiporo nodded, trancelike, and then bowed to Hannya. "My lady, thank you."

Enashoma bowed quickly too, and then darted outside. Motekeru said nothing to Hannya nor showed any special reaction to her. Iniru returned her attention to Kemsu. She had removed his parka and shirt to expose the three wounds that were still oozing blood. The reitsu had stabbed him twice in the stomach and once near the heart. Turesobei knelt beside him.

"Pierced lung," Iniru whispered.

Kemsu shivered; his teeth were chattering. "So cold."

Iniru placed a star stone beside him and tapped it to full strength. "I don't have time to bandage the wounds. And there's not much I can do."

Hannya said telepathically to Turesobei, "The boy is fading into the Shadowland already. There is nothing you can do for him."

"Watch me try," Turesobei thought back at her.

"Wait one moment, then," she said.

She finished the healing spell on Zaiporo. He thanked her profusely then said, "I'll help Shoma and Motekeru. There's nothing I can do here but get in the way."

Hannya knelt beside Kemsu. "Do you know the *spell of blood binding*? That would stop the bleeding and aid the healing spell."

"I know of it from Chonda Lu's grimoire, but I can only do Kaiaru spells that involve storm energy, and those only at risk of becoming the dragon."

"I will do it, then." Hannya chanted the spell. The bleeding stopped.

Turesobei then cast the *spell of winter healing* and put everything he had into it. A white cloud of energy formed over Kemsu's chest and seeped in. Kemsu's eyes brightened, and his color improved. Turesobei felt relieved. Maybe Kemsu would be okay. Maybe Hannya was wrong.

Kemsu convulsed and coughed up blood. Not good. The magic hadn't sealed the wounds inside well enough. There was only so much that accelerating natural healing could do when the damage was extensive, or when it affected internal organs.

Turesobei opened his kenja-sight and sighed. The problem wasn't just the wounds. The reitsu had stolen most of Kemsu's vital energy, too. Hannya was right. Even if the spell had fixed his wounds, it wouldn't have been enough.

"I'm ... I'm not going ... to make it," Kemsu said. "Reitsu ... took a lot of warmth ... that's why I'm so cold." He coughed up blood again. His eyes met Turesobei's. "Not wrong ... am I?"

"This is my fault," Turesobei said. "All of it. I'm so sorry, Kemsu."

"Don't be," Kemsu replied. "Had ... adventure of a lifetime ... if a bit short. We nearly got you ... there."

"Thank you," Turesobei said. "I will be eternally grateful." He sat back with exhaustion and disbelief.

"Leave us out on ... the ice. That's ... our way." Kurine lay nearby. Kemsu reached out and touched her hand. He strained a smile as tears welled in his eyes. "You will ... see to her ..."

"I will," Turesobei said. "I promise."

"Niru, I ..." She took his hand. Wracked with spasms, he retched up more blood. "Do you think ... you and me ..."

She leaned in and kissed his cheek and whispered something in his ear. He smiled and let go. His last breath seeped out.

Iniru closed his eyes. She began to sob, and Turesobei took her in his arms. What could he say?

"At least he could smile at the end," Turesobei said.

"At least," she replied numbly.

"What did you tell him?"

"A lie."

Hannya healed Iniru and returned to Fangthorn. Motekeru carried both bodies out and placed them on the ice, away from the scene of the carnage. With his claws, he etched a big circle in the ice around them and wrote their names beside them. Turesobei allowed Hannya to leave the blade. As the Earth Dragon, she hovered over them like a shroud. Lu Bei recited an ancient poem honoring fallen heroes, and Turesobei asked the Crimson Sun to bless the two goronku. Enashoma spoke the *Prayer to the Greater Deities*.

When it was done, Hannya said, "Their spirits have now passed on to the beyond."

"You can know that?" Iniru asked.

"I am deeply connected to the Shadowland," Hannya replied.

"Did they ... did they go on to Paradise?" Enashoma asked.

"That I cannot say. What I do know is that they did not wander the Shadowland aimlessly, and they passed on peacefully. I believe that means they found Paradise or Oblivion. I do not think a peaceful soul goes to Torment."

"Thank you," Iniru said, wiping a tear away.

They pulled their reduced-to-essentials packs onto their backs and marched, painstakingly because there was no other way to do it, over the slippery ice. Turesobei gave Iniru the white-steel dagger, since he had Fangthorn. Lady Hannya walked with them in her human form, carrying a pack for them. They spoke little to one another. Even Lu Bei remained silent, staying in book form. After all the dangers they had knowingly faced, death had struck — silent, swift, and unexpected. It seemed unreal, and yet far too real at the same time.

Turesobei had known this was bound to happen eventually, that they would lose one or more of their group, but that didn't make this any easier. He felt powerless. What if Hannya hadn't woken him? What if the reitsu had then killed Shoma and Iniru? He tried to block it out of his mind. He could blame himself later for not sending Motekeru out with them, or for not doing another scan. He still had the others to save. And Kurine. He wanted to make certain at least one of the goronku made it through this.

"Sobei," Iniru said, "if the yomon catch up to us, can you beat them?"

"I really don't want to find out," Turesobei said.

"We might not have a choice," Iniru said.

"If it comes to it, yes. The yomon didn't have any way to counter the Storm Dragon before. I could fly above them and rain lightning down on them. I really don't see how anything could resist that."

"You underestimate your enemies," said Lady Hannya. "The Shogakami imprisoned the yomon here for a reason. The last one hundred and eight out of the thousand that invaded Okoro — the Shogakami could not kill them. Think about that. Nine Shogakami could not beat these yomon. Trickery imprisoned them here. That is all they could do without white-steel, which was exceedingly rare here in Okoro."

It had all but disappeared by the time the baojendari had arrived. Turesobei had been surprised to see Amasan and Tepebono use the arrow in the vision Hannya had shown him.

"But I destroyed twenty of them!" he said.

"You caught them off guard," said Lady Hannya, "but they will be ready for you next time. After a few minutes of exposure, yomon naturally recalibrate to the kenja signatures used near them. Once they are in synch, they are resistant to those signatures. So next time, your lightning will not harm them, and neither will Motekeru's fire burn them. You will have to fight them on the ground, and they will be able to hurt you, while it may be impossible for you to hurt them at all."

"Good thing I didn't transform to fight them earlier," Turesobei said with relief. "I'd be stuck as the Storm Dragon, and the rest of you would've died."

"Comforting," Zaiporo muttered.

"What about you, Lady Hannya?" Iniru asked. "Could you destroy the yomon? Are you as strong as the Storm Dragon?"

Eyes aflame, her voice crackling with power, Hannya rounded on Iniru and yelled madly, "I have always been stronger than Naruwakiru! Only when she took on the jade heart was she more powerful than me."

Turesobei put a hand on Hannya's arm. "Iniru doesn't know about your history with the Storm Dragon. Relax. Focus."

Hannya took several deep breaths, and then her features began to soften. After a few minutes, she spoke again, though she didn't apologize for the outburst, just as she hadn't apologized to Turesobei for what she had put him through.

"The binding limits me in my dragon form, because I cannot fully emerge from the sword. Still, as a dragon, I am certain I could beat a fair number of them, but I would not be able to defeat them all or shield the rest of you during the battle. And this Awasa, she has a white-steel sword. Should she attack me with it ... that would be very inconvenient."

As the sun was setting, Hannya said. "We have arrived."

"I don't see anything," Iniru said. "Just more ice."

"The edge of the world and the doorway to the Nexus are just three hundred paces ahead." Hannya crooned out a song. A stone archway matching the Winter Gate appeared. The portal wasn't active, though. "Our doorway. I just need to open it. But I cannot do that from out here."

"Better get to it fast, then!" Lu Bei shouted from up above. "Trouble's arrived."

The eighty yomon and Awasa, riding on the back of one of them, appeared on the horizon. Awasa screamed. The yomon charged.

Hannya shifted into her Earth Dragon form, billowing out into a black cloud the size of a house. She roared into the sky. The yomon slid to a halt. With the Earth Dragon drifting along behind them, Turesobei and his companions ran, as best as they could. When they reached the gate Turesobei cast the *spell of the moon mirrors*.

"Careful!" Turesobei said. Step past the pillars, and you'll step into nothingness."

Hannya returned to her human form and stood before the gate.

"What about the yomon?" Zaiporo said. "They won't be afraid now."

"Sorry," Hannya said. "I cannot do this part in my dragon form."

In the distance, Awasa shouted, "It was just a trick! Get them!"

Bellowing war cries, the yomon charged again.

"Without the Shogakami, I can only open the gate for a few moments," Lady Hannya warned. She began chanting the words of a spell, words that sounded like a form of Ancient Zaboko.

"Everyone get ready," Turesobei said, facing the oncoming tide of yomon, Fangthorn at the ready.

Enashoma hooked her hands under Kurine's arms, so she could drag her through the portal. That way, Motekeru could fight the yomon if he had to.

"Sobei, we've got to get out of here fast," Iniru warned as the yomon closed to two hundred paces.

A portal shimmered within the gate ... and disappeared.

It shimmered again ... and disappeared a second time.

"What's wrong?" Enashoma asked.

Hannya shook her head.

"Do you need help?" Turesobei asked.

Hannya again shook her head.

Lu Bei zoomed down and hovered beside Lady Hannya. As she began her chant a third time, Lu Bei spoke the same words in perfect unison with her. His eyes glimmered.

The gate sparked to life again ... and it held.

"Is it safe?" Turesobei asked.

Still chanting, Hannya nodded.

"Everyone, go!" Turesobei yelled.

Zaiporo grabbed Kurine's feet and helped Enashoma carry her through. As thudding steps cracked the surface of the ice, Turesobei glanced back. The yomon were nearly on top of them. This was cutting it way too close. The hounds bounded into the portal. Ceasing his chant with a nervous frown, Lu Bei turned into a book. The portal remained live. Turesobei handed the diary to Iniru.

"You've only got a few more seconds," she said as she darted through.

"Can you maintain the portal on the other side?" he asked Hannya. She shook her head no. "Motekeru, go now!"

"Master —"

"Go!"

Motekeru stepped into the portal and disappeared.

Hannya tapped Turesobei on the arm.

"Another moment," he said. "The yomon won't kill me. Awasa will want to face me herself. So when I say go, we go together."

The yomon were so close Turesobei could hear them panting and grunting as they strained to run as fast as possible. Their steps were so heavy that cracks in the ice preceded them.

"Turesobei!" Awasa cried out. "I won't let you get away!"

Sword in hand, Awasa leapt forward off the shoulders of the yomon she rode. She flipped once in the air and came down with a kick. Turesobei dodged aside. As Awasa landed in a crouch, she swung Sumada and sliced through Hannya at the waist.

Hannya's form dimmed. Her chant ceased. Screaming, she disappeared back into Fangthorn.

Chapter Fifty-Nine

The portal flickered. The yomon were only paces away. Turesobei lowered his shoulder, charged, and tackled Awasa, knocking her through the sputtering gate.

A blinding light ... skin tingling with a million pricks ... thoughts scrambled ... bright swirls of gold and crimson and emerald ... the pinging of a thousand wind chimes ... orange blossom and cloves ... a lullaby with nonsensical words ... pain ... laughter ... darkness ... nothing ... they weren't going to make it ... they were being torn apart and spread out into ... Oblivion ...

Though it was hard to think of anything, Turesobei locked onto his love for his friends and focused his mind on the Nexus, on Fangthorn in his hand, and Awasa tucked against him.

"Hannya ... the Nexus."

"I can't help you," she replied with a strain in her voice. "Your storm kenja ... release it into the pathway to keep the connection alive ... or we'll never make it."

For once, he didn't worry about becoming the Storm Dragon. There was no fear, because there was no other choice. He opened the channel to the *Mark of the Storm Dragon* all the way and projected the energy outward, as best as he could. He heard himself roar. He felt his body shift into that of the dragon. The darkness vanished. Lightning flashed all around them, so that it seemed they were flying through a tunnel in a storm cloud. And he was the Storm Dragon, carrying them through.

Suddenly, all that vanished, and Turesobei stumbled onto the other side of the gate, fully human, with Awasa still in his arms. He threw her aside as he crashed onto a flagstone surface.

Relief spread through him. He wasn't the Storm Dragon, and his friends were already here. They had made it through safely. They had escaped the Ancient Cold and Deep and reached the Nexus of the Realms.

He glanced behind him. The portal within the matching gate on this side was closed. Half of one yomon had made it through. Blood poured from the severed torso.

Turesobei stood. They were on a raised, octagonal platform in the middle of an empty courtyard. A temple complex circled the open space. High above burned an orange ball that mimicked the sun. The sky was a faded purple instead of blue, with no trace of clouds. On the edges of the platform stood eight gates, and there was a closed trapdoor in the center of the floor.

Awasa flipped up off the ground and brandished the white-steel blade. Turesobei, Iniru, Zaiporo, the hounds, and Motekeru formed a wide circle around her. Lu Bei popped out and hovered overhead. Enashoma backed far out of the way.

"Just give up, Awasa," Iniru said. "You don't stand a chance."

"I am Ninefold Awasa," she snarled as she touched the amulet on her chest. Eight copies of Awasa, but with blank faces and claws, appeared beside her. "You will die first, filthy k'chasan."

The eight copies of Awasa leapt into action, but they didn't make it far. Iniru flicked her wrist, and the reitsu's white-steel dagger spun through the air and struck the amulet of Barakaros the Warlock.

With a sharp crack, the iron amulet split in half and fell, clanging, onto the platform. The eight copies vanished, and Awasa staggered back with a dumbfounded look on her face. The tip of the dagger had pierced her chest. She pointed Sumada at Iniru.

"This will end here, you —"

"Hai-yah!" Lu Bei yelled.

The fetch plunged from up high and drop-kicked Awasa in the back of the neck. She fell unconscious.

"Darn right this will end here," Lu Bei said. "I'm sick of running from you, you crazy ... mad ... whatever you are." Then he sparked her in the face three times for good measure.

Iniru lunged in and grabbed Sumada. Turesobei sheathed Fangthorn, and sighed with relief as Iniru passed Sumada to him. He'd recovered his father's white-steel sword at last.

"Keep that thing away from me," Hannya said telepathically.

"Are you all right?" he asked her.

"I will recover sufficiently in a few minutes. The strike of the white-steel sword disrupted my energies, and the tunnel didn't do much for me, either. I helped as much as I could."

Iniru pulled the white-steel dagger out of Awasa's chest.

"Nice shot," Zaiporo said.

"Is she okay?" Turesobei asked.

Iniru felt Awasa's pulse. "Her pulse is strong. We'd better tie her up."

Motekeru pulled rope from his pack and got to work on it. Turesobei checked Awasa's wound. It had already sealed and was rapidly healing on its own. Looking at Awasa this close, with her purple eyes, the throbbing veins on her face, her sharpened features, the bruise-colored star on her forehead, her increased height and muscled form — the Warlock's power had warped Awasa so much that it was hard to believe it was actually her and not some sort of poor, demonic copy. How could this be the delicate, insecure, and immature girl he'd once fancied?

"You stayed to the last second to capture her, didn't you?" Iniru asked him.

"Would you expect otherwise from Sobei?" Enashoma asked.

Iniru kissed him on the cheek. "No, and that's why we all love him. But —"

"I nearly got myself killed. I know. It was risky. But I just couldn't leave her back there. She was my responsibility. I had to try."

With Awasa bound and gagged, they all sat down to rest.

"And what do we do with her now?" Enashoma asked.

"I'll figure out something," Turesobei said.

"I think we should open the portal and toss her back to the yomon," Lu Bei said, arms crossed. "But of course, no one ever does what I think is best."

"Half of us wouldn't be here if it was up to you," Iniru said, half-smiling.

"Oh, yeah?" Lu Bei said pompously. "Do your math again. It's more than half."

Everyone laughed until tears came from their eyes. It was more from the relief of having survived than Lu Bei's antics. Laughing as well, Lu Bei stuck his tongue out at Iniru and settled into Enashoma's lap.

"Lu Bei," Turesobei said, "how did you help Hannya back there? The spell didn't work until you joined in."

"I just added another voice, master, and gave what little power I could, which wasn't much." He tapped his forehead. "I've got perfect memory, so I learned the words easy enough after she went through the first time, though I'm not sure what I was saying."

"You sure that was all?" Turesobei asked. "You do keep secrets sometimes."

"The fetch speaks true," Hannya said out loud through the blade. "And he did help, not with his power but with his voice. I am not certain why that helped, though. Magic is finicky that way. Apparently, a chorus was needed." She took on human form and knelt before Turesobei. "Will you honor our bargain now?"

"It shall be honored," Turesobei replied.

"Are you sure that's wise, master?" Lu Bei asked.

"I'm with the fetch this time," Iniru said. "I mean no offense, Lady Hannya, but how do we know we can trust you?"

"We can't know," Turesobei answered. "But she got us this far, and I made a deal with her. I will keep my word. I know Lady Hannya well from our experience together in the Lower Stacks. I trust her."

With Hannya standing nearby, Turesobei carefully grabbed the black-steel sword by its blade and lifted it, placing the *Mark of the Storm Dragon* on the hilt against the larger, matching mark on his cheek. He focused a trickle of energy onto the hilt and spoke the common version of the *command of unbinding*. He thought it might work, since Naruwakiru had cast her command simply, using brute force instead of intricacy. With a flash, the mark on Fangthorn's hilt disappeared. With that done, he closed his eyes and pictured Tepebono trying to break the bindings on the sword. Matching the memory, he recited Tepebono's commands. The runes on the blade disappeared, one-by-one, until the last vanished, unleashing a wave of earth and fire kenja.

"Lady Hannya, you are hereby free to live as you once did. I, Chonda Turesobei, possessor of the Storm Dragon's power, claim no authority or control over you."

Hannya shuddered with delight and took in a deep breath. She twirled on her tiptoes with her arms outstretched. "You have no idea how good this feels after so many millennia being trapped in that sword." She kissed Turesobei on the forehead. "Bless you, Chonda Turesobei, you brave fool. Now, follow me. You can leave your packs here. There is something I *must* show you."

With Motekeru carrying Kurine cradled in one arm and dragging Awasa along with the other, they followed Hannya through the trapdoor and down a staircase that led to an empty courtyard with barren soil and dry ponds and fountains. Hannya shoved open a door on one edge of the encircling temple complex, and they entered a long, lavishly-built hallway of cedar and stone that ended with a set of elaborate rune-carved doors. Hannya breathed in deeply, and then pushed them open.

At the end of this rectangular chamber, a steep staircase led up to a high dais and a throne carved out of pure jade. Turesobei's breath caught; his heart raced. He wanted to run, but couldn't bring himself to move.

On the throne slumped a Kaiaru with sea-dark hair and skin the pale color of fog. He wore a simple gray robe like that of a monk. It hid all of his kavaru stones, save the one on his forehead and the ones on each hand. His eyes were closed, but his chest heaved up and down with breath.

Hannya knelt at the foot of the steps. "Blood King of the Nine Realms, I beseech you, awake and rise again!"

"No!" Turesobei shouted.

Eyes alight with blue-white flame opened. As their color turned to flickering vermillion and then deep green with specks of gold, a sinister laugh rumbled free from parched lips.

Afterword

Thank you for purchasing this book. If you enjoyed this tale, please leave a review at your favorite online retailer or Goodreads. All it takes is a sentence or two!

You can follow me at twitter.com/dahayden, or you can like my page at facebook.com/haydenverse. I love chatting with my readers, so don't be shy.

For a full list of all my books available, or to learn more about me, please visit dahayden.com or typingcatpress.com.

Want to get an email when my next book is released?

Sign up at tinyletter.com/dahayden.

More Stories In ...

The Storm Phase Series

THE MAKER'S BRUSH
Storm Phase Interlude One

LAIR OF THE DEADLY TWELVE
Storm Phase Book Two

THE FORBIDDEN LIBRARY
Storm Phase Book Three